Outbreak

Growing up in the enchanting west of Ireland gave Rory McCormac a love of nature and an individualistic outlook on life, while veterinary practice there and in Malta and Oman has 'unfurled new perspectives'. Despite his enthusiastic wanderlust, he still calls Connemara home. He is married, with two grown sons.

Outbreak is his second novel. His first novel, *Playing Dead* is also published by Arrow.

For John Wilson and Lawrence Butler, who both know
why

The two quotations from James Joyce's *Ulysses*, are taken from the end of chapter one and the beginning of chapter three and are made with permission of the Estate of James Joyce.

OUTBREAK

Rory McCormac

ARROW

Published by Arrow Books in 1998

1 3 5 7 9 10 8 6 4 2

Copyright © Maurice O'Scanaill 1998

Arrow Books Limited
20 Vauxhall Bridge Road, London, SW1V 2SA

Random House Australia (Pty) Limited
20 Alfred Street, Milsons Point, Sydney, New South Wales 2061, Australia

Random House New Zealand Limited
18 Poland Road, Glenfield, Auckland 10, New Zealand

Random House South Africa (Pty) Limited
Endulini, 5a Jubilee Road, Parktown 2193, South Africa

Random House UK Limited Reg. No. 954009

A CIP catalogue record for this book is available from the British Library

Papers used by Random House UK Limited are natural,
recyclable products made from wood grown in sustainable forests.
The manufacturing processes conform to the environmental
regulations of the country of origin

ISBN 0 09 960731 X

Typeset by Deltatype Ltd, Birkenhead, Merseyside

Printed and bound in Great Britain by
Cox & Wyman Ltd, Reading, Berks

I

'. . . and damn me but when I went back up to see them a couple of hours later, wasn't she deader than the Christmas tree in July! The fastest bit o' work you ever saw.' Tom Ryan, short, wiry and fiftyish, looked earnestly up at me as I turned from the back of the Land Rover. A small angular face with dark, darting eyes gave him the expression of a quizzical bird, the sharp nose made even more beak-like by the subsidence of grey-stubbled cheeks into spaces once occupied by teeth.

'By God, but that's a quare one alright,' I said, closing the door. I picked up my case and looked towards the hill. Far above us, the brown cone of its summit notched into the skyline, spoiling its straightness as a snagged thread would a hem. The lower flanks were a patchwork of fields, all looking as if they were part of a creeping landslide. The heifer was in the last field up.

'Are you *sure* the Land Rover can't get closer than this?' I asked.

'I'm sure. The tractor can cross the river lower down but she's out of order at the moment. You couldn't cross in that. Too many big rocks.'

He led me across a wooden footbridge which shook alarmingly with each footstep. 'I hope it's nothin' takin',' he said, as we regained terra firma. 'There's another fourteen with her.'

Walking by the river, I started taking the case history,

building background, assembling details. 'How long since she died?'

'About an hour. Just before I rang for you. That would be,' he looked across a mile of fields to the steeple of the village church, 'half-elevenish. But I don't know how long before *that* she died. I put them to the high field this mornin' – it was a little after eight when we got there – so whatever got her, got her inside three and a half hours. She was perfect when I left her. It must be somethin' quick, huh?' He darted me another bird look.

'Oh, very.' Lush, wet after-grass dragged heavily at my boots, shining them and spangling them with golden buttercup pollen. All about us, grasshoppers chig-chigged industriously, unseen in the warm sward; in a whitethorn hedge a robin paused briefly in his song, but only long enough to let us pass.

Some twenty minutes later the relentless climb came to an end in the farthest corner of the highest field, a corner which might well have been ceded to the mountain by whichever of Ryan's ancestors had built the ancient dry-stone boundary wall, for it was little more than an abrupt marshy pit at the upper end of the constant slope of reasonably good land, a boggy depression, spiky with rushes. Despite my fitness, I was relieved to have arrived.

The moment our figures broke the skyline above the hollow, scavenger birds arose, alarmed. Two grey crows flapped off protesting raucously, and several black-backed gulls from the coast screamed their annoyance as they wheeled above us, glaring resentfully down the lengths of their great orange beaks.

I looked down at the dead heifer in the pit, and began to feel uneasy.

She lay on her right side, belly facing us, legs stuck out from her already bloated body, like an overstuffed rocking horse that had fallen over. There was a faint greenish tinge in the rich tan of her skin and, even though she'd only been dead a short time, from twenty feet away, the sickly miasma

2

of decomposition wafted towards us on the morning air. The marshy ground at her hooves, fore and hind, had been scarred into wet, black crescents by her paddling death throes. I took it in at a glance and knew that all the possible causes I had thought of on our way up the hill had been miles off – none of them could explain the copious pools of dark blood which had spread out from her mouth and nose, and from beneath her tail at the back.

'You never mentioned the blood,' I said. In the deeps of my mind, rusted cogs were beginning to clank into motion.

'There wasn't that much of it when I found her. Although,' he continued after a brief reflective pause, 'there must have been. She was dead for sure and, if the heart was stopped, then where would all this blood come from? Eh?'

'Good question,' I said absentmindedly. I was still trying to dust off Dr Whitty's bacteriology lectures in my head.

'Come to think of it,' he said, 'she wasn't that bloated either . . .'

The blood was the clue. Why was it still flowing? Why hadn't it clotted? As if to emphasise its liquid nature, the leading edge of the blood-sheet at her rear half-oozed, half-slithered, with a small, slurping plop, into a hoofprint. At the head end, it looked as if there were maggots seething just below the gory surface, but it was only gas bubbles being expelled through her nose and mouth by the ever-mounting pressure inside.

'Well,' said Ryan. 'What d'you think of *that*, now?'

'It's a strange one, no doubt.' I wasn't going to name names until I had done a final search through my memory.

'Did you ever see the likes of it?'

'Never.' Nor, I thought, had ninety-nine per cent of the vets in Ireland.

'So . . .' He looked at me expectantly. 'Aren't you going to open her?'

If I was right, then opening her was the last thing I should do. If I was right, what I really needed was a shotgun to kill the gulls and grey crows which were still hanging about hopefully, before they spread bits of her all over the place. They'd already had her upper eye and had started on the delicate underside of the protruded tongue.

'No,' I said. 'I'm not.'

'You're *not!* Well then, how are you going to find out what killed her?'

'I think I know already. All I need is a blood sample. I think she died from anthrax.'

'Never heard of it.'

'That's because it's so rare. But . . . the sudden death, all that dark unclotted blood, rapid decomposition, slow onset of rigor mortis – I'll bet you a pound she's not stiff yet. I can't think what else it could be . . .'

'Anthrax,' he repeated and thought for a moment. 'Is it serious?'

'What d'you mean, is it *serious?*' I pointed in amazement down at his dead heifer.

'I mean will the others get it? Is it contagious?'

'Well . . . in a way. The bacillus that causes it can live in the soil for the best part of a century – seventy or eighty years anyway – and during that time, it lives inside a very hard shell, called a spore, which protects it from damn near everything – sun, wind, heat, cold, you name it. With the normal turnover of soil, by worms or ploughing, the spores come to the top again and are eaten by animals. They invade the blood, multiply very rapidly, until the blood is *teeming* with them and the animal dies within hours, like your heifer.'

'Well, damn me,' he shook his head. 'So what happens now?'

'Anthrax is a Scheduled and Notifiable disease so, by law, I have to report it to the local Veterinary Office.'

He reflected a moment. 'Are you one hundred per cent sure it's anthrax?'

'Ninety-nine point nine nine.'

'Well is there any point in stirrin' up the whole county until you're sure? Even for your own sake . . . Won't you look a bit of a twit if it turns out to be somethin' else?' Tom Ryan had the universal fear of getting caught between the

4

merciless quernstones of bureaucracy, and the universal ability to make it seem that, in trying to wriggle out of it, he was really only concerned about me.

'Maybe, but I'll look a *hell* of a twit if I don't report it and it turns out *not* to be something else.'

'Aye,' he allowed dryly. 'I suppose so.'

Opening my case, I took out a pair of heavy rubber gloves, a roll of cotton wool, a small bottle of surgical spirit, a scalpel blade and a 20cc syringe, both in their sealed, sterile packs. I handed Ryan a purple-capped screw top vial.

'Don't open it until I tell you to. It's got anti-coagulant in it to keep the blood from clotting any more than it has already.'

'Well there's certainly no shortage of that about.'

'That blood on the ground will be contaminated and I may as well take a proper sample now, while I'm here. If it's not anthrax, I'll need routine bacteriology and I'm not facing that climb again.'

I sidled crabwise down the slope and made a wide detour around the heifer, approaching her from the back. Squatting behind the bloated shoulder, I pulled on rubber gloves, then reached across to catch her forelimb; it bent easily. 'See?' I peered up at Ryan, who was now surrounded by the fourteen survivors, all looking down at me with intense, uncomprehending interest. 'The leg bends, no bother. No rigor.'

He nodded and flicked a hand back at a heifer which was about to pull his cap off; this caused immediate panic amongst the tight-packed cattle – they shot backwards and sideways, startled by the small movement, but only for a few steps; then the heavy breathing and serious investigating began again, wet, quizzical muzzles thrust forward on fully-extended necks.

I poured surgical spirit along the jugular furrow and picked up the blade. Ryan and the heifers watched, rapt. A length of the thick skin parted effortlessly under the honed sliver of steel, exposing the underlying loose connective

5

tissue like moist, tough, spiders' web. Dragging the blade broadside through this, I laid bare the dark blue, finger-thick, jugular vein, then carefully nicked it. A blob of black blood squeezed through. I left the blade to one side on a wad of cotton wool soaked in spirit, then slowly, carefully, and with some difficulty, drew about 10cc of the semi-clotted gore into the syringe. I dropped the blade into the incision, teased off a wad of cotton wool, wiped the nozzle of the syringe on it, and covered the blade with the wad. Then I soaked the lot in what was left of the surgical spirit, checked carefully about me, and retraced my steps up the steep side of the marshy hollow. The syringe, which I carried nozzle up, didn't even waver.

Ryan stared in fascination as I ascended from the pit, his gaze fixed rigidly on the syringe. Even when I reached him, he continued to stare at it, though by now it was so near him that he was almost cross-eyed.

'You can open the vial now, but hold it very steady so I don't get blood on the outside of it . . .'

He stopped breathing as the gap between syringe and vial closed and I had a sudden flash recall of an old black and white film I'd once seen, at the part where the hero (a poet with rampant consumption and a wooden leg) defused an evil-looking (Luftwaffe) bomb in the cellar beneath the room of the (sweet-faced, uncomplaining, bedridden, wid-owed) mother of the heroine (a beautiful ambulance driver).

The docking successfully accomplished, I began to transfer the blood from the syringe to the vial; it had to be done carefully as its semi-clotted consistency made it difficult to keep a steady expulsive press on the plunger; done forcefully, it might have come shooting out in a sudden burst, squirting blood all over.

'Cap,' I said.

He reached to screw it on.

'*Careful!*' I warned and his hand jerked away so quickly he almost dropped the bottle.

'*Christ*, man, don't *shout!*' he said testily and had another go.

6

I peeled off one glove, everting it so that the syringe ended up inside it, then repeated the procedure with the second; the syringe was then enclosed in both and I put the resulting bundle into a plastic sample bag, poured in strong disinfectant and sealed the bag. 'Make sure this goes in the fire when they're burning her,' I warned, placing it on the ground beside him. I took the vial, wrapped it in a cocoon of cotton wool, placed it in one sample bag, then another, and carefully placed the lot in a compartment of my case. 'God help the germ that tries to escape through that,' I said, sitting down on a rock beside Ryan. I removed my boots and swabbed each thoroughly with disinfectant, paying special attention to the treads on the soles; I left the last of the cotton wool and disinfectant to him, admonishing him to do the same before he left. 'It shouldn't be very long before someone arrives to take over. In the meantime, as I said, keep everything away from her.'

'Okay,' he replied. 'You can phone from the house. Tell the missus what's goin' on or she'll think I'm lost. And ask her to bring up a big sheet of plastic – it'll keep away the birds and the flies. And tell her to make sure it's an old piece. I suppose it'll have to go on the fire?'

'They'll burn everything that touched her bar the two of us,' I assured him.

He nodded glumly. 'I'll be hearin' from you, I suppose?'

'You will.'

As I walked away from him, the assembled heifers parted before me; then they gambolled and galloped about me all the way to the gate. Obviously they hadn't had as much excitement in ages.

Neither, for that matter, had I.

2

It wasn't until I was clattering across the cattle grid of the Regional Veterinary Laboratory that I remembered that the recommended procedure in cases of suspected anthrax was to sever an ear and cauterise the resultant cut surfaces. At least I *thought* it was. Or was that for something else? I shrugged – it was too late now, and blood was blood. Anyway, with what would I cauterise it, dear Liza, dear Liza? I didn't carry matches or a cigarette lighter and it was a safe bet that Tom Ryan didn't either – he couldn't steam up and down that hill at the rate he did and be a smoker, too.

Inside, I told the girl in the glass-walled cubicle that I had an urgent and dangerous sample and asked to see somebody senior. She leaned towards her PA microphone, put on her sing-song, airport-announcer voice, and said: 'Mr Corless to reception, please. Mr Corless to reception.' Then she flashed me her on-off, receptionist smile. 'He'll be with you in a moment. If you'd care to take a seat?' Duty discharged, she turned away and attacked the keyboard of her computer.

Mr Corless arrived just as I sat down.

'What have we here?' He eyed the packet.

'Anthrax,' I said, trying not to sound like I was probably the most interesting thing that had happened to him all year.

9

'Hmm,' he said, not taking it big at all. He reached out a hand. 'Anthrax, eh?'

Having my momentous news met with what amounted to little more than an 'Oh yeah?' took me aback slightly, and I was just beginning to think that this must be the most laid-back, poker-faced lab technician in the whole world, when he looked sharply at me. Ah, I thought, It dawneth upon him. At last. Maybe what I'm faced with here is just the *slowest-brained* lab technician in the whole world.

'You are a vet, I take it?' he asked with sudden suspicion. No mention of anthrax.

'M.V.B., M.R.C.V.S.,' I assured him. 'Fully paid up.'

'It's just that we can't have laymen driving around the country with suspect anthrax samples thrown on the dashboard.' He spelt it out, obviously marking *me* down as one of the slowest-brained *vets* in the whole world. 'You're new around here, aren't you?'

'Yes. Doing a locum for Mark Daley of Ballintaggart. Frank Samson.'

'Nice to meet you. How's Mr Daley's leg coming along?'

'Fine now. Plaster comes off tomorrow, then another week or so and he should be as good as ever.' What was this guy up to? Small talk about Mark Daley's leg when we were talking *anthrax* for God's sake . . .

'Good.' He looked down at the package. 'Okay, Mr Samson, I'll get started on this right away. In the meantime, could you fill out one of our forms? Kathryn will give you one.' He turned to go, then stopped. 'You'll wait, I presume?'

'How long will it be?'

'Ten minutes. Fifteen. Not long.'

'I'll wait.'

'I'll be as quick as I can.' He vanished whence he had come, through a swing door with all kinds of signs on it warning unauthorised persons not to even *think* about it.

Wondering about Corless's blasé reaction, I made my way to the canteen and pushed through the swing door. Operating-theatre clean, it contained about ten four-seater tables, and was decorated all over with 'Have-You-Washed-Your-Hands?' notices. I was the only person there. Some industrious but limited graffitist had used a red felt-tip to cross out 'Hands' in most of the notices and substitute various other parts of the anatomy. The obvious, school-boy-smutty wobbly bits had been exhausted a few posters in from the door and, from then on, they become more arcane – the one above the pile of formica trays at the start of the counter wondered if I had washed my medulla oblongata.

'Hello?' I called to the person I could hear making noises in a room at the back. A huge-busted, earth-mother figure appeared in a door in the wall behind the counter. *Lunch?* She was very sorry, but lunch was over and there was nothing left. The staff was small and they never had extra people – well *almost* never – so she knew exactly how much of what to cook, she should do, as she had been here for fifteen years, started in Mr Berry's time, did I know Mr Berry? A *lovely* man . . . No? Before my time possibly . . .

'Well, is there anything at all?' I got in when she made a compulsory pit-stop for an air-change. 'I'm starving. I haven't had a bite since eight this morning.'

'Maybe some chips. I'll see.' And she vanished back into the rear of the premises. I'd obviously pushed the correct button and ended up with a plate of chips, a bar of dark chocolate and a cappuccino. She produced a tooth pick which, she told me, was for the chips – presumably in case I *hadn't* washed my hands. Most of the chips were hard and dry, so she refused to charge me for them. I found a table at which a previous diner had left a paper and scanned the headlines as I ate. Twice, a staff member came in, but neither was looking for me. Each had a coffee and a cigarette and both left as soon as the cigarette ended. Neither one got more than a quarter way down the coffee.

The notice above the payphone in the corner expressed the hope that I had washed my earhole. I called base and found that things were pretty much under control, nothing urgent. I bought another coffee. The clock above the service hatch told me I'd already been there for twenty minutes.

I was just starting back over the stories I'd skipped on my first run through the paper, when the door opened, and a man looked in. 'Frank Samson?' he called to the room in general. As I was the sole occupant, I thought this a bit odd.

'Yes?' I answered, and waited for him to say something more, but as far as he was concerned, the conversation was at an end, and he just stood there, holding the door open, waiting. He wasn't exactly drumming his fingers or tapping a foot but he managed to convey an air of impatience. Suddenly riled, I took my time. I had him taped at once – one of those institute types who look on us general practitioners as the labourers in the field, the pedestrian journeymen who didn't do post-grad degrees because they weren't quite up to it. I swallowed my last mouthful, neatly quartered the paper, and pushed back my chair. On the way to the door, I paused to call my thanks to the lady whose whereabouts were, once again, detectable only through the racket of pots being soundly walloped in the back room.

'Yes?' I inquired again, stopping in front of him. He was a couple of years my senior and radiated an aura of smug, proprietorial authority.

'Come with me, please.' The pale face beneath the carefully-parted, short hair split briefly into an insincere smile, the smile of the managing director, who, while putting in a dutiful appearance at the wedding of one of his more lowly employees, finds himself buttonholed with unwanted and unwonted familiarity by the half-drunk workmates of the groom. He didn't bother to introduce himself but I couldn't decide whether this was because he didn't think I warranted it, or because I could read my own introduction off the name-tag pinned to the lapel of his lab coat. It told me that he was Dr Simon B. Harbison, that, so far, he had accumulated enough letters to fill the next line without having to space them too far apart, and that he was

Deputy Director. No doubt he was at present working on yet another clutch of letters. More power to his elbow.

'I presume,' I said, deciding to break the ice as we squeaked along the polished corridor, 'that the Deputy Director would hardly have come in person to tell me that my sample was negative and that I could go home?'

'No.' Another thin smile told me that the Deputy Director would not have come at *all*, under any circumstances whatever, had there not been a severe shortage of messenger boys or runners or whatever. 'You took venous blood,' he noted disapprovingly.

'Yes. Jugular.'

'One would have expected the severed pinna. *Preferred* the severed pinna.'

That finished me. I hate people who use the impersonal 'one', and if they also call a lug a pinna, then that said it all. I had a prize one here.

'One would have severed the pinna had one had any cauterising agent at one's disposal, but one was halfway up the side of a mountain and one's vehicle was miles from one, and one didn't have matches. In fact, *two* didn't have matches – that's the farmer and me,' I explained, making a joke of it, keeping it pleasant. But my antipathy nudged through, just as his God complex wriggled through his laboured civility. 'May one take it, however, that the sample was still testable?'

He nodded. 'The lab staff have done their Giemsa. Anthrax. Unequivocally.'

As we turned a corner into a short corridor, he developed a frown, his pace slowed and I changed down a gear to keep with him. His face wore the unmistakable look of a deputy director to whom something has just occurred. 'You said,' he said, stopping altogether, 'that your car was miles away?'

'That's right.' As he had reverted to plain English, I decided not to bother pointing out that I had said 'vehicle'. I also decided that it was a pretty odd remark to make to somebody who had just brought in one of the more rare and notorious diseases.

'Why was that?'

'Why was what?'

'Why was your car so far away?'

'Because the road didn't come any closer to where the heifer died. Which, as I said, was up the side of a hill. Mountain,' I amended.

'Odd,' he said, as he stopped at the last door along the corridor. It had a shiny brass nameplate telling me that Dr F.X. Johnson (plus even more letters than my guide had on his label), Director, resided within. Harbison opened the door without knocking.

'Frank,' he said, and for a moment – until I sussed that F.X. could only stand for Francis Xavier – I thought he was suddenly coming over all matey and addressing me, 'this is the GP who brought in the anthrax. Frank Samson.' Turning to me, he announced: 'Our Director, Dr Johnson.' Boswell, I imagined, might often have used less reverend tones when introducing *his* Dr Johnson.

The director was a large man with a pleasant, if bluish, face. His chest heaved as he leaned across the desk and extended a hand. 'Pleased to meet you, Mr Samson. Excuse my not getting up. Blasted emphysema. Only firing on one lung . . .' He tailed off, wheezing.

'Rotten dose,' I said, and at once regretted it. It seemed to relegate his condition to the status of a temporary inconvenience, on a par with a touch of acid indigestion or a boil on the bum.

'So,' he heaved, 'anthrax.' He pointed towards a microscope on a small table by his desk, and indicated that I should have a look. I did. The sample was teeming with bacilli – millions of them, their rod shapes all but obliterating the blood cells. Some had clear oval areas in the centre, the beginnings of spore formation.

'Not much doubt about that, is there?' I said.

'None at all. Now for some details.' He pointed me towards a chair, picked up the form I had filled in, posed a few questions which the form hadn't, expanded on some which it had, and finally asked me if I could mark the exact

14

location of Tom Ryan's farm on the large scale map of County Galway which covered most of one of the walls of his office.

The map was a new one, unmarked except for a couple of pins, a green one in the north-east near Tuam and a red one south of it, near Gort. I located the village nearest the Ryan farm, oriented myself and traced a finger along the roads and byroads. 'Here,' I said, turning to look over my shoulder at Johnson, my finger held on the spot.

Harbison, who was standing nearby, said: 'Roughly a triangle.'

I presumed he meant my finger and the two pins and I was about to ask him if he meant an *equilateral* triangle as any three points not in a straight line form a triangle, but I let it go. I was too curious. Were those pins anthrax cases too? Recent cases? The map was new, the pins shiny. But a rare disease making one of its sporadic appearances hardly merited a wall-sized action chart.

'I'll mark it,' Harbison said eagerly, obliterating Tom Ryan's farm with a biro dot. Ignoring me, he went to Johnson's desk. 'It's grey today, isn't it?'

Johnson checked a document which lay on top of his in-tray and nodded. 'That's right. Grey.' He trawled a pudgy forefinger to and fro through a flat plastic box full of pins of various colours; locating a grey one, he pinched it carefully, lifted it out, and dropped it onto Harbison's extended palm.

Grey? I wondered at the strange choice of colour. Green and red were gone but what about blue, black, white, orange, yellow, purple? *Grey*?

'Those two pins aren't anthrax too, are they?' I asked.

'Yes.' Johnson nodded.

'Since when?'

'Twelve days ago, the red one. Nine, the green.'

'Three cases in a *fortnight*! Have the others been confirmed?'

'Indeed they have.'

'Well, isn't that ... odd?'

'Very.'

'Do you have any ideas why?'

'We have some theories. Nothing conclusive.' He broke off, stricken by another bout of wheezing.

Harbison had picked up a scientific publication with a picture of a rotavirus on the cover, and seemed to have withdrawn from the conversation, probably in protest at the director's answering my questions. Generals should not entertain the inconsequential questions of foot soldiers.

'Why grey?' I asked, when Johnson had stopped gasping. 'Surely there are lots of colours you would normally consider before grey?'

'An astute observation, Mr Samson. Why do *you* think it's grey?'

I shrugged. 'It sounds like you're running out of colours, but you've only used green and red . . .'

His eyes flicked to the opposite wall and I followed them – the wall was covered by a map of the whole country and I was about to turn away when, with a chill shock, I realised that the map was covered in pins of all the colours I had put before grey – in fact grey seemed to be the only colour missing. My eyes zoomed at once to County Galway. It had just two pins – a green one near Tuam and a red one near Gort. The teddy-bear profile of Ireland suddenly took on the sinister look of a voodoo doll run through with death pins.

'All *anthrax*?' I asked in disbelief.

Johnson wheezed resignedly. 'All anthrax.'

'Since when?'

'Today is the sixteenth day of the outbreak,' replied Harbison, re-entering the proceedings as the director was seized by another attack and turned an alarming navy blue.

I shook my head. At least it cleared up the mystery of Corless's reaction. Anthrax was becoming common! 'There must be *some* theories?' I said, turning back to the map. How come I hadn't heard about it? It should be front-page stuff. Half the epidemiologists in the country would be working round the clock on this one.

'Sure there are,' Johnson panted, regaining some control. 'None very good, though, I'm afraid.'

'Of course, one must bear in mind that, until a few days ago, there hadn't been enough reported cases to see any trends,' Harbison offered in defence of the high command. The comment was directed more at his boss than at me.

'How many pins?' I asked Johnson.

'Simon?' He looked at his deputy.

'One hundred and twenty-seven up to and including yesterday – an average of eight point four six six six recurring, per diem.' We were back to the fancy language. 'In the previous ten years, the average per *annum* – and I stress per annum – has been two point three.'

'So what are the current theories?' I stared at the map.

'Tell you what,' the director replied with a watery-eyed smile, 'see what you can make of it. It'll probably be every bit as valid as what we've come up with.'

Harbison sucked in his breath. Blasphemy!

I stood back and stared hard at the map, looking for patterns. One thing was obvious: this was no case of one highly potent source of bacilli suddenly surfacing after many years – not with *that* range. After a few moments' consideration, I nodded to myself, then began reasoning aloud.

'Okay. The disease hasn't spread along the course of any water system – if it had, there would be clear bands along a river or around a lake, and it could never have covered the country like this,' I waved an expansive hand at the map. 'And it hasn't spread radially – there's no sign of a focus with concentric rings spreading out from it. Nor does it look as if it's been spread by the prevailing winds – there would be fronts of different colours, bands following one after the other. By the way,' I glanced over my shoulder at him, 'I'm assuming a constant incubation period and a constant wind direction.'

He nodded. 'Go on.'

I turned back to the map. 'Okay. Let's see now. Wind and water are out, so how about animal vectors? First mammals. I don't think so, because it has spread too quickly. It would also have spread out from an original point, which it hasn't, and would have been stopped short by natural barriers like rivers, lakes, bays, mountains, bogs. And there's no evidence of that. So they're out. That leaves birds and flying insects. But they don't look likely either. It would take *thousands* of birds to cover the country so thoroughly and, offhand, I can't think of any species which travels so much – it's too early for migrants to be heading off. There *does* seem to be some vague banding, though – for instance, here, and along here,' I traced them with a finger, 'but I can't think why birds should fly along certain bands. Following areas of special food, maybe? But we don't have such specialised birds in Ireland, as far as I know, nor such clearly demarcated feeding areas either. So I don't know. Still, they *are* there, those vague bands, and that's about all I can see.' I turned to find out how I was doing.

Johnson nodded, beaming. Harbison, without closing the magazine, glanced up. 'What, if anything, do you make of "those vague bands", as you put it?' The soupy smile was back – it was time to put the lower orders back in their place.

'Well, it's hard to be *sure* at this point, but they *seem* to follow the road system.'

Johnson beamed again and nodded so vigorously that he brought on another severe coughing fit. Harbison had the chagrined look of a magician who, having plunged his hand into the hat, finds that not only has the rabbit gone A.W.O.L. but is, at that very moment, being produced by a member of the audience from behind the pinna of his neighbour. When I stopped feeling smug, I began to wonder how anthrax could spread by road.

The director, having again staged one of his flash recoveries, was delighted. 'Exactly!' I wondered if, secretly, he wasn't pleased to see his supercilious deputy put down. 'And Simon,' he added, convincing me that he was, '*he* didn't know what *we* knew when *we* worked it out. I'm afraid, Mr Samson, that we haven't been entirely honest with you. Look at Northern Ireland. Not a pin in it. Not a single pin.'

'I thought that that was because they were looking after their own cases up there . . .'

'They don't *have* any cases up there to look after, so far. Not a single one. We're in constant contact. Needless to say, they're watching the situation very closely.'

'I'll bet they are. Well that puts paid to any possibility of natural spread, doesn't it? Nature is no respecter of artificial boundaries.'

Given a few more moments' reflection, I could probably have reasoned up to the point at which the official theorising had arrived, and stuck, but Harbison, smarting at being so recently upstaged, was determined to get back in and reveal the last few minor points before I worked them out for myself.

'Of course, it would be ridiculous to think that one single solitary vehicle could have travelled the country in such a short time, wouldn't it?' What a creep, I thought, what a boring pedantic creep. 'So we are led to the next conclusion,' he continued, 'which is that *several* vehicles must be involved . . . okay? And, what's more, that they all operate from a central location in which a long-forgotten reservoir of *Bacillus anthracis* has suddenly and inexplicably surfaced. Are you with me?'

'Just about. Don't go too fast.'

He missed it by a mile. 'Oh? Alright. Obviously we've searched every cattle mart in the country, all the big dealers' yards and farms, and cross-questioned every farmer who has lost an animal but, thus far, without finding any common link.'

'There is *one* common factor,' Johnson butted in, tired of Harbison's laboured talking-to-idiots approach. 'In every case we've traced, the deaths have occurred in fields by a road.'

So *that* was why Harbison had thought it odd that I'd been miles from my car . . .

'Ah *hah!*' Harbison gloated, a finger held aloft in triumph. 'But not in *this* case, Frank. Not in this case. *This* animal died in a field up a mountainside, far from the nearest road.'

Simultaneously, the director and I spoke. He asked if the dead animal had been moved recently, while I volunteered the information that a mere few hours before death, she had been in a field, not just close to, but right *beside* a road.

'You actually went to *see* the field?' Johnson asked, surprised at my certainty. Or maybe my thoroughness. Harbison, in his blushing confusion, was ignored by both of us.

'No. The farmer told me. I was thinking of stuff being dumped over the fence – some form of poisoning, perhaps lead . . .'

'*Lead poisoning!?*' Harbison made one last attempt to salvage some dignity. 'There isn't the *slightest* similarity, except, of course, for rapid death in both cases. Lead poisoning! With all that *black blood* around?'

'This was before I saw the animal. I was just getting the case history as we walked along.' That put him out for the count. I turned back to the director. 'So that's the theory? A fleet of vehicles spreading spores as they travel the roads?'

'That's the best we can come up with so far,' he shrugged almost apologetically. 'And even *that* has only shown up in the past few days. Despite the obvious pointer of Northern Ireland not being affected, you need a hell of a lot of pins to even *begin* to pick out the road system. The thing now is to trace the source before the cattle population of the country is decimated.'

'The *cattle* population? All those pins are cattle?'

'Yes.'

'No sheep? Sheep are equally susceptible and there are as many fields of sheep along the roads of Galway as there are cattle, probably more.'

'None reported. The reasoning goes that farmers don't get so worked up about the odd ewe keeling over here and there – they're always doing it with the various clostridial diseases. They'd probably blame it on one that missed her vaccination, that sort of thing.' He broke up into a fresh fit of coughing. While I waited for him to get the tubes under control again, an image came to my mind of a photograph in some long ago newspaper, of four men dressed like astronauts or workers in a nuclear power plant, trying to decontaminate a Scottish island called Gruinard, which had been deliberately seeded with anthrax spores fifty years before. With the sun behind them and the bleak landscape, they looked like the last people in the last place on earth.

'Could it be a bovine specific strain?' I asked when he seemed ready for further conversation.

'That's been checked, but I'm told that it's just the normal strain, nothing fancy. We thought at first that we might be dealing with a new, highly active, supervirulent, mutant strain.'

'Do those pins mark individual animals or individual farms?'

'Animals. A few farms have had two animals die, but not many. And none has had more than two. In all those cases both deaths took place in the same field.'

'I suppose a supervirulent mutant would have killed all the animals in the field – not just one or two.' I looked again at the map. There was something else odd about it. Mentally, I ran my eye along the courses of the main arterial roads, Dublin to Galway, Cork to Limerick, and so forth. Any traffic covering the country as a whole should spend a lot of time on these roads; yet there was no clear clustering of pins strung out along them – if anything there were actually *fewer* pins along the main roads than along the minor ones, many of which I recognised – doing locums, a fortnight here, a month there, soon teaches you your way around. 'Have you superimposed a road map on this one?'

'Not here. At headquarters, of course. Why?'

I explained my observation and both of them looked hard at the map, Johnson rising laboriously to do so. Harbison remained seated, clutching his protective magazine.

'What point are you making?' Dr Johnson wheezed, lumbering back to collapse into his chair.

'More an observation. Either these mechanised Typhoid Marys are travelling all over the place using the sideroads mainly, which seems odd, or there's something in the sideroad environment which activates anthrax spores, which is even more odd. Or there could be something in the main-road environment which *inhibits* their activation, which seems not only odd, but ludicrous.'

That seemed to put an end to the open forum on anthrax. I had the impression that, any second now, Johnson would start looking at his watch, so I slapped my palms down on my thighs and said breezily: 'Ah well . . . must go. I've got a practice to look after and it's not even mine! Mark Daley will be thinking I've taken early retirement.'

'How is Mark coming along?' Johnson asked, extending his hand.

'Fine.'

'Tell him I was asking for him,' he said. He held on to my hand. 'And by the way, keep this quiet for now – you know what the media would do with this. We'd end up with a glut of cattle on the market, prices crashing, farmers up in arms . . . you know yourself. Remember the BSE. It's not The Official Secrets Act or anything, but the order *has* come from on high. The minister himself, no less.' He let my hand drop.

'I understand.' I nodded. 'Well, goodbye. Nice meeting you.'

In reply, he smiled and began yet another coughing fit.

At the door, I turned. 'Goodbye, Dr Harbison.'

He looked up, trying to give the impression that he had forgotten I was there. 'What? Eh? Oh! Goodbye. Goodbye.'

3

The fourteen heifers became hypochondriacs by proxy – through Tom Ryan. He moved them back down to a paddock near the house so that he could keep them under observation, and he spent a large part of each day draped across the wall, staring morosely at them. If one stretched out in the sun, or elected to stay out in a shower rather than join her companions under the dubious shelter of the dripping whitethorns which ringed the paddock, he phoned the surgery. A strange bovine noise, time spent gazing instead of grazing, or a brief cessation of chewing the cud sent him into a panic and, convinced that his heifers were going to be picked off, one by one, his sepulchral tones became depressingly familiar to Jacqueline, the receptionist. One day I went to his farm three times.

'Look, Tom,' I told him on the last of these visits, when I was more than slightly exasperated, 'there's nothing *wrong* with her! Or any of the others either. You're worse than an old dear with her poodle. All these calls are a waste of *my* time and *your* money. Like I said, there's very little chance that another one's picked it up, but if she has, then there's nothing you or I can do about it anyway.'

'But there's been cases of two animals gettin' it,' he insisted. 'The government vet told me.'

'Very, very few, Tom. Very few. You'd have to be dead unlucky.'

'If I had ducks, they'd drown,' he replied in gloomy pessimism.

On one of these visits, Tom cadged a lift into Ballintaggart. The tractor had been repaired and had been promised for that day.

'If it's ready,' he said dolefully as we rolled out the gate.

I braked. 'Shouldn't you ring first?'

'No,' he said. 'Keep goin'.'

'How'll you get back if it's not ready?' I let out the clutch.

'Someone'll drive me. Jack himself will. Or the wife.'

'Jack being?'

'The mechanic. A *great* mechanic. He can do anythin' mechanical – tractors, cars, boats, radios, televisions, radar, fridges, depth sounders. Probably even planes.'

'He sounds like a right man to know.'

'The best. Only, he's inclined to be a bit slow . . . The brother-in-law left in a radio four years ago and it's still in the workshop.'

'You think your tractor could be there for *four years*?'

'No. There's the field the heifers were in,' Tom said, returning like a homing pigeon to his pet subject, pointing out the field the moment we came in sight of it; he'd been waiting for it, the high point of the trip to town. 'Before I put them up to the high field.'

I slowed down and eventually stopped. I had to, partly because it was obviously expected of me, and partly because I couldn't see where I was going – his arm had swung across in front of my face, blocking my view. 'This is where she picked it up,' he announced dolefully.

We had come to a halt on top of a low hill. Behind us was the valley where Ryan's house and home farm lay, against the backdrop of the hill on which the heifer had died. Today, it climbed into a crown of cloud which obscured its summit. In front of us, the land dropped sharply away, fanning out into a spectacular panorama of moors, lakes, bays, islands, and distant blue mountains.

'*This* field?' I asked, looking out at a bank about eight feet high, topped by another five to six feet of tall hedge of hawthorn and fruit-laden blackberry briar. I wondered how anything could have splashed off the road and got through, or up and over, that lot.

'Aye,' Tom sighed morosely. 'It's the only field I have on this side of the valley.'

'Begod, Tom, but I think you were right when you said if you had ducks they'd drown. Look at those other fields! They're all at road level with only sheepwire between them and the road . . . and yet *your* field with its high bank and thick hedge was the one that got splashed with the stuff.'

'Didn't I *tell* you?'

'How come anyway that you've got such a fine hedge while the others have only wire fences?'

'It was all hedges once, up to a few years ago. There was always a lay-by in front of my field, a parkin' place for lookin' at the view, because it's a kind of beauty spot; but seven or eight years back, the tour coaches started comin' up here and the county council had to widen the road. They took bits off all the other fields to bring them back level with mine and all the fine hedges were cut down and carted off. They replaced them with that . . . wire thing. Rubbish is all it is! There's neither shelter nor shade in it, nor hidin' enough for the wren to build her nest.'

I could see cattle in several of the wire-fenced fields further along; it was obvious from the short yellowed grass, that the fields had been overgrazed. I presumed that the cattle had been in them since before Tom's anthrax case had come to light and I asked him about them.

'They're Jimmy Power's. He was told not to move them because if one of them has the bug, it'll only die somewhere else and contaminate another field. But he'll *have* to move them soon – they're runnin' out of grass. He asked the government vet what if they hadn't picked up the bug yet but the field *was* contaminated? She said to put in an electric fence to block off a strip about twenty feet back from the road because she didn't think anythin' would have splashed in further than that. But he had to take it down in the end – the cattle were goin' mad to get at the grass along by the road.'

I studied Ryan's high bank and thick hedge again. 'There isn't even a *gate*, for God's sake.'

'The gate's just up here, but you can't see it because of a bend in the track.'

We crawled slowly on to the end of the hedge. Reaching the first of the wire fences, I changed up into third and we continued towards town. I offered to drive him to the garage but he assured me that there was absolutely no point in even trying for the tractor until much later in the afternoon. 'You always have to give Jack twenty-four hours,' he told me. 'At *least* twenty-four hours.'

I dropped him off at The Champion Bar and Lounge, declining his offer of 'a little somethin'. It was the first time I'd seen anything like joy on his face and there was a newly-acquired, almost lamb-like spring in his step as he skipped towards the pub door.

Towards the end of the week, Mark Daley felt he was fit enough to start work again, and I left for Dublin after afternoon surgery on the Friday.

4

It was getting on for nine-thirty when I pulled up outside Claire's flat in Ballsbridge, one of Dublin's more genteel suburbs. I stood beside the Land Rover and stretched away the small cramps of three hours' nonstop driving. Claire had the top floor of a well-preserved Georgian house, halfway along a graceful crescent of them and, though there was a distant rumble from the busy roads which passed at either end of it, on Claire's tranquil backwater no traffic stirred to disturb the century-old peace. Across the road, behind heavy railings, a balding man in shirtsleeves thrust a hand-mower over a tiny square of grass, sending fountains of daisy heads dancing briefly into the air. Between a lilac bush and his neighbour's wall, a wisp of acrid smoke wavered into the still air above a smouldering pyramid of grass clippings. I heard the mower and I smelled the smoke and *déjà vu*'ed back to childhood holidays with grandparents, now long dead, in a similar, tidy suburb, not more than a mile or two away. A few houses down, someone was practising arpeggios on a piano, but I couldn't tell from which open window the notes cascaded into the street; I wasn't even sure which house. I let myself in, checked the letter box and climbed the stairs.

Even from the landing I could hear Claire splashing about in the bath, belting out her favourite opera of the moment – Tosca, she had told me it was. I winced. Though perfect in almost every way, Claire is no singer, but she maintains that she is unable to sit in a bath without bursting into song. I often wonder why the neighbours don't object. Perhaps they think she's great.

'I'm back!' I called from the hall, but she was at one of the noisier bits and didn't hear me. I eased open the bathroom door and called 'Hi!' into the peasouper.

She was in the middle of telling some character called Scarpia what she thought of him. All in Italian. *'Eeeek!'* She broke off.

'Only me.'

'God, Frank! You nearly scared the *life* out of me. Don't you ever knock? Or even *shout?*'

'I did. I shouted "Hi!"'

'That was almost in my ear!'

I bent to kiss her wet face and folded my arms along the side of the tub. 'How's it goin'?'

'Fine.'

'Didya miss me?'

'Don't I always?'

'You've got suds on your forehead.'

'Well, wipe them off.'

'You've got suds all down your front, too.'

'That's because I'm in the bath.'

'Would you like some coffee?'

'Are you going to make some?'

'Yep.'

'Then I will.'

'In here?'

'No. I'll be out in a minute. I've almost finished.'

'But what about the bit where you go "Mario Mario" and jump off the battlements?'

'I'll do it next time.'

'Well, mind that you do. We can't have you shirking bits. Beethoven would turn in his grave.'

'Puccini.'

'I'll make the coffee.'

I went out, leaving them to sort it out between them, not

28

quite sure that she hadn't already killed Scarpia and wasn't just singing away to his corpse. Opera is funny like that.

I set the kettle and wandered back into the living room. Spacious and high-ceilinged, it had an alcove at each of its tall windows: one, described rather grandiosely by the estate agent as 'the breakfast alcove', held a glass-topped table and two high, wing-backed chairs, all in wicker – very Raj and very much more suited to an apartment in Poona or Lahore than a Georgian flat in Ballsbridge – while the other was occupied by a swivel chair, set side-on to the window and facing an old roll-top desk. The room was dominated by an enormous ornate fireplace, though all it framed now was a tame, electric, mock-coal fire. The mantelpiece held Claire's more valued books, securely clamped between two Zell Osborne bronzes of the stallion Catamaran, presents from a grateful syndicate in appreciation of our part in unravelling the knots of his mysterious disappearance a year or so ago.

I drifted towards the desk. The screen of the word processor glowed greenly, showing a chunk of text and the cursor winking on 'existentialism' – enough said. Maybe an article for her paper, *The Daily Instructor*, or some heavy features piece, or perhaps it was just a bit of private study – Claire was into that sort of thing. When I first began to get serious about her (some two hours after we'd met), it used to worry me that my tastes were so mundane, but it had never bothered her, so I didn't think about it now either. Except sometimes when I detected a tiny kernel of unease in my head, as if it was a potential enemy that might some day come between us.

I perched a hip on the desk and sifted through the accumulated mail: there was nothing of interest. Claire handled all the bookings for Veterinary Locum Services (VLS), my business, only consulting me when two or more clients were clamouring for my services for the same, or overlapping, periods. It had been hard work getting VLS going, but once the idea had caught on it had snowballed, and I was now at the stage where I had to consider taking on help, certainly during school holidays when most of my clients wanted time off and asked VLS to cover for them. I could use six vets during school holidays, no bother. Success had just one downside; I was away for long periods at a time, so Claire and I lived our life together in short intense bursts. So far it hadn't caused us problems – when I was on a locum, she often joined me at weekends, while I usually managed a couple of days in Dublin between jobs. But we had a deal: as soon as either of us began to feel the pressure, that was it. Finito. End of the locum business, at least with me as its sole employee.

Beautiful, damp and glowing, Claire came through from the bathroom, her drop-dead perfect figure wrapped in a white bathrobe, her rich auburn hair turbaned in a soft towel. She hugged me from behind as I poured boiling water into two mugs of instant, then went to the fridge for milk. We sat at the kitchen counter and compared weeks (both tough), how we felt (both absolutely knackered), whether we should go out (no, no), what to do about food (omelette, Spanish, to be cooked by me), while Claire dried her hair.

After supper, we played five or six games of Boggle, yawned a bit, cuddled some, talked about having a last coffee, decided against it on the grounds that it might keep us awake, and went to bed.

For all the sleep we managed, we could have had ten last coffees. What with making love and chatting about this and that, the most either of us managed was some interrupted dozing and, as we lay in bed at the crack of noon next day, bemoaning the fact that we were still absolutely knackered, I wondered if, in future, we couldn't make love *and* hold our discussions at the same time, and use the time thus saved for sleeping. '*Philistine!*' Claire hissed, before trying briefly to smother me with a pillow and flouncing off to make breakfast, muttering about some people's insensitivity. As I stepped under the shower, I could hear her rattling about in the kitchen, going 'Mario! Mario!' and, presumably, preparing to leap from the battlements.

Later we drove out into the Dublin mountains and climbed up to The Hellfire Club. We got soaked to the skin on the way back down, bushwhacked by some clouds which had lain in wait for us behind Three Rock Mountain – the sky had been a perfect blue when we'd set out.

That evening I got dragged off to see Cocteau's 'The Human Voice' and afterwards, we ate Italian in a nearby bistro. Between courses (in the middle of a discussion about whether people speaking on a phone express themselves differently than they would if they could see each other) my attention began to drift. In the soft table light, Claire was almost ethereally beautiful and I watched her with a glow of wonder seated like a small lump in my chest.

'What do you think?' she asked, having animatedly made some point about the importance of gestures. Large grey eyes regarded me seriously across a candle in a wine bottle encrusted in wax stalactites.

'What I think is, I think you are incredibly beautiful and I am the luckiest man I know. And I love you.'

Her expression softened and a tiny smile began at the corners of her mouth. She reached for my hand, raised it to her lips and kissed my knuckles. 'I love you too, Frank. One of life's happier coincidences.'

The ritual of Sundays hadn't varied much since we met: one of us would cook a mammoth breakfast, while the other went for the papers. This wasn't quite the pigout it might seem, as it was usually the only meal of the day. It had come into being as a kind of a stoking up for me, because on Sunday afternoons I would normally be heading off for one of the many corners of Ireland to begin a new locum on the Monday. Claire was cook this weekend so I walked round to the newsagents.

Strolling back in the warm sunshine, my eye was drawn to an item in the lower right corner of the front page of *The Sunday Instructor*. I leaned against some railings and read the article, which went under the poetic headline:

CATTLE DEATHS BAFFLE VETS

Vets throughout the country are mystified by a recent outbreak of Anthrax, a killer disease which can affect man as well as animals, but has, so far, only been reported in cattle. The disease is caused by a bacillus and is rapidly fatal. A joint statement by the Departments of Agriculture and Health cautions people who work with cattle, against touching any animal found suddenly dead or extremely ill, and advises them to contact a veterinary surgeon at once.

A spokesperson for the Department of Agriculture said that, by comparison with the figures for other years, the present outbreak amounted to nothing less than an epidemic. He said that, while the source of the outbreak remained unclear, the Department was following a definite line of enquiry and a breakthrough was expected soon. Pressed by leaders of the farmers' organisations on the government's attitude to compensation, he said that the matter was under discussion but that a decision had yet to be arrived at.

Mr Matt Rush, General Secretary of the Irish Veterinary Union (IVU), which represents the country's general practitioners, stated that his members were doing all in their power to stem the spread of the disease. 'There is a full and ongoing liaison between the IVU and our colleagues in the state service,' he said.

The lid had come off. I wondered whether someone had blown the whistle, or if the article had the blessing of the powers that be.

Claire read it over breakfast. I watched her and decided that her beauty of last night had owed nothing to the soft lighting of the bistro; with the midday sun streaming through the window, she was still unlike any woman I had ever seen – there was a serenity about her, a tranquillity; she looked as though she could never age. I smiled to myself, a small smile of happiness. Claire caught it.

'What's the joke?'

'No joke.'

'Then why were you grinning like a baboon?'

'Not grinning, smiling. Smiling like a baboon.'

'So smiling. Why?'

'Believe it or not, because I'm so happy and you're so beautiful.'

She snorted in happy dismissal.

'I'm dead serious. If you weren't such a lousy singer you'd be perfect.'

'You're no nightingale yourself,' she retorted and returned to the article, reaching one hand across to cover mine. A tiny breeze wandered lazily in and out through the raised window; the net curtains billowed and fell, billowed and fell, while, on the table, a floral-patterned shadow-tide ebbed and flowed languidly across our breakfast. She lifted her head. 'Some headline, huh? Cattle Deaths Baffle Vets. It rhymes perfectly.'

'Never mind the headline. What do you think of the contents? Anything strike you as odd?'

'The oddest thing is that this is the first time I've ever seen a man referred to as a spokesperson. I thought it was a misprint but it says "he" twice, so I presume it's right. It's always women who are spokespersons – I don't know why we ever bothered to change it . . .' Claire rarely passes up such opportunities.

I shook my head. 'That is *not* what I meant.'

'I'll bet you didn't even notice it. What then? Odd that the disease is cropping up all over?'

'No.'

'Stop playing guessing games, Frank! Am I getting warmer? Animal, mineral, vegetable? What's odd? Animal diseases are hardly my field!'

'Relax! Look at the timing.'

'What? The disease has been around for a month and it's only now that the Department is issuing warnings about how dangerous it is to touch carcases, and so on?'

'Bingo!'

'Maybe the provincials have been running it all along?'

'Is that likely?'

'It's possible, though I'm sure the local correspondents

33

would have filed it and it's certainly big enough to have made the nationals – at least the agricultural sections. Have you seen any of it?'

'Just one. Last week.'

'Did you touch the carcase?'

I smiled at her sudden alarm. 'I suspected what it was and took all due precautions.'

'What a clever little sausage my Frank is,' she beamed. 'I wonder though,' the reporter in her began to stir, 'why it took a month for them to get all steamed up about the public health aspect. I'd have had it in the papers from day one. And on TV. And radio.'

I told her about Dr Johnson's caveat to me and the danger of panic selling, falling prices, mutinous farmers. As I went on, her jaw became more and more set. She wasn't too pleased about the cavalier attitude of the authorities, she said. The establishment putting Sean Citizen's life on the line again, she said. And for what? To keep the fat farmers of the country happy. The landed gentry. What about the inner cities? We argued back and forth a bit. I pointed out that in this case, it was the fat farmers and the landed gentry who were in danger, the denizens of the inner cities being, by the very nature of their location, not given much to coming across suddenly dead bullocks, or inexplicably ill ones either, for that matter . . .

'Hmmph!' she said and, grey eyes sparking like indignant arc lamps, announced that she would certainly be putting some awkward questions to some civil servants first thing in the morning.

'And proper order too,' I said, drawing a suspicious glance.

When we eventually got round to our other time-honoured Sunday custom, the crossword, I was presented with a rare chance to feel smug, solving at once a clue which Claire had obviously been working on for some time. I was immersed in the Sports Section when Claire read out: 'Seven across, Frank. Six letters, second letter, T. The clue is: "Make a start, reorganising rock bands." I thought it might be "Stones" – but why?'

'"Strata",' I said. 'Anagram of "a start" . . . Strata, bands of rock. The word "reorganising" signals an anagr . . .'

'I *know*!' she said. 'You don't have to explain.' And she turned, slightly huffily, to write it in.

I retreated back into the lee of the Sports Section.

When she went to dress for some family occasion which was scheduled for the afternoon, I went with her, the idea being that we finish the crossword, me doing the writing while Claire did the dressing, but the man has yet to be born who could concentrate on the intricacies of fifteen down – 'Fitting that turnover should be important in the millinery business.' Seven letters, second letter 'A', fourth letter 'S' – while Claire sat at her dressing table in diaphanous, lacy, tan and cream lingerie (*café au lait*, was the official colour, she told me), rhythmically brushing her hair with long graceful strokes. I watched mesmerised as the movements of her arm caused her breast to rise and fall. Interpreting my silence unerringly, she stopped brushing, arm still above her head. In the mirror, she arched an eyebrow at me and said in mock warning: 'Back to fifteen down, Frank. Second letter "A", fourth letter "S" . . . What's the clue again?'

'Who knows?' I said, rising from my seat on the bed. 'Who cares? Who can remember that far back? Besides, I've just thought of a poem about you.'

'Oh yeah?'

'Do you want to hear it?' I cleared my throat.

'Sure.'

'Okay. Here goes:

"Rose's are red,
And Violet's are blue,
But *café au lait* looks only incredibly sexy on you . . ."'

'It's a lovely poem, Frank. I'm honoured.'

35

'You don't mind me knowing what colour Rose's and Violet's are?'

'It's the loose world we live in. Frank!' she protested half-heartedly as she saw me approach in the mirror. 'I'm going to be late!'

'I know.' I slid my arms around her and buried my face in her hair.

'Well, don't you care?'

'No. Do you?'

'No,' she murmured and leaned her head back, rubbing it against my shoulder. She turned her head to kiss me and, without taking her mouth from mine, stood slowly and turned into my arms. I led her to the bed, gently laid her down, and we made love with the urgency of clandestine lovers stealing precious moments.

Afterwards, she lay napping on my chest. I stroked the silkiness of her back and resisted the urge to doze peacefully off – I knew I'd have to wake her so I just lay there, thinking for the nth time how lucky I was. In a little while I shook her shoulder. 'Hey! Wake up, Sleeping Beauty. Time to go.'

'Awwwh!' she groaned and, with a deep sigh, struggled sluggishly out of my embrace.

I walked her to her car and watched as she drove to the end of the crescent. As she edged out into the traffic, she turned, waved back and blew me a kiss. I returned to the flat, did the wash-up and sat down to finish the papers. Suddenly, apropos of nothing, the answer to fifteen down came to me. I filled in the C P IZE of CAPSIZE in red biro, drew an arrow to the margin, signed:

'F. "The Brain" Samson. XXX,'

and left for my next job, a stint for Gino Callaghan in Limerick.

5

The road to Limerick turned out to be something of a road to Damascus for me. Though the revelations were by no means complete, by the time I'd reached my destination, I'd come to the conclusion that there was something definitely odd about the anthrax outbreak. It would take about another week before I realised exactly how odd.

Traffic was light, at least in my direction. Flashing by on the other side, weekenders from the city were beginning to stream back towards Dublin, reluctant early starters hoping to beat the jams – on a fine summer weekend like this it would be bumper to bumper in a couple of hours. But my side was wide and open and I gave the Land Rover her head. I played about with the radio and listened to the tail end of a football match, the top few songs in the charts, and the pros and cons of a theory that the people of the west coast of Ireland were not Celts at all, like the rest of the country, but the descendants of intrepid Phoenicians. Coming into Nenagh, I checked my watch, decided I had time, and broke my journey to call on Bill Howell, classmate, flatmate, and best friend from college days. We didn't see each other very often anymore, didn't even keep in contact much, but we had one of those maintenance-free friendships which survived undiminished, no matter how much we ignored it.

We almost collided in his gateway. As usual, he was

driving like a maniac. As I shuddered to a halt, I could see a broad smile of recognition forming on his face.

'Hey, Frank!' he grinned, squeezing alongside.

'Hey yourself, you loony. Where's the fire?'

'Just on my way to a call. Hop in.' He began to move things off the passenger seat of his elderly, battered Mercedes.

'I haven't got much time, Bill.'

'It'll be less than an hour. Leave the Land Rover here.'

'Okay,' I said and pulled in tight to the side of his driveway.

'Where are you off to this time?' Bill asked as we headed out of town.

'Limerick. Gino Callaghan.'

He shot me a concerned look. 'There's nothing wrong with Gino, is there?'

'Jeez, Bill! You make me sound like some kind of vulture or . . . hyena! He's off on holiday with Sylvia and the kids. That's all.'

'Lucky sod. God knows when I'll get a break. I can't afford to even *think* of one at the moment.'

'Well, when you do, the locum'll be on the house. You know that.'

'Thanks, Frank, but don't pencil me into the diary yet.'

'What's the call anyway?' I asked as Bill eased out to overtake a bus which had been holding us up for all of ten seconds or so. Suddenly I could see beyond the bus, and my heart froze in horror. Squeezing my eyes shut, bracing my arms against the dashboard and ramming my right foot into the floor, I prayed, for Bill had committed us suicidally to an almost nonexistent gap between the bus and an oncoming oil tanker.

'Lame horse,' I heard him say as the thrum of huge diesels and blaring horns pressed in and down on me from all sides. I telescoped my neck into my chest, awaiting the inevitable, hating Bill passionately at that moment for taking me with him. One second, two . . . The roaring maelstrom of noise mysteriously evaporated, the expected

time of impact miraculously passed . . . I opened my eyes
tentatively, squinted about me and found that we were
inexplicably in the clear.

I cleared my throat and said hoarsely, 'That's hardly a
Sunday afternoon call, is it? Unless he's broken the leg.'
My hands were shaking and slick with sweat.

'It happened suddenly, according to the owner, but then
again he hasn't seen the horse since Wednesday – so what's
suddenly? Anyway, we'll soon know.'

We careered through, over and around the hills over-
looking the broad silver sickle of the Shannon and, ten
minutes later, turned into the driveway of a large house.
Bill raced straight past, round the back to the stable yard,
accompanied by a yapping pack of canine outriders.

A red-bearded giant appeared from one of the loose
boxes as we pulled up. 'Bill,' he said.

'Geoff,' said Bill in reply. Obviously an area where they
weren't given to effusive greetings. 'Frank Samson. Geoff
Collins.'

Collins ducked his head once in my direction. 'Frank.'

'Geoff,' I said, returning the duck. When in Rome . . .

'What's the problem?' Bill asked, fetching his boots from
behind the back seat.

'Right fore. Can't put it to the ground.'

'Which horse is it?'

'Jebali.'

'Jebali? You still haven't decided where to send him,
then?'

'Not yet. I've got a possible three but I'm waiting for a
decision from two others before I make the final choice.'

'Well we don't want anything happening to Jebali. Let's
have a look.'

There was a good-looking grey gelding pulling hay from
a net which hung from a ring in the back wall. He was
favouring his right fore, barely touching the toe to the
ground. The leg had swollen up above the fetlock and I
could imagine it throbbing like hell. It looked like it had
been that way for at least a couple of days. When the horse

39

turned to get a better look at us, he took none of the weight on his sore foot but turned in a series of small hops on the left.

Bill and Geoff entered but, as the space was hardly big enough for the two of them and the horse, I stood by the door. Bill lifted the leg and gently squeezed the hoof with the hoof-tester; predictably, the horse nearly hit the roof. When he had settled him again, Bill began to probe the sole with a hoof knife. The horse winced once or twice and tried to pull its foot away but otherwise gamely stuck it out. Bill interrupted his scraping and looked up. 'Geoff,' he said, 'if you'd been caught coming out of Garvey's sandpit with this horse, you could have been arrested for stealing – there's enough gravel in here to fill a small truck.'

Jebali bore the pain bravely as Bill pared back the sole until he located and released a nasty abscess, and a bead of grey pus oozed out. An application of iodine, an antitetanus shot and an antibiotic injection completed the job, and we prepared to leave. 'Put a poultice on that, Geoff, and change it in the morning. I'll look in tomorrow afternoon about threeish – he'll need a couple of days of injections. Okay?'

'Right,' Geoff said.

Bill packed his stuff away in the boot and opened the driver's door. 'Geoff,' he nodded.

'Bill,' Geoff said, then turned to me. 'Frank.' They obviously weren't into lavish goodbyes, either.

'Geoff,' I said.

Driving through the gate, being seen off the premises by the same yapping canine escort, I asked Bill. 'What was Geoff looking for? A trainer for the horse?'

'Yes. He had Jebali at Northfield. Stuck it out until the bitter end, until Murray lost his licence. I don't know if he was being loyal or just foolish, but he persevered longer than most.'

'You've lost me, I'm afraid.'

'It's a long story.' He thought a moment, deciding where

to start. 'I know you're not a racing man, Frank, but even *you* must have heard of Northfield?'

'Ah, no. Sorry. It doesn't ring a bell.'

'Jeez! You've got to be the only one in the whole country.' He shook his head. 'Well you've heard of George Harty, surely?'

'Who hasn't? Aaarrrghhh!' I gargled irreverently, rolling my eyes.

George Harty's life had been famous, but his death had been nothing short of spectacular. He had dropped dead in the winner's enclosure at some big race meet – I didn't remember which – while being presented with yet another prestigious trophy. That in itself was spectacular, but what followed made it stupendously sensational: when George turned waxy and collapsed, the cameraman in the enclosure decided to record the drama in full – he later claimed (somewhat disingenuously, it was thought) that he assumed George was just having 'a bit of a turn', and that it would be helpful for his doctors if he captured it on tape; he also maintained, reasonably enough, that the person in the outside broadcast control truck should have switched at once to another camera. But unfortunately the person in the OB unit, knowing that the next few minutes would be devoted to close-up, uninterrupted, laudatory speechifying, had chanced a quick visit to the loo. To make matters even worse, the winning owner, a stout party by the name of Madeleine Fingal-Symms, became unwittingly involved in the spectacle when she squatted down to tend to the stricken man. From that moment on, the country's television screens were filled with the double image of the contorted face of the dying trainer in the lower right diagonal half while, suspended above him, the upper left field was filled with an expanse of pink flannel drawers which clasped their wearer some three inches above her pudgy knees. And so, TV viewers in bars and bookie shops, pubs and parlours all over the country had been treated to over a minute of pure sex and violence. Live. It took three weeks for the nation to settle down again.

'Quite,' said Bill in a clipped tone. 'Well, be that as it may, Northfield was George's home place. He started training there, local horses at first, but then his reputation grew and he needed to expand so he bought a place in Kildare and operated from there for twenty-five years or so. Then he suffered a mild heart attack and was warned to slow down, so he sold the Kildare place and moved back to Northfield. Most of the owners moved with him because, over the years, he had built up a great team, and so he continued to prosper. Until, that is, his . . . rather vulgarly exhibitionist demise.

'There was only one heir, a nephew called Joe Murray, George's only sister's sole offspring. Joe had none of George's ways, with either horses or owners, but he managed to hold on to most of the owners by paying way over the odds for top quality staff, and they did the training while Joe himself strutted about and developed a mega drink habit. Then the money ran out and he couldn't pay the classy help any more, so the slide began in earnest. Joe should have stayed in vet school. He dropped out to take over from his uncle.'

'Sad. But it doesn't explain why you don't know whether Geoff was being stupid or loyal . . .'

'A lot of people stayed loyal, though few as long as Geoff. Despite problems at the yard, both real and rumoured, a surprising number of owners stayed. There were a good many reasons, the main one being that George Harty had become an almost mythical figure, and North-field was like a shrine – like . . . like what The Cavern was to The Beatles. You kind of expected magic and greatness to be constantly hovering in the air of the place. That's one reason.

'Then there's Joe himself. Like I said, he's in danger of becoming an infamous baddie, but a while back, he finally showed some character and got himself off the booze. He probably thought it would cure all his ills, revive the yard, but by then, the place was pretty much in free fall. Some owners stayed on, knowing that a mass exodus would make it that much harder for George's nephew to dry out. They probably felt that that was what George would have wanted them to do. But racing is a business and I reckon that hanging on at that point was where loyalty and stupidity began to get mixed up.

'Yet another reason for holding on was Murray's wife – she's said to be a really nice woman and though she doesn't know horses from ice cream, she was working like a slave to save the yard.

'So, with most of the good horses gone, and most of the good staff, too, the aura of magic evaporated. Joe's boozing only compounded the fact that he's a fairly surly bloke who's got no way with horses or people and probably never had. There was also talk of cruelty, negligence, starving the horses, cheating owners, and God knows what else, but no one pressed charges, so some super-fairminded citizens like Geoff, going on the principle that a man is innocent until proven guilty, refused to join what they saw as basically a lynch mob. I hate to say it but there's no smoke without fire and the rumours had been pretty well substantiated. I think it was definitely stupid of Geoff to have stayed to the end, laudable maybe, but stupid.

'There were other little things too, which put people off, some really petty like. As soon as he took over, Joe tried to cash in on the George Harty connection by calling himself Murray-Harty. That kind of thing doesn't go down well and everyone began to call him Moriarty, even the papers. When they dehyphenated him, I suppose he thought, what's the point? So now he's back to just Murray, though he calls himself Joss instead of Joe. That hardly matters; he finally lost his licence a week or two back. From what I heard, he'd have lost it long ago if it wasn't for the industry's respect for his late Uncle George. But Joe, I'm afraid, is now history. Which means, of course, that all the local small owners who began to fill the spaces left by the exodus of the bigger clients – at much reduced rates, of course – now have to find new homes for their horses.'

'Sounds like a right mess. Do you know Murray?'

'I've seen him around – at the races and such – but, no, I can't say that I know him. I knew old George alright, very well. He and my parents were great friends. He was a really nice man . . .' (Aw shit! I thought, recalling my irreverent miming of George's death throes) . . . 'but Joe I know only by his rather dodgy reputation. I don't go to Northfield – it's too far away, damn near sixty miles.'

We drove on in companionable silence.

'What do you make of this anthrax epidemic, then?' Bill asked, skilfully skinning by a tractor which seemed to me to fill the whole lane from hedge to hedge, and sticking a hand out the window to wave back at the driver.

'Jeez! Go easy, will you, Bill!' I clutched the dashboard and, for about the tenth time, drove my right foot into the floor. 'I'm a lousy passenger.'

'That's alright,' he grinned, 'I'm a lousy driver.'

'Very funny,' I growled – wasted, of course. 'The anthrax?' I got back on topic. 'A bit of a mystery, isn't it? Have you seen any?'

'Yep. Two in fact. On the same farm, in the same field, three days apart. There were over thirty dry cows in the field and I thought we were going to lose them all. How about you?'

'Just one. In Galway. I was covering for Mark Daley.'

'I believe Mark broke his leg?'

'Fell off a horse.'

'Really? I heard he'd been *kicked* by a horse.'

'Uh-uh.' I shook my head.

'How is he?'

'Fine, now.'

'But what about Stephen Blake? Isn't that something?'

'Stephen Blake from Fermoyle?'

'Yes. He's got to be the most unfortunate poor bastard of all time.'

'Why's that?' I asked, trying not to slip into vulture/ hyena mode. Or at least not to let it show.

'He was called in by some local bigwig – an American film producer or director or something. One of his prize

Pekes was sick. Anyway – you know Stephen – anxious to make the big impression, he comes hurtling up the drive, all biz, in his new, top of the range, state of the art, Range Rover . . . and runs straight over a Peke.'

'The sick one.'

'No, Frank. *Not* the sick one. Another one. A totally different Peke. This guy has three of them. Stephen leaps out and checks the Peke which is plainly going toes up but still has a way to go. The owner is at high doh, so Stephen says he's going to rush it back to the surgery as it needs instant attention. He chucks it on the back seat, throws himself back into the sexy Range Rover and – you're not going to believe this, Frank – in his hurry, reverses over the *other* goddam Peke, killing it stone dead!'

'The sick one?' I asked once more, groping frantically for the silver lining in what looked like shaping up to being one of the blackest black clouds of all time.

Bill shook his head gravely. 'Uh-uh, Frank. *Not* the sick one. The sick one is lying in the drawing room, reclining on satin cushions, wheezing and gasping, in dire need of the attentions of the vet, who is otherwise occupied outside, publicly slaughtering its healthy fellow Pekes with his new, top of the range, state of the art, how is your father, Range Rover.'

'God almighty!' I breathed in horror. 'Are you serious?'

'I can't believe you haven't heard it! The whole country is talking about it . . . Did you not hear the latest one? "Who's been on top of more "peaks" then Sir Edmund Hillary? Stephen Blake . . ."'

'That's not funny. Can you *imagine*?'

'I agree. Not funny. Anyway, what can Steve do, the poor bastard? The Peke he reversed over is as dead as a maggot and the first one he squashed is expiring noisily on the back seat, so he rushes off to the surgery with it . . . but it dies anyway, on the way . . .'

'Oh! Nooo!'

'. . . and not only *tha-at*, but the one he'd originally been

45

called in for, but never actually got to, dies too. Of pneumonia.'

'This,' I said solemnly, 'has got to be the very worst thing I have ever, in my whole life, heard!'

'Me too,' Bill said, equally solemnly. 'A hat trick of own goals . . .'

A few reflective seconds later we caught each other's furtive glances and exploded into uncontrollable shrieks of unholy laughter.

Recovering some small measure of professional decorum, we promptly surrendered it again by getting into a farcical debate over whether the bereaved owner – who, being an American was bound to sue the Y-fronts off Stephen Blake – had a case. Bill reckoned the Yank could take Stephen to the cleaners, whereas I was of the opinion that he had no case at all.

'Malpractice? C'mon, Bill. It was just a traffic accident, for Chrissakes! Maybe the guy can get the cops to summons Stephen for careless driving, and even *that* would be dodgy because The Incident, if I may refer to it so, didn't take place on the public highway . . .'

'Well, why didn't he at least go and see the one that was dying of pneumonia?'

'Because there was another one dying *faster* on the back seat of his Range Rover.'

'Yeah! Because he ran over it.'

'That's what I've been trying to tell you. It was an accident, a straightforward road traffic accident. You think we should treat RTA victims differently, depending on who it was that did the running over? Is that what you're saying? Or should vets be allowed to run over, say children, and be treated like anyone else, but get singled out for special punishment if we run over a dog or two? Would this guy be able to sue for millions if it had been the electrician or the plumber or a guest of his that ran over the pooches? If you ask me, Stephen did everything in the correct order.'

'Aw bullshit, Frank!' said Bill, recognising one of my awkward moods. 'By the way, this is the farm where they had the anthrax.' We were driving along by a high, ivy-covered wall on our right. 'He's one of my biggest clients. Milks about two hundred, two-fifty Friesian Holsteins. Rears his own replacements, doesn't buy in anything, does it all by the book.' He slowed down as the high wall continued to unwind on our right. There seemed to be no end to it.

'Big farm,' I said.

'Used to be the estate of the main local aristocracy. Apart from milking, he also grows cereals. He's almost self-sufficient. This is the field they died in.' He indicated a section of the high wall.

'Are there cows in there still?'

'I think so. Why?'

'Just comparing your case with mine. In the one I saw, the VO told them to leave the cattle in the field, but to fence off the area nearest the road.'

'There were three or four of these which should have calved by now so he'll have had to move those back up to the milking herd, but I don't know about the rest. If you like, we can have a look.' He slowed to a stop at the entrance to a narrow lane. 'The gate's just down here a bit.'

'Naw. It's not important. Just curious. Go on, head for home.'

I stayed for an hour or so, parrying all attempts to feed me, then, promising to call on my way back from the locum, continued my journey.

Squinting into the lowering sun I concentrated on driving directly west, and it was only when I turned a few degrees south and had some relief from the glare, that I began to think of anthrax again. I thought how odd it was that, in Tom Ryan's case in Galway and Bill's case in Tipperary, both fields had been separated from the road by almost impenetrable barriers, Ryan's thick hedge and eight-feet-high bank and Bill's huge estate wall. I wondered if there might not be some connection between the protection afforded by these barriers and the successful development

47

of dormant anthrax spores into the virulent form. But what would anthrax spores need to be protected from? Not natural things like frost, sunlight, desiccation – anthrax spores were one of the most resilient creatures in nature. I passed through a tiny village on a crossroads, checked a signpost and turned left. So what about unnatural things like (in view of the road factor), exhaust fumes, or oil droplets? Maybe anthrax was particularly sensitive to them? This could explain why the cattle in the wire-fenced fields had not been affected – perhaps those fields had been sprayed with anthrax bacilli *and* oil droplets, which inhibited them. But, hold on ... if oil and/or exhaust fumes killed anthrax spores, bang went the theory of the bacilli being spread by vehicles travelling the roads. And anyway ... why should bacilli blow over the high barriers, but oil droplets and fumes not? I came to this impasse as I reached the outskirts of the town of Ward in County Limerick and made straight for Rock Hill, the small hotel I had stayed at on my previous visit.

'Ah, *Mister* Samson!' Mrs Foley, owner and manager, theatrically clasped her hands in front of her pert bosom, then threw them apart. 'Back again and still looking like a teenager!' She beamed at me for a moment, inspecting me for changes. I beamed back. She was a widow, a slight woman in her late fifties with backcombed hair so black it must have been dyed, and the jollity usually associated with people twice her size. Her voice too, was that of a much larger woman; it almost boomed.

'It's good to be back, Mrs Foley,' I said, bringing the mutual beaming session to an end. I set down one of my cases and extended my hand. 'I see you've redecorated the reception.'

'*And* the dining room,' she smirked.

I swayed backwards to glance through the glass door. 'Why, so you have!'

'Do you like it?'

'Yes indeed. Lovely. Very cheerful. It gives a feeling of space.'

She smiled happily. 'That's what I think, too. Spaciousness.' She beamed around the tiny foyer again, then back at me. 'I've kept your old room for you.' Her tone suggested that she had almost had to give her life in its defence from hordes. I picked up my bag and followed her towards the stairs – there was no lift. 'I suppose you know that Sheila has left us?'

'Really? No. I didn't know.'

'Of course. You didn't keep in touch, did you?' I thought I detected a faint note of disapproval and I remembered the previous year when she had taken an almost unhealthy interest in trying to get me and the pretty receptionist together. 'Yes, she's gone. She got a job as a receptionist in The Senator Hotel in Killarney. A very good job.' We reached my room and she turned to me, her hand on the doorknob. 'I'm sure you'll miss her,' she said, throwing open the door with a flourish the room hardly warranted.

'Indeed I will,' I said. Secretly, I was relieved. Last year, before I'd met Claire, Sheila and I had had some memorably good times, and it had crossed my mind as I approached Ward that she might be all keen to resume where we'd left off, a definite no-no in my new circumstances. I set down my luggage and looked around; as far as I could see, nothing had changed, but as Mrs Foley continued to lurk expectantly in the doorway, I thought I must be missing something and checked again. Still nothing. 'What can I say?' I shrugged and flapped the arms. 'Home from home!'

'I expect you know she got engaged. It was in the papers.'

'I must have missed it.'

'To the young man whose father owns The Senator.'

'Oh! I must send her a card. Is he a nice bloke?'

'Almost as nice as yourself, Mr Samson.'

'Why *thank* you, Mrs Foley.' I made an exaggerated bow.

'Now.' She got all businesslike. 'What would you like to eat? You must be *starving*.'

'Not this evening, Mrs Foley. I've already eaten, thank you. But I am looking forward to night upon night of gastronomic bliss at Rock Hill!'

'*Now* who's the shameless flatterer?' She smirked and went out.

After I had unpacked and changed I went round to call on Eugene Callaghan – Gino to his friends. In fact, Gino to everyone, as far as I knew.

The Callaghan household was pure confusion. Half-filled suitcases, buckets and spades, inflatable air beds, a large wicker picnic basket, canoe paddles and fishing gear littered the entrance hall – the chaos was even worse than last year. My arrival was met with great excitement by the children as it officially inaugurated the holiday; from this moment on, their father was off duty, theirs exclusively for the duration; if the phone rang now, I'd be the one who'd have to head off, not him. To mark my arrival Gino and Sylvia declared a coffee break.

I knew the practice well enough not to need a familiarisation tour or introductions to the staff, so we sat in the bright kitchen, sipping hot coffee, and chatted. Stephen Blake's spectacular fall from grace came up early, brought up by Gino, and though this time there was no overt hilarity, black comedy bubbled barely beneath the surface. There was much sympathy for all three late Pekes and their bereft owner, but the general feeling was that Stephen had met his comeuppance.

'If I told him I'd delivered a rhinoceros of twins last week, then you can bet your life he'd have done a *Caesarean* on a hippopotamus with triplets the week before,' Gino summed it up. 'Under hypnosis,' he added. 'And probably under water.'

I laughed. 'Still,' I lifted my cup, 'it shouldn't happen to anyone.'

'True. But if it *did* have to happen to someone, then it's just as well it was Stephen that it happened to.'

I nodded sagely, not quite sure what he meant.

Gino gave me an update on cases that needed it, and that part of the business was soon dispensed with. Sylvia made second cups and, taking hers with her, left to resume the packing. Within minutes, inevitably, anthrax had come up. It was clearly going to be *the* topic of conversation for months to come, it and Stephen Blake.

'Have you had any around here, Gino?'

'Nearly every practice in the area had a case'

'In the whole country, if you ask me. I saw one in Galway, Bill Howell in Nenagh saw two; I met Dick Barnett from Carrigaline and he had also had two. Who lost the animal here?'

'Bobby Young.'

'The Joker?'

'The very man. But it didn't stop him making his lousy jokes. He's got an old donkey which had a touch of colic last week. Of course Bobby reckoned that what we were up against here was A Pain in the Ass. The only advice I can give you is: laugh at once, even if the joke is dire. If you don't, he'll repeat it until you do.'

'Tell me, Gino,' I said casually, loth to abandon my theory of an hour ago, 'is there a high wall around the field where Bobby's animal died?'

'You've already met him, then?'

'No.'

'Then how do you know about the high wall?

'Just a guess.'

'Guess bullshit, Frank. Come on, why did you ask about the wall? You *must* have been talking to Bobby.'

'I wasn't. Cross my heart and hope to get anthrax. Like I said, it's just a guess. I've seen two fields where the disease appeared and both of them had these bloody great walls or hedges, which should have prevented *anything* from splashing in from the road, so I began to figure and I came up with this crackpot theory . . .'

I explained my theory to Gino, who, early on, began to

shake his head in disagreement, but nevertheless heard me out. 'It won't work, Frank.'

'But there must be *some* connection with the high wall . . .'

'The Joker, Frank, is building a hay shed and silage pit right in the middle of *his* field and, for months now, there's been nothing but cement mixers, JCBs, diggers, tractors, dumpers, compressors and generators working in it from dawn to dusk, spreading fumes and oil over the whole area. In fact so much so that's he's being taken to court for contaminating the stream. Which might wipe the smile off his face for a while. He's had to fence off the stream and he's been piping water into that field for the last two months.'

'Ah well. Exit the Nobel Prize. But dammit Gino, it can't be just a coincidence. Three out of three . . .'

Gino's eyes slipped out of focus. 'Actually, now that I think of it, it's four out of four. Last week, I was on my way back from town and I saw one of our local VOs on the road. I don't know many of the government vets working out of the city, but I knew this one so I stopped to have a chat, and he was on an anthrax case. That field had a high wall too − I remember because as I was driving off, I was keeping an eye out for a low spot or a gate so that I could have a quick peep, but there wasn't one.'

The kitchen door burst open. 'Daddy! Daddy! Can I take my tricycle? Can I can I can I?' The little five-year-old, a scale model of her mother, asked breathlessly, hurtling herself onto her father's lap.

'Of *course* you can, Lucy! How could we *possibly* go on such a long journey without a back-up vehicle? Do you want a sip of coffee?'

But Lucy had already squirmed off his knee and, shooting back out the door as quickly as she had shot in, was gleefully crowing: 'Now Ben! I *told* you!'

'That little lassie rules us all,' Gino sighed and shook his head. 'Now we're stuck with having to fit the goddam tricycle in somewhere. A kid's tricycle must be the most awkward design ever thought of.'

Sylvia stuck her head round the door, ostensibly to see if we were alright, but obviously to let Gino know that it was time to come out and help.

I took the hint. 'Okay then, Gino. Unless I can give a hand here, I'll be off. I'll pop round to the surgery and have a looksee.'

I wished them a happy holiday and, on my way out, making a pantomime of much mystery and secrecy of the transaction, slipped Lucy and Ben a fiver each.

6

Gino's easy-going manner was deceptive. In fact he was a workaholic who drove himself mercilessly, and he certainly didn't spare me. The appointments book at the surgery was full for the next few days, crammed with routine work from morning until nightfall. Towards the end of the week, the days became progressively less busy and there were hardly any appointments at all for the following week. This had nothing to do with Gino relenting and deciding to go easy on me; it was a fairly common phenomenon of one-man practices – the clients got so used to seeing the same face all the time, that many preferred to postpone their routine jobs until 'the boss himself' got back. And so Gino had crammed as much work as he could into the first four days, before it became common knowledge that he was going on leave. Despite his best efforts at subterfuge, I knew there'd be cancellations; there always were. Needless to say, clients with really sick animals quickly discovered that in fact they weren't quite as fussy about waiting for 'the boss himself' as they had thought.

Back at the hotel, I phoned Claire. I usually clocked in on the first evening of a locum, just to let her know I'd arrived; this time, however, I also wanted her to check out my high wall theory and she promised she'd try to visit a few of the farms over the next few days. I didn't tell her that Gino had shot the oil droplet scenario down in flames, mainly because I still thought it had potential – the Joker's building site I wrote off as the inevitable exception that proved any rule.

In the following days I was much too busy for further theorising, but on one or two occasions I caught myself checking patients for anthrax before considering more mundane, and likely, diagnoses.

On Friday evening, Claire was on the 6.15 from Dublin. I was almost late – a horse with a colic at the far end of the practice and the Friday rush hour had really snarled up my plans – and I made the station just as the passengers debouched onto the platform.

She moved through the crowd with her long graceful strides, her auburn hair like a halo, backlit by the sun which had just dipped beneath the awning of the platform. She waved and gave a huge happy smile when she saw me. We'd been together for more than a year now, and that smile still gave me goosebumps. Turning to the tall, grey-haired man, who walked beside her, she pointed towards me, led him over and introduced him as Jim Darby, Chief Veterinary Officer for County Limerick. They must have discussed me minutely because, as we shook hands, he asked me how I was enjoying my second locum in Ward (fine, fine), and if I'd heard from Gino (no); then he said how delighted he was to shake the hand of the man who had solved the 'Catamaran business' (shrug and simper) last year, and told me, glancing meaningfully at Claire, what a lucky man I was (cheesy smile). Then he let my hand go. When he turned to take leave of Claire, she gave him the full works – the goosebump smile at full voltage, the grateful look, the lingering handshake – and thanked him for his most enjoyable company all the way from Dublin. She doesn't like to admit it but Claire uses her femininity to gather potential contacts as assiduously as a squirrel which expects a long, hard winter, gathers nuts. As I steered her through the thinning crowd and out into the car park, I said: 'D'you mind telling me why you were doing the Mata Hari number on the local CVO?'

'He's a nice man, Frank. And he *was* good company.' She slung her canvas holdall into the back and said: 'God, this wagon is a tip! First thing tomorrow morning, the big clean up.'

Not to be put off, I asked her if her meeting with the CVO had been totally fortuitous. It hadn't, of course – she'd met him when she visited Agriculture House, discovered that he was the Limerick CVO, ascertained that he was in Dublin for the week working on 'this anthrax thing' and determined that he'd be on the afternoon train home on Friday. She'd been planning on driving down, but had promptly changed her plans, and she'd been gratified to see how pleasantly surprised Darby had been when she slipped into the seat opposite him. He had also, it transpired, been talkative.

'The first case of this anthrax epidemic was in Limerick, did you know that?'

'No,' I said, 'I didn't.'

'And d'you know what else? I've checked on your high walls. I visited five around Dublin and I discussed another three with Jim, Limerick cases. All the Dublin ones, and two of the Limerick cases, had high walls. In case you're worried, he didn't realise I was probing.'

'Five out of six? Well how about that, now,' I said, with a happy smile, taking my prepaid ticket off the dashboard and slotting it thoughtfully into the automatic barrier raiser.

We had to go back to see the colicky horse, which, after a couple of hours respite, had relapsed and was now actually *worse*. I was surprised – I'd thought the first injections would have solved the problem. The owner was worried. So was I, only I couldn't show it.

I checked the pulse – as a rule of thumb, the faster and more thready the pulse, the worse the colic. This animal had a pulse of about sixty-four (it had been below sixty last time and should be forty to be normal). The Capillary Refill Time was good, indicating that the peripheral circulation was in working order, a positive sign. Another optimistic pointer was that the gums and conjunctiva were still a healthy pink – not dark red to blue/black which would signify toxaemia. On the other hand, the gums were tacky and the skin had lost some of its elasticity so the horse was dehydrated. I hoped I had enough intravenous fluids with me – horses often need gallons.

The internal examination I had done on my first visit hadn't been of much help diagnostically, but this time I could feel a stodgy, doughy mass, the pelvic flexure of the colon. The rectum itself was empty – nothing was passing back through that impacted colon. By the time I'd given my patient a couple of buckets of salts and liquid paraffin through a nasogastric tube, twelve litres of (slow) intravenous fluids, and various painkilling, antispasmodic and antitoxic drugs, also I/V, it was pushing on for ten-thirty.

It took us another thirty minutes to get back to Ward, by which time the only establishment still serving food was a van outside the town hall where the regular Friday night disco was just warming up. A knot of the local young swains horseplaying around the entrance fell into awed silence as Claire bought two cod and chips and drenched them with all the condiments and sauces on offer. When she headed back to the Land Rover, and they knew it was safe, a few of the braver lads began to call out to her, offering to take her to the disco, to bed, to incredible orgasmic heights, et cetera. If she'd turned back, I reckoned they'd have taken to their heels in panic.

Whether she'd been trying to make some unsubtle point or not, I couldn't say, but Mrs Foley had put Claire in Sheila's old room. When I'd told her the day before that Claire would be coming to stay for the weekend, she'd immediately said, in what I felt was a slightly frosty tone: 'Oh! How nice for you. I'll prepare a room for her at once.' It was said so reflexly that I reckoned she'd been rehearsing. Perhaps she felt I was being disloyal to the memory of the absent Sheila (whose praises she had been enumerating at every opportunity since my arrival) or maybe she had strong feelings on extramarital cohabitation;

or it could even have been a bit of both – she might just have been one of those most perfectly balanced of creatures, a person with a chip on *both* shoulders. Either way I had no interest in discussing the matter with her, so I thanked her and let it be.

We ate in Claire's room, then fled the smell of greasy chips to mine.

That night, by the light of the gibbous moon which hung outside the window and laid a pale-white track, like an extra sheet, across the bed, I stared at the sleeping face of Claire and thought back to the chic city girl I'd first met, a woman who had thought it odd that there were roads which didn't have public lighting and couldn't believe there were no taxis prowling the streets of Knockmore-on-Sea (pop. 500, give or take) at all hours of the night. Her transformation had been as swift and remarkable as it had been complete. She had come to stay for a few days, ostensibly to work on an article she was planning on *A Day In A Vet's Life*, but, even at that early stage there was already a strong personal interest and it seemed clear that only some unforeseeable disaster could prevent our relationship from developing further. Possibly in anticipation of this, Claire had arrived, bowed under the weight of little black numbers, red numbers, blue, green and beige numbers, with shoes and accessories to match, a jewellery box, and enough cosmetics to open a small shop. The first morning, when I'd collected her from the hotel, she was dressed for country life a là *Horse and Hound*. Around eleven that same morning, when it became obvious that this was country life a là *Cow and Sheep*, she asked me to pull up as we passed a general haberdashery in a little town we were driving through and, fifteen minutes later, arrived back in a woolly jumper, and jeans tucked into sensible wellingtons. The *Horse and Hound* stuff, now wrapped in brown paper and tied with hairy white string, was consigned to the back and I don't believe I've seen it since. Now, she only brings style when I warn her that there may be a fancy do in the offing, and she lives her weekends from a canvas holdall which contains her toothbrush, a few warm shirts, a couple of pairs of jeans – clean but well marked with healthy farm stains, a woolly jumper or two, a tartan-lined Barbour, and thick, woolly socks. Between visits, her hiking boots and wellies live in the Land Rover. She can now hold an obstreperous calf or foal, restrain a cow by sticking her fingers into its wet nostrils, and she has even, under my direction, delivered a couple of lambs from ewes too small for me to handle. Most telling of all, she has stopped, long ago, wrinkling her gorgeous nose at such jobs.

The weekend was busy and we were on the road most of the time. The horse with the impacted colon was fluctuating wildly, one minute seemingly recovered, the next, down again. We were back and forth to him, giving him fluids, tubing more purgatives into him, keeping his drugs levels topped up. It was all costing money and I could see that the owner was beginning to wonder if the economical thing wouldn't be to have him put down. He asked about surgery and I told him, if he wanted his horse operated on, then he'd have to take it to one of the specialist equine hospitals which were properly kitted out for the job, and they'd be looking for big money before they even started. When we called on Sunday afternoon the owner had reached a harsh but necessary decision – if the horse wasn't showing clear signs of improvement by the following evening, then he'd put him down. This time I had a stern word in my patient's ear, gave him a few encouraging pats, and pushed the dosage rates of all his medications through the roof. Claire warned the horse that she fully intended visiting him next time she was down, so he'd better get the finger out right away and *do* something. On this occasion, she didn't come into the stable; she was in her city clothes because we were going straight from there to the train station and back to Dublin.

The second week began at a less frenetic pace. Towards evening on Monday, on my way back from seeing the colicky horse – he was much improved (he must have been eavesdropping when his fate was being discussed) – I remembered that I hadn't yet got around to checking The Joker's field. There'd been no time. Still harbouring a forlorn hope of salvaging my anthrax/oil-droplet theory, I turned off a few miles outside Ward and went in search of the field, and some way of explaining away the construction site and its machinery. I only had a vague recollection of where The Joker's out-farm was – I'd been there last year, but at night, and The Joker had been driving. After a wrong turn or two, I eventually came to a T-junction I recognised, turned left, rounded a bend and there it was up ahead, the high wall.

It was one of those well-built estate walls that still box off large tracts of the better land of rural Ireland, the former parks and estates of a rapacious and hated gentry. Half boundary, half defensive perimeter, they had been recommended by astute estate managers, decreed by absentee landlords, overseen by tyrannical agents, and built by the forced labour of a resentful tenantry a mere smouldering generation away from concerted revolution. These walls had been made to last, and they have, in most cases outliving the fine houses they were built to protect.

I parked and, locking the Land Rover, walked by the wall until it turned off down a narrow, untarred lane. By then I had looked through four gates into four fields, none of which had contained a building site. The fifth field, on the corner, didn't have a gate on to the main road, so I followed the wall down along the rough track, its gravel surface and grassy sides churned up by the passage of heavy vehicles. Here and there were lumps of dried cement, presumably the droppings of a bulk carrier as it squeezed along between the wall on one side and the briars and birches on the other. I followed this spoor until it turned in through a tubular-steel, five-bar gate, now locked. Inside, the trail of muddy wheel-tracks continued for some fifty yards, ending at a half-built hay shed and silage pit surrounded by various machines. The field. Leaning my elbows on the top bar of the gate, and resting a foot on the bottom, I took stock.

The actual site was cordoned off by an electric fence, as was a twenty foot strip of grass parallel to the wall by the main road. To my left, a line of bushes and small trees grew along the course of a stream, presumably the one that was about to land Bobby in court. In the breathy quiet of the evening I could hear its faint gurgle through the clicking pulses of the electric fences. I tried to count the grazing cattle and ended up with a rough figure of twenty, all black whiteheads, all about twelve hundredweight, a nicely matched bunch without a quarter hundredweight between any of them. Excluded by the electric fence from the lush grass by the wall, they were cropping a threadbare area, and I presumed that The Joker, too, had been advised not to move them, just in case. But, like Ryan's neighbour in Galway, he'd have to move them soon – big cattle like those get through a lot of grass. I studied the field, trying to resuscitate my theory, and though I twisted it every which way with Procrustean singlemindedness, I finally had to admit that, in light of the reality before me, it was untenable. As Gino had put it, the machinery would have emitted enough fumes and spray to kill all the anthrax bacilli in County Limerick.

For all their legendary dumbness, cattle are insatiably curious creatures and, as soon as they spotted me, they began to drift my way. Within a few minutes, I had a three-deep, twelve-ton audience standing in a rough semicircle, a wary five feet away, sussing me out. As I wasn't moving, the front row decided it would be safe to check me out further and shuffled cautiously closer. Then one, a real hero, began to edge in on his own and was soon sniffing at my hands from a mere foot away. Closer and closer he inched until at last his dewy nose briefly touched my hands; instantly he backed a few steps and stood, sending his tongue up his nostrils in a thoughtful, considering way, evaluating the results of his experiment. Emboldened by my stillness, he returned, but this time, he didn't retreat –

he couldn't, even if he'd wanted to, as the others had all shuffled forward a few steps too, and were now packed tight behind him. Instead, he produced about a foot of pale tongue, rough as sandpaper, and gave my hand a rasping, slobbery lick. He licked again, then tried to curl his tongue around the hand to draw it into his mouth – his investigations had obviously led him to conclude that, despite the fact that he was a strict herbivore, I was, if not actually *edible*, at least chewable. When another commenced cannibalistic efforts on my shoe leather, and a third was about to sample the material of my jacket, I decided that enough was enough. I waved a dismissive hand and said '*Shoo!*' and caused immediate panic in the ranks. Bullocks weighing over half a ton were almost falling over each other in their hurry to get away. They halted uncertainly a short distance off but, when I pushed myself away from the gate, immediately took to their heels again and galloped further away.

On my way back along the lane, I suddenly began to feel uneasy, although I couldn't quite figure out why. The feeling was so strong that I took a nervous look back along the darkening track, half expecting to see a menacing figure following me, but I was alone. My uneasiness persisted even when I emerged onto the tarred road, and I was beginning to wonder if I wasn't becoming paranoid, when, with a shock, I suddenly realised what was behind it: I had just identified *another* factor common to all the anthrax locations I'd seen, a factor which suddenly made me a dangerous threat to someone unknown. In each case, the only entrance to the field was through a gate hidden from the road. And that meant it couldn't possibly be a coincidence – somebody had to have *chosen* those fields. Lost in thought, I walked back to the Land Rover, the setting sun casting a long shadow ahead of me.

As I drove back to town, I reviewed all my facts. Up to a few hours before her death, Tom Ryan's heifer had been in a field with a high bank and hedge between it and the road, and an out-of-sight gate up a narrow crooked path; Bill

Howell's site had a high estate wall and I recalled him offering to drive me down a narrow lane to check (presumably through the gate) if there were cows still in the field; Bill's and The Joker's cases were almost identical. During dinner I decided to add Gino's reported case to the list – he'd told me he'd been trying to get a peep into the field as he drove away but that there hadn't been a break in the high wall. I reckoned therefore that it was legitimate to conclude that the gate, not being along the road, must have been down a side track. Four out of four, a perfect score.

Twice I phoned Claire, but she wasn't in either time. I walked around town for a while looking for The Joker – I thought he might have come in for a drink, but if he had, I didn't find him. In several of the pubs, I was recognised, and people insisted on buying me drink; in less than an hour, I'd drunk four pints, not one of which I had wanted, so I gave up the pub search and walked by the small river which bustled self-importantly through the centre of Ward. Just before going to bed, I tried Claire again and, this time, got through.

Her first question was about the colicky horse and I reported the progress. That took about five minutes as the new Claire, now quite knowledgeable about such matters, was eager for technical details – was he still dehydrating? did his colon still feel stodgy? any sign of toxaemia? was I worried about laminitis? and so on. When I told her about the hidden gates, she went suddenly quiet and I could almost see her working out the implications.

'Are you sure, Frank?'

'I'm sure about the ones I saw. Can you remember any of yours?'

She thought for a while, then reckoned that some were the same, but as she couldn't swear to them all, she'd have a quick look around in the morning – it wouldn't take long as she now knew where she was going, not like last time.

'I wonder if anybody else spotted the gate angle?' I asked. 'I wonder if the cops are on to it?'

'Why don't you ring Peter Potter? He'll tell you, or at

least, he should – after all the help you gave him last year with Catamaran.'

'Good idea. And, if they're not aware of it yet, then it's high time that they were.'

As neither Inspector Potter nor I would have been able to do much in the hour that was left of Monday, I put off phoning him until morning. I rang early to get him before he left home, remembering from last year how difficult he was to get hold of once he was snarled up in work at the station. He was full of beans, chatting about old times, telling me – with good-natured sarcasm – how surprised he was to find he could still function without having me to solve his cases for him ... As soon as I worked the conversation around to the anthrax epidemic, he clammed up and, though he refused to confirm a Garda investigation, he wouldn't deny one either and it was abundantly clear that there was. He asked me why I thought there might be and I told him that it was just a wild unfounded guess on my part. Two can play the clam game. I gave up after a while, said I'd talk to him soon again, and hung up.

Halfway through the morning rounds, Claire called me on my mobile phone. She'd visited all but one of the fields (she'd been unable to find the last one) and all had checked out positively – not a single one had a gate which was visible from the road. So the score was now eight out of eight. We discussed the significance of this for a while and I told her about Potter's uncharacteristic reticence.

'Why all the secrecy?' she asked.

'Who knows?' I said as I pulled into a farm and waved at the farmer who immediately started anxiously towards me. 'Listen, I've got to go. Call you this evening.'

One of the last calls of the morning round was to Bobby Young. The call was non-specific – 'Cow, fresh-calved, off food,' – so I hadn't rushed. He was crossing the yard when I swung in and brought the Land Rover to a halt beside him. 'Howya Bobby,' I said, before sliding the window shut against flies.

'Ah!' he beamed. 'Would you look who it is! The hard man himself. Back again to us, I see! Can't stay away now, can you?'

'Sure, I have to come back for a laugh every so often, Bobby. Apart from yourself, they're a fierce dry bunch out there.' And I nodded dismissively over my shoulder at the rest of Ireland.

Bobby beamed. 'And you're lookin' damn fit too, young fella. You'd be a hell of a man entirely if you'd only stop cuttin' the hair!'

He began to laugh and, remembering Gino's advice, I added a quick bark too. With a surname like Samson, the joke was old and hoary; I was pretty certain that he had used it last year too. A couple of times, if memory served.

'You're looking pretty good yourself, Bobby.'

'Acch! The age is beginnin' to take its toll. I'm thinkin' of changin' the name by deed poll . . .' He waited, funny bit at the ready, exactly like someone who has just said: 'Knock knock . . .'

'To what, Bobby?' I asked, knowing full well to what.

'Bobby *Old!*' He cackled and I brayed dutifully again.

While I was at the back of the Land Rover getting my case, Bobby extricated a dead, dried-up bee from under my windscreen wiper and was holding it by its one remaining wing when I rejoined him. He grinned at me and I could see that there was another one coming.

'What,' he asked, eyes crinkling in anticipation, 'is the first thing that comes into a fly's mind when he hits your windscreen?'

'Go on.' I said, with a shake of my head. 'What?'

'His *arse!*' And he guffawed. I laughed too, even though I'd heard it before. I'd forgotten it – I'm no good at remembering jokes.

'Be that as it may,' I said, trying to bring the curtain down on the vaudeville act, 'you've got some trouble then, aye?'

'Not me. The cow!' He creased into giggles again, and this time I was damned if I was going to join in. He stopped suddenly but didn't repeat the gag – perhaps he realised how truly sub-standard it was.

'What's wrong with her?' I enunciated pointedly, daring him to answer that if he knew that he wouldn't have had to call me.

'Couldn't rightly say, Frank. She calved two days ago and she has an awful grunt now. Kind of unkh.. unkh.. unkh. Like that. All the time.'

'Is she eating?'

'Nothin'.'

'Drinking?'

'A cupful. If that.'

We came to the gate into the inner yard. Beaming hugely, he pointed to the three big notices wired to it. The first said 'NO ENTRY', the second, 'BEWARE OF THE DOG' and the bottom one, 'SURVIVORS WILL BE PROSECUTED'. I smiled thinly and passed on into the yard, keeping a sharp look out – vets learn these things early. We rounded a shed corner and suddenly, there it was. The Dog. Stretched out asleep in the dubious sunshine, it was an ancient and obese sheepdog, so fat that its upper legs stuck horizontally out from its gross torso, and didn't go anywhere near touching the ground.

'*That's* the dog?'

'That's him. That's Assassin.'

As we drew nearer, I could see that Assassin's ancient lips had fallen slackly away from his ancient gums and that there wasn't a tooth in his ancient head. 'The world's only toothless watchdog!' I scoffed. 'Hah!'

Bobby, his face creasing for laughter again, was in like a shot with a hoary old gag. 'Toothless he may be, but *watchit* – he could give you a damned nasty suck!' We passed the prone Assassin, hooting. He never even heard us; only the faintest rhythmic quiver in the fat over his ribcage betrayed the presence of life.

As soon as I saw the cow, the laughter stopped. Sunken-eyed and hunched, she stood facing the wall, stiffly turning her neck to look at us when the opening door flooded her dark stable with light; then she turned away again, disinterested, and resumed her lonely, agonised grunting. I went to her head but she paid no attention whatever to my presence until I caught her stone cold ear; then she made a few feeble twitches to free it but gave up long before I let it go. As I went on with my examination, my face became grimmer. Bobby obviously realised how serious it was and suspended the stand-up comic routine. I removed the stethoscope from my ears and put it in my pocket.

'Not a sound in her abdomen, Bobby. Her guts are all seized up.'

'That's bad?'

'Very.' I put on a rectal sleeve and did a quick internal examination. 'Acute peritonitis.' I said grimly. 'She's a goner, Bobby.'

'A cute what?'

I ignored the pause in 'acute' – perhaps I had only imagined it. 'Peritonitis. Acute *diffuse* peritonitis. She probably got it when she was calving. If her womb was damaged, then infection could seep through into the peritoneum . . .'

'What's that?'

'A slippery lining on all the organs in the abdomen, and on the body wall, too. It's to let everything move around in there without friction. When an infection gets in, the slippery surfaces get inflamed and start to stick together. Poisons build up and in no time enter the bloodstream, at which point the animal becomes toxic. That's the stage she's at now. You get the same thing in humans from a ruptured appendix or a burst ulcer. Did she calve on her own or did you have to help her?'

'She needed a bit of help alright, but I wasn't here. The pharmacist was on duty and he helped.'

'*Pharmacist!*' I exclaimed, affronted. 'What pharmacist? What the hell does a pharmacist know about calving cows?' Recently there had been some ill-feeling between vets' and pharmacists' organisations: The vets claimed that farmers who went to a pharmacy, and explained their animals' symptoms, would invariably be sold something, anything; they would try this ju-ju for two or three days and, when it didn't work, they would call the vet. Vets contended that pharmacists were not qualified to diagnose illness, and that nobody, *including* vets, could reach a diagnosis from afar, without even seeing the patient. On the other hand, the pharmacists (and farmers) maintained that it didn't take a vet to know the simpler conditions, and that vets wanting to be called to treat every single minor or common ailment were only trying to monopolise the whole thing out of self-interest. 'Which pharmacist?' I demanded indignantly, intending to do something about it, even if it was nothing more than reporting him to Gino on his return. Calving difficulties were *definitely* not minor ailments.

'Oh, he's not a *real* pharmacist. I call him that because this is a farm and his job is to assist . . .'

'Aw *shit*, Bobby!' I groaned. 'Be *serious*. Did the goddam 'Farmassist' handle her, then?'

'I don't know.'

'Well, can you find out? Is he assisting today?'

'Aye. I'll get him.' He went to the door and bellowed 'Sammy!' so loudly that the deaf Assassin stirred his head. The cow, on the other hand, didn't even twitch an ear.

In a moment Sammy, a medium-sized, dissolute-looking, spotty teenager, arrived at the gallop and stood peering unsurely at us.

'Did you handle her when she was calving?' Bobby nodded at the cow.

'I had to,' Sammy replied nervously, defiantly. 'The head was back and if I didn't straighten him he'd be inside in her belly yet.'

I looked at Sammy's arms. Short. That was probably what had happened. When the head is back, the neck is bent and the calf's muzzle nestles against its shoulder or even behind it. To correct this, the calf must be pushed gently back into the roomier part of the womb before an attempt is made to bring the head forward. If the head is pulled around without first pushing the calf back, the uterus, stretched taut as it is, can burst open from the pressure or, more likely, be sliced open by the calf's sharp teeth raking across it. If Sammy had pushed the calf back, then the calf's muzzle would have been out of his short-armed reach. He might however have slipped a snare over the calf's jaw so that he could hold the jaw in its original position while pushing the rest of the calf back. This is a little more risky – and difficult – but can be used, provided every effort is made to cup the tiny muzzle in the palm of the hand.

'Did you put a rope on the jaw?' I asked.

Sammy's eyes darted about shiftily as he tried to decide which way to answer this one. He chose the right way. 'I did.'

'Did you use lots of soap and water?'

'Yes.' No worries about *that* one.

'And disinfectant?'

'Oh yes.' He nodded briskly. This was getting to be a breeze.

Maybe he had and maybe he hadn't. Perhaps the peritonitis was from something else altogether. 'Okay,' I told him. 'You did your best.' He was off out the door before I could finish. You could see the relief in him, even from the back.

'So I'd better get the truck and ship her off to the factory.'

'She'd be condemned, Bobby. Waste of time and diesel.'

'So what'll I do? I can't just leave the poor oul' bitch suffering . . .'

'If she was mine I'd shoot her and call the knackers. Do you have a gun?'

'I have, but I wouldn't like to shoot her. She was a kind cow. Acch! The knackers are only along the road. They'll be along in a few minutes. Let *them* do it.'

Walking back across the yard, Bobby got back to the one-liners again. I couldn't believe it. 'God, Bobby, you're amazing: You've got a cow dying from peritonitis; you lost a bullock with anthrax and *still* you crack jokes.' There was no admiration in my tone, but Bobby chose to take it as a compliment.

'Sure, isn't it better than hittin' the bottle?' he answered proudly, as if that was the only alternative. 'Gino told you about the anthrax, then?'

'He mentioned it.'

'Now *there* was a messy job for you. Blood everywhere!'

'I know. I saw one myself.'

'Around here?' he asked with sudden interest.

'No. Up in Galway. A few weeks ago.'

'Isn't it damnable how it's spreadin'? By road, the government vet said. But I still can't figure out how it got into my field – there's no mart out that way. It must have been from one of the farmers further along the road comin' back from the mart, because I haven't been to the mart myself in ages. I was *supposed* to be goin' in another few weeks with a load of bullocks, but it was one of them that got the anthrax. Now I have to keep them, for the moment anyhow. Blast it. I can't do them much better because my land isn't great for finishin'. They're fine cattle, but it's high time they moved on.'

'They're a nice bunch alright.'

'You saw them?' he asked in surprise. 'When?'

'Oh I just happened to be out that way, so I had a quick look.'

'Well the one that died was as good as the best of what's left. He was my profit. Tell you the truth I bought them a bit dear in spring. Now I'm goin' to have to keep them through the back end of the year. I'll have to buy feedin' for them. I wouldn't mind but I nearly sold them a couple of weeks back. There was a jobber lookin' at them.'

'Was there a big difference between ye?' I asked automatically, closing the back door of the Land Rover. Vets spend half their lives listening to the financial details or implications of sales, near sales, near misses, hard luck stories, going to the mart a week early, a week late . . .

'We didn't get that far. He didn't ask me what I was lookin' for and he didn't make me an offer.'

71

'So why did he call, then, if he wasn't going to bid?'

'He didn't call. I came on him lookin' in over the gate at the cattle and started talkin' to him.'

My heart gave a sudden lurch. 'What?' I asked carefully.

'I said that he didn't call on me. I came on him at the gate lookin' at the bullocks but he said they weren't his type. He said he was only buyin' cull cows, but when I invited him to the house – I've a few of those oul' ladies too, that I wouldn't mind partin' company with – he said he wasn't workin' that day and that he'd call back some day when he was. An odd kind of a lad, he was.'

'What was odd about him?'

'Well who ever heard of a cattle jobber havin' a day off? I know one who was standin' by the graveside as they lowered his wife in, and while everyone else was prayin' for the poor woman, he was mumblin' prices at the man who owned a bunch of heifers in the field the other side of the graveyard wall. Day off, how are you! And him all decked out in his oilskins and wellin'tons.'

'*Did* he come back another day to see the cows?'

'Nary a sight of him since.'

'Did you know him? Had you ever seen him before?'

'Never. He's not from around these parts. I don't know what county his car reg. was but it wasn't Limerick, city or county, Tipperary, north or south, and it wasn't Clare, Kerry or Cork.' He listed off the neighbouring counties.

'I suppose you don't remember the reg?'

'God no! Sure it was *weeks* ago!'

'What kind of car was it, d'you remember?'

'It was blue, light blue, and it was the same make as the one Gino's wife had before he got the new one and gave her his old one. I'm not great on the makes of cars – there's so many different breeds of them about nowadays – but I think it was a Renault.' He pronounced the last syllable to rhyme with 'salt'. 'I can't swear mind you, but I know his car was the same make as Gino's wife's, only light blue.'

'Did you mention the jobber to the department vet?'

'No. I forgot all about him until the wife mentioned him

the other night. Why? Do you think he's the one? Going around the country, spreadin' anthrax unbeknownst to himself?'

'No, Bobby,' I answered truthfully. The reluctant jobber could quite easily be the spreader of the anthrax but if so, then it was entirely 'beknownst' to himself. 'Anyhow, don't worry about it. I'll mention it to the government vets and let them look into it.'

Subtle questioning didn't add much more to the picture of the jobber. He was clean-shaven, of average height, weight, age and had no strong accent. His hair colour was not known because his sou'wester came well down. I left Bobby to organise the disposal of his dying cow and drove back to town, my mind buzzing in overdrive.

7

Over lunch I continued to worry at the problem, despite constant interruptions from Mrs Foley. Her other guests had gone off on a day trip to some local landmark or beauty spot so she had me at her mercy and treated herself to a vicariously romantic monologue about Claire and me and what a lovely couple we'd make. (I'd been under the impression that we already made quite a lovely couple). As she moved from table to table, straightening a fork here, polishing a glass there, reshaping an imperfectly fanned pink napkin yonder, I tried to ignore her and make sense of what could be behind the seemingly senseless slaughter of cattle up and down the country.

'Oh she's very beautiful, I admit,' Mrs Foley fiddled with the place settings on the table next to mine, 'but' – she examined her reflection in a knifeblade – 'what I always say is that these city girls are a mite too . . . sophisti-*cated* for the likes of us, do you know what I mean? And her a reporter, too! It must take a special kind of person, never mind a special kind of *woman* to do that sort of thing. Someone tough and shrewd.' (Resilient and resourceful were the adjectives I would have chosen, but never mind). 'Now *Sheila* . . .' and she droned on, extolling Sheila's virtues, while I tried to impose some order on my random thoughts. At last, failing to elicit any reaction from me, Mrs Foley moved on to a distant table, leaving an unpleasant little swirl of prejudice eddying in her wake.

I tried to find a motive for the anthrax and, now freed from my hostess's distracting chatter, soon began to make some headway. It was unlikely to be the work of a madman or someone with a grudge – it was too methodical and there were too many farmers involved. Therefore it was logical to assume that it had been done for personal gain of some sort, possibly extortion, a kind of pay-up-or-it'll-happen-again racket.

It was much easier to figure out *how* it had been done. The bacillus could only have been passed to the victims by one of three routes: injection, inhalation or ingestion. The first two didn't really rate: injection using a syringe would require the animal to be restrained, while a dart gun would make noise, cause the animals to stampede, and probably leave a telltale dart either stuck in the animal or lying about in the field to be discovered later. Inhalation would require the use of a nasal spray or atomiser, up close. Getting close wouldn't be a problem because cattle, being insatiably curious, investigate almost anything. The biggest problem with the airborne route was that it would require a calm day or at least a day when the wind was blowing *away* from the poisoner and towards the cattle; this, I figured, would make the job so complicated that it would be ruled out on logistical grounds, never mind the very real danger to the poisoner himself from lethal droplets being blown willy-nilly about.

Ingestion was by far the most suitable route of administration. All one would have to do would be to lace a piece of turnip or other bait, wait for the cattle to come close, then let one of them take it straight from the hand. Simple.

I was surprised when my 'solution' stuck at that. New questions kept crowding in, but I could find no answers: Why, for example, organise a *nationwide* spread? Why not just drive around and throw a laced turnip into any field of cattle and trust that one of them would find and eat it? Why go to the trouble of locating fields with hidden gates? Did he/they need to be one hundred per cent sure of their kills? If so, why? Why not infect some sheep, too, just to

76

make it look less suspicious? Maybe they just hadn't bothered with sheep – they'd need lots of dead sheep to equal the dramatic effect of one 600kg bullock bloating like an airship; then again, maybe it was just because sheep aren't particularly curious animals . . .

An incongruity suddenly struck me, one that I ought to have spotted before, and I headed for the foyer and the phone. I found Bobby's number in the book and dialled. 'Bobby,' I said. 'That day you saw the jobber – was it raining?' The summer had been one of the best on record.

There was a short silence, then: 'It wasn't rainin', Frank. It was a beautiful day.'

'Then why do you think . . .'

'. . . would a man who wasn't workin' be wearin' oilskins? I don't know, Frank, but that must be the reason I thought he was workin'. Sure why else would a man be wearin' oilskins on a fine day?'

I knew the answer to that one but I said nothing. If I'd been handling virulent anthrax bacilli, I'd have been wearing protective clothing, too. Hail, rain, or shine.

Back at the table, sipping coffee, I tried to put flesh on the bones of my faceless culprit. He obviously knew his animal behaviour and he also knew where to acquire anthrax bacilli, how to store them, grow them, handle them. Could he possibly be . . . a *vet*? There couldn't be many other professions which would satisfy all these criteria. Not, mind you, that *all* vets were an exact fit – ninety-nine per cent of GPs, including me, wouldn't know where to even start looking for live, virulent anthrax bacilli . . . I was just beginning a delightful little reverie about pinning the whole thing on that stuffed academic white coat, Harbison, even if it meant framing the bastard, when Mrs Foley came in and announced that there was an Inspector Potter of the Garda Síochána on the phone for me.

Without even an opening hello, Potter got straight down to

77

business. 'Why did you think that we might be investigating this anthrax business, Frank?'

'Good afternoon, Peter.' I reminded him of the civilities.

'Oh, eh, good afternoon . . .' And he repeated the question at once.

'Because the whole thing stinks.' And I spelled out the pointers that had led me to that conclusion.

'Fair play to you, Frank,' he said when I'd finished. 'You never lost it. Listen. You are now officially on notice that you are what we call "helping the Gardai with their enquiries."'

'That's a euphemism for being under arrest, right?' I said after a pause.

'Not in this case, Frank. Superintendent Downing will be at your local station at five-thirty this evening and he would like you to call round for a chat.'

'Who's Superintendent Downing?'

'He's from HQ in Dublin, and he's in charge of the anthrax investigation.'

'He's coming all the way from Dublin just to talk to *me!*'

'No. He's in the neighbourhood, anyway. But he does want to see you.'

'Okay, then. Maybe I'll have something for him to make it worth his while.'

'Yeah?'

'Maybe it's nothing – a possibly suspicious character seen at the gate of a field where an animal subsequently died from anthrax . . .' And I went on to tell him of Bobby's jobber.

'Hell, Frank. That could be the lead he's been waiting for. Oh, by the way. I nearly forgot. There's an official news blackout on this one. Tell Claire, will you?'

'Sure, Peter,' I said drily. 'She'll be thrilled skinny.'

On my afternoon rounds I had a call to Richard O'Malley's, the man who had had the colicky horse which had staged the prudently-timed, eleventh-hour, photo-finish recovery, thus pipping the far more fancied *Euthanasia* at the post.

78

This time it was to attend another animal, but I had a look at last week's patient anyway and was gratified to see him in seemingly perfect health. 'No more problems there,' I smiled, pleased with myself, and gave the horse a matey slap on the neck.

'No health problems, anyway,' O'Malley replied gloomily.

I gave him a searching look, then asked him if anything was wrong – I knew it couldn't be the bill; it would be a whopper alright, but he wouldn't get it for at least another week.

'I was just thinking I might have been better off if he'd kicked the bucket the first day.'

'Bit late for that now, isn't it, Richard?' 'God,' I thought. 'Some people.'

'Hey, don't get me wrong! I'm not complaining. You did a great job. The problem is, what do I do with him now?'

'How do you mean?'

'I paid a lot of money for him; he's been in training for yonks with nothing to show for it except a large hole in my pocket. Out of six starts, he has a nicely balanced record – two third-lasts, two second-lasts and two lasts – in that order, so I can't even fool myself that he was improving. When you add up the money I've lost in backing him, training fees, what it cost to buy him, and veterinary fees, he owes me a small fortune. I don't know now whether to give him a chance with a decent trainer or forget about him. I might just be throwing more good money after bad. What would you do if he was yours?'

I snorted wryly. 'If I had that gift, Richard, you would now be beholding the countenance of one of the richest men in the world. Are you sure it's the trainer's fault?'

He gave what is called a hollow laugh. 'I'm sure. So are many others. That horse was abused. Look at those scars. He didn't get *those* racing and they certainly weren't there when he went into training.'

'Who was training him?' I asked, though, remembering

my conversation with Bill Howell, I reckoned I already knew.

He immediately flared up. 'Who do you think? That great genius, Joe Murray, up at the Northfield-Auschwitz University for young horses, is who! Who else? I don't care what Gino Callaghan or anyone else says, but that horse has been beaten badly. Excessive use of the whip, and him not even on the goddam track. I wish to hell I'd moved him ages ago.'

Because I'd been focusing on the colic on my previous visits, I hadn't paid much attention to the marks and weals on the horse's body. They had healed and so needed no attention from me. But now, viewing them forensically, it was difficult to see how they could have arisen 'legitimately'. There was a long, almost horizontal raised scar along the right ribcage. Whatever had caused that mark – whip, fall or scrape – couldn't have happened while the horse was being ridden – the area would have been covered by saddle, saddle cloth, bellyband, stirrup-leather and rider's leg. I ran my finger slowly along the raised track; it wasn't uniform because the weal was thicker over each rib where the damage had been greater – the yielding flesh in the spaces between the ribs had got off a bit lighter, though not much; what was more significant was that the scar was complete from end to end without any break in its continuity. Clearly the horse had not been tacked up when it was inflicted. Even the *angle* of the stripe would have been impossible for a rider to achieve – it slanted upwards gradually from front to back. The ugly weal was also longer than any jockey's whip I'd ever seen. In my opinion, the scar could only have resulted from the skin-splitting lash of a long whip or stick, delivered from near the horse's right rump. Likewise, two almost-bald parallel tracks on the right buttock could only have been made from a position behind the horse and to its right. There were other knocks on the legs, fore and rear, which, I supposed, could have been genuine racing or training injuries. Even more disturbing were some scars on the head, though these too, could be explained away as accidents. Just about.

'So what do you make of those?'

Knowing that even a mildly damning answer from a vet could be used to harden the rumours of cruelty at Northfield into some sort of proof, I had to be circumspect. I wasn't afraid of getting embroiled in a cruelty case – it wouldn't be the first, or last – but I preferred to wait until I knew a little more before pointing accusatory fingers. I had the impression, from what O'Malley had said earlier, that Gino had taken a similarly evasive line. On the other hand, I thought it quite likely that the horse *had* been seriously abused, so I didn't want to discourage the owner. 'He looks as if he's tangled with the infamous No. 11 bus,' I said.

'Deliberate?'

I shrugged. 'Who can say for certain, without a proper investigation? If it *was* deliberate, then it probably isn't an isolated case.'

'Bloody sure it's not! I know of at least four others and I've heard of . . . oh . . . ten more.'

I shrugged again. 'So what do you want me to say? If you know for sure that that's what happened, then why don't you go to the police? Cruelty to animals is a criminal offence, not civil.'

'I know, but how could I prove it? And if I didn't prove it beyond a reasonable doubt, and the case got thrown out, then I could be screwed for defamation, libel, slander, and Christ knows what else.'

'I'm not sure if that's true. The state would be prosecuting, not you.'

'Aye, but the state could only prosecute if someone went and made the accusation in the first place.'

'I'm afraid I can't help you there, Richard. That's lawyer's turf.'

I don't know what else he had expected me to say but he had a distinctly let down look about him as I drove out of the yard to continue my rounds.

Before I reached the next call, I was summoned back to Ward. Superintendent Downing had suddenly decided to bring our meeting forward and was already impatiently awaiting my arrival at the local Garda barracks. It looked as though my possible lead had brought him running. They must be stuck, I thought. Very, very stuck.

8

Downing was large, bulky and awkward-looking, with tufts of sandy hair clinging to the sides and back of a shiny bald head. He had disconcertingly pale eyes set wide on either side of a fleshy nose and an enormous gap between his two front teeth. His complexion suggested that he didn't spend enough time out of doors. There was an air of vagueness about him which, I soon found out, was misleading. He met me at the counter of the garda station and welcomed me like I was the prodigal son. When I entered, several officers, plainclothes and uniformed, stopped talking amongst themselves and drifted across to stand around me. If I'd been a suspect, my lawyer would have been screaming intimidation and harassment. Even pure as a babe in arms, their crowding was none too comfortable. As I unwound my story, two of them scribbled rapid notes; when I came to the part about the jobber in the oilskins, Downing interrupted me to issue orders and send a local man to drive his men out to interview Bobby. I wondered how long it would take him to get on to the jokes when confronted with serious-faced, no-nonsense lawmen. Then he invited me into the back. For a 'little chat'.

We sat in the office of the local sergeant, with a cluttered, government-issue desk between us. The desk had a scalloped border of cigarette burns all around its edge, like brown fingerprints. Above us, flickering slightly and humming loudly, a single fluorescent tube augmented the meagre daylight that dribbled in through a small window, the only source of natural light in the room.

He started slowly, as if we had all the time in the world now, asking me about my locum business, when I'd started it, why, how it was going, where I'd been working over the past three or four months, what kind of practices they had been ... He had a strange habit of staring at the ceiling when he was talking to me and gazing out the window when I was talking to him. The window gave on to an air shaft and, as I waited for him to get to the meat, I wondered what inspiration he was picking up from a rectangle of red bricks and a grey tangle of PVC pipes.

'I've spoken to Inspector Potter,' he started, turning to face me, eyes sliding upwards to traverse the ceiling from corner to corner, 'and he gave me a general account of how you worked out so much by yourself. It *was* by yourself, wasn't it? Nobody told you, I mean?' The pale eyes stopped their wanderings aloft and dropped briefly into normal position like two lemons coming down together on a one-armed bandit.

'No. No one told me.'

The eyes slid up again, as if someone had just put in another coin. 'Now tell *me* about it. From the beginning.' And he turned his head away again to resume his inspection of the uninspiring wall.

I spoke to his left ear for about five minutes. Not once did he turn my way. Keeping it all in chronological order, I led him step by step onwards from the case I had seen on Tom Ryan's farm, through my visit to the laboratory, and how, as I travelled around the country, I had begun to notice a pattern, finally twigging the significance of the hidden gate. At this point he interrupted me to compliment me on my 'deductive faculties'.

'Well,' I shrugged modestly, 'you must have travelled much the same path yourself to have arrived at the same conclusions.'

'No, actually, we didn't. It would be a bit "specialised" for us. A detailed knowledge of rare diseases of animals is not an entry requirement for joining the force.' He flashed me a gappy grin, meant to neutralise any hint of the patronising.

'By "you", I was referring, of course, to the Authorities In General. The government vets would have worked it out,' I concluded, giving the recently fêted deductive faculties an early outing.

'No, Mr Samson, they didn't. They didn't have to. They were informed that the sudden increase in anthrax had been deliberately engineered.'

'Really?' I said, wondering if I ought to have been able to deduce this, too. 'How come?'

He reached down and hefted a battered leather briefcase onto the desk. He rooted in it briefly before extracting a large manila envelope which he passed across to me. 'Have a look at that and see what you think.'

The envelope contained a sheaf of maps, one for each of the twenty-six counties of the Republic. Each was about double foolscap size and had a number of X's marked on it. I riffled through them quickly until I found the map of County Galway. It had some twenty X's, but I was looking for three in particular – one in the region of Tom Ryan's farm outside Ballintaggart, one near Tuam and another near Gort. I found them at once, then looked at the other X's.

'Jesus! Has Galway had that many more cases? There must be twenty crosses here.'

He consulted a notebook. 'County Galway has had six cases up to this morning.'

'Six? Then what are the other crosses for?'

'Read the letter.'

I turned to the flimsy sheet at the front of the pile of maps.

Department of Parasitology,
Veterinary College of Ireland,
Shelbourne Road,
Ballsbridge,
Dublin 4.

Notifiable Diseases Section,
Department of Agriculture,
Agriculture House,
Kildare St.,
Dublin 2.

Date as postmark.

Dear Sir or Madam,

I am at present conducting research into the possibility of predicting outbreaks of Sheepscab, based on microclimatic and other ecological data. I have marked with red crosses, on the enclosed maps, a number of locations in which I expect heavy infestations to occur this winter. I should be most grateful if you could keep these maps on your files and check them against actual outbreaks as they occur. I need not point out that, should my research confirm my hypothesis, the benefits to sheep farmers and the agribusiness sector in general would be considerable. Thanking you in anticipation of your kind cooperation, I remain,

Yours faithfully,

It was signed: Gordon Harris, MVB, MRCVS. I read it a second time and looked up. 'I presume that all these X's,' I tapped the maps, 'mark the places where anthrax has occurred or is likely to?'

He nodded in confirmation. 'In your line of business, you must know most of the vets in the country. Do you know a Gordon Harris?'

'No. Have you checked the register?'

'We have. As you might guess, he's not on it, though

there was a letter for him at the vet college – being kept in case he turned up.'

'*Yeah!*'

'That's what I thought, too.' He snorted at the gullibility of mankind. 'It was from the Department of Agriculture acknowledging receipt of *this* letter.'

'Of course.' We exchanged sheepish grins.

'And the maps and the X's?' I enquired.

'The places which, presumably, have been seeded with anthrax. All the cases which have come to light to date coincide with X's on the maps. A pity the maps aren't on a large enough scale to pinpoint the actual farms or even the fields. Nevertheless, they'll serve their purpose nicely. With these on record, nobody's going to accuse him of jumping on the bandwagon of a "natural" disaster when he claims later on to have actually *caused* it. As, I presume, he will. Notice the date stamp showing when it was received at Agriculture. By then there had been a mere fourteen cases, and yet here's this letter with those and all *future* cases marked in.' He paused. 'Also,' he continued, 'the people in Parasitology tell me that it would be impossible to predict the occurrence of Sheepscab with the accuracy which the letter suggests.'

I shrugged. 'Probably. Who spotted the tie-up?'

'A young lassie, straight out of school. She'd only joined the civil service six weeks before. Obviously she's still green enough to actually read letters as if they were important,' he replied cynically.

'Still . . .' I handed the letter back into his reaching hand. 'Any idea why all this is going on?'

'No. Oh, there are theories alright – lots of them, none of them watertight – but I think we're going to hear from him soon, so there's not much point in running off half-cocked. We've nothing to go on and it's probably a better strategy to sit tight. If he thinks we haven't yet connected his sheepscab letter with the anthrax, he may get careless.'

'Have you considered the possibility that Gordon Harris might actually *be* a vet?'

Downing stared hard into my eyes for about five seconds. It seemed more like five minutes and it struck me that I would hate to be a guilty party pleading innocent and have old Superintendent Basilisk Downing give me the dead-eye treatment.

'Actually, I had considered the possibility that it was you.'

'*Me!*' I squealed. 'On what basis for God's sake?'

'Purely an idle thought, but consider. It must be someone who knows animal diseases, Anthrax and Sheep-scab. And who, besides a vet, would know that the Department of Parasitology is the one which would deal with Sheepscab? No one. Or very few. However, there was no vet anywhere in the picture until you phoned our friend, Potter. You just might have been checking to see if you were still safe, if anyone had cottoned on yet, maybe getting a little nervous or anxious ... So I asked around a bit and found that you were, if you'll pardon the expression, a kind of vagrant vet of no fixed abode, and suddenly you began to look like a prospect. You see, whoever did this must have spent *weeks* checking the countryside and doing the rounds; a vet with his own practice would probably have found it difficult to get away, whereas someone with more time on his hands would have had no problem. However, you'd told Potter that you had been working in Ballintaggart in Galway, so we checked how long you'd been there.'

'Six weeks.'

'And two days. I know. We also asked the vet there – a Mr Daley, I believe? – if he knew where you'd been before coming to him, and he did, so we checked there too, and you ended up with a watertight alibi. You'll be glad to know that Potter wanted to bet his pension you were clean.'

'Did you take him up on it?'

'No. The evidence was too circumstantial.' And he smiled goofily at the ceiling in general.

'So why did you ask me to come here?'

'First, to see you – you can tell a lot by being face to face with someone ...'

'A suspect you mean.'

'. . . Second, to see if you had come up with anything we hadn't thought of. After all you are a vet, a vet in practice, and I wanted to talk to someone like you but kept putting it off because of the blackout. Potter told you about the blackout, I take it? Third, you seem to have a good head for these matters – you'd make a good policeman. Or criminal. The way you handled that business with Catamaran last year has won you a few admirers along the way, myself included. Finally, I wanted to see if you had any ideas about a motive.'

'Well, thanks for all that. I think. As to motive, I had thought it might be a protection racket and the anthrax just a case of the guy giving a pretty awesome demonstration of his power; but the letter to the Department rules that out, and frankly,' I shook my head, 'I haven't a clue now. It doesn't make sense to give this big demonstration and then tip off the authorities.'

'He didn't *mean* to tip off the authorities. Yet. He was just laying in the proof in an almost perfectly camouflaged way.'

'But to what purpose? If he intends to extort money from farmers he has already shown what he can do. Unless . . . Naw!' I paused and grimaced. 'That'd be crazy!'

'What would be crazy?'

'Maybe he's going to try to screw the government. Hold the whole country to ransom?'

'Perhaps it's not so crazy. Who knows? Maybe the BSE business gave him ideas. We'll just have to wait and see, won't we?'

I left soon after, having been given a cup of lousy coffee as a reward for my information. We parted outside the station, Downing lumbering off in the direction of a squad car to go out to see Bobby for himself. I reckoned that the farmassist would be doing all this evening's milking on his own.

I had a call to Bobby Young's farm two days after my meeting with Downing.

'How did you get on with Superintendent Downing?' I asked.

'Great, Frank! We're on first name terms. He calls me Bobby and I call him Superintendent!' Gales of laughter followed, to which I added the merest breeze, just enough to prevent him from repeating it. 'Ach . . . He's a bit of a pain, stuck-up like. And, like a lot of Dublin jackeens, he seems to think that we're all ignorant yobbos down the country. I should have told him about the record Pub Quiz between Cloonaminna and Srahglan . . . It's into its fifth week now, ten solid hours of *mind*-bendin' concentration, hundreds, if not *thousands*, of questions, the greatest battle of minds this parish has ever seen, and they're *still* locked in a tie . . .'

'Yeah?'

'Yeah. Still nil all!' And he doubled up. I should have seen it coming.

'Did either of you tell the other anything startling?' I asked, steering him back towards Downing.

'I don't think so. He told me nothin' and he seemed to know all I knew about my mystery jobber. He wanted to know everythin' I could remember, down to the colour of the oilskins, which were green, and he had a paint chart from the Renault dealers in Limerick for me to pick out the *exact* colour of the car. The only other thing I could think of was that the car had a tow-ball and the left taillight unit was broken and had a straight up and down crease in the body beside it, like someone was backin' a trailer but it jack-knifed. A fat lot of good that did him, my good friend the superintendent.'

'You never know. Cops are trained to piece together all kinds of things which would mean nothing to the likes of you and me.' I saluted, pulled the door to, then made good my escape without having to listen to the usual blitz of parting gags.

Another horse, another owner. This one had a gash on its shoulder which, like beauty, was only skin deep. Still, it needed five stitches. I tied the last one, spread some of Colm Walsh's magical wound cream along the suture line, and began to gather up my gear. 'We'll take these out in about a week,' I said. 'It should heal well, probably won't even leave a scar.'

Lady Merrisen tucked an errant wisp of greying hair back into place behind her ear, and said, with a most unladylike snort. 'Oh I shouldn't worry about *scars*. He's had more than his share.'

'He does look as though he's been a bit accident prone,' I agreed, eyeing the grey gelding.

'It's more a case of him having spent a year in a war zone.'

I looked at her, lost. 'Sorry?'

'Northfield House,' she said, as if that explained everything.

Not another one, I thought.

Walking me to the Land Rover, she explained that she had warned her brother-in-law (who actually owned the horse) against sending it to Northfield, but, because of loyalty to the late George Harty ('dear, sweet, Georgie', she called him), and some other hidden agenda, he had insisted, and, (serves him right), had ended up with much the same results as my colicky patient's owner – high vet bills, special expenses, and a big round zero in prize-money. The brother-in-law, not having much sympathy with losers, had wanted to have the horse put down, but she had insisted on taking it and giving it a good home. She seemed to feel that, having been through the rigours of Northfield, it deserved a kind of veteran's pension. Had I not already heard much the same story from Richard O'Malley, and seen those very suspicious marks, I might have been inclined to take her ladyship's tale with the proverbial pinch of salt. With grim satisfaction she told me that she had managed to convince her brother-in-law to take his other five horses away, *before* Murray had lost his licence. Like Richard O'Malley, Lady

Merrisen also seemed to want to involve me. She explained that, as she was not an owner, she herself couldn't pursue Mr Murray through the legal system, and that her brother-in-law refused to do so despite her constant urgings. She seemed to think that if I were to have a word with him, I might persuade him to unleash retributive proceedings against 'that contemptible, execrable man'. I declined, politely but firmly, and told her she should approach Gino about it on his return. I smiled inwardly as I thought of Gino trying to work his way out of that one. 'Or a lawyer,' I added, feeling instant remorse.

Back at the surgery I asked Christy, the taciturn yard man, what he knew about Northfield House. For a man who spoke to no one, Christy seemed to know everything. He had no known family or friends and lived in a small cottage a few miles outside town. Despite his outwardly sullen appearance, I always found him okay and we had the odd pint together. He told me that he wouldn't have sent even a horse that he hated to Northfield, and, though I did my best to winkle more information out of him, that was all he would say.

That evening, I ought to have tackled some overdue paperwork, but managed to talk myself into leaving it for an evening less beautiful than this, and went for a long jog along country lanes instead. Normally, I keep myself in good shape but, despite working hard physically, I'd been neglecting regular training lately and felt it keenly. Coming back into town after a punishing twelve kilometres, I bought a paper in a newsagents which was just closing for the night and went into the first pub I met for a cooling drink and a quiet read. Just short of closing time, refreshed, rested, and well ready for bed, I left the pub and strolled back towards the hotel, savouring the gentle chill in the night air, the near empty streets, the town closing down for the night, and congratulating myself that so far, I hadn't had one single night call. I turned the corner into the quiet street which led to my hotel. There were no pubs in this street and it seemed to have shut up earlier than the rest of Ward – there wasn't a single lighted window in the whole street, upstairs or down. Apart from two men leaning against a parked car, chatting quietly and smoking, the whole place was deserted.

As I drew abreast of the men, one of them looked at me and said, 'Aren't you the vet?'

'Yes,' I said, kissing goodbye to nights without calls. I looked inquiringly at them and, when neither of them spoke, I said: 'What's the prob . . .' I broke off, suddenly uneasy as they dropped their cigarettes in unison and, eyes locked on mine, pushed themselves purposefully away from the car.

'We've got a message for you,' the younger of the two said with a cool, tough-guy smile. He was well over six feet, with long blond hair, blue eyes, and a wide set of perfect teeth. He stood facing me confidently, feet planted firmly apart, arms hanging loosely by his side.

'Yes?' I looked warily from one to the other, adrenaline coursing through me, trying to figure which of them would make the first move. Again there was no comment from them. 'Eh . . . who from?' I asked through a dry mouth.

A barely audible footstep came from behind me, and I knew I was for it. Before I could react, agonising pain scythed through my lower back, kidney to kidney, and, winded and half-dazed, I felt myself buckle at the knees. The smaller, older of the two men in front lashed out with a heavy boot as I fell forward, and caught me an excruciating, crumpling kick in the groin. In a blaze of agony I went down and folded into an anguished foetal position in the gutter, my head and shoulders almost under the car. I don't know how many kicks they landed on my ribs, my legs and my chest, and I didn't care – the intense fire throbbing and pulsating in my groin was all-consuming. Then I felt rough hands haul me out from under the car and I began to fear that they were going to attack my head.

A voice from beside my ear said with quiet menace: 'Open your eyes, Mr Vet!'

I did, very warily. The young blond giant was squatting beside me, smiling. He slapped my face a couple of times, though not hard. He was probably being cool again and, even through the pain, I found myself wondering what mental image he had of himself. Even now he was posing. 'The message,' slap, slap, 'is: keep your opinions to yourself and keep your big mouth shut. Kapeesh?' Slap, slap.

I nodded. 'Kapeesh?' In a broad Dublin accent?

'Else you might have to have it *wired* shut and you wouldn't like that, eh?'

I shook my head.

He smiled a brilliant smile, gave my cheek a few friendly pats, and languidly stood up. I noticed that he had put on leather gloves – presumably to protect his hands while he slapped me – and he now began to take them off again. That was another Oscar performance; he tugged fastidiously once or twice at each fingertip, one after the other, then went back along the row until the glove came off. Then he spent a moment looking down on me, smiling enigmatically and tapping the gloves into the palm of his left hand, seemingly now in Gestapo officer mode, before nodding to his men and walking off down the street. The third one, the hero who had snuck up from behind, hesitated, then swung a vicious kick into my side; luckily for me, most of the venom was dissipated when he connected with the mobile phone in the pocket of my tracksuit jacket. He tried another kick lower down but his heart wasn't really in it and he caught me just a glancing blow on the thigh before scurrying off after the others.

Now that the immediate danger of further onslaught had passed, I gave myself over to the incredible pain in my groin and I lay in the gutter for a long time, suppressing groans and panting and wondering why there'd been nobody about to help me or at least raise an outcry. Moving very gingerly, I uncoiled myself and got to my hands and knees. As I half crawled and half stumbled away from the gutter, I noticed an abandoned wooden fence-post which, I presumed, was what had been used on my back. I leant against a lamppost for a moment, then, slowly set out for the hotel.

It took me fifteen minutes to travel the few hundred yards, another ten to make it to my room – the scissors action necessary for climbing stairs, even though I stopped for a rest on each step, was murder – and another five to get all my clothes off. I took strong painkillers, filled a barely tepid bath and submerged myself up to the nostrils in it, adding cold water until it was as cold as I could bear. After half an hour of steeping, I took my bruised body to bed and, incredibly, managed to fall asleep fairly quickly.

9

The painkillers wore off just before dawn. In the paling dark, I lay quietly on my bed, stiff and sore, and relived the night's events. I'd been warned to keep my mouth shut and my opinions to myself so I reasoned that the attack had been initiated either by The Anthrax Man (because of my chat with Downing, however he might have heard about it), or Joe Murray (who could have resented my comments to Richard O'Malley and/or Lady Merrisen), take your pick. My money was on the trainer.

I began to test the various battered bits, and gradually discovered that, all things considered, I was in reasonable working order. I swallowed more pills, stripped off and took stock in the full-length mirror which doubled as the door of the walnut-veneered wardrobe. The colours had come up while I slept and my torso was now covered in purplish-black patches. Minutes later, I stood at the loo and was very relieved that the pink-tinged urine of last night had cleared – I'd been half-expecting painful clots.

Covering the signs of battle with clothes seemed to lessen the pain; perhaps it was psychological or perhaps the analgesics were already kicking in. Whichever, I went down to breakfast, walking almost normally, though lowering myself onto the chair was difficult. The waitress noticed nothing – from my face and my hands, nobody would suspect a thing.

I called to the police station on my way to the surgery. I

reckoned the cops would trace my assailants in a matter of hours. I could describe the handsome blond with the twisted mind to a T, and have a fair crack at the other two, so the cops would only need a quick word with Richard O'Malley and her ladyship to find out whom they had spoken to about my comments. Then, hey presto. I was shown into Sergeant Rhea's office, where Downing and I had had our *tête à tête*. I told him my story and showed him a selection of my bruises, and a few moments later, left, with his assurances following me out the door.

I managed to hide my twinges and winces during morning surgery and left for morning rounds, hoping not to encounter too many cases involving brawn as well as brain.

About ten-thirty, my battered mobile phone wheezed into life – last night's kick had left a long crack in its casing which I'd closed with surgical tape, but it had obviously sustained internal injuries, and I had to shout for Jeannie, the receptionist, to speak up. Eventually I managed to decipher from the crackles that the Minister for Agriculture, for some reason which he hadn't explained, wanted me to call him back as soon as possible.

'Do you want the number?' she shouted.

'No.' Not much point in trying to use the terminally-ill mobile. 'I'll be there in about ten minutes.'

On the way in, I mulled over the minister's call. I presumed it had to do with the anthrax – he could only have heard of my interest – or, for that matter, my existence – from Downing, who would also have provided my phone number. So far so good; the deductive faculties were coasting along nicely but, by the time I reached the office, they hadn't helped me to figure out why exactly the minister wanted me to phone him.

Thomas F. Hilliard was the consummate political animal, the great survivor. Adored by the less morally encumbered of his party's supporters, he had an unswayable following upon whose vociferous support he could call at any moment, and this was all that had saved him when, on more than one occasion, the creaky ship of scandal had sailed very close to his shore. He had come from relatively humble origins – *very* humble, if the party hagiography was to be believed – and had clawed his way up by any and all means to become one of the richest and most powerful men in the country. The wonder was that he was not Taoiseach, but, the story went, even his most blindly loyal supporters would draw the line at giving him the actual headship of a government. To the opposition, and to most neutrals, he was anathema, and there was no shortage of suggestions as to what the F in his name stood for. Personally, I wouldn't have voted for him if his was the only name on the paper.

When I told the woman who answered the phone who I was, she reacted so quickly that it was clear she had been awaiting my call. She told me to hold on, she would put me through right away. It seemed that I was getting top priority. I heard a click and then she said, whether to the minister or to me, I couldn't tell: 'He's on the line now, sir.'

'Mr Samson?' The unmistakable gravel tone came down the line to me.

'Yes, sir.'

'Ah! Good man. You're well, I hope?'

'Yes, thank you, sir.' I replied, wondering if I ought to have added: 'and you?' On balance, I thought not.

'Good man,' he repeated, this time in a praising tone which seemed to suggest that 'well' was either a surprisingly clever or an unexpectedly pious thing for anyone to be. 'I'll tell you briefly what I want, without going into too many details over the phone. You've spoken to Gerry Downing and this ties in with what you discussed. I'm at my house in Limerick. I want you to come here as soon as possible. At once, in fact, unless there is some very pressing reason why you can't. Treat it as an urgent call.'

'Do you mean a sick call?'

'Yes. A sick call. Actually, it really is a sick call.'

'Can you tell me what the problem is?'

'No. Not on the phone. And – I know this may raise an ethical problem for you – but I must ask you not to contact my own vet to tell him that I've called you in. That would be the normal procedure, would it not?'

'Yes, sir. It would.'

'Well don't. I'll explain when you get here. What time can I expect you?'

'I should be there in about an hour. I can leave straightaway.'

'Good man. I'll send word to the guard at the gate. What do you drive?'

'A Land Rover. Long wheelbase. Green.'

'Reg?'

I gave it to him and he said 'Good man' again, and hung up.

In fact, heavy rain along the way slowed me considerably and I was a good twenty minutes late. An incongruous wooden prefab cabin nestled by the wall in the space between the imposing limestone gate pillars and the road; it looked as though it had been hastily emplaced during some security alert, purely as a temporary measure – many years ago. I waited, engine idling, while two pairs of eyes scrutinised me through dusty glass. A hand rubbed circles on the inside of the window but it didn't seem to reduce the opacity much. The eyes continued to regard me balefully, hoping, I presumed, that I would go away. I blew my horn and, in a moment, the owner of one of the pairs of eyes, dressed in a blue cape, grudgingly descended the three wooden steps and splashed slowly across towards the jeep. He eyed me with dislike and distrust as if he expected me, at any moment, to poke a Kalashnikov out the window at him, then vanished round the rear. In the mirror I could see him backstepping to read the number plate, which he then compared with a clipboard that he magicked out from beneath the waterproof cape. He approached my open window but I didn't turn my head until he actually spoke. It's amazing how trivial hostilities can arise from nothing.

'Name?'

'Frank Samson.'

'Business?'

'Vet,' I answered his slightly ambiguous question.

'Business *here*,' he amended warningly. The rain had grown suddenly heavier.

'Minister's request. Urgent request. He was supposed to have passed the message on to you. So that there would be no delays,' I added dryly.

'Any identification?'

I rooted about under the dashboard and behind the seats until I eventually found an envelope with my name on it. I turned back to find him looking very cheesed off. The shower had by now become a full monsoon, drumming a tattoo on my roof and, presumably, his head.

'That's all I have.'

He produced a visitor's book from somewhere else beneath the cloak, ordered me perfunctorily to sign and, when I had, snapped it closed and turned away. I was the first visitor on the day's page. Before he got back to the shelter of his cabin, his colleague had pressed whatever buttons it took to make the massive wrought-iron gates swing smoothly apart.

Through regular gaps in the shrubbery which lined the long curving approach, the house flickered briefly in and out of view, giving a jerky, silent movie effect; rain trails on the windscreen made definition grainy, adding to the image, but the impression was of a large plain house, more or less cubic beneath its shirt of Virginia creeper and ivy. The driveway, emerging from between its laurel and rhododendron walls, opened on to a generous forecourt, too near the house to afford a good overall view. I suddenly remembered a controversy from five or six years back, a nine-days wonder at the time. Hilliard, then Minister for Local Government, had bought a large estate just outside Limerick, from a couple who had been trying for years to have the site designated as building land, but had eventually given up. Within six months, he had managed to get the elusive permits (from his own department) and, a short while after, had sold the land to developers for, it was said, many times what he had paid for the whole place, house and land. Estimates of his profit varied, depending on which paper you read: the opposition and independent papers talked of seven hundred per cent; his own party press (which would dearly have loved to ignore the uproar, but couldn't) talked of 'a substantial profit,' while a fanatical local rag from Hilliard's home town brazenly maintained that 'Poor Tom just about broke even.' Anyway, I thought, viewing the stately pile, whichever way you looked at it, it seemed that 'Poor Tom' had ended up with a fine house set in spacious grounds for free, and a whole pile of money to boot.

I parked close to the door which opened almost at once to frame the minister himself. He wore a grey chalk-stripe suit and a large professional smile which said that, if it hadn't been pissing down, he'd have come out *all* the way to greet me, but there was no point in both of us getting soaked, now was there? With scant regard for my aches and bruises, I jumped out of the Land Rover, slammed the door and, neck hunched down into my collar, galloped up the steps as quickly as was seemly in the circumstances. He moved aside to let me in.

Now that I was on the same level as him, I was surprised to see that he was quite a short man, less than five-six. On TV, he seemed a six-footer plus. His features were so sculpted and his mien so patrician that I was surprised that the noble head was supported, not on an alabaster plinth as one might have expected, but on a disappointingly mottled and wattled neck.

He pumped my hand. 'Good of you to come so quickly, Frank,' he said with a patronising familiarity which rankled – I had the distinct feeling that the last thing he'd done before coming to the door was read a cue card with my name on it and that he was using it early so as not to forget it. Frank. Frank. Frank ... 'That's a nasty one!' He nodded out at the curtains of water as he closed the door.

'Yes sir. Is my Land Rover alright there? Not in anybody's way?'

'Fine, Frank. Fine. Come on in.' As I followed him through the spacious hall, I could almost see an aura radiating from the enormous energy crammed into his stocky frame.

He stood aside at an open door and said: 'After you, Frank,' and we entered a spacious study. 'Sit down.' As I headed for a wooden ladderback job, the minister pointed to a deep armchair. 'That one is much more comfortable. Now what would you like, Frank? Tea or coffee?'

'Coffee would be good, thank you, sir. Black.' I lowered myself gingerly into the 'much more comfortable' chair and immediately wished I'd had the gumption to insist on the upright one.

'Good man!' He beamed as if I had just given the correct answer to a very difficult question. 'Black coffee. A good strong beverage for a good strong man. I always say that tea is all very well for women and members of the opposition, hey?' And he laughed as he pressed a bell behind his desk. Being a supporter of the opposition – and of women too, for that matter – I ignored the remark. Claire would have leaped at his throat.

The minister placed his elbows on the desk, knitted his fingers into a hammock for his chin and gave me an earnest look. 'This anthrax business seems very fishy, doesn't it, Frank?' The sincere man-to-man approach.

'Yes sir. It does. Have there been any new developments?'

'We'll come to that in a moment. Cigarette?' He pushed an exquisitely ornamented silver cigarette box towards me.

'No, thank you.'

'Good man. Too early for you, eh?'

'No sir. I just never started.'

This got me another 'good man', awarded through lips that clamped his cigarette into brief immobility for the application of flame from a table lighter that matched the box. 'Wise man, Frank. I envy you.' He squinted suddenly and jerked his head back as smoke dissolved in the tear ducts of his eyes, searing them.

The door opened and a uniformed maid came a few steps into the room. 'You rang, sir?'

'Yes Annie. My usual, and . . .' he turned to me, eyes running, 'what would you like, Frank? Tea or coffee?'

'Black coffee, please,' I said to the maid, flabbergasted at the utter shallowness of the man.

'So, Frank. What's your opinion, then?' he asked after the door had closed behind the maid.

I cleared my throat and sat forward a bit. 'Hard to say, really. I think I know how it was done, or at least how it *could* have been done, but as to why, that's another matter altogether. And as for where the stocks of bacillus came from . . .' I grimaced and shook my head.

He had been nodding through my short speech. Now he continued to nod, pushing himself back from the desk to make space to open a central drawer; from it, he took a white envelope which he placed face down on the desk and spent some silent time, a fingertip on diagonally opposite corners, squaring it precisely within some private reference points. 'We've got a problem, Frank.' He moved the envelope infinitesimally to the left. In the ashtray his cigarette smouldered, ignored, the smoke rising straight until it broke and scrolled away on the eddies of some undetectable air current. 'A problem we could do without right now.' Annie knocked and, without waiting for a summons, brought in our coffees.

Hilliard moved the envelope to one side to make room for the cup and stubbed out the dying butt.

While we sipped coffee, I tried to find out why he had called me, what the sick call was, but he ignored my questions and went on speculating on reasons for the anthrax.

'I reckon he's going to blackmail us,' he said, and I thought cynically that he should recognise the early preliminaries of blackmail, having, it was strongly rumoured, often used that tactic himself.

'The farmers?'

'No. Not the farmers. The government. The nation.'

'Well ... But surely there must be easier ways ... Threaten to blow up a power station, hijack a plane or even ... eh ... kidnap a politician.'

'Different people have different methods, Frank. Horses for courses and all that.' Again, I thought, he should know. He fingered the envelope and began: 'About this ethical business Frank ... (*I was about to get a lecture on Ethics from Tom Hilliard. Wait 'til the grandchildren heard this one.*) ... Gerry Downing contends, and I agree with him, that the longer we can pretend we don't know that the anthrax is deliberate, the better chance we have of catching our culprit. Or culprits. Now, the reason I called you in is that you're already aware of what's going on, whereas my vet isn't. It's not that I don't trust him – I do – but something else has come up which seems to be a new development and, to avoid all kinds of explanations and complications, I thought it better to let you handle it ...'

'I see sir. Handle what?'

'This.' He slid the envelope across the polished desktop.

I picked up the envelope and turned it over. It was addressed to Mrs Veronica Hilliard and marked 'Personal'.

'It was very shrewdly sent to my wife. If it had been addressed to me, I probably would never have seen it; even marked 'Personal', my secretary would have opened it and probably dumped it. It looks like a real crank effort. You can take it out, Frank. It's already been dusted for fingerprints. The envelope too.'

Inside was a single sheet of white A4, folded. I opened it and looked at the verse which had been typed on it:

A FARCICAL POEM

Young Miss Molly Hilliard's
Quite different from Moll Flanders,

> *But she'd better take up billiards*
> *Because her horse has . . .*
> *By A. Mallei.*

I read it again and felt the gravity of what the verse said creep in on me. The missing last word was 'glanders'; the word 'Farcical' in the title was a pun on 'Farcy' which was the old name for glanders, and the subscript, supposedly indicating the writer's name, stood for the name of the causative organism, a bacterium called *Actinobacillus mallei*. The thing that made it extra scary was the fact that there hadn't been a case of glanders in Ireland in years; the disease, one of the earliest animal ailments described, had been eradicated from western Europe in the early nineteen hundreds.

The minister obviously thought I'd had enough time to think it over. 'Glanders is what they're talking about, isn't it, Frank?'

'Yes, sir. There doesn't seem to be much doubt about that. Is this the sick animal you mentioned?'

'Yes.'

'How long has it been sick?'

'Lawrence will know. That's his domain.'

'Has it been seen by your own vet?'

'Yes. A few times. He thought it had a stubborn infection in the nose.'

'I believe that that's the way it starts. Did he treat it?'

'The vet had him on a course of antibiotics but they didn't seem to be doing much good, so he changed the medicine. Without great results, it seems. He's still discharging and he now has what you might call running sores on his legs. Does that sound like glanders to you?'

'I'm afraid it sounds exactly like glanders. I've never seen the condition, mind you, but it's one of the things you remember always, one of the famous ones.'

'Like anthrax?'

'Like anthrax.'

'You know, Frank, if it *is* glanders and it *has* been caused by the same man, then God knows how many more kinds of germs he has in his bag and what he intends to do with them . . .'

'Maybe I should get started and have a look at the horse. Is he here?'

'He's here. Out the back. We'll see him in a moment.' He looked at his watch. 'I'm waiting for Downing to phone – he should be on any minute, and I suppose that time is hardly of much consequence to poor old Frosty now.'

I didn't think there was much point in telling him that, when I suggested we begin, I'd been thinking of my time, not Frosty's.

'What happens if it is?'

'It's a Scheduled and Notifiable disease.'

'Like anthrax?'

'Like anthrax.'

'So he'll have to be put down is what you're saying. Can you tell for sure by just looking at the horse?'

'If it's classical glanders like you described, then I think so, yes. To be one hundred per cent sure, a few laboratory procedures would be needed. Or I could inject him with the glanders antigen and see if he develops a reaction, a swelling at the site of injection. That's called the mallein test.'

'Do you have this injection with you?' he asked.

'No. If it's available at all, it will be through your department only. But I don't think we need it. The laboratory will give us quicker confirmation. They can have a look at the organism in a sample of the discharge. They can also do the blood test, an S.A.T. test – provided of course that they have the proper reagent, or can get it. They may not have it as it's been many years since there was a case.'

The minister was just beginning to tell me that, if the materials weren't available, then he'd make sure that they quickly became available, to leave it to him, when the phone rang. He covered the mouthpiece and said 'Gerry

Downing' to me and then into the phone, 'Yes. Put him on.' After a lengthy conversation he said: 'Okay, Gerry,' and hung up. 'He'll be here in about twenty minutes. Now let's go and have a look at Frosty.'

IO

We stopped at the Land Rover for me to put on my boots. The minister had already donned his, and a raincoat; our journey to the horse, he explained, would take us through soaking, long grass. Thankfully, the downpour had ceased, a mere temporary respite if the plump, dark clouds roiling above us were anything to go by. We followed a meandering flagstone path through flowerbeds and herbaceous borders, across well-tended lawns, up and over a grassy knoll with a sycamore sapling sprouting from its summit like a banner on a castle, and down the other side to a tall yew hedge which had a narrow wrought-iron gate set into it. The yew arched unbroken above our heads as we passed through into a sodden, sad, dilapidated paddock.

Coarse grasses and bindweed clambered relentlessly over the scattered skeletons of practice jumps, overrunning rusting tar barrels and fallen poles painted with flaking bands of red and white; where the paint had come off altogether, mosses, lichens, and vivid, clammy fungi colonised the decaying wood, nature patiently reclaiming her own. The paddock was bounded on its other three sides by high walls of bare breeze-block, totally at odds with the house and its spacious, gracious grounds. Above the back wall, a stubble of TV aerials indicated the presence of many houses, the end result, I presumed, of the elusive, but finally granted, planning permission.

Hilliard stood and looked around as if he hadn't been

there in a long time. 'A couple of years ago, while she was still at school, Frosty was the love of Molly's life. Now . . . this mess!' He spread a helpless hand to encompass the whole area. I reckoned Lawrence must be one lazy sonofabitch to have let it come to this.

'Oh, she's not unusual in that, sir. I see it all the time, especially with young girls. One day their pony is the most important thing in the whole world, the next, I'm called in to vet him on behalf of a buyer. All of a sudden they become wrapped up in their friends . . .'

'Friends!' he gave a bitter bark. '*Friends*? A bunch of useless layabouts. All of them.'

There didn't seem to be any reply to that, so I didn't even try.

We headed across the paddock, towards the row of sheds in the corner. Like the wall they backed on to, the five boxes were constructed of plain cement blocks, noteworthy only for their stark, utilitarian ugliness. A skim of plaster and a lick of paint would have gone a long way towards making the place a little more inviting, possibly even have kept Molly interested. The minister led me to the second box from the right. The half-door, I noticed, had a large crescent chewed out of it, the work of a totally bored horse which spent too much of its life locked up.

Even without the benefit of the poem, I reckoned I would have diagnosed glanders in short order anyway. Frosty was a dark bay gelding, about fifteen hands. I assumed that his name had arisen from the same reasoning that had made a woman I once knew christen a totally black cat 'Snowflake'. He looked wretched, eye dull and lacklustre, head hanging as though too heavy for his neck. There was a purulent discharge from both nostrils, heavier from the left. So far, it could have been any URTI – upper respiratory tract infection – but the nodules and suppurating ulcers on his legs had nothing to do with any URTI I had ever seen; to me, they acted as a reflex memory trigger for glanders, just as the dark blood-flows of Tom Ryan's heifer had immediately produced the thought: anthrax. I wondered about Frosty's vet and why his memory of lecture notes and textbook pages hadn't been sparked.

'Ah! Here's Lawrence, now,' said the minister, and I turned and looked towards the man who had come through a wide gate in the end of the hedge and was now making his way slowly towards us. He was elderly and walked with an odd gait, his upper body over to one side, as though he was carrying a heavy suitcase. The condition of the paddock was understandable now – with that disability, Lawrence couldn't do much in the way of physical work. 'He can tell you more about Frosty than I can.'

Lawrence eventually made it and wheezed to a halt beside us. 'He's worse, Tom,' he said in the unmistakable accent of Hilliard's part of the country. 'A lot worse. He started gettin' them sores on his legs a few days ago. I'm washin' them with Dettol but they're gettin' worse. I was thinkin' of callin' the vet again to let him see them. There was no sign of them when he was here last week.'

Mentally I apologised to my unknown colleague – without the classic lesions on the legs, no one would have thought of the supposedly extinct disease.

'No need, Lar. Frank here, is a vet.'

'A horse vet, Tom? A specialist like?' Lawrence didn't even look at me. Seemingly all he knew or would ever need to know came from 'Tom'.

'Aye, Lar,' the minister mendaciously confirmed, falling back into the speech patterns of his youth. All things to all men. I'd have been willing to bet that Lawrence was one of the unquestioning, unthinking hardliners who believed that 'Poor Tom just about broke even' on the house deal. They both turned questioningly towards me.

'I'm almost certain it's glanders,' I said. 'To be one hundred per cent sure, I need to take a couple of swabs and possibly a blood test for serology. They probably won't have glanders antigen in stock, but the serum will keep for a while.'

'Like I already told you, if they don't have it right now,

then they soon will, believe you me.' Hilliard turned to the older man. 'You stay here, Lar, and help the vet. I've things to do at the house. Will that rain keep off?'

Lar squinted up at the sky. 'It won't be as bad as it was, Tom; but still, it'll be a better day for lookin' out than lookin' in.'

'Aye, Lar,' the minister said and he turned and headed back towards the house. I went with him, to get what I needed from the Land Rover.

'I wonder how the person who did this got in,' he mused as we crossed the paddock. 'The guards are on the gate, day and night, and anyone climbing over any of the walls would be in full view of the houses – their back gardens come right up to the walls. And even if they did manage to cross without being seen, Lawrence is always pottering about. He breeds canaries in that shed at the end of the row. Or budgies or pigeons or something – birds anyway. He's always here except on Wednesday afternoons when he goes into town for a few pints with some other old codgers.'

'So maybe they came in on a Wednesday afternoon. Or at night.'

'Yes, but like I said, the guards are at the main gate and there's a whole housing estate of nosy busybodies directly outside the wall, minding everyone's business but their own.'

'In the dead of night?' I stood aside to let him through the gate.

'It wouldn't surprise me.'

'Did Frosty usually stay in his box or was he normally out in the paddock? Before he got sick, I mean?' Remembering the chewed door, I guessed it was the former.

'Bit of both, I imagine, but you'd better check with Lawrence. Why?'

'If he was in his box, it would have been that much easier for someone to pass him a doctored sugar lump or whatever.'

'I see what you mean.'

I collected my equipment from the Land Rover and returned to the stable where, with the help of Lawrence, I took the samples I needed. Frosty was too sick to notice when I took blood from his jugular vein and lanced an unopened nodule for a pus sample.

'He's done a fair job on that door,' I remarked when we'd finished, working my way around to giving Lar a firm ticking off for having kept the unfortunate animal boxed. The vaunted deductive facilities could visualise it all: Frosty in solitary confinement, eating the timberwork in boredom, being a sitting duck for the deadly blandishments and Greek gifts of his poisoner . . .

'That wasn't Frosty. That was Little Darlin', the first horse himself bought. We sold him after a month or two. If we kep' him any longer, sure he'd have et his way out of the stable!'

'I see.' Slight trim of deductive facilities required. 'Why didn't you just let him out into the paddock?'

'We did, but he started eatin' the jumps then.'

Back to straightforward questions. 'Before he got sick, was Frosty mostly in or out?'

'Out.'

'All the time?'

'Except in the dead of winter. Otherwise, he could come and go as he pleased – the door was always left open for him.'

'Was he fairly approachable when he was out?'

'Not specially. I could walk up to him alright but if he didn't know you . . . for instance he wouldn't let Mr Hogan, th'other vet, near him. Prob'ly afraid of injections . . .'

As we crossed slowly back through the paddock I noticed that Lar grimaced with pain every time he moved his right leg; I felt chastened – compared to his for-life disability, my crop of bruises from last night's ambush palled into total insignificance. When Lar headed back for the large gate, our paths diverged and I was able to move at a normal pace.

As I closed the gate in the hedge behind me, I looked back; Lar, still wincing, had progressed a mere few feet from the spot where I'd left him.

When I rounded the side of the house, the ministerial Mercedes was waiting to take the samples to the local Veterinary Laboratory. The minister had already spoken to the director, impressing on him the need for secrecy. Gerry Downing came in as I wrapped the samples in layers of self-sealing freezer bags, then placed them in a Tupperware box, well wadded with soft kitchen paper. Annie was asked to furnish fresh black coffee – this time I wasn't offered a choice, but I'm quite sure it wasn't because Hilliard remembered.

The minister went out with the samples and Downing turned to me. 'You've seen the horse, I gather?' His pale gaze slid briefly up along my forehead, bound for the ceiling.

'Yes. It's glanders for sure. The samples are just to confirm it.'

'So . . .' The eyes came back to mine. 'What else do you have to do here now?' He made it sound like: 'Why are you hanging about then?', so I made up bits about having to be on hand when the test results came in. I realised that, even if that was true, I could have waited outside. To draw his mind away and at the same time remind him that he owed me, I said: 'And tell me, how did you get along with Bobby Young?'

He snorted. 'He provided us with very little more than you had already told me. And at an infuriatingly slow pace. He has the primitive sense of humour of the true peasant, and no concept at all of the word "enough".'

The minister returned and handed the poem to Downing. While he read it, I had a brief tussle with my conscience: strictly speaking, though I was hardly idling, I was neglecting Gino's practice. In the end, I compromised – I'd phone the surgery as soon as I'd heard Downing's report. Fifteen minutes later his longwinded 'progress' report began to grind to an end – it could really have been summed up in two words: 'none' and 'minister'. Finally, more from desperation than a wish to involve me, he turned my way. 'Our man, it seems, has a varied arsenal of germs to choose from, wouldn't you say, Mr Samson?'

'I was just thinking the same thing.'

'Makes you wonder, doesn't it?'

'About what?' demanded Poor Tom, feeling left out.

'I was just wondering, minister, if storing microbes would need an elaborate laboratory?' He turned back to me.

'No. It wouldn't. A culture of bacteria can be kept pretty much forever on what are called "slants", small screw-cap bottles of media. Once you have one viable slant and a supply of the right medium – there's an optimum, or selective, medium for each type of germ – you can have an endless supply; all you do is remove a fleck from the parent colony and place it on a new slant, and inside a couple of days, you'll have a thriving new colony. And so on. Anybody could do it, though very few people would know that; even fewer would know which selective media they needed, or where to get them, and practically nobody would know where to get the bacteria.'

'Would *you* know Frank?' the minister asked.

'No sir, I wouldn't. If I wanted a supply of anthrax or glanders for legitimate purposes, whatever they might be, I'd contact the Bacteriology Department at the Vet College and ask their advice.'

'I'll check with them.' Downing, clutching eagerly at straws, uncapped his pen.

The minister looked hard at me, and leant forward over his desk. 'Suppose I said to you, Frank, that you had to get supplies of these germs but that you couldn't ask anyone for help, how would you go about it? And money was no object.'

'That'd be a tall order.'

'Tall is not impossible, Frank. And after all it seems someone has done just that.'

'True, sir,' I answered, the admonition deserved. I

thought for a while. 'The organisms could only come from the wild or from captive stocks in laboratories. With a single species, for example anthrax, it might just be possible, by travelling to a country where the disease is endemic, to take some from an actual *case* but this would take organisation, luck, and . . . and the idea is ridiculous, even without thinking of a second organism.

'So that leaves the laboratory. The only people who could get at stocks of bacteria would be those who actually worked there – nobody else would know where they were kept, how to recognise one type from another, etcetera. So, the question now is: is our man actually a bona fide lab worker himself, or has he acquired the bacteria from someone who is?' I paused, trying to work out the next bit.

'Well?' asked the minister. 'Keep going. Don't stop now. What about burglary?'

'An ordinary burglar, stealing to order, would hardly even know where to start looking. An insider would be a more likely prospect. Even if he wasn't stealing for himself, an insider might do it for money or because he'd been blackmailed, threatened . . .

'The big difficulty as I see it is how to find out, at the outset, which labs were working on which organisms. I suppose it could be done by going painstakingly through scientific journals but, as it would be highly unlikely that any one research lab would be working on the two organisms he wanted, anthrax *and* glanders, he'd need to pinpoint two labs, find two separate bendable employees . . .' Then it struck me. 'Of course! A vaccines laboratory! That's the only place you'd find all those different animal pathogens under one roof. And it would be simple finding out which labs produce which vaccines . . .'

'It would?' The minister looked dubious. 'How?'

'Vaccine companies bombard us vets all the time with lists of the vaccines they produce. To produce a vaccine against any organism, virus or bacteria, it's essential to have live stocks of that organism.'

'You think it's a vet, then?' the minister asked.

'Or someone in our field.'

'How many companies in Ireland produce vaccines?' Downing asked. 'Any idea?'

I shook my head. 'I don't know, but I can tell you now that there won't be any producing vaccines for anthrax or glanders. We're not allowed to even use those vaccines here, let alone produce them. I'll get you a list of the major international producers by tomorrow.'

'Are we going to have a glanders epidemic now, Gerry?'

'I doubt it, minister. My guess is that your horse is a one-off, just to show us that he can go where he likes, even past security men. Of course, by attacking your horse, in your home, he may also feel that he can gain some kind of psychological advantage over you. But the most important thing from our point of view is that he has now shown us that he has at least two organisms in his arsenal.'

'You think there may be even more?'

Downing shrugged. 'He has already managed the hard part, finding a source, so why stop at two?'

'I doubt there'll be a glanders epidemic,' I weighed in, 'because it would be very difficult to organise: for one thing, there are relatively few horses; for another, few of them would be in outlying fields out of sight of their stable yards. And besides, there's no guarantee that a horse, seeing a stranger hanging about, would come across to check him out.'

'What about this sheepscab letter, Frank? Do you think he has the bacteria for that too?'

'Sheepscab is caused by mites, not bacteria. And anyway, it's endemic. Spreading sheepscab would be pointless.'

At one point I mentioned that both anthrax and glanders were also *human* pathogens, and the minister immediately began to talk of poisoned city reservoirs and contaminated baby foods. Downing was trying to convince him that there was no evidence to suggest that that was the intention, when there was a knock on the door.

'Come in.'

I glanced around. A girl stood in the doorway, very

pretty, with shoulder-length, straight, blond hair, wide-set blue eyes, a generous mouth exactly like the minister's and a cutesy button nose. In denims and a sweatshirt, she'd have been a knockout; in clothes and make-up which were far too old for her, she was neither one thing nor the other, a kind of teenaged woman. She looked ill at ease. I turned my head forward again.

I heard a little cough. 'Eh . . . Sorry to interrupt your meeting, gentlemen,' she said to the room in general, and then to the minister: 'I'm off, Dad, and I'm in a bit of a hurry . . .'

'Off?' he replied curtly. 'Off where?'

'Back to Dublin.'

'But you just *came* from Dublin last night!' I began to feel awkward. There was obviously a row brewing. He didn't seem at all put out by the fact that he had an embarrassed ringside audience sitting in front of him. Over my shoulder, I could sense the girl's growing uneasiness.

'Da-ad . . .' She began in a tone which was part pleading, part warning.

He ignored it. 'Why did you come home last night, then?' he demanded angrily. 'If it was only for a few hours, why didn't you stay in Dublin?'

'*Dad* . . .' she said again, a bit louder.

'I want an answer, Molly! Why did you drive a hundred and fifty miles just for a few hours sleep? Three hundred miles in twelve hours. For no *reason?*' When there was continued silence from behind, he said: 'I'm waiting for an answer, young lady.'

Downing, blushing scarlet, studied the blank cover of his pink folder, while I rubbed at a deep scratch on the side of my shoe and tried to pretend I wasn't there.

'Can we talk about this in private, Dad? Please.'

Her distress finally got through to him. For the first time, he seemed to realise that this was not a good time to air their differences. With a sharp sigh of exasperation, he shook his head as if to clear it. 'Okay, Molly,' he sighed resignedly. 'I suppose we can do that. When will you be back?'

'Sunday week, about noon.'

'I'll probably see you up in town before then. Drive carefully, won't you?'

'Well . . .' She hesitated, cleared her throat again, and dropped her voice to as near a whisper as she could. 'Can I . . . eh . . . borrow a hundred pounds until then?'

Downing almost dropped the pink file. I just froze.

There was a long silence from across the desk. Finally, Hilliard gave a little laugh, sank his chin onto his chest and rolled his head back and fro a few times. Then he leaned to one side, took his wallet from his hip pocket and counted out the requested hundred. 'Here, sweetheart,' he said holding the money towards her, 'and it's not a loan. It's a prize. For having such incredible *neck*.'

When she went to the desk I could see that she was about eighteen, maybe nineteen, but no more. She was blushing and she looked steadily and self-consciously at the carpet all the way, avoiding her father's eyes. When she reached the desk she looked up, blushed even more, then said: 'Thank you, Dad. Eh . . . sorry,' in another attempted whisper, and turned to go. Her father watched her as far as the door and, just as she was about to go out, suddenly remembered.

'Oh, Molly! Wait a minute. I'm afraid there's some bad news about Frosty . . .'

'Wha . . . what bad news?'

'I'm afraid it mightn't be a simple cold like we thought at first. It could be serious. A disease called glanders, and . . .' He stopped.

'And . . .?' she echoed, fear rising. I turned again to look at her. She stood rigidly, her hand on the doorknob, blue eyes wide with worry. 'He's not going to *die*, Dad, is he? Can't he be cured? I'll phone Mr Hogan. He'll know what to do.' She rushed to the desk and caught the phone.

Gently, he covered her hand with his. 'Now Molls, don't panic. Frank here is a vet and an expert on horses,' he lied glibly, 'and he's done some tests to see if it really is glanders. It may not be, but if it is, then it's by far the best thing to put Frosty to sleep. If it's glanders, he would suffer a lot in the last stages. Right, Frank?'

I nodded gravely.

'And I don't want that, indeed won't allow that, to happen. Are you with me on this, Molls?'

She sniffed miserably, nodded and then turned towards me. 'How could he have got it?' she asked plaintively, her eyes pleading for explanations.

I didn't answer at first, expecting her father to tell her, but he had obviously decided to leave it to me. 'Well . . .' I began slowly, looking to the minister for guidance, 'it's usually picked up from another horse . . .'

'But Frosty hasn't been near another horse in *years*!'

'The contact doesn't have to be direct. If someone who had been in contact with an infected horse handled Frosty, there could have been some of the bacteria on their hands or clothes or shoes . . .'

'I haven't been near other horses – I've been to the races, of course, but not near the horses. The only other person who ever goes near Frosty is Lawrence and he never leaves this place.'

I felt rotten. She was looking at me as if I was a saviour, and all I was doing was fishing. 'There must be others. The vet, the farrier . . .'

She looked at me in wide-eyed bewilderment. 'You think *they* . . .'

'No, not really – they visit lots of horses, so there would be an epidemic of glanders about if it was one of them. I just meant you should think before you say there was nobody near Frosty except you and Lawrence. It's import-ant to think of everyone, even the most unlikely. What about friends of yours? Have any of your friends been here to ride him?'

'My friends are all in Dublin.' A chilly little frisson passed between her and her father, and then, suddenly, her expression went stony. Perhaps it was because I was the only one in eye contact with her that I was the only one to notice her stiffen and see the spark of realisation that flashed in her eyes and was just as quickly quenched. 'No,' she answered quickly, too quickly, 'I can't think of anyone else who visited Frosty. How long back are we talking?'

Reasonable question. 'Oh . . . Six weeks. Two months.'

'No, then. No one in that time.' She looked at me defiantly, knowing I'd spotted the hesitation.

'Pity,' I said, going for broke and hoping that neither Downing nor her father would butt in. 'If I could pinpoint when the exposure occurred, then there might be a chance of treating it.' It was a lie, and a cruel one, but it was the only thing I could think of which might get her to come out with whatever she was hiding. It almost worked. I could see the indecision in her eyes, weighing one thing against the other; then she turned and rushed for the door, sniffing tearfully that she was going to see Frosty.

'Why did you say that? About treating the horse?' the minister asked as the door closed. He looked puzzled and annoyed in equal parts.

'Well, I assumed you didn't want her to be told the whole truth yet, or you would have explained it to her yourself. I didn't really feel it was my place to do it. But apart from that, it's not good to be too brutal and blunt. It's better if reality dawns on her bit by bit,' I said lamely. 'At least, that's what I've always found.' I didn't want to say that it was because I thought his daughter was holding back something. As it was clearly to do with her friends, and I knew his attitude towards them, I thought her reticence might have been due to her father's presence. I reckoned she might tell me if he wasn't around.

They both looked at me in silence for a long moment, then, deciding that I was the expert in the field of delivering such bad news, they resumed the interrupted conference. As soon afterwards as I could, hoping to catch Molly before she left, I asked to be excused on the grounds of having a practice to run. I promised to call later when the lab results were back and to take it from there. The minister thanked me for being such a help and asked Annie to show me out.

Annie told me that Miss Molly had already left and that seemed to bring my investigating to a sudden end. As I headed to the Land Rover, I decided that the only course now was to tell Downing and let him question her. But not now, not in front of her father. I'd phone him later, when he got back to his office.

There was a folded sheet of white paper lying on the floor of the Land Rover. It had obviously been slipped in through the closed window. I unfolded it and read the hurriedly scribbled note:

PLEASE MEET ME COTTLESTONE'S
(PUB ON RT APPROX 2 MLS FROM GATE)
TURN LT AT GATE. V. IMPORTANT!
M.H.

The massed clouds which had lurked threateningly over-head had shuffled off towards the east, leaving a mere screed behind, a reminder to us below not to get too complacent. As I drove slowly along, keeping an eye out for the pub, the sun worked its way through the thin cover and lit up the lush countryside in all its fresh-washed greenness.

I saw the first tacky sign, nailed to the gable-end of a shed:

COTTLESTONE'S COUNTRY SALOON – 800 YDS.
MUSIC FRI & SAT.

The wording was framed loosely by awesomely bad paintings of motifs of the Wild West – a six-gun, a cowboy boot with spur, a cactus, an animal which could have been a steer or a hoss (it could just as easily have been a sheep or a gnu, but I narrowed it down to the steer or hoss because of the context), a ten-gallon hat and a half-pint glass; the glass had nothing, as far as I could see, to do with the Old West, so I presumed that it was just the artist's way of introducing a note of realism, making sure that people didn't get carried away, that they'd realise it was a *pub* we were talking about here, not some kind of theme park.

I came upon a second sign, a repeat of the other except that this one said 1 ST TURN RT. instead of 800 YDS.

The quadruped, though equally vague in body shape, was slightly more identifiable inasmuch as it seemed to have *paired* organs on either side of its conical head and I concluded that it was a somewhat underdeveloped longhorn steer. The other cartoons were the same and I was just trying to figure out how many half-pint glasses it would take to fill a ten-gallon hat when the 1ST TURN RT. loomed up and I swung across the road and in.

It should have been called a barn, not a bar. The place I entered was enormous and soulless, all formica and beautyboard with scores of tubular metal tables and leatherette chairs spread three deep around a central wooden floor, polished for and by the feet of dancers. In one corner, a small stage was crammed with amplifiers, speakers and a few microphones, so it seemed that the MUSIC FRI & SAT was live. The walls were plastered with posters showing the same picture – a group dressed in cowboy outfits sitting on horses; two held guitars, two had rifles (presumably Winchesters) and one actually held one of each. The subscript informed me that they were the resident group, Davy Crockett and the Alamo Heroes. The fat one weighing down the middle horse (gun *and* guitar) topped off his bulging buckskin suit with a coonskin cap so I reckoned that he was The Man. The other four wore Stetsons. I could picture the heaving, sweating scene at eleven on a Saturday night. Not a pretty sight. And I was willing to bet that the sound would be nothing to write home about either.

I was the only one in the place. 'Hello!' I called, and in a moment, a head came through a door, said: 'Hang on a tick,' and vanished again. I spotted a payphone on the wall between two of the slot machines that lined the place, and called the practice. The work was piling up but not too bad, and there were no emergencies. I told Joannie I was tied up and would contact her as soon as I was free. In the meantime, she should ask any other callers if it could wait until tomorrow and, if not, then I would get to them late this evening. If *that* wasn't suitable, she should pass them on to Jamey Mulligan, the other practice in town.

The barman came back as I finished the call – I thought he was one of the Alamo Heroes, the one on Davy Crockett's left. 'Now, then. What'll it be?'

'Cappuccino, please.' *Another* coffee. I'd be swimming in the stuff. I put more money in the phone and called the Ward barracks. Luckily the sergeant was in.

'Well?' I asked once I'd introduced myself. 'How did it go?'

'Not much joy, I'm afraid. Lady Merrisen hasn't mentioned your conversation to anyone, but Richard O'Malley reckons that he might just possibly have alluded to it. In the pub.'

'Aw hell! The *pub*!'

'The pub. He's a frequent visitor. I spoke to a couple of lads who were there, and he didn't *allude* to it as such, he spent most of the evening telling anyone who'd listen, that you had told him that his horse had been abused at Northfield, that it would undoubtedly have been a winner only for that, and that you had advised him to sue for cruelty and loss of earnings and God knows what else . . .'

'The bastard! I never said *any*thing like that.'

'In vino verbiage.'

'Damn! So what happens now?'

'God knows who heard him – half the town probably, and they probably told the other half. If I were you, I'd have a strong word with O'Malley and forget the rest of it.'

'Gee, thanks.'

'You're welcome,' he said, clearly missing the irony.

Seething with anger, my bruises suddenly very painful again, I hung up and chose a seat by the window where I could watch the gate leading from the road, and soon, a bottle-green Porsche turned in and vanished around the side towards the car park. Though I couldn't see the driver, because of the tinted windows, I knew it was Molly. When she came in a few minutes later, I stood up to meet her and tried to judge her emotional state after her visit to Frosty.

The carefully applied make-up was now smudged, especially around the eyes, but otherwise she seemed quite composed. Perhaps she really believed I could cure him.

'How come you're in here?' she asked. 'There's quite a nice bar across the corridor.'

'Oh? I didn't know. Shall we move there, then?'

'It doesn't matter. Here's fine.' And she sat.

The barman came across. 'Howya, Molly?'

'Yo, Des.'

'What'll it be?'

'Soda water and lime. I'm on my way to Dublin,' she said as though she needed to explain or excuse the soft drink.

'And for yourself?'

'Another cappuccino, please.' Yucck.

When he left, I asked Molly if he was one of the Alamo Heroes.

She threw her eyes to heaven and said that he was.

'What are they like?' I nodded up at the posters.

'Brutal. The horses would make a better fist of it than they do.'

I thought once she had mentioned horses she might get on to why she had asked me to meet her, but she didn't. She rummaged in her bag, produced a tube of mints and offered me one.

'No, thanks,' I said and wondered if I should wait for her, or come straight out and ask her why she had slipped the note through my window. I decided to give her another minute. Des approached with a tray which he slid inexpertly onto the table, slopping some coffee into the saucer.

'Oops!' he said. 'The oul' hands must be shakin' a bit this mornin'. Haven't seen *you* around for a while Molly.'

'That's maybe because I haven't been around, Des.' As he showed no sign of leaving, she asked him how the band was going. 'The Heroes', she called them.

'Great! Doin' a few gigs here and there. We even had one

as far down as Tramore. A cousin of Jack's, a guy called Ronnie McAuliffe, got it for us.'

'Jeez, it'll be The Point Depot next, Des. Full house.'

'Heh!' he snorted. 'That'll be the day.' Then he got serious, coy almost. 'We might try a trip to Nashville next summer, though. Try to crack it there . . . You'd never know . . .' Self-consciously he wiped the perfectly clean table-top and picked up the tray.

'You'd never know is right, Des. Stranger things have happened.' When he had moved out of earshot, she added, sotto voce: 'But not many. And not in modern times.'

She went suddenly quiet, twirling her glass. I tore the top off my sugar sachet and watched the grains lie for a while on the creamy surface of the cappuccino before they found a weak spot and disappeared all together with an almost audible plop.

Molly looked up suddenly. 'When you said it was important to know how long ago Frosty picked up the disease . . . By the way, I don't know your name. I don't think we've been introduced.'

We had, but she'd been stressed. 'It's Samson. Frank Samson.'

'Frank is okay?' I nodded. 'How can that affect the course of the disease?'

Since finding her note, I'd been wondering how to play it. It seemed that whatever Molly knew would be forthcoming only if there was the chance of a pretty good dividend at the end. So I had decided to lie like a good thing, keep dangling specious carrots in front of her, and felt more louse-like than ever. 'Different drugs have different effects at different stages of the disease, Molly. Some can actually be *dangerous* if used at the wrong time. Being able to pinpoint a time is very important in coming to a decision on which drugs to use . . .' I let it hang there, let her make up her own mind.

'I see.'

There was silence so I decided to prod a little. 'Why? Do you have any idea how long ..?'

She shrugged. 'Well . . . not really. I mean, how *could* I be sure of something like that?' She stopped and stared into the pale green translucence in her glass. 'But eh . . . when you asked me back at the house, Frank, if any of my friends had been near Frosty? I didn't think of it at the time but in fact a friend *did* come to see Frosty – but only once. And for a very short while. I very much doubt that that had anything to do with it . . .'

'Probably not. But we can't afford to ignore any possibility. When was this?'

'Five weeks ago? Six? Something like that.'

I nodded and pursed my lips. 'Well that would be about right – it certainly looks like a month, month-and-a-half case to me.'

'Is that a good time for a cure, Frank? Now that you have an idea which drugs to use? If that is when it happened, though I can't see how, would it be a good time?'

'It could be better and it could be worse, Molly. I won't try to fool you. It would also help to know which strain of the organism we're dealing with . . . Have you any idea where your friend might have come across the bug?'

'No. None in the world.'

'Pity. The sooner I can find that out, the sooner I can get on with treating it.'

'But . . . eh . . . didn't Dad say that if it *was* glanders, you'd have to . . . that it would be incurable?'

I thought she'd forgotten about that, but he had said it, and I had backed him up. 'He did, and that's usually true. But a small percentage of cases pull through, and Frosty is young and strong . . .'

'He's nearly twenty and he's as sick as a dog.'

'Still, I don't think we should write him off without giving him a chance, do you?'

'No,' she shook her head. She'd have to have been totally heartless to answer 'Yes' to that one. If she wondered why I had suddenly changed my story, she didn't ask.

'So, like I said,' I picked up the coffee cup and took a

swig from it in order to at least partially cover the cruel lie, 'it would help if we knew what strain.'

'What about the lab, Frank? Can't they tell you?'

'Sure, but it would take about a week.' I lied again, piling on the pressure. 'And we don't have a week. In fact, if something doesn't turn up soon . . .' I sipped again, watching her like prey.

'I honestly don't think that my friend was responsible. We were only there for a few minutes. He originally planned to ride Frosty but then he changed his mind, so we just watched him running around the paddock.'

'Why was he running?'

'Oh, he always got excited when he saw me; probably thought we were going to do some practice jumps or something. He loved jumping – though he wasn't the world's greatest, mind you.'

'Surely you must have patted his neck or something?'

'Hardly. My eh . . . boyfriend gave him an apple.'

The bubble of anticipation that had been growing inside me popped, and the hairs on my arms and on the back of my neck tingled. I waited a moment but she didn't go on, so, hoping that it wasn't going to sound too suspicious, I said: 'An excellent consolation prize for missing the jumping session. Lucky for Frosty that your boyfriend just happened to have an apple on him.'

She smiled dreamily. 'The apple may have been more for my benefit. He knows how much I love Frosty . . . He bought a basket of exotic fruit for me, which we ate on the journey down, and a special apple for Frosty.'

'He brought the apple all the way from Dublin? Wow! Now why can't I ever think of romantic things like that.' And I shook my head in mock annoyance. 'So what happened then?'

'That was it really. We left almost immediately. We had to get back to town for the Lord Mayor's Charity Ball. It was in the Mansion House. A very grand affair. *Très splendide!*'

'I'm sure it was.'

'If it turns out that my boyfriend *was* responsible, he'll be so upset!' Her brow furrowed. 'I wonder though where he could have come across a horse with glanders. It's quite rare, isn't it?'

'Not "quite". "Very".'

'He was abroad a few months ago, just before we met. At Antibes? But he was hardly in contact with any horses there. He's not a horseman. His brother does some show-jumping and his father and uncle are both Masters of Hounds, but Mark – his name's Mark – he's the black sheep of the family in that respect. He's not particularly fond of horses, even a teeny bit scared of them, I think.'

'Except for Frosty.' I gave her a conspiratorial grin.

'Like I said, his desire to ride that day was probably to score Brownie points with me. I must admit I'd love it if Mark and I *could* ride together – we've got lots of friends near town who own horses.'

'Mark what, Molly? What's his surname?'

'Why? What difference does that make?' She shot me a puzzled look.

'None. I just wondered if I'd heard of his brother, the show-jumper.' At this stage it didn't matter if she told me or not – it would be simple to find out. Molly was, I presumed, one of the present crop of bright young things about town and all the other bright young things about town would know who her boyfriend was, at least the boyfriend named Mark whose brother show-jumped and whose father and uncle were masters of hounds and who had been her escort for the Lord Mayor's *trés splendide* Ball. If it came to that, his signature would be in the visitor's book at the gate, on the same date as the Ball.

'His brother's name is Christian. Christian Glasser – have you heard of him?'

I shook my head. 'Can't say that I have.'

'He's younger than Mark. That's Marc with a "c", by the way.'

'They're French?'

'No. Just Marc with a "c". But please, I don't want my

father to know anything about this. He's such a pain when it comes to my friends, and he disapproves of Marc in particular. He'd kill me if he knew I was going out with him – ground me forever!' And she downed the drink she had until now merely toyed with, in one gulp.

'He won't hear a word from me, Molly. Where does Marc live? Just in case I need to have a chat with him.' I had no intention of talking to 'Marc with a c' Glasser; all I wanted was to set the law on the bastard and the quickest way to do that was to get his particulars and, as soon as Molly left, phone Downing. If he wasn't the poisoner – at least of Frosty – I'd eat my wellingtons.

'In Dublin, but he's actually staying with friends just along the road. He asked me to drive him down yesterday. He had some business or other, I don't know what.'

'Long trip, just for the day. But you're obviously used to that. That day he wanted to ride Frosty, was that a special journey, too?'

'Kind of. It was such a lovely day and Marc suggested we go for a drive in the country, said he'd like to try riding and thought Frosty would be a good one to start on.' She looked at her watch. 'Jesus, I'll be killed!' She sprang up. 'Your talk with Marc. Will it take long?'

'No. I shouldn't think so.'

'Okay then. If you follow me, I'll lead you there.'

This put me on the spot. I hadn't expected anything this sudden and I didn't particularly want to get any further involved. On the other hand, I could hardly do a complete U-turn and back out. 'Just let me ring the practice first. I want to make sure there aren't any urgent calls.' I went back to the phone, fishing in my pocket for the number Joannie had given me that morning, hoping that Downing was still with the minister. It was a relief when Molly went off to powder her nose.

'Listen,' I said conspiratorially, 'I've got to make this fast. I'm with Molly, the daughter – she's just gone to the ladies now – and she's taking me to meet a friend who brought an apple all the way from Dublin to give to the horse. His name is Marc Glasser, that's Marc with a "c". I don't know exactly where he is right now and I can hardly ask without making it look fishy; Molly has no idea that the glanders was deliberate . . .'

There was a pause from the phone, then a restrained, 'I see.' Obviously the minister was nearby. A distant cough confirmed it.

'You can't talk?' I said.

'Eh, no.'

'Well that's not much help, now, is it? I rang you for advice. Okay. Let me tell you my options as I see them. One. I can go along, pretend I think the glanders is accidental and there's just a vague chance that he might be an innocent source. Or. Two. I can tell her I've got urgent calls and so can't go to see Marc. But that'll look very odd as Frosty *is* an urgent call and I've been hinting all along that if I'm to have any chance of saving him, I have to talk to Marc. Also, if I don't go, she'll tell him I suspect he may be the source, which might scare him into emigrating on the spot. Which option do you suggest?'

'Eh . . . The first.'

'You want me to go and meet this guy?' I made sure.

'Yes.'

'Okay, then. I'll be in touch.'

Molly was back at the table, studying her repaired make-up in a small mirror. She looked up at me. 'Well?'

'Let's go. No urgent calls.'

She replaced her compact in her bag and stood up. Pausing in the doorway, she looked back, and waved. '*Ciao*, Des.' As we walked across the car park, she said: 'You wouldn't believe it but I used to fancy him something rotten.'

'Not a bad-looking guy, Des.'

'Oh, *very* good looking. That had nothing to do with it. I just reasoned that anybody who can butcher a helpless twelve-string like Des does and still think he's Waylon Whatsit has to be inherently flawed. Nashville! Jesus! Hah!'

With a flash of thigh, she swung into her Porsche. 'I'll go slowly,' she said.

'Why, thank ye kindly, miss,' I responded with a subservient tug of the forelock.

She laughed. 'You know what I mean. Actually I think Land Rovers are great.'

'But not for speed?'

'Wouldn't you agree?'

On the way, I tried the mobile phone again but by now it was totally defunct. Nothing, not even the 'Battery Discharged' icon, appeared on the LCD.

12

The house to which she led me was of much the same period, size, and opulence as her own, but the forecourt was appreciably smaller and I had to berth the Land Rover carefully between a shining Mercedes and a tiny, blue, rust-pitted Fiat. Molly, who had parked right by the door, had already rung the bell when I joined her. She looked anxiously at her watch.

'I really meant it, Frank. We're in an awful hurry.'

'Five minutes. At most. I promise.'

The door was opened by a pretty, uniformed maid. Uniformed maids seemed to be sine qua nons in these large houses.

'Good afternoon, Miss Hilliard.' She glanced at me and bobbed her head. 'Sir.'

I bobbed back.

'Afternoon, Maeve,' Molly returned brusquely. 'Can you please tell Mr Glasser that I'm here.'

The maid opened the door, admitting us to a large, airy, hall. 'Miss Roberta is by the pool and Mr George hasn't come down yet.'

'I'm not staying, Maeve. I've just come to collect Mr Glasser.'

'Yes miss. I'll tell him you're here.' Her rubber soles squeaked off across the polished marble.

While we waited, Molly examined herself critically in an enormous mirror with an ornate, gilt frame. Now that her

Marc was in the immediate offing she seemed to have forgotten all about Frosty. She primped her hair, touched up her lipstick, brushed delicately with three fingertips at her fine cheekbones and said (several times): 'Jeez, I look a mess.' These self-deprecating remarks were delivered more or less sotto voce, so I said nothing. She also said: 'Where the hell is he?' and 'C'mon,dammit, Marc! We're going to be *late*!', but here too, she was talking to herself and I kept out of it. Besides, I had my own problems, the main one being how to avoid stampeding Glasser. He'd freak at being questioned about Frosty already – with the poem only posted the day before. I'd have to keep it very unthreatening, very casual, then leave equally casually and hand it all over to Downing.

The man who emerged from a door on the left was anything but romantic, in either appearance or bearing. Everything about him was 'ish' – figure plumpish; hair longish, fairish and dampish; face fattish, not exactly florid, but looking like he had stepped straight from a bath, Turkish; expression, vaguely owlish. He wore a whitish towel dressing gown over bluish silk pyjamas and slap-slapped across the hall in well-worn leather slippers, the backs of which had gone under long ago. He was halfway across the hall before he noticed us.

'Molly!' he squeaked. It came out like it was his first word of the day and he coughed a couple of times to clear the pipes. 'How goes it?' he continued in a more normal voice.

Molly, who had turned with a sparkling smile when she heard the door opening, was obviously disappointed. Almost rudely so. 'Yo, Pinky,' she said unenthusiastically, and with a melodramatic sigh, turned back to the mirror.

'Care for some brekkers?' Pinky had obviously missed the tone of her 'greeting', or maybe he was just used to it.

'I had breakfast with the normal people. Hours ago. Where's Marc? Is he furious with me? I'm very late.'

'I don't know where he is or whether he's furious or not.

Haven't seen him, but then I've only just got up. You know me, up every day at the crack of noon, no matter what – hail, rain or snow. Who's this?'

'A friend. Frank Samson. Frank, meet George Summers, better known, and more accurately described, as Pinky. Oh, isn't Marc the monkey!' she said, returning petulantly to her pet subject. 'We were supposed to leave at one, and now it's nearly half past. He should be ready and waiting. We'll barely make it!'

'Probably playing silly buggers. It would go against his macho grain to be kept waiting by any woman – even you, Molly. Come through and have some coffee. Maeve'll round him up. He can't be far away. I'll call her.'

'I've already spoken to Maeve,' Molly said in a long-suffering tone. 'Who do you think let us in?'

'Oh. Of course . . . Silly of me. I don't function properly until after breakfast – you know that, Molly.'

'I should. You've told me a hundred times.' She turned to me, put on a bored face, tapped her open mouth with her palm in a feigned yawn, and pronounced in a flat monotone: 'Pinky's body never ever wakes up until the early afternoon and his brain continues to sleep until he's had what he has the infernal gall to call "breakfast".'

'Well, lucky old you!' I beamed at him.

'Oh, pay no attention to her,' he said, as he playfully (and unsuccessfully) tried to catch Molly's eye. 'She just wishes she could do it herself. Well, no point in letting it get cold, what?'

He led us into a dining room with a long table down its centre. It looked as if it would seat twenty, but now it was set for just one. Heading straight for a sideboard with more domes on it than the Kremlin, he began raising the gleaming cupolas, one by one, liberating glorious aromas from beneath each. 'Kippers anyone?' He moved on. 'Eggs, fried, scrambled, poached?' Gentle clang. Next one. 'Bacon, liver, kidneys, sausages? Pudding, black and white? Tomatoes, fried or fresh? Mushrooms from the fields? No, Molly? Can't tempt you?' Molly was totally disinterested. I, on the other hand, was hungry. 'Then how about you, Frank? Some breakfast?'

'Call it lunch and you're on.'

'You can call it supper if you like. Just help yourself.'

While Pinky and I were digging in and Molly was impatiently sipping coffee, Maeve came back.

'Mr Glasser doesn't seem to be in the house, miss.'

'But he must be. It's after one. Where could he have gone, Pinky?'

'Search me.' Pinky punctured an egg yoke with a finger of toast.

'Oh!' Molly pouted in exasperation, but whether her annoyance was directed at Pinky or at the absent Marc, I didn't know.

'Perhaps he's in the garden,' he suggested.

'If he was, he'd have seen me arrive.'

'True. Maybe he went for a jog along the road?'

'I'd have met him.'

'Not if he went the other way at the gate.'

'Up that *hill?*'

'I guess not.' He nodded at Maeve, who turned and left. 'I bet he's found another woman, a new love, and that he has eloped with her.'

'Yeah. Thanks, Pinky. It's all very well joking but we're due on court at 4.30 sharp. Quarter finals, mixed doubles.'

'Who are you playing?'

'Sam and Moira Walters.'

'Ring in sick, Molly. Save yourselves the petrol money. Sam'll annihilate Marc, and you and Moira cancel each other out – you're both useless.'

'Look who's talking!'

'But *I* don't claim to be able to play tennis, Molly.' Pinky got up and returned to the sideboard with his still-heaped plate. It seems he had forgotten a sausage because that was all he took. Or maybe he hadn't forgotten it – maybe he just thought it was easier to fetch a new one rather than disinter the original from beneath the mound. 'Frank?' he asked, holding the dome aloft.

'Not for me, thanks.'

'Maybe they won't have it all their own way this time, Pinky.' Molly ignored the interruption. 'Sam injured his ankle a couple of months ago and it's not a hundred per cent yet. Marc reckons that if they don't hammer us in straight sets, 6–1 or 6–2, then we're away with it. If it goes beyond seventeen or eighteen games, we have them – Sam's ankle will never hold out.'

'Dream on, Molly.' Pinky shovelled another load into his mouth.

'Would you like to put a tenner on it?' Footsteps in the hall drew Molly's eyes expectantly towards the door but, once again, she was disappointed.

A tall and statuesque woman drifted gracefully into the room and said: 'Hello all.' She had a slender athletic physique and a crown of copper hair, piled above her heart-shaped face. A high brow, startlingly green eyes, a delicately thin nose, and fine, chiselled lips gave her a noble, classical beauty. She looked to be in her late twenties. She wore a multicoloured kimono over an electric-blue one-piece swimsuit, and the few straggling tresses at the base of the Audrey Hepburnesque neck were damp. She had obviously been swimming. Rather her than me, I thought – the day, though now bright and cloudless, still held the cool clamminess of the morning's deluge and the breeze was a mite too boisterous.

'Hi, Bertie. Marc isn't out at the pool with you, is he?'

'Haven't seen him for hours, not since early this morning.' Bertie poured herself a tiny cup of black coffee and sat opposite me. Her eyes smiled across the table at me above the rim of her cup; then she took a small sip and looked towards her brother and Molly for introductions. But Molly was preoccupied with her Marc, and Pinky was busy stoking up the awakening grey cells, so I smiled back and said: 'I'm Frank Samson. I'm with Molly – kind of.'

The Worrier and The Scoffer made belated attempts to atone for their deplorable manners, but Bertie had already given me her hand across the table. 'Bertie Garrison,' she smiled again. 'Nice to meet you.'

'Bertie is Pinky's sister,' Molly explained perfunctorily. 'Where did you see Marc this morning, Bertie?'

'Heading off down the forest path. He said he was going for a walk.'

'What time was that?'

Bertie made a moue and shrugged. 'Well before the rain . . .'

Pinky said, around a poised forkful of assorted breakfast: 'Rain? What rain? Has it been raining?'

'Half-ninish?' She ignored her brother completely. 'Isn't he back yet?'

Molly's impatience instantly switched to alarm. 'I hope . . . I hope he's alright.'

'Oh I'm sure he'll be along in a moment,' Bertie said in a brisk, reassuring voice, but Molly wasn't reassured and she kept glancing towards me with increasing worry in her eyes. After a minute or two I said, as if I'd just thought of it: 'Tell you what. Why don't I go along the forest path and see. Maybe he's stretched out, dozing in the sun.' If he was, then he had to have chosen the worst day ever for it; the downpour might have stopped but the ground would be sodden for days. What worried me was that, for whatever reason, Marc with a 'c' Glasser might have panicked, and already made a bolt for it.

'That's probably it,' Bertie agreed. 'It's pretty warm now, as long as you're sheltered from the breeze. I think I may have had forty winks myself.'

I dabbed at the corners of my mouth with my linen napkin, excused myself, and stood up. 'Can someone show me where this forest path is?'

Bertie Garrison and I walked by the front of the house. She had put on a turquoise tracksuit bottom and an olive-green army-surplus sweater, one of those ribbed ones with patches on the shoulders and the elbows, and, despite the jarring combination of colours and textures, still looked stunning. I stopped at the Land Rover to change into boots.

'He's probably jogging,' she said, watching me tieing the laces.

'I thought he told you he was going for a short walk?' I glanced up at her, smothering a wince as one of my bruises protested the sudden movement.

'He did, but that was hours ago, so he can't be walking still. Perhaps he came back, hung about for a while, and then went jogging. I'll bet he's puffing along the road now, in the gold lamé Christian Dior jogging ensemble, giving the cardiovascular system what for and pummelling the washboard abdominals.'

'Maybe,' I laughed, making a loop in the last lace and pulling it tight.

'Marc leaves Dublin so rarely that he's inclined to OD on fresh air when he has the chance. He's into his image in a big way, into keeping the body beautiful, beautiful.' There was a faintly derisive note in her voice all through and I had the feeling that she didn't take Marc very seriously, that, had the words still been in common usage, she would have referred to him, with a sneer, as a fop, popinjay, or dandy.

Rounding the corner to the side of the house, Bertie stopped me with a light hand on my forearm. 'If you *really* want to go, there's the forest path. But I bet he'll be back in the house before you get round the first bend. Molly fusses so much.'

'Does the path go on for long?'

'It's a bit more than ten minutes to the clearing. Would you like me to come with you?'

'Oh, I think that's hardly necessary . . .'

'I'm sure it's not but would you like me to come with you anyway? I could pop back to the house and get some sensible shoes . . .'

I smiled and shrugged. It was her forest path. 'As you like, but . . . hadn't I better get going at once? Molly tells me she and Marc are in a big hurry. Important tennis match or some such.'

'You're right. I'd only delay things. Just stick to the main path – no one would go for a walk along the side paths. They're very rough.'

The turf was damp and springy underfoot, and the still-dripping young conifers formed muffling walls so that I walked in total silence. The path was about ten feet wide and twisted and turned for no apparent reason. Every so often, a lesser path would head off, plunging to left or to right into the forest, but I kept to the main one. I wondered, as I went, how Glasser knew so much about animal diseases – from the general conversation, I got the distinct impression that he was a confirmed city type, a pretty unlikely villain in this case. Maybe he was totally innocent; maybe I had jumped to an unwarranted conclusion, but somehow, I didn't think so. I looked at my watch – seven minutes. I decided to give it another five, then call it a day. On the return journey, I'd call his name as I went, though I was now convinced that he'd done a bunk, made his way to the main road, then hitched a ride.

Abruptly I found myself at the edge of a small clearing. It was as far as the path went; the only opening in the silent surrounding ranks of trees was the one I stood in. There was a large whitish rock in the centre, and off to my left a wooden hut, its back against the trees, its blind side towards me. Its door, which was wide open, faced the rock. I presumed it was a kind of tea-hut or shelter for the foresters.

'Hello!' I shouted, not wanting to startle Glasser if he was sitting inside, 'Anybody in?' In the silence, my voice sounded like I had used a loud hailer. 'Hello?' I called again but there was no reply. I headed for the door, but, a few paces short of it, came to an abrupt and uneasy stop – my nose had picked up a faint but unmistakable trace of blood on the clean forest air. I paused, listened to the total silence, swallowed hard, then stepped forward into the doorway, and came face to face with the hacked corpse of Marc Glasser.

Reflexly squeezing my eyes shut, I stumbled the few

yards to the rock where I promptly and painfully retched up all of Pinky's brekkers. Holding my forehead against the cool wet stone, I waited for waves of shudders to pass over me, then, swallowing back the acid and bile which scalded my throat, I looked again.

At first I had to force myself, but the longer I looked, the less appalled I became, and, after a few queasy minutes, I managed to impose a sense of clinical detachment on myself. I approached the door, but, wary of obliterating footprints or other evidence, I stopped well back and examined the macabre contents of the foresters' tea-hut.

Glasser was wedged pathetically into a corner, as if he'd been trying to escape by shrinking into it. I could see several deep gashes on the forearms, as if they had been bludgeoned down out of a paltry defensive cross. The arms, resting on his thighs, were crossed at the wrists. There must have been twenty other wounds, mainly to his head, face and neck. The right eye was open, staring sightlessly through a ragged fringe of clotted blood. The floor was almost covered in congealed gore, and blood had sprayed all over the walls. Looking like rusting nailheads, a diagonal row of dark, evenly spaced spots ran across the wood, spurts from a severed artery. Swarms of fat, metallic-green flies had already found him. On the floor lay a short-handled axe and it struck me that when it was lifted, it would leave a perfect outline of itself in the congealed blood. I took one last look and tried to memorize all the details – Downing would want to know if anything had changed since I found the body – then turned back towards the house.

The return journey was eerie. I'd seen enough death to know a fresh carcase from one that had been dead a while, and I kept telling myself that whoever had killed Glasser had long since gone, but I was uncharacteristically spooked, and I moved quickly, as anxious to put space between me and the abattoir in the clearing as I was to pass the whole bloody mess to Downing. The path now felt claustrophobically narrower, as if the trees had shuffled towards each other. I approached the side tracks with trepidation and put on an extra spurt as I passed each one, with just the quickest of anxious glances down its green length. When I was almost at the house, I heard, or thought I heard, a rustling in the trees and my hackles rose and stayed up until I reached the end of the path where it joined the lawn. There I pulled up short, and waited, catching my breath. What could I tell Molly? Your romantic friend has been hacked to death in the woods? Sam and Moira Walters are going to have a bye into the semis, ankle or no ankle? I peeped around the last tree.

The two girls were leaning against the Porsche, Molly drawing circles in the gravel with a preoccupied and uneasy toe. Bertie was talking earnestly to her, as though giving the younger woman advice, and, once or twice, Molly nodded. Pinky stood motionless in the middle of the lawn on the other side of the forecourt, contemplating the sky and smoking a cigarette; he was still in pyjamas and dressing gown and, for some reason, was standing up to his insteps in rich wet grass about two weeks overdue a mowing. He spun his cigarette into a flowerbed and came across to join the others. I decided that it was time for him to take charge. I didn't know any of them from Adam – it had nothing to do with me.

There was a short path leading towards the back of the house and I took this, arriving at the edge of the large, neglected kitchen garden which separated the forest edge from the house. Maeve had obviously seen me approach and she was at the door before I reached it. She expressed no surprise apart from a slight elevation of the eyebrows. 'Yes, sir?'

'Em . . . can you ask eh . . .' I couldn't think of his real name, 'Pinky to come here, please. I don't want anyone else to know, so get him away on his own. Tell him that there's a phone call or something, then get him to come here.'

'Yes, sir.' Her eyes went beyond me, searching, sensing it was serious.

Pinky came into the kitchen looking mystified and slightly worried.

'I've found Marc . . .' I started, without preliminaries.

'And . . .?'

'And he's dead.'

'Dead?' He gaped, and groped behind him for a chair. 'Dead?' He flopped heavily down, suddenly panting. '*Dead*?'

'I'm afraid so. He's been murdered with an axe in that shed in the clearing at the end of the path. You're going to have to tell Molly. Don't give her any details, though. It's fairly brutal.'

'Oh God . . .' His head sank on to his chest.

It suddenly struck me that I was *assuming* it was Glasser. It takes two to have a murder, killer and victim. Maybe Glasser had killed the man in the shed and then fled. 'Well, I think it's him.'

Pinky looked at me sharply. 'What do you mean, you think it's him?'

'I never met the man.'

'I thought Molly said you were a friend of hers?'

'Only since today.'

There was silence while Pinky fumbled in his pocket for cigarettes and lit one with a shaking hand. 'Aw *Bollocks!*' he swore as if I'd just made the whole mess immeasurably worse.

'Maybe you should come and check for yourself.'

'Not for all the tea . . . It has to be Marc! Tallish – six-one or two maybe, slim, late twenties, dark brown hair, greenish eyes, scar on his right cheek, handsome . . . eh . . . in an effeminate sort of way . . .'

I thought back to the hut. 'It's hard to say what he looked like; he was covered in gashes and blood, all about the head area. I couldn't even swear to the colour of his hair . . .'

Pinky had gone green. 'God! An axe!' He puffed at the cigarette for a few moments and pulled himself together. 'This is terrible! What about the clothes?' he asked suddenly. 'Blue windcheater? Cream shirt? Pale fawnish trousers? Light tan shoes?'

'Well again, that's difficult to say, but I'd say you're right. There was a blue anorak thing, the shirt was cream – what little of it wasn't soaked in blood – and the trousers were definitely fawn.'

He took another thoughtful drag on his cigarette and then ground it out. 'It's Marc alright.'

'Well if you're satisfied . . . Hadn't we better call the cops? If you like, I'll do that while you break the news to Molly and your sister.'

He stood up shakily. 'Yeah. Okay. There's a phone in the hall.'

13

I sat on an antique ladderback chair beside an ornate, Louis the somethingth, brass-inlay table; in most houses it would have had pride of place, but in this house, it was the phone table. In the directory I found several numbers for Garda HQ in Limerick and asked for Downing.

'What news?' he asked.

'Well, bad, I'm afraid. I found Marc Glasser. Murdered.'

'*Murdered?*' squeaked the previously unflappable Downing; this flapped him like washing on a stormy Monday.

'With an axe. In a shed in a forest.'

There was a long pause. 'When? What forest?'

'I don't know how long he'd been dead – some hours, I'd say – but I found him about twenty minutes ago. The shed is in a forest behind the house of people called Summers or Garrison, I'm not sure which, but I can describe exactly how to get here.' And I did.

Downing asked me to hold a moment and I could hear him barking instructions to assemble a team, get cars ready, etcetera. Then he came back on. 'Anything else?'

'He was last seen at about 9.30 this morning going for a walk along the path that leads to the shed.'

'Who saw him?'

'A Roberta Garrison, a member of the household. I think. I haven't sorted out who's who yet.'

All I could hear was his breathing for a few moments, then: 'Tell me about Glasser.'

'There's not much to tell, apart from what I told you earlier. He was Molly's boyfriend, though since when I do not know. Her father disapproved strongly of him, again on what grounds I do not know . . .'

'Does Molly know yet, that Glasser's dead?'

'They're breaking the news to her now.' As if on cue, out on the forecourt, a long thin scream rose to a barely-human pitch, held for the length of two breaths, then collapsed into desolate wails and sobs. I could hear Pinky and Bertie's voices raised in urgent consolation as they tried to break through the horror which must have been smashing through her brain. 'Listen!' I held the phone towards the door for a few seconds. 'Did you hear that?'

'Poor kid. Just stay where you are and make sure no one goes near that shed. We'll be there as soon as we can. If anything else comes up I'll give you an unlisted number for here. Got a pen?'

'Fire away.' I picked up the ballpoint which was attached by a long plastic coil to a holder stuck to the side of the phone, and jotted down the number on a message pad – I had to turn over a new leaf as the top page was covered in an elaborate tracery of curving doodles. I repeated the number, Downing said: 'Correct', and we hung up. I tore out my page, let the top sheet fall back down again and, as I replaced the pen, my eyes caught the words: 'Molly – 1p.m.'. The message occupied a small clearing near the centre of the page – the doodles swooped and looped and coiled towards the words, but, at the last moment, arabesqued gracefully away to lose themselves in the intricate filigree of scrolling lines. In all, there were three messages on the page, all appearing in little clear windows amongst the swirls: at the top, in a strong backhand was: 'Tue. 10a.m. Dentist'; beneath this, in the next clearing, was a six-digit number which had obviously been gone over many times, as the individual numbers were considerably thickened; then came the 'Molly – 1p.m.' message. The number I'd written and the dental appointment were in black ballpoint and both had smudged on the first character, so I figured that they'd been written with the pen attached to the phone, but the 'Molly – 1p.m.', the phone number, and all the doodling were in pale blue ink, and were in the same stylish hand.

The maid came rushing into the hall, drawn by the scream and the forlorn howling it had now become.

'Maeve!' I checked her as she glanced apprehensively towards the half open door. 'There's nothing you can do out there. I found Mr Glasser's body in the woods. He's been murdered.'

'*Jesus, Mary and Joseph!*' Her hand became a fan, spanning her bosom.

'As you can hear, poor Miss Hilliard is taking it very badly. I've just called the gardaí and they're on their way now. They'll take charge. In the meantime I think it's best if we leave Miss Hilliard be.' I picked up the pad. 'Tell me, Maeve, would you recognise the handwriting of the household?'

'Oh yes, sir. I've been here nine years now.'

I showed her the pad. 'Can you tell me who wrote these?' Outside, the wails of grief continued. I had to call for the maid's attention. 'Maeve?'

'Oh ... Pardon me, sir. Let me see. The dentist's appointment is in Miss Roberta's writing, and the others – the phone number and the note about Miss Hilliard – that was ... Mr Glasser. I dialled this number for him this morning.'

'Yeah? How come?'

'He asked me to. He'd been trying to make a call for about fifteen minutes, and getting nothing but the engaged signal. He said he thought he might have been doing something wrong because he wasn't used to country phones, so he asked me to try.'

'So what happened?'

'The number was engaged, sir.'

'Are you sure it was this number?'

'Yes, sir. I read it off the pad. Then he asked me to call Faults to check if the number was out of order, but they said it wasn't. When I told Mr Glasser, he got angry and snatched the phone from me and told Faults that the line had to be faulty, that it couldn't be engaged because the other party was expecting his call. He told them it was a very important call and asked them to cut in on the line to check, but I gather they told him they couldn't do that because he became even more angry and slammed the phone down so hard I thought it was broken.'

'What time was this?'

'Between half past eight and ten to nine.' She must have noticed my look of wonder at her precision because she went on: 'I finished doing the hall at ten to nine and left for the study to continue my work. There's a very fixed system. Clean the drawing room first and set the fire in there; then the hall, then the study and the family sitting room, then Mr and Mrs Summers' bedroom – though I didn't have to do that this morning because they're away – then Miss Roberta's room. Sometime between noon and one o'clock, whenever he wakes up and rings his bell, I prepare Mr George's breakfast and set the table for him. Then I do his room while he's eating breakfast, and . . .'

'Fine, Maeve. I get the picture. You weren't, by any chance, within earshot when Mr Glasser finally *did* get through?'

'No, sir. I don't even know if he did.'

Outside, the wailing went on, unabated. I looked again at the thickened digits. 'Could this be Miss Hilliard's *private* home number?' Presumably a minister would have one or two ex-directory numbers.

'I wouldn't know, sir, but, if it is, it'll be in the address book.' She opened a drawer and produced the book. I flicked through to the H's and found Hilliard. There were five numbers, but none was the number on the pad. This all of a sudden began to look very interesting indeed. Certainly worth reporting to the command centre.

'Well, thank you. You've been a great help. Listen, why don't you make us all a cup of coffee? Strong and black. It might help.'

'Of course, sir.' Glancing dubiously once more towards the hall door, she hurried off.

I phoned the number Downing had given me. They'd obviously been told I might call, and there were no preliminaries. 'Ah, yes, sir. And what can I do for you?'

I read out the mystery number. 'The victim, Marc Glasser, was trying to call this number this morning, shortly before he vanished. The super will want to know the name and address.'

'No problem, sir.'

Molly exploded through the door. She stood before me, almost accusingly, and demanded that I tell her *exactly* what I had found. I toned it down as best I could but she had already heard the words 'murder' and 'axe' from Pinky, and it would have required a tongue far more silvered than mine to contrive a euphemistic version of a story containing those particular two words in the same sentence. Despite my best efforts, she went off into hysterics again.

Bertie hugged her and patted her back. Pinky did his bit by asking if she wanted a cigarette and, when his sister snarled at him that he knew full well that Molly didn't smoke, said oh, and lit one for himself. Maeve arrived with four black coffees on a tray. I put the phone on the ladderback chair, took the tray from her and placed it on the cleared Louis phone table. Several times, I pressed the strong brew on Molly and Bertie, but neither showed the slightest interest.

There was renewed uproar when Molly decided she wanted to go to the shed, to see for herself, and had to be physically restrained. Bertie steered her firmly into the sitting room, pressed her down on a sofa, then sat beside her, arm clamped around the shaking shoulders, murmuring consoling phrases. At last, after a huge brandy produced by Pinky, she calmed down enough to let Bertie drive her home.

'What happens now?' Pinky asked, as we stood on the forecourt, watching the Mercedes vanish round the corner in the driveway. 'Did you get on to the law?'

'They're on their way.' I looked at my watch. 'Do you mind if I make another few calls? I'm supposed to be running a practice.'

'Help yourself.' He led me back into the house and excused himself. 'I'd better get dressed.'

I rang the practice and cried off for the rest of the day. Joannie assured me that the neighbouring practice would cover – they owed Gino a day, anyway. I could tell she was dying to know what was going on. Next I rang Hilliard who told me that the lab had confirmed glanders. He said he would like me, if I wouldn't mind, 'to see it through', and I said that I would. I was trying to get through to Claire when Pinky came in, fully dressed.

'I ought to follow them to make sure they're alright. I'll be back soon.' Watching him wheeze away, shoehorned into the tiny Fiat, I wondered if I oughtn't to have held everybody until Downing arrived, but I hardly had the authority. Anyway, as Pinky had said, they'd be back soon.

Claire wasn't in the office so I left a message for her to contact me later at the hotel.

At a loose end, I made my way towards the kitchen to see if Maeve might have remembered anything more about Glasser's phonecall.

'Sir?' She looked up guiltily from the ironing board; the radio was playing a requests programme, though very low, and she switched it off at once.

'That little Fiat,' I said, more to open a conversation than for any other reason, 'is it Pinky's?'

'Mister George's. Yes, sir.'

'Is the Merc his, too?' His surroundings and seemingly idle lifestyle suggested something more salubrious than the aged Fiat.

'No, sir, just the Fiat.'

'Oh. He must be very fond of it. Sentimental value, or some such.'

'I couldn't say, sir. He's had it for a couple of years now. The Mercedes is Miss Roberta's.'

'Ah now, that reminds me ... How can she be *Miss* Roberta if her surname is Garrison, while her brother's is Summers?'

'Actually, sir, her name is Mrs Garrison but her husband died in a skiing accident last year so she moved back in with us. I'd always called her Miss Roberta and she'd only been gone from the house a little over two years, so when she came back, I just carried on, same as ever. I was mortified at first because I kept forgetting to say 'Mrs Garrison', but she said it was all right to call her Miss Roberta so ... so that's why. Eh ... May I ask, sir, what exactly happened to Mr Glasser?'

I told her.

'Oh, how awful!' She clicked her tongue and shook her head solemnly for a while then asked: 'Would that be the clearing with the rock in the centre, sir?'

'Yes.'

'That shed must be a new addition, then. My husband works in the forestry and often we used to walk along that path. There was no shed in it then. Though I haven't been along there since we got married last May – we're too busy with the new house.'

'Did you know Mr Glasser well?' I asked.

'Not really, sir. He probably stayed ten or twelve times during my time here, but he hasn't been for over a year now. I didn't even know he was here until I saw him this morning – he hadn't arrived by the time I left last night. If I'd known, I'd have made up the room.'

'Those other times. Did he stay long?'

'No, sir. Nearly always just overnight. He never came with more than an overnight bag.'

His luggage! I hadn't even thought of his luggage. 'And this time?'

'Just the usual overnight bag. Do you want to see it?' Clearly, Maeve thought I had some sort of official standing. No wonder, with all my questions.

I hesitated. I'd surely be exceeding the limited 'powers' which Downing had conferred on me if I continued snooping, but on the other hand, there might be something *really* important lying about in his room, a name, a diary . . . I'd almost convinced myself that I should take a quick peek, but not touch anything, when Downing arrived with a sergeant and a uniformed driver. He immediately sent them off to 'secure' the murder site but decided that he would wait at the house for the main team, which was on its way. I set the two men upon the forestry trail, told them to keep to the main path, and returned to join Downing.

Standing in the hall, I repeated all I had told him already and answered some questions he had thought of in the interim. I showed him the notepad and told him that Glasser's luggage was in his room.

'Oh? And just how do you know that?' He looked at me sharply and I was glad I hadn't gone solo.

'Maeve, the maid, told me.'

'Just came up in the conversation, did it? Have you been up to the room?'

'Hey, c'mon!' I said. 'Give me some credit!'

The search took less than five minutes. The leather overnight bag was empty. On the dressing table, there were two small matching cases, one containing hairbrush, clothes brush and comb – all silver-backed – and a set of manicure instruments; the other held a veritable arsenal of male toiletries, all in miniature bottles, and four condoms in a special little pouch which had 'Be Prepared!' on it in flaking gold lettering. Four? In an *overnight* bag?

There was nothing in any of the dressing-table drawers or in the drawer of the bedside locker. The travel alarm clock was set for just before eight. The only item in the wardrobe was a kind of short raincoat. Despite what had been a threatening sky since dawn, he hadn't bothered to take it with him. The short walk he had told Bertie he was taking, was clearly meant to be just that – a short walk; and the blue windcheater would have been adequate against the early autumnal chill.

'This his?' Downing raised a cuff of the raincoat.

'Yes, sir,' Maeve replied. 'Everything in here is.'

Downing felt the pockets, then took it off its hanger. The left pocket was empty but the right yielded a soft leather wallet and some small change. The wallet contained a long-expired Visa card in the name of M. H. Glasser, two ten pound notes, three fives, and three pound coins, all in a zipped pocket; scattered throughout the other pockets and compartments were a list of names, addresses and phone numbers – mostly of women, several bills from tailors, wine merchants and trendy clothes shops, and a fold-out plastic concertina of photograph holders. All the photographs were of Glasser. In some – posed studio shots – he was on his own, but in most he was with women, not one of whom appeared more than once. Molly Hilliard didn't appear at all.

He was indeed very handsome and the scar on his cheek gave him the swashbuckling air of a derring-do adventurer. He'd probably got it when he was a kid – falling off his tricycle or something equally banal, but it certainly looked the business, the real Heidelberg duelling item. I could see Molly falling for him like a stone. I could see most women falling for him. *Four?* Oh, the dog . . . There was a letter from a modelling agency which even I had heard of, discussing the possibility of an assignment with a fashion magazine which I had also heard of. The letter was seven months old and I wondered why he had kept it – either the job had happened or it hadn't; maybe he'd just kept it so that he could glance quickly through it if there wasn't a mirror handy. There were several different business cards – all his, and all describing different professions. One said he was an interior designer, another an actor, a third had him as a photographic model, while an impressively embossed fourth offered classes in 'Social Accomplishments' *(sic)*, whatever they might be. The last thing Downing found was a piece of paper with a telephone number written on it in pale blue ink – the same hand and ink as the doodle-scrolls by the phone, and the same number, only with the digits 061 in front, the local area code.

Propped by the window, there was a black shiny heavy-duty plastic laundry bag with a plastic yellow zip and the legend, in mauve, 'LAUNDRY – HIS'. Downing emptied the contents onto the bed and spread them out. There was a glossy gold-coloured shirt with wide sleeves and narrow cuffs, like the ones worn by flamenco dancers on postcards, a pair of designer jeans, a fluffy cream bath towel with a matching hand towel and face cloth all bearing black tabs with M.G. in gold Gothic needlework. There was a pair of silk boxer shorts and a pair of blue cotton socks, and these too bore the Gothic monogram.

Downing put the wallet into a large manila envelope and left everything else. He prodded the wastebasket with his toe. 'Was there anything in this when you did out the room this morning?'

'No sir. Nothing at all.'

Back downstairs again, he compared the phone numbers.

'They're the same,' I assured him. 'I've already passed it on to that number you gave me and asked them to find out who owns it. I reckon you'll have your killer then, dead to rights.'

'Do you now?'

'Why not? The way I see it is: Glasser eventually got through, had an argument with the person, or made some threat, so they agreed to meet somewhere nearby – in the shed – and he gets himself killed . . .' I tailed off, suddenly and embarrassingly conscious of the fact that I hadn't given much thought to this half-baked conclusion.

Downing soon put me straight. 'No, no, no. The suggestion of a face to face meeting couldn't have just "come up" during this morning's phonecall – it had to have been arranged, at the very latest before he left Dublin yesterday evening. If the business could have been concluded by phone, or by post, or by carrier pigeon, then he could have done so without having to leave Dublin. Take it in steps, man.' He began to count off on his fingers:

'Molly told you that the only reason she came down from

Dublin last night was because Glasser had "some business" to attend to, and she drove him.

'We also know they left Dublin late yesterday evening, so he didn't have time to attend to his "business" when he arrived last night. But he knew he'd be going back early today – 1.00pm – so his business must have been scheduled for this morning. Also his alarm was set for before eight so he wasn't having a lie in as you might think he would, and him, so to speak, on holiday. Of course, there's nothing to say that he set the alarm especially for *this* morning, but he was up, and busy, pretty early.

'Now. Maeve says he told the Faults people the call was prearranged and expected by the other party. Right so far?'

I nodded, feeling dumb.

'Okay. Now I agree with you that the call was, let's say almost definitely, to the killer, but I can't for the life of me see how it could have been to *his* phone, either home or office.'

'Why not?'

'If the call was prearranged, and we know that it was, the killer would have made sure that the line was free at the time. That's if he was in control of the line. But as the number was not free, then I suggest that he didn't control the instrument. So my vote goes to a public phone, a very busy public phone.'

'A street phone?'

'I can't think why it should be busy continuously for such a long time. It wouldn't be a pub; they wouldn't be open at that hour. Perhaps in a building like a hotel, railway station or bus depot – a long queue of commuters, businessmen, sales reps ringing their offices or homes before starting out for another day on the road . . . And,' he added, 'it would have to be reasonably close to here, wouldn't it? If, say, Glasser got through at nine o'clock, and was headed off up the forestry path by nine-thirty, we can assume the meeting was for tennish. So Mr X was on the phone to him at nine and at the shed in clearing by ten. So, by definition, the phone has to be within an hour's travel from the shed in the woods, including walking time . . . And that narrows it down a lot, wouldn't you say?'

I tried another tack. 'Don't you think that a forestry shed is an odd place to hold a meeting? Why not meet in the town? In a hotel, for instance.'

'The town is quite a distance from here, and Glasser didn't have a car. It had to be somewhere close by and, presumably, private. Both of which the shed is. If he's visited here ten or twelve times, he would have known of the shed's existence. It was about the only place around here they *could* have met. After all he could hardly have invited strangers into his friends' house just like that.'

'Actually,' I said, thinking back to my recent chat in the kitchen, 'that shed, in the clearing, has only been there for the past few months, long after Glasser was last here. There never was a shed before . . .'

'Are you sure of that?'

'That's what Maeve told me. So Glasser couldn't have known of its existence.'

'Now that,' Downing's eyes began to drift out of focus, 'could be really interesting. If Glasser didn't know of its existence, then . . .'

'It means the killer knew of the shed, and it was he who suggested the venue?'

'Possibly.'

'*Possibly?* If they agreed to meet at the shed and Glasser didn't know of its existence then, it had to be the killer who suggested it.'

'Let's not be hasty. Perhaps they just agreed to meet on the path and in the course of a stroll came upon the shed.'

'Aw hell!' I said when I noticed him smiling at me, teasing me.

The main team pulled into the forecourt at this point and, once everyone had been accounted for and assembled, we set off for the forestry path.

Downing, who was a very slow walker, led the shuffling procession, the police doctor to his left, me to his right;

several times he came to a complete halt in order to ask me a question or make a point, and, each time he did, he caused a multi-cop pile up behind him. As we breasted the little rise before the clearing, my queasy feeling returned, though much less strongly.

The two men who had been sent on ahead were leaning casually against the side of the hut, obviously inured to its horrific interior – I actually heard one of them laugh in response to a comment from his companion. They stopped talking and straightened up as soon as they spotted us. On entering the clearing, our column fell silent too, and as it wended its way towards the shed, I began to sidle off in the direction of the rock. But Downing caught me by the sleeve: 'Come on. I want you to tell me if everything is exactly the same as it was when you left.'

This time I didn't find the sight quite as horrific and I looked clinically around, taking my time. I told Downing that nothing had been disturbed and he nodded before waving me away and turning to the medical examiner. I went and leaned against the boulder, nursing the chastened deductive facilities and keeping out from under everyone's feet, my thirst for amateur sleuthing thoroughly under control. I saw Downing and the photographer go in and re-emerge after five minutes. When they came out, the doctor went in. At that point Downing called the men into a group around him and spoke spiritedly and urgently for several moments – I was reminded of the captain of a fancied rugby side which finds itself unexpectedly on the wrong side of a half-time 21–0 scoreline. When they dispersed to their allotted tasks, he came across to me, wiping his shoes in the long grass, dragging them through the sward over and over, swabbing gore, real or imagined, off their wet, polished sides. Spotting the splash of vomit, he stared suspiciously at it. Maybe he thought the killer had thrown up, sickened by what he had done.

'That was me,' I said, embarrassed. 'The first time.'

'Oh? Feeling better now?'

I nodded. 'Fine.'

'Well, I've done all I can here. Come on. The men know what to do.'

We walked back through the woods and emerged onto the crowded forecourt. A uniformed garda, who had stayed behind with the cars saw us, dropped his surreptitious cigarette, and came across. 'That number, sir, is the public telephone kiosk in Cloughbeg, sir.'

'Which public telephone kiosk in Cloughbeg?'

'There's only one public telephone kiosk in Cloughbeg, sir.'

'Oh. And how do you know that?'

'I'm from Cloughbeg, sir.'

'Are you now? Well then, would you just go down that path, find Sergeant McCarthy, and tell him to take yourself and two other men to Cloughbeg and do a door to door for anyone who might have seen a man hanging about the public phone this morning between 8.30 and 9.00.'

'Yes, sir.' The man from Cloughbeg headed off.

'Oh!' Downing called after him, 'and find out what chatterbox was on the phone all that time.'

I stayed around for another short while but there was nothing for me to do, so I left. It took some natty navigating to worm my way out of the parking area – Molly's abandoned Porsche and the police cars were all parked haphazardly, blocking me in.

Passing through Cloughbeg, I noticed a squad car parked by the phone box and gardai standing on doorsteps nearby.

14

Pulling up at Hilliard's gate for the second time in the one day didn't qualify me for the snappy salute and the friendly wave through. In fact, this time, both gatekeepers came out and crossed to the Land Rover. I said out through the window: 'Frank Samson, here at the minister's request . . .' and would have gone on with the routine, registration number, and so on, but the elder of the pair held up his hand.

'We know. The boss said you'd be coming back. He told us on his way out.' He leant an elbow on the window. 'Tell us. We heard someone got murdered over Cloughbeg way. You wouldn't have heard anything about that, would you?'

'A fellow by the name of Marc Glasser was murdered. Someone took an axe to him.' Talk about bad news travelling fast.

'That's what I heard. An *axe*, bejasus. Na-sty.' He whistled. 'He wasn't local, was he?'

'No. From Dublin. Did you know him?'

'No. Should I?' The hostility of the morning seemed to have vanished with the rain.

'I thought you might have recognised the name. He was here some time back, with the minister's daughter.'

'With Miss Molly?'

'Good golly, Miss Molly.' The younger one spoke for the first time and sniggered. I had the feeling that he said the same thing every time anyone said: 'Miss Molly' – and probably sniggered, too.

I ignored him. 'Yes.'

'Glasser? Glasser? When would that have been?' The older man ignored him too.

'Oh . . . say, six to eight weeks ago?'

'Then I certainly should know him. Or at least of him.'

'Maybe you were off duty.'

'Even so, I always do the weekly returns. The names of all the visitors. A name like Glasser, I'd remember for sure.' He opened the visitors book. 'Six to eight weeks, you say?' He began thumbing back, running his finger down along the entries for each day – there weren't many on weekdays, three or four at most; weekends were busier, but still no more than about fifteen. He went back ten weeks but found no Glasser.

'If he came in with a member of the family, would he still have had to sign the book?'

'Oh yes. All visitors. Everyone. Even the super.' And he turned back to today's page. 'See? Right after you this morning. That's meant to be Gerald Downing, though you'd never think it to look at it, would you? He should've been a doctor, the super – he has the writing for it.' He thrust the book at me and handed me the pen.

'Again?'

'Aye. Every time you go in. All except members of the family.'

I signed. The heavily back-sloped signature two above mine was R. Garrison and the one between us was a J. Alton, not Pinky's as I would have expected; presumably he had decided not to go in – once he'd established that the girls had reached the gate safely, he'd have been happy enough to leave the hysterical Molly to his sister.

'Who told you about the murder? The minister?'

'No.'

'Ah! Mr Summers, then?'

'Who's Mr Summers?'

'The man who came shortly after the minister's daughter and her friend arrived. In the tiny Fiat?

'Nobody came here since the Mercedes. I was on to H.Q. a while ago and they told me.'

So much for making sure that the girls were alright. Pinky hadn't even bothered to follow them all the way. Probably headed for the nearest pub to cure the shock. Why was I not surprised? 'The minister has left, you say? Will he be long away?'

'He's gone to Cork. He'll probably stay overnight.'

'Oh. Is Mrs Garrison still here?'

'No. She left just before the minister. There's just Miss Molly at the house.'

'Good golly, Miss Molly,' said the young one, unerringly spotting his cue.

'Would you ever go and open the gate, Seán,' said the man with the Visitors' Book, rolling his eyes to the skies.

With Hilliard gone, I reckoned I'd sneak in, find Lawrence, do the job, sneak back out again, and avoid the stricken Molly altogether; anyway she was probably already doped to the eyeballs and passed out in her bed. But as I abandoned the Land Rover on the empty forecourt and headed for the corner of the house, the front door opened. Molly, puff-eyed and drawn, but very much awake, stood there.

'You've come to kill Frosty, haven't you?' Her tone was sepulchral.

'Well . . .' I said uncomfortably. Personally, I've always thought that there are some spades which ought to be called manually-operated, topsoil-turning implements.

'The gravedigger has already arrived, complete with JCB.'

'Oh. I see.' J. Alton, I presumed.

'You know something? I envy Frosty. At least he'll have no more suffering.'

'Well . . .' I repeated, momentarily stuck for a nimble reason as to why instant oblivion should be a great idea for the miserable Frosty, yet a lousy idea for the equally miserable Molly. 'Frosty is terminally ill, Molly. You'll pull through . . . believe me. People always do.'

'What a rotten world,' she sniffed. 'Will you tell me about Marc, now?' First things first.

'I don't think we should talk about that, Molly.'

'Was it very bad?' she asked, not caring what I thought.

'You should remember him as he was, a very handsome guy.'

'You could tell?' There was a slight twitch in the curtains of despair which hung about her. 'Pinky said his face and head had . . .'

'Pay no attention to Pinky!' I snapped. 'Pinky didn't see him. I did. He looked very handsome and . . . at peace. Is your father here?' I tried to change the subject.

'No. He's gone to a meeting in Cork. You'd think nothing had happened.'

'You told him? About Marc?'

'No. Of course not. Not yet, anyway, though I suppose he's bound to find out, now.'

'Well then.., Aren't you being a bit hard on him?' This was good; we were getting to talk about the murder, but a few important orbits out from the epicentre. 'What did he say when you came back without your car and . . . in such a state?'

'He didn't see me. I went straight to my room. Bertie came with me. On her way out she told him I had a very bad migraine and had decided against driving back to town after all. He came up to see me before he left, but I pretended to be asleep and I had the blankets up over my head.'

'Then you're not being very fair on him, are you?'

She sniffed, discomfited at having her shiningly right- eous cause for complaint dented. 'Well, he knew about Frosty, didn't he?' Suddenly there was life in her voice, even if it was only the petulance of the spoilt brat.

'Your father was very upset about Frosty, Molly. I know he was. But if a minister has a meeting scheduled, then he'd need a very grave reason to cry off.' I listened to myself defending Tom Hilliard to his daughter, and couldn't believe it.

'Will it be quick?' she asked, changing tack without warning, again.

'Very.'

'Is it painful?'

'A lot less than the antibiotic injections he's been having.'

'Will he know he's going to die?'

'Death is an abstract concept, Molly, and animals don't think in abstracts. This injection won't mean any more to him than any other injection he's ever had in his life.'

Molly sniffed, unconvinced. 'I've got a friend who works for a vet and she says that some animals know when the vet comes at them with the needle . . .' She looked defiantly at me out of red, swollen eyes.

'What do you mean: "Comes at them"? You make it sound like the Charge of the Light Brigade. Look, Molly,' I said gently, 'just think this through a minute. As far as Frosty is concerned it's just an I/V shot and he'll react to it the same as he would to any intravenous injection – no more, no less. That's the truth.'

'I'm going with you,' she said suddenly, as if she'd been debating it for a long time.

'Fair enough. Maybe you should. Just be calm if you can.'

In a corner of the paddock a yellow JCB scooped soil from an ever-deepening hole and deposited it on the crumbling black pyramid growing at one side. Nearby were six plastic sacks of quicklime. Molly averted her eyes as we crossed the paddock towards the stable.

'We'd better get his head collar,' I said after she'd spent a few minutes stroking Frosty's nose and whispering to him.

'I can hold him. He's very good with injections, aren't you, boy?'

'Actually, Molly, what I mean is, it's probably best if we

lead him across to where we're going to bury him.' She rounded on me, eyes blazing. 'I just felt it might be more dignified for him to walk, that's all,' I said placatingly. 'Otherwise we'll have to drag him with the JCB.'

She thought a moment. 'We'll walk. Can you please get his halter? It's in the next shed.'

Molly slipped the halter over Frosty's head for the last time, then slid her arms round his neck. Oblivious to my presence, she clung to the tired, drooping neck, whispering goodbye, goodbye, to him over and over, goodbye, goodbye, until I began to think that she might be bidding farewell to the final link with the innocent years of her own youth as well. Feeling like an intruder I went outside and unwillingly eavesdropped on the urgent, intense, whispering, as Molly tried, all at the same time, to console her doomed pet, excuse her recent neglect, and reassure him she would never, ever, forget him. Then I heard her ask the horse if he was ready, and, a moment later, she emerged, leading Frosty gently from the shed and across the paddock, talking quietly to him all the way.

It was over in seconds. I filled two 50cc syringes with Euthatal and shot them, one after the other, into Frosty's jugular vein. He sagged unconscious to the ground before the first had gone in fully, and the second finished him off. The instant stillness which developed was unmistakable but I pressed my stethoscope against the ribcage, all the same – just in case.

We watched Frosty being committed to his grave as delicately as is possible with the front bucket of a JCB, and stayed while J. Alton came down from his cab and dumped the lime into the grave. When he climbed into the machine again and began to claw the soil back in, Molly buried her face in my shoulder and, though loud sobs wracked her, when I looked at her face, her cheeks were dry. She was cried out. There were no tears left for Frosty. In one four-hour period, an eighteen-year-old girl had run out of tears, and that was as rough a break as you could get. She was doing alright, considering.

Back at the house, I suggested we wash our hands thoroughly, as glanders can infect humans.

'Would you like some coffee?' Molly asked when we met in the hall as I was about to leave. When she saw me hesitate, she added: 'I'm having some, anyway.' She carried a green leather writing case under her arm.

'Well then, yes, thank you. I would.' I didn't like the look of that writing case, but it would have been cruel to refuse.

She led me into the room opposite her father's study and sat us down on either side of a low table. With a little grimace of annoyance at her own forgetfulness, she rose again immediately and pressed a bell by the fireplace. In a moment Annie appeared and was given the order. Molly moved a heavy glass ashtray and a bowl of flowers to one side and pushed the writing case towards me; then, without a word, she went and stood at the window, looking out into the garden.

After a few moments, I said: 'Am I supposed to open this?'

'Yes. I want you to look in it.'

The case contained between twenty and thirty photographs, all of Glasser either on his own (more of the studio portraits I had seen in his wallet) or with Molly. I leafed through them, not knowing what, if anything, I was supposed to be looking for. There were three copies of one shot, with him looking like a fifties' matinee idol. On impulse, I slipped one into my pocket.

'Nice photographs,' was the most neutral comment I could think of when the silence looked like it could go on forever.

'Have you looked through them all?'

'Yes.'

'Please put them back in.'

I did. 'Okay, they're in.'

She came back to the chair and sat. The puffy red eyes regarded me earnestly across the table, boring into mine, warning me not to even think of lying. 'Now tell me – truly – did Marc look much different?'

I looked back steadily. I was beginning to think that she was more worried about his good looks being ruined than she was about him being dead. 'No,' I lied again. 'Hardly any different at all. I told you. He looked at peace. Very peaceful and very handsome.'

Annie came in with a tray, bringing the third degree to a natural end, and, when she went out again, it didn't resume. I decided to chance a question or two myself. After all, she'd started it.

'How come, Molly, that Marc's name wasn't in the visitors' book at the gate?'

'You checked *that?*' Her eyebrows shot up in disbelief.

'Yes. Like I said, if I could have pinpointed the exact date of infection . . .'

'I told you. My father would have hit the roof if he knew I was going out with Marc. If he found out he'd actually been here, at the house, there'd have been holy war! So we used another name. Christian something or other. Christian is his brother. The surname is distinct too, so we had to change that also, but I don't remember what name we used.'

'Can you tell me why your father had such an aversion to Marc? Are the Glassers powerful political or business rivals?'

'Oh no. Nothing like that.'

'How did he even know him?'

'Well . . . It's a long story. My aunt, my father's sister, my hysterical, frustrated, frigid, tiny-minded, tight-assed, begrudging, maiden aunt, *she* was the cause of it all. She bought a house in Dublin – one of those big old houses on Landsdowne Road?'

'I know them. I had a flat in one. Three minutes walk from the vet college.'

'Anyway. She needed to have it decorated and obviously someone recommended Marc – this was last year, long before I met him – and . . .'

'He didn't finish the job?'

'Actually, he didn't even start it.'

'Well . . . so what? Couldn't she have got another interior decorator?'

'Sure . . . but em . . . She'd already paid him a fifty per cent deposit – three and a half grand.'

'Oh. I see.'

'She's loaded, for God's sake! You'd think she was about to die of malnutrition or something!'

'Aw, come *on*, Molly. Be reasonable.'

'I'm sure he would have got going on it soon, but to hear my father and herself in full cry – "That repre-*hens*-ible man, Thomas!" she trilled in a strident spinsterish voice. I laughed and was delighted to see that it drew a small smile, albeit a wan one, in response. Then the mouth twisted down again. 'I wish to God we'd never come down here last night.'

'Did Marc say why exactly he needed to come?'

'No. And I didn't ask. We didn't even talk about it. We just talked about general stuff, you know – clubs, people, clothes, restaurants, parties. You know? General stuff.'

'Did you stop anywhere along the way?'

'We had sandwiches in a place just outside Naas – this side.'

'Did you meet anybody there?'

'No. It wasn't the kind of place we would normally go, so we wouldn't have known anyone. We were both broke – I only had four quid and Marc had no money at all!'

I thought of the thirty-eight quid nestling in his wallet and felt like telling her. Only the thought that he could have borrowed it from either Pinky or Bertie last night stopped me. Though that seemed highly unlikely – thirty-five maybe, or forty, but who'd ask for a loan of thirty-eight quid? And it couldn't be change – he couldn't have gone shopping last night; it was late, there were no shops about, he didn't have a car . . . What a parasitic bastard.

'Did he make a phonecall while you were in the sandwich

place, or leave you for longer than a call of nature might take?'

'No. No to both. He did try to make a phonecall but not from there. It was later. Much later.'

'From the public phonebox in Cloughbeg?'

She looked at me with sudden suspicion. 'How could you know about that . . . ' Indeed how could *anyone* know about it except from herself or from Glasser? And as she hadn't told me . . .

'Oh. It was on a piece of paper in his wallet,' I said casually.

'Yeah? Why?'

'I was hoping you could tell me. I don't have a clue.'

'Well, I'm sorry. Because neither do I.'

'You said he tried to make a call. How do you know he didn't get through?'

'Because he wasn't in the box long enough to have dialled, let alone spoken to anyone. Do you think that he might have been trying to call the person who did this?'

'Who knows? Who knows?' The brief stop at Cloughbeg might have been just to jot down the number, or check that it hadn't been changed lately – there were new exchanges going in all over the country. 'What about when you got to the Summers' house? Who was there?'

'Pinky, Bertie, Marc and me. Just the four of us.'

'Anyone call by later?'

'No.'

'Maybe after you left?'

'I didn't leave until the early hours. Bertie and I were talking.'

'What about Pinky and Marc? Where were they?'

'We had dinner, just the four of us. Then we played pontoon for an hour or so. Then Pinky made coffee and took his with him up to his room. He didn't come back down. Marc, Bertie and I played for another while, forty-five minutes, an hour,' she shrugged, 'I don't know. Then Marc went off to bed. After that Bertie and I talked for maybe a couple of hours.'

'Did Marc leave the house at all?'

'No. Unless you count getting his bag from the car. That took about two seconds. He needed the bag because it had his things in it – Marc would use only his own towels. He was very fussy about that. As I said, he was back in seconds, and went straight upstairs.'

'And that was the last time you saw him?'

She looked as if she was about to dissolve into hysterics again, but didn't. 'Not exactly. I went up to say goodnight later, but he was fast asleep.' She sniffed and her lower lip trembled but she held it together. '*That* was the last time I ever saw him.'

'I'm sorry, Molly. Maybe I shouldn't have asked you all these questions.'

'Why not? I mean, it's all that's in my head right now. It's not like I'd managed to forget. I may as well be talking about it as thinking about it.'

'Very sensible.'

'Anyway, it'll be a good dress rehearsal for the cops. I'm sure they won't be far behind you.'

I left shortly after. Molly assured me that she'd be alright, that Bertie Garrison would be back soon to spend the night, and, while thanking me for my offer to wait until Bertie arrived, told me that it wasn't necessary. At the door, she thanked me for being so good with Frosty and that knocked her back a bit again. She walked with me to the Land Rover and, as I was unlocking the door said: 'Jesus. It seems like ten years ago since I slipped the note in through that window . . .' She managed a wan smile and a wave as I drove off.

I hooted at the gate and Seán came to open it. I drove over to the hut and went in. There were three guards inside, seated around a formica table with mugs and plates on it, the remains of a pound of butter in its silver paper, a sliced loaf in its waxed paper, and cheese slices in cellophane. Flies droned listlessly around, landing with impunity on spiral strips of fly paper which hung from the wooden ceiling and had long since ceased to be sticky.

'Hello,' I said to the one I knew but whose name I never found out. I looked at the reinforcements.

'Changing of the guard,' he said. 'Did you not see the busloads of tourists outside with the cameras?' He laughed, then turned to the other two who were holding steaming mugs halfway to their faces and wondering who the hell I was, walking into the hut like I was the goddam Commissioner or something: 'This is the one who found the body at the Summers' place.' That settled, they each took a mighty mouthful in perfect synch. I produced the photograph and handed it to my friend.

'Ah, Jays, I remember yer man alright, now. Came through one afternoon with the daughter and acted like he owned her, the car and the whole blessed place. They weren't here for more than half an hour, but.' He was already thumbing back through the pages. 'This is the lad that was murdered,' he said to his colleagues without looking up, and he passed the photograph to them. 'I hear he was the love of the young one's life. Tough on her, the poor kid. And now the horse, too.'

'He called himself Christian something,' I offered helpfully.

'Here he is. Christian Peters is what he signed. I *knew* no Glasser came through. Now, why do you think he was giving wrong names? Mmmm?'

'Haven't a clue,' I said, turning the book around so that I could see it. The signature was in the same hand as the messages on the pad by the Summers' phone. The date was about seven weeks ago, a Wednesday, and I wondered if it was pure coincidence that Glasser's visit happened to fit in with Lawrence's afternoon off.

I refused the offer of tea, thanked him for his time and left. Seán was walking around the Land Rover, inspecting it with the eye of the off-road enthusiast. Not that there was anything special on it that would have rewarded inspection, no winches or jerry cans – it didn't even have a shovel strapped to the back door, for God's sake. As I sat in, he appeared from behind the back. I waited for him to speak but he just gave me a wide, beaming smile.

I beamed back as I closed the door. I slid the window open: 'Don't lock the gate too tightly,' I advised. 'Mrs Garrison will be back soon. She's going to stay the night with Miss . . . Hilliard.' I emphasised the surname. I raised a hand in salute and began to move.

'Good golly, Miss Hilliard,' the twit sniggered, returning my salute. You'd want to be up and about before your breakfast to sneak one past *him*.

I arrived back at the practice just in time for evening surgery and was confronted by a full waiting room; by the time I'd seen the last one out and locked the door, it was pushing on for nine and I was totally knackered. Having been, perforce, ignored all day, my bruises were now clamouring for their proprietor's attention.

I sat at Gino's desk, yawning, and wondered what to do about Frosty's charge sheet. I'd spent the entire day on Hilliard's horse but it had been part of the whole anthrax business and I could have been said to have been on national service, pro bono publico, so to speak. It was up to Gino. I did out a normal call sheet and stuck a note on it for Joannie not to do anything with it until Gino got back. Then I pulled the phone towards me.

Claire answered at the fifth ring – I'd interrupted her bath.

'Murdering Tosca as usual, I suppose?' I made a tired attempt at banter.

'Tosca died at the foot of the battlements.'

'Whatever. Things have turned nasty here – a guy was murdered this morning. With an axe.'

'An *axe*? Yeccch!' She gave a low whistle. 'Who?'

'Bloke called Glasser. Marc, with a c, Glasser.'

There was silence at the other end. I thought we'd been cut off.

'Claire? Can you hear me?'

'You're putting me on, Frank. Marc Glasser? Murdered?'

'Do you know him?'

'Of course I know him.'

'Why "of course" and how do you know him?' I had a sudden nightmare flash of me opening Glasser's wallet and finding a shot of Claire and himself, thick as thieves, smiling knowingly to camera. Almost simultaneously I felt guilty for even thinking it and I wondered how Molly Hilliard was going to cope with the experience when the time came for her, as no doubt it would.

'Every woman in Dublin who isn't actually repulsive knows him. Mosquito, they call him, because he only comes out after sunset and is unerringly attracted to any area of exposed skin. Jeez! Mosquito murdered. Where?'

'Just outside Cloughbeg, in Limerick.'

'Limerick? Mosquito *never* leaves Dublin. Are you sure you've got the right guy? Very good-looking, with a scar on his cheekbone?'

'I'll tell you, Claire, I wouldn't know about the good-looking part or the scar either, only I saw photographs of him. He was hacked beyond recognition.'

'How awful! Poor Marc. There'll be a lot of broken hearts around town when this breaks. Do you have any idea who did it?'

'Nothing definite.'

'Well, with all due respect to the dead and all that, but the cops are going to be able to interview suspects by the busload – fathers, husbands, boyfriends, sons and lovers, you name it.'

'I think he may have been killed by his partner in crime. Anthrax Man.'

'Mosquito involved in *that*! You've got to be joking. He'd never even have heard of anthrax. In fact, I'd be surprised if he'd have heard of cow.'

'He was hired to do a bit of wooing, gigolo-ing.' And I went on and told her the whole story. I finished by urging her to try to get herself sent to Limerick for a few days to cover the story, hope springing eternal.

'Wouldn't that be nice?'

'Very nice.'

'But I doubt it. If the paper sent anyone, it would probably send Sinéad Farrelly.'

'Who's Sinéad Farrelly?'

'Gossip Column.' It seemed that Claire's respect for the dead had already evaporated.

Finding Downing was a harder job but I eventually traced him to his hotel and interrupted his dinner. I told him what I had found out from Molly, which, when you boiled it all down, wasn't a lot. I gave him the pseudonym which Glasser had used and the exact date of his visit, told him about Molly's aunt being ripped off, about their journey from Dublin and the stop at Cloughbeg.

'You seem to have asked a lot of questions.'

'No, I didn't actually. After I'd put the horse down, we had some coffee and Molly talked. She was on her own – TF had gone to Cork. Bertie Garrison had left too, though she was due back shortly – so Molly talked and I listened and . . . well perhaps I did steer the conversation a little bit.'

'Does she know that you put down the horse?'

'Does she know? Sure, she was there with me. She *held* him for me.'

'A tough young lady. We've had a bit of luck with that phonebox. There's a local woman who doesn't have a phone and whose daughter works as a night telephonist in New York. Once a week the daughter phones her at the public phonebox at eight-fifteen, when the woman is on her way back from morning Mass – it's the middle of the night in New York. They've been known to talk for hours, which explains why it was engaged for so long. They've been doing it for years . . . Our man knocked on the door several times, but she couldn't tell us much about him. What she *could* tell us tallies with what your friend, the comedian/

farmer told us. And there was a blue Renault 16 parked nearby at the time – a local shopkeeper noticed it. He said that you wouldn't expect to find strange cars in Cloughbeg so early in the morning. I've sent descriptions of him and his car to all the police stations and petrol stations in the area – about thirty-miles radius. And we're checking the Central Vehicle Registration Office for all Renault 16 owners in the same area. After that it will be a matter of visiting each one.'

I was surprised by his sudden willingness to talk to me so openly. 'Good luck. I don't see how, but if there's any way I can help . . .'

'Thank you. You've been quite a help so far, but it looks like legwork from now on. I'll call and see the Hilliard girl first thing in the morning – it seems she's up to answering a few questions, or at least amenable to having the conversation "steered" along helpful lines.'

He wished me good night and went back to his dinner. I stretched as much as the bruises would put up with, yawned, and began to think about mine. It had been a long day.

Outside, the dull, blustery day was in its last few minutes, and a fresh wind, moist off the Atlantic, scudded tattered shreds of cloud eastward, directly into the path of the inexorably advancing dark.

15

The following Monday, an oppressively close and dark day, I was sitting at Gino's desk, filling in reports after morning surgery and at last devoting my entire efforts to looking after his practice, when the post arrived. Amongst the usual sheaf of bills and fliers was a letter addressed to me in a strong backhand which looked vaguely familiar. As I slit the envelope, it came to me – Roberta Garrison's writing, or as near as dammit. Intrigued, I unfolded the two sheets of cream vellum and saw I was right. Now even more intrigued, I began to read – I couldn't even hazard a guess at why she should be writing to me, but I assumed it had to do with Glasser's murder. I was wrong.

> *Dear Frank,*
>
> *I hope you'll excuse the familiarity of my address when our brief association would make a 'Dear Mr Samson' more apt, but as you read on, you will see why, in this particular instance, the more correct address would be nothing short of laughable. I've been racking my brains for a subtle way to introduce what I want to say, but having failed dismally, must resort to straight talk: Are you free next Thursday evening? I think I need to explain myself.*
>
> *You may or may not know that I've been a widow for almost a year now. In recent months, at the insistence of friends, I've been trying to ease back into a 'normal' lifestyle – I'm afraid I have little appetite for this as yet, but people will*

keep inviting me to dinner parties, and it has become impossible for me to turn them all down. To be truthful, it probably is best for me to get out once in a while – it's just a bit hard to face it as my hosts invariably feel obliged to invite a 'spare' man to even up the numbers; the rather unpalatable upshot of this is that I am inevitably regarded by one and all as the spare man's 'partner', which, on several occasions, has placed me in embarrassing situations. Personally I've never understood why it is considered essential to have an equal number of men and women placed alternately around a table in order to enjoy some food and conversation, but it does seem to be an immutable rule. Enough background, now for specifics.

One of these dinner parties is scheduled for next Thursday. I'd already accepted the invitation when my hostess mentioned (with a suggestive smirk) that she intended to invite the inevitable spare man. The man she mentioned has been been my 'date' four times already, and I can only assume, from the knowing leer she gave me, that there is some rumour going the rounds now that we have begun an affair or some such. In fact she asked me if I wouldn't prefer to invite him myself. I was horrified, as this particular man is one of the more unwelcomely persistent ones; and, I suspect, the source of the rumour. Quite apart from this, he is also a man whom I would not touch with the proverbial bargepole, whatever the circumstances.

You will appreciate, therefore, that I was in somewhat of a dilemma: having accepted the invitation, I could hardly then refuse it mere seconds later, at least not without my 'weird mood swings', as no doubt this action would be instantly dubbed, becoming a matter for general discussion and speculation by one and all; on the other hand I couldn't very well accept the invitation but veto her choice of spare man, without adding grist to the rumour mill – no doubt, had I done so, it would immediately have become gospel that he and I had had a lovers' tiff! So I did the only thing I could think of at the time: I told her I already had a date for that evening, and if she didn't mind, I'd like to bring my date along. I was in a panic as I didn't/don't have a date. However, I didn't mention any *names, so you won't be letting me down if, for one reason or another, you can't make it.*

I would appreciate an early answer – if you can't come, then I either need to recruit someone else, or cry off. I am reluctant to take the latter course as I feel I have been presented with an ideal opportunity to send out the message that I neither need nor wish to have spare men arranged for me. If I can't re-establish my independence, then I don't see how I can ever get back into so called 'normal' life.

I've just read back over this very embarrassing letter. It makes me sound soulless, callous and calculating, and I can see how you could feel insulted by it. Let me assure you that no insult is intended. On the contrary, when I suddenly found myself in dire need of an escort, I don't mind admitting that you were the first person to pop into my head. I've thought of a few other possibilities since, but they are (comparatively) very sub-standard and would make poor substitutes. I do hope you can make it on Thursday.

Yours brazenly,

Bertie. (Roberta Garrison).

I laid the letter aside and thought: how did she know I wasn't a married man with a wife, family and fireside to whom and to which I returned every evening? She must have checked me out. It was both flattering and faintly frightening. I re-read the letter, searching for hidden meanings between the neat, back-sloping lines, but failed to find any. As a straightforward plea for help from a put-upon widow, there was no question about it – of course I'd do my bit to help out. The slightly flirtatious tone of the last paragraph made me a little less sure, but as we had met for the merest of minutes, it was unlikely that it was anything more than an awkward way to end an awkward letter.

I pulled the phone towards me and began to dial Claire's number, then stopped. Ringing her specially to tell her (ask permission?) would be making a big deal out of the invitation – I'd no intention of not telling her but I'd do it during the course of another call. I lifted the receiver again and dialled the number at the top of the letter. Bertie herself answered it. 'Hello?'

'Hello. Frank Samson here.'

'Ahhh . . .' A little cough came down the line. Eh . . . How are you?' she enquired nervously.

'Oh . . . Sitting up, and taking a little light nourishment,' I joked, a teeny bit nervous myself.

'Sorry?'

'Nothing. Just a silly remark. I got your letter, by the way, and Thursday'll be fine for me.'

'Well,' she sounded relieved, 'that's great. Thank you. As I explained . . .'

'No explanations needed – you put it all very clearly in your letter.'

'I ought to have phoned, but . . . em, I thought you might need time to think it over. So I wrote.'

Bertie was uptight during the whole conversation, confining herself to the details: the dinner would be in Limerick city at eight o'clock; she wouldn't hear of me driving out to her house to collect her because then I'd have to drive her home too, all of which would add miles to my journey – it was bad enough, she said, my having to make the long journey from Ward to Limerick, just to get her off the farcical hook she had stupidly got herself onto. Eventually we agreed to meet at seven-thirty at a hotel a street or two away from her hosts' house, have a drink, get our stories straight, then arrive together in one car. She told me she was looking forward to it and I said so was I. As I hung up, I realised, with a guilty little start, that I actually *was*.

Outside, the first plump drops of rain plopped onto the concrete yard, making a sound like the patter of surreptitious footsteps.

I finished work late again that evening. Claire rang as I was going to bed. Towards the end of the call, I said: 'Oh by the way . . .' and mentioned, as if it had almost slipped my mind, my Thursday appointment with Bertie, playing up the doing-the-needy-widow-a-favour side and leaving out altogether anything in the nature of physical description.

'I see,' said Claire in a thoughtful tone. 'Is she, by any chance, young and beautiful?'

'Oh . . . Just, you know . . . a . . . a widow,' I said lamely, wondering how the hell she'd worked that out. 'Just an ordinary widow, you know.' After a longish silence, I said: 'Well, I could hardly refuse the woman, could I?' And I read out the letter, terminating it slightly prematurely at '*no insult is intended*'. I also changed the signing off bit to '*Yours sincerely*'.

Claire went quiet while her feminism had it out with her possessiveness and finally decided that a sister in need of protection from a rampant male chauvinist pig deserved the break.

'I'll be down on the Friday evening train,' she said.

'Great. I'll be at the station. Assuming, of course, that I'll have managed to escape from the widow's clutches by then.'

'Don't push it, Frank. Goodnight.'

'Goodnight. And I love you.'

'Me too.'

Uncharacteristically, sleep eluded me. I lay in the dark, trying out different ways of saying: '*I've agreed to chaperone the widowed sister of a client to a dinner party on Thursday evening*', and wondering which nuance, which stress syllable, had given the game away, which part of it had made it sound as though she was young and beautiful.

On the Wednesday, just before noon, I was thrust suddenly back into the thick of the national crisis of which, thanks to the continuing official news blackout, the nation was still blissfully unaware. The minister called again, and this time there were no niceties – without explanation or an enquiry as to whether I was busy or not, he summoned me to an urgent conference at his house. I set out at once and, a little over an hour later, was met at the door by a secretary who propelled me, almost physically, into the study. The minister and Downing were huddled over the desk and the air was thick with tension and cigarette smoke. Without any of the fulsome bonhomie of my last visit, Hilliard thrust an envelope at me. 'Read this.'

The envelope contained another poem, after the fashion of the first:

> *'I bet you've squawked and talked to the law.*
> *You may even have been and seen the vet.*
> *You're probably frantic about what you saw,*
> *But hey! you ain't seen NOTHIN' yet!!'*

Underneath, with no effort at further poetastry, was: '*Look at the base of the road sign nearest your gate. See what you CAN find.*'

Hilliard placed the *CAN* on the polished surface of his desk, pushed it across to me, pointed at it and said: 'Open it, Frank. It's been dusted for fingerprints.'

The can looked just like an ordinary sweet-can; in fact it probably was an ordinary sweet-can, large enough to hold about half a gallon of water. Removing the tight lid which had been sealed with adhesive tape, I peered cautiously in. It was packed tight with newspaper, except for a column in the centre which was occupied by another tin can. This in turn was packed with more newspaper, except at *its* centre, where a narrow cardboard cylinder, like the core of a roll of fax paper, was cocooned. Protruding slightly from this was a green rubber stopper. I looked up, puzzled. Both men were watching me.

'You can take it out,' Hilliard said, 'but be careful.'

'What is it?' I asked, not being at all interested in taking it out until I knew what it was. The way they were watching, it could have been nitroglycerine.

'Foot and Mouth Virus,' Downing said glumly, speaking for the first time.

My heart lurched. 'You're joking, of course.'

'I wish.'

'How do you know? There's nothing in the poem . . .'

'There was a letter in the can.' Downing again.

'Take a look at the tube first, Frank,' the minister said. 'See what you think.'

'Think about what, sir?'

'Just take a look.'

The glass test tube was three-quarters full of clear liquid. A label said: 'DANGER – LIVE FOOT AND MOUTH VIRUS. EXTREME CARE!!' in red ink. Gingerly I slid the doomsday tube back into its protective cylinder. My fingers felt contaminated and I rubbed them briefly on the paper in the can and then on my jeans. So this was what it had all been leading up to. Anthrax and Glanders, horrifying in their own right, were mere botherations compared to a full-scale outbreak of Foot and Mouth Disease.

'Well, Frank? Is he bluffing?'

'I very much doubt it sir, but I can't tell by just looking. It will have to be checked at a lab, and that may take days.'

'Show him the letter, Gerry.'

Downing opened a folder and passed me the top sheet. It had a sheen of fingerprint powder all over it. 'This was in the can.'

It had been typed on the same, cheap, flimsy paper as the poem.

Minister,

I most earnestly urge you to take this letter seriously. The tube does contain live, virulent Foot & Mouth Virus and is to be treated with the utmost care. DO NOT OPEN IT! Obviously you will want it checked independently as I do not expect you to take my word for it. As far as I know, it will have to be sent to a virology lab – your veterinary staff can advise you on this. I will wait until noon next Tuesday to allow for the testing to be done and for any other problems that might crop up. But that is all. Under no circumstances will an extension of this time be granted. You are to assemble ten million pounds in small, used, unmarked banknotes, none larger than a twenty. You will be told what to do when the time is right. For now, all you have to do is be ready.

If there are any hitches, then the results will be devastating. I have lots more F&M – though, as you know, just a tiny drop will do the trick! I also have a good stock of Rabies virus and the viruses of African Swine Fever and Newcastle Disease – we must not forget the pig and poultry industries! I don't have any more Glanders (sorry about your daughter's horse), but there's plenty of Anthrax – it just goes on growing and growing! There's also a thriving colony of Colorado Beetles which, I believe, play merry havoc with crops. Obviously, all these will be turned over to you when the money is safely in my hands. Equally obviously, they will be turned loose if I have any problems with police or marked notes or anything else of that sort. Believe me, it's not worth taking a chance. The way I see it, you're getting a bargain. If any of these bugs gets loose, it will cost the country ten times that. Or more.

You know I mean business. The Anthrax outbreak proves I can do it. I have done it! If in doubt take a look at my letter of 4th ult to your Department re. Sheepscab. If you haven't seen it already, it should make very interesting reading!!!

I'll call you on your home phone at noon on Tuesday. When I ring, don't talk. Just listen. Your instructions will be clear, simple and precise and will require absolutely NO discussion. They will take exactly fourteen seconds to deliver. Be a good minister and protect the environment and the livestock of the country. All you have to do is Be Ready by Tuesday! Remember . . . Unmarked notes.

There was no signature but the name, Gordon Harris, was typed.

As I handed back the letter, all I could think was that it could have been a lot worse – he could have asked for twenty million or fifty and I couldn't see how the government could refuse. Like he'd said, ten million was a bargain.

'Any ideas, Frank?' The minister looked at me expectantly.

'No, sir. Not just at the moment. I must confess to being a bit shocked. I mean . . . Foot & Mouth!!'

'And the others? Rabies, and so forth,' Downing put in. 'I believe that they, too, are all serious animal diseases?'

'About as serious as you can get. Some, like Rabies, are human diseases, too.'

'This guy knows his stuff, Gerry, doesn't he?' the minister tapped the letter with the backs of his fingers.

'We've been working on the assumption that he's a professional in the agribusiness sector from the outset. It seems even more likely now.'

'If he really does have all these, then that's an incredible list,' I said. 'There can't be too many labs worldwide with all those under one roof. I realise the tight situation he's put us in, but in order to pressure us, he has had to give a little, too. I reckon we can now justify narrowing down the field a lot. Unless Gordon Harris has contacts in *several* labs, which seems highly unlikely, his source can only be one of a handful of labs, worldwide.'

'What about the beetles?' The minister interrupted. 'He said he also has Colorado Beetles.'

'They may or may not have come from the lab. I doubt it. I think they're fairly common in certain places.'

'Where?'

'I don't know, sir. They're not my field, really – more of a horticultural problem.' I shrugged. 'Possibly Colorado?' I hazarded an educated guess.

'Maybe we can find a lab in an area where Colorado beetles also thrive . . .' mused the minister, making what at first looked like a silly question, not so silly after all.

Downing waited respectfully to see if the minister was going to develop the beetles theme, then asked me if I could name the main vaccine labs who would handle such 'germs'. I couldn't, certainly not a comprehensive list, but I gave him pointers as to where he might find out.

'Give us a quick run down on Foot and Mouth Disease, Frank,' Hilliard interrupted again. 'Just the bare bones.'

'Briefly, it's a highly contagious viral disease of all animals with cloven hooves. It spreads very rapidly and up to one hundred per cent of exposed animals develop the disease. The symptoms are lameness and heavy salivating, with blisters in the mouth and on the skin between and just above the hooves. The actual mortality rate is not high – but animals which recover are thin, unthrifty and unproductive. Because of this, slaughter of affected and in-contact animals is the policy we follow, though in countries where the disease is endemic, they vaccinate the whole susceptible population . . .'

'I take it that vaccination is out in this case, Frank?'

'Between this and next Tuesday? I would say so. Yes, sir.' I went on. 'The virus persists in products like meat, milk and cheese, which is why all countries would ban imports from us. All trade in the agricultural sector, local, national, and foreign would stop at once. There would be restriction on travel in rural areas, quarantine of people on affected farms, cancellation of all sporting fixtures and other gatherings. The price of cattle would plummet, meat factories closed, people out of work . . .'

'In other words a national disaster.'

'Yes sir. I think ten million is a bargain. Unless Interpol comes up with something inside six days.'

That transferred the spotlight neatly on to Downing. 'Give us your report, Gerry. What's happening?' The minister sat back and stared at the sweet-can on his desk.

Downing cleared his throat and took a wire-backed notebook from his pocket. His voice becoming a drone, he read a sad litany of clues which had led nowhere and promising leads which had petered out, but, like the last time, he had no progress to report. With regard to Interpol – he paused to turn the notebook around and started from the back – they had been finding it difficult to get replies from some of the countries . . . but, blah, blah, blah. And that, in substance, was it.

'What are Interpol finding out for you?' I asked, when it was plain that he had run out of steam. A while back.

'Three things,' said Downing eagerly, relieved to have someone to talk to, another voice in the unimpressed silence emanating from across the desk. 'One,' he grabbed an index finger and shook it a bit, 'the names of all institutions in member countries which handle the germs of Anthrax and Glanders – I'll send them this revised list at once of course. Two,' the middle finger got snared as well, 'if any of these institutions reported a theft or a break-in in the last six months, and,' he stuck the appropriate number of digits into the air, 'three, if any of them has an Irish citizen on the staff, or someone who has a known connection with Ireland or an Irish citizen. I'm assuming our blackmailer is Irish. We have to narrow it down somehow.' He broke off his lame narrative as a helicopter clattered in overhead and landed. It had come to ferry the lethal sweet-can to the virology laboratory. A lab technician packed the sweet-can in about five different polystyrene containers, sealing each one as he went, then packed the resultant parcel in a stout metal carrier case. As we watched the young pilot carry it out of the room, not one of us harboured any serious hopes that the vial might be nothing more than a gigantic bluff. I hoped, as I heard the helicopter roar into the sky, that they'd have a safe journey, especially over agricultural land.

16

I'd cancelled Thursday evening surgery the moment I'd accepted Bertie's invitation, and five pm found me picking fastidiously through Gino's wardrobe. He was the same size as me, and, fortuitously, a snappy dresser. I'd started out just looking for a jacket or blazer to go with the one respectable pair of trousers and shirt I travelled with, but, seduced by the enormous choice, I fitted myself out with a full ensemble, including shoes. I placed my booty in a small suitcase and headed back to the hotel. By six, I was standing in front of the wardrobe-door mirror, admiring myself in Gino's full splendour – a slightly conservative navy blazer, pinkish shirt, Veterinary Council tie, and grey trousers which broke, just so, over his highly-polished black brogues. The socks and underpants were my own, as was the cologne – I'd forgotten to have a rootle through Gino's formidable stockpile.

Mrs Foley told me I looked gorgeous and asked me if Claire was down from Dublin. I said, no, I had to go to a meeting and she said it was a strange hour of the day for a meeting; I handed her the key and turned away from the reception desk. As I crossed the foyer, I could feel her eyes boring into my back, like lasers.

Nearing Limerick, catching the tail end of rush hour, I wondered again just what I was doing here. Sure, Bertie Garrison had asked me to help her out and and that was fine, but it was unavoidable that there were some sexual undertones. There just had to be. For a start, no red-blooded male could view a date with Bertie Garrison detachedly and dispassionately. Add to that the strong 'I-am-interested' signals in her letter and the whole thing became one giant ego trip; the only thing which stood in the path of a singularly auspicious chase was the fact that I loved the faraway Claire and she loved me and, worse, trusted me unreservedly, as I did her.

I arrived early at the hotel and sat sipping a pint of Guinness, the only patron of the plush lounge bar. I chose a stool from which I could see the foyer, just in case I'd come into the wrong bar, like I had at Cottlestone's the day I met Molly Hilliard. Dead on seven-thirty, Bertie walked in. The thick copper tresses were now down, cascading luxuriantly onto her shoulders and neck; her understated, off-white, linen dress managed somehow to look both demure and extremely sexy and, for a second, all I could do was ogle. She came towards the softly-lit bar, gold high-heeled sandals clicking on the marble floor and I slid off my stool and went to meet her.

'Oh my!' she smiled. 'But don't you look handsome and elegant.' The unsureness of her letter and the phonecall seemed to have ebbed.

I inclined my head graciously. 'I was hoping to match what I imagined you'd wear, but I see I've failed miserably. What a beautiful dress you are wearing, Mrs Garrison.' I tried to inject some reserve into the mutual admiring and complimenting by addressing her formally.

My reserve was lost on her. 'Why, *thank* you. What did you imagine I'd wear?'

'Well, having only seen you in a bathing costume and some odds and ends, I had to forego the details and go for the overall effect. I underestimated. It's hard to guess with someone you've only ever seen for ten minutes. Approx.' I set another tidy little barrier in place.

Again, she didn't seem to notice. 'I didn't see you as a blazer and slacks man.'

'I'm not. These are borrowed. Even the shirt and tie. What did you think I'd be wearing?'

'I really didn't know ... Shining armour, I guess. Thanks for coming.'

'Hey! My pleasure. I'm honoured.'

I steered her to the bar and bought us drinks. We sat in a booth and argued good-naturedly about the drink. Bertie wanted to pay, claiming that as I'd been good enough to help her out, there was no way I was going to be out of pocket as well. I said that if that was the deal, then I'd have to ask for specimen charges of my time, depreciation on the Land Rover, wear and tear on the tyres and several gallons of diesel, not to mention hire of the clothes and so forth to be taken into account. We finished our drinks and drove the couple of streets round to the party in her car.

Ten people ranged around a rectangular table – the host and hostess at either end and the guests spaced man-woman-man down the sides. Bertie sat across from me, and one to the left. Stella, the hostess, immediately to my right, had been full of meaningful looks, winks and smiles as we chatted before dinner and she didn't let up after we'd sat down to table. Her husband and the other guests were fine, but Stella was a pain. Hardly a comment came from her that didn't have a silly little innuendo tagged on. Regarding the roast Connemara lamb, she reckoned she had gone very easy on the garlic because: 'I'm sure Bertie doesn't want her breath tasting of garlic *tonight*!' (Sheepish smile). The cheeseboard was passed to Bertie with the caveat that: 'some of these are supposed to be aphrodisiacs, so don't pretend tomorrow morning that I didn't warn you!' (Cheesy grin). Coffee would be served in the drawing room 'as soon as you two have stopped playing footsie.' There were many more. To her credit, Bertie fielded them all with finesse, without a sign of irritation, and somehow, without confirming or denying anything by either look or word. I pretended not to understand any of them and the rest of the company, a decent bunch, just talked over them. Stella was a worse busybody than Mrs Foley – if there were rumours about Bertie, then Stella had to be a prime suspect for the position of *fons et origo*.

After dinner, she buttonholed me and gave me a long and sincere lecture on what a special person Bertie was, how precious, how ... *vulnerable*, how, how, how *fragile*, *brittle*, and yet how strong, resourceful, and 'indomital ... indomible ... in-*dom*-itable, dammit!'. She also reckoned she had never seen her so radiantly happy, even before THE TRAGEDY, and how lucky she was to have found me and how lucky I was to have found her ... and that everything that had happened might be for the best, who could tell ... ? She went on, in a confidential whisper, her lips almost nibbling my ear, that not only was Bertie beautiful, as everyone could see, but that she had also been left, how could she put it ... ? 'Loaded? Very comfortably off?' if I got her drift?

'You mean, rich?' I asked aloud, fed up with her intense conspiratorial whisperings.

'*Shhh!*' she hissed urgently and, clutching my arm, glanced furtively around. As nobody seemed to have noticed my indiscretion, she put her mouth back to my ear. 'You could, I suppose, put it like that,' as if 'rich' was a very odd word to use to describe having lots of money.

Soon afterwards Bertie announced that it was time for us to be off and we took our leave amidst a slurred blaze of ribald remarks and *double entendres* from Stella who, for the past ten minutes, had been impressively, if only just, making a mockery of the law of gravity.

'I'm sorry you got stuck with Stella,' she said as we pulled out from the kerb. 'She's back on the booze and she can be a handful.'

'More like a menace,' I snorted. 'Maybe it's none of my business, but I'd strongly suggest you have a chat with her. She doesn't know me from Adam, yet she told me lots of private details about you, including that you were seriously rich. I don't think you should have that kind of stuff broadcast to every Tom, Dick and Harry. Do you?'

She smiled. 'I'm touched by your concern, Frank, but it

is common knowledge. My late husband left me six-point-eight million. Net. It was in all the papers not so long ago.'

'Oh. But not in the sports pages, aye?'

She laughed. 'Don't worry. I'd never tell Stella anything private. Nobody would. But, as I said, thanks for worrying about me. It's a nice feeling to have someone worry about you.' She took her hand off the steering wheel to squeeze mine.

We were still in third gear, though the engine wasn't racing – it was just that Bertie was driving very slowly. 'You're still in third,' I observed, ever the bad passenger.

'Why, so I am!' She changed up but didn't increase speed, so the engine now laboured and shuddered excruciatingly. Suddenly she flicked on her indicator and rolled to a stop outside a fast food joint. 'Come on,' she said. 'Buy me a coffee.'

'I'll buy *me* a coffee.' I grumbled. 'You, with your countless millions, can buy your own.'

While we sat at a window table with attached plastic chairs moulded to fit the contours of someone's backside, though not mine, Bertie talked and I listened. At first it was all light-hearted, but, bit by bit, out leaked the little problems – the insecurity, the lack of self-confidence and esteem, the loneliness, pessimism for the future and basically, the lack of an understanding friend or companion to talk to, to share things with. I listened to it all and wondered why it was that people always seemed to think they could lay their grief on me – I remembered Claire doing it shortly after we'd first met. My relations and friends were always at it, too. Not that I objected – I just wondered why me.

'Sorry, Frank,' she eventually smiled. 'It was bad enough me propositioning you by letter without treating you as a shrink as well.'

'Speaking of shrinks . . . Did you hear the one about the man who was talking to a shrink at a party and said he knew it sounded crazy but, at one stage in his life, years before, he had firmly believed he was a dog?'

'No.' Her face took on a delightful expression, eyes widening and fixed on mine, her lovely mouth widening, anticipating laughter.

'Well the shrink says that must have been *aw*-ful, and the guy says it was, though, thank God, he's totally over it now, and has been for years. The shrink says he's delighted to hear that but, as he's very interested in this syndrome, could the man come to his clinic sometime? So the guy says okay and, a week or so later, calls. The shrink is delighted to see him and gives him the big welcome. Then he leads him into his office and says, "now then, you'd better lie on the couch there and tell me all about it". And the guy says: "Gee, I'd love to Doc, only . . . I'm not allowed on the furniture."'

Bertie burst into laughter, pushing herself back against the chair. She had a very nice laugh. I grinned at her, growled 'Woof, woof!' and got some more mileage out of that. When she stopped laughing, she told me I was a tonic, and insisted on going to the counter for two more coffees 'for the road'. My untimely joke (one of the Joker's) wasn't quite as inapt as it might have seemed. I needed time to think. As I saw it, I had just two choices: I could be boorishly indifferent to her problems, or I could point out to her that she had all kinds of things going for her and that the world was, whether she realised it or not, hers for the taking. I was a bit reluctant to embark on this latter course as it was quite clear from her conversation that she viewed me as pretty much the embodiment of all she was missing. All very flattering, not to mention tempting, and all almost guaranteed to mess up the good life which Claire and I had made for ourselves.

When she came back with the coffees, I said: 'Bertie, I've been thinking,' and, throwing caution to the four corners of the fast food joint, told her how beautiful she was, how desirable, what a lovely person, what great company, how intelligent, and any other confidence-boosting thing I could think of – hackneyed no doubt, and pretty obvious, but nevertheless the business. As I heaped it on, I hoped she hadn't just been fishing for compliments. I also hoped she wouldn't start getting ideas about me.

She watched me steadily all the time I was speaking and, when I hesitated, said: 'But . . . ?'

'But nothing. That's it. If there is a but, it's but you must be crazy if you can't see it. Seriously, Bertie, you can't expect not to be a bit low so soon after such a drastic upheaval in your life. Believe me, though, it'll all come to you. Just as soon as you're ready. You're very much in charge of your own life. Just give it time.' Having done my bit, and probably overdone it, I was anxious to get going. I began to wind down the evening and, a few minutes later, looked at my watch. 'God, would you look at the time. Bottoms up!' and I drained my coffee at a gulp.

On our way to the Land Rover she tried to return to the subject; if, as I had said, she was all those great things, then why was she so miserable and lonely? I wasn't going to get sucked back onto that track so I made light of it. 'I thought that was standard fare for spoilt little rich girls?' I smiled to show that the serious part was over.

'Spoilt little rich girls get what they want or they throw wild and fierce tantrums. You don't see any sign of a wild or fierce tantrum being thrown now, so how can you say I'm spoilt?' I smiled again, feigning non-comprehension. At this point we were at the gate of the hotel carpark and a few silent seconds later we pulled up by the Land Rover. 'I wish we could do this again, Frank, this time without Stella and the mob. But we can't, can we?'

I picked up her hand in what I hoped was an avuncular way. 'Not really. It wouldn't be prudent. Not from my side, anyway. It could get to be a habit.'

'Ah well. Story of my life. Wild and fierce tantrum time, I think.' She sighed and, pulling her hand away, turned to look forward into the dark carpark.

Ever so gently I touched her bare shoulder. 'Goodnight Bertie.'

When I opened the door and the inside light came on, she turned to me as though she was about to speak.

'Sssh . . .' I whispered and, leaning towards her, kissed her gently on the lips. Her hand came up to caress my cheek. When I moved, her hand stayed there, her eyes remained closed, and her lips half-parted. It was as if she didn't realise that my face was no longer there.

All the way back to Ward, I regretted being so reserved – hell, I'd almost treated her like she had some dread disease. I mean, would it really have made any difference if I'd put my arms around her and given her a comforting hug? Or kissed her a few times instead of a fraternal once? Or if, before kissing her, I hadn't dispelled the cosy intimacy of the warm, dark car by making sure that the door was open, the cool draught coming in, and the interior light on? Or if I'd given her a playful nibble on her bare shoulder? The answers, I had to admit it, were all emphatic 'yesses'. A hell of a difference.

That night, for the first time since I'd met Claire, I dreamt of another woman, and, as I sat at breakfast next morning, sipping orange juice, riven with guilt, I tried to imagine how I'd have felt if anything *had* happened last night, when I felt this lousy just because I'd dreamt it. Later on, I began to feel better about myself and, later still, quite proud of how I had handled the evening. Still, I was glad I didn't have to go through the test again. I'd drop Bertie a quick note, thanking her for an enjoyable evening and wishing her every happiness in her future life, and that would be that.

At two pm, Bertie strode into the surgery. I gawked, then invited her into the office. Recovering slightly I said: 'You look too chipper to have a sick animal.'

She laughed. 'Don't panic. My aunt and her husband are down from Dublin for a few days. We've been for a drive to the coast and we were passing when I spotted your Land Rover. I thought I'd stop and get some worming tablets for the cats. Kill two birds with the one stone, you know? I also wanted to say thanks for last night.'

I smiled. 'Like I said, it was my pleasure.' Passing? The

surgery was some four miles of complicated country lanes and winding streets away from the coast road. She seemed suddenly unsure as to what the next step might be. 'Would you like some coffee?' I said.

'I'll have to take a rain check on that, Frank. I've got two senior citizens out in the car, rumbling mutinously because they're overdue their naps.' The insecure look returned. 'Listen, I'm sorry if I got a bit serious last night, laying all my woes on you. I'm out of practice at just going out for a companionable evening. When I said I wished we could do it again, that's all I meant – that it would be nice to share a meal again sometime.' I smiled and inclined my head, which was no great help to her. After a moment, she swallowed and said: 'Eh . . . What do you say you join me for the most fabulous dinner that six-point-eight million can buy one of these evenings? No strings attached. Cross my heart.' And she did, wittingly or unwittingly outlining perfect breasts.

Again, I was stuck. If I refused what she was at pains to point out was nothing more than a harmless suggestion that two people who had had a bit of a laugh together, should dine together, it would be tantamount to accusing her of having ulterior motives or designs on my body, or, looking at it another way, expressing a fear that I might not be able to keep my hands off hers. On the other hand, if I accepted, all the above might come true, which was not what I wanted either. 'Why don't you call me on that?' I kicked for touch.

'Sure,' she said. 'When?' she opted for the quick throw in.

'Well . . . not this evening, tomorrow or Sunday, anyway.'

'Oh! You're . . . tied up?' The green eyes became distant for a moment.

'Yes. As I told you, I'm not exactly a free agent.'

She was flustered and I didn't make it easy for her. 'So then, how about Monday?' she said at last, in a smallish voice.

'We'll see.' That was when I ought really to have told her to forget it.

She stood to go. 'Okay then, Monday. I look forward to it, though . . . I wish it could be sooner.'

I followed her to the front door, just to be polite. As she turned on the doorstep to face me, I said: 'Haven't you forgotten something?'

She hesitated, frowned briefly in puzzlement, then, smiling, took a quick step forward, reached up, and kissed me.

'Your worming tablets,' I said and immediately regretted it.

She blushed a bright pink and looked as if she wished Gino's doorstep would open up and swallow her. 'Eh . . . There's no hurry,' she stumbled. 'Perhaps you can bring them . . . Monday evening.'

I was as embarrassed as she was – certainly too embarrassed to point out that she was going to *phone* on Monday, that we didn't have a date – so I said nothing. Nor did I ask her, as I had planned to, if she needed directions to get back on to the coast road. She was much too flustered for sarcasm, and besides, despite my better judgement, I'd begun to feel protective towards her.

I stood and watched the Mercedes reverse away from the kerb, then turn towards the general direction of the coast road. Bertie didn't look at me but she gave me a big salute, a flat hand which acted like a visor and shielded her still bright pink face from me; the tiny aunt beside her stretched her neck to get her nose above the dashboard, then shielding her eyes with her hand, like an Apache scanning the prairie, stared malevolently at me until her neck could turn no further. In the back, unable to wait any longer, the old man had already commenced his overdue nap.

Claire's visit that weekend was memorable, mainly because it was almost a disaster. I met her off the train and, for the first mile or two everything went well. Then she asked me how dinner with the widow Garrison had gone. 'Fine, fine!

Not half as gruesome as I thought it would be.' I immediately began to feel bad and from then on it was all downhill: I didn't tell her there was now a second date on the cards – Claire would obviously surmise that the widow was chasing my bones, which certainly seemed to be the case and, whereas I could tell myself that I'd be well able to handle the situation (which I reckoned I would), it might not be that easy to convince Claire. She'd at least want to know why I was putting myself in this position, and wasn't once, as requested, enough? So I told her nothing and felt rotten. When she asked what was wrong with me, and said that I didn't seem myself, I told her it was probably a touch of 'flu. That night, she noticed the fading bruises on my body and arms and jokingly asked if that was what the widow had done to me? This would normally have led us into a teasing session, but I just said: 'No. Remember I told you I'd been set upon by three thugs?' and stared at the ceiling. She looked worriedly at me again and asked me if I was *sure* I was alright.

Saturday and Sunday were a bit better, and by Sunday evening, I had rationalised my lying and omissions enough to be almost my old self. Then disaster struck.

There were less than ten people waiting for the Dublin train, but three of them were Bertie Garrison and her aunt and uncle. No escape. If I didn't acknowledge Bertie while Claire was with me, it would be a clear signal to her that I thought of her as more than just a platonic companion; it would also show that I was quite willing to keep secrets from my girlfriend. As I tried frantically to decide on the best course, the matter was taken out of my hands; the diminutive aunt began to tug at Bertie's sleeve and point excitedly at me. To make matters worse, Bertie looked even more beautiful than usual – the effect no doubt of getting rid of the aunt and uncle, who, she'd told me, were nigh impossible to please.

'Oh! There's Mrs Garrison,' I said brightly, my heart slipping down towards my boots.

'Where?' Claire's gaze roamed the platform. It passed

straight over the trio, dismissing them instantly, as neither of the females fitted, even vaguely, her mental image of the Mrs Garrison I had sketchily described to her.

'There. With those two elderly people.'

'*Her?*'

'Come and meet them. Hello!' I called, setting off for the group.

Conversation wasn't great for the few moments that were left to departure time, and I was relieved when it was time to go. The senior citizens were travelling in a smoking carriage – the aunt was a forty a day woman – so Bertie took them off. She shook hands with us, said how nice it was to meet Claire, and went off.

'Your powers of description, Frank, are obviously deserting you.' Claire observed aridly as she watched Bertie moving up the train. She looked particularly great from the back, I noticed. '"Typical" widow sounds to me like a greying, respectable, middle-aged-and-upwards lady. Your . . . friend . . . Mrs Garrison is quite the beauty, isn't she?' There was a bleak frost on her voice.

'Do you think so?' I gave innocence a last forlorn shot. 'Mmmm, I suppose she's not that bad, come to think of it.'

'You hadn't noticed, I suppose. Of course, you *can't* have – mousey, timid, late thirties, you told me. Didn't you get a look at her teeth? I thought you vets could always tell by the teeth . . .'

'C'mon, Claire! You know I love you and only you.' I put my arm around her and felt her stiffen. I steered her towards an open door. All along the train, doors were slamming. Claire closed hers with a bang and turned at once for the carriage. 'Claire,' I said urgently, through the open window. 'Don't leave without telling me you love me. You've never done that. Please, don't do it now. Please! No matter what you think, nothing's changed.'

'I love you, Frank,' she said in a robotic tone without expression, then continued on into the carriage. She took a seat on the far side, though there were many vacant seats on the platform side. I stood, helpless, and watched as she thumbed unseeingly through a magazine, never once raising her eyes. In due time, the train lurched and pulled out, leaving Bertie Garrison and me alone on the platform.

To hell with it, I thought, and asked Bertie if she had either time or the inclination to join me for a hamburger and chips in the nearby Burger King. Surprise, surprise, she had both.

I got home in time for Claire's phonecall but she didn't ring – another first. I rang her about eleven and spent a long time trying to set things right. It was an impossible situation – my sin was not so much what Bertie and I might have got up to; it was that I had not trusted Claire enough to tell her the full facts about how attractive Bertie was, but rather had to glide over them as if she (Claire) was just some bimbo who couldn't be trusted not to react in a purely kneejerk jealous way.

'So in your book, telling the odd white lie for what I consider to be in our best interests – that's yours and mine, Claire – is a worse sin than screwing around? Is that what you're saying?' I asked belligerently.

It wasn't exactly what she was saying and I knew it. And what 'best interests', pray, might they be that I was referring to?

'If I'd said Mrs Garrison was young and . . . good-looking, wouldn't that sound like I was gratuitously trying to tease you or make you unsure, or . . .?' I was finding it difficult to appreciate the closeness of her reasoning. The way I saw it, Bertie had needed someone to escort her. I'd done nothing underhand, as I'd told Claire about it on the phone, which I needn't have, indeed *wouldn't* have if I was intending to be unfaithful to her. Okay, I'd neglected to mention that the woman in question was our age group, 'reasonably attractive', but what should I have done? Eventually, after it became clear that I was getting nowhere, I said that as the 'heinous crime' had already been committed and could not now be undone, the only course left was for her to make up her mind about what she wanted to do about it, and, if it wasn't too much to ask, let me know her decision. I repeated that I loved her, and she said she knew that, and hung up.

Oh what a tangled web . . .

17

Sleep, proper sleep, remained out of reach all night. What little rest I managed came in brief bouts of troubled semi-consciousness, and, shortly before dawn, I gave up expecting even the dubious comfort of these. I lay in the greying silence of the room, my mind a seething jumble of problems. Claire, who I still thought was being unreasonable and bloody-minded, was the major problem by a mile; Bertie, who was being sweetness personified, was really no problem at all – except to herself; and the fact that the country was within twenty-four hours of biological Armageddon was everybody's problem, if only they knew it. After some minutes of fruitless worrying, I threw off the covers, swung my legs onto the floor, and pulled on warm clothes.

Night's grip on the world was weakening as I walked the path that led to the peat bogs at the back of the hotel, my legs from mid-shin down lost in shrouds of dense ground-hugging mist. Hunched into my anorak, I shuffled through the thinning dark, mulling over every disease the black-mailer had mentioned, looking for some link which hadn't struck me already, but could find none. I turned back when the first pinkish sliver appeared above the eastern horizon and watched my shadow develop beside me as the sun crept up the sky. The birches and rowans along the path were beaded with dewdrops. Like a suddenly arrested rain shower, they hung from every leaf, twig, and berry, refracting the changing colours of the dawn. Spider-webs beyond number, sagging paunchily beneath their water-weight, began to materialise out of the mist as it retreated, along with the dark and the cold, before the warming of the strengthening day.

I passed quietly through the still-sleeping hotel and back up to my room. A short while later, as I was soaping my neck in the shower, a sudden thought came to me which brought me up with a jerk. Standing immobile in the warm jets, I turned it over and over in my head, amazed that I hadn't spotted it days ago, and wondering if it could really be as significant as it looked. As I towelled and dressed, I began to think I'd been jumping to conclusions – there could be hundreds of innocent explanations. However, by the time I arrived at the surgery, nearly an hour later, I hadn't managed to come up with even one.

After surgery, I sat in Gino's office, and reviewed my new 'lead'. To be honest, it didn't amount to much – it was just a contradiction that had cropped up in a conversation which might or might not be significant; it was certainly nothing tangible enough to pass on to Downing – with only one day to go, he would have his hands full. Besides, it seemed to me that whereas I might be able to work another casual chat around to the point where the slip-up might be unwittingly repeated, the unexpected appearance of Down-ing or his men would be enough to make anyone, innocent or guilty, clam up. Not only that, but if the police appeared and my 'slightly suspicious character' was indeed guilty, then they'd have tipped their hands and the guilty one or ones would know that the investigation was closing in. They could then take action to cover themselves, destroy evidence, scatter their lethal germs about . . . whatever. It was now accepted that the person who had killed Glasser and the one who was threatening to inflict multiple plagues upon the country, were one and the same. After thinking it over for a few minutes I decided that the best course would be for me to see if I couldn't contrive to get the remark repeated, innocently mention the fact that it seemed contradictory, observe my interlocutor's reaction and then accept his explanation so that he'd believe that I was satisfied with it. Whether I was or not, I'd stay on chatting brightly for a while, make him feel sure I suspected nothing, then, depending on what my impressions had been, report him forthwith to Downing as someone who might repay investigation.

I glanced at the clock above the door – it was almost ten, much too early to head off.

With a couple of hours to kill, I made a start on the day's farm rounds. The last call happened to be to Bobby Young. Of course I was subjected to the usual crop of gags and one-liners but my mind was not on them and he had to repeat some of them several times before I remembered to go ha, ha! I was finding it hard enough to concentrate on his wheezing, puffing calf, never mind the relentless comic routine.

'You seem a bit off colour yourself today, me lad,' he observed after a while.

'I didn't get much sleep last night.' I said, fishing the stethoscope from my pocket.

'Ah . . . What you need then is one of them new microwave beds. Have you heard of them?'

'No.'

'Oh, they're mighty things altogether – you can get eight hours sleep in four minutes.'

I tried not to laugh, but it came out just the same.

'This little fella's got pneumonia, Bobby,' I said.

'I thought as much, when I heard him coughing. I was going to give him a hefty dose of Epsom Salts, the best cure for the cough known to medical science.'

'For the *cough?*' I asked in surprise, thinking he was confusing the powerful laxative with something else.

'Aye. In people, anyway. A quarter-pound of Epsom Salts in the morning and you'll be afraid of your life to cough all day!'

Boom, boom.

Just before I left, Bobby got serious and told me he thought he might have seen the 'jobber' on TV once, but he wasn't sure. He couldn't remember if it was before or after he'd met him at the gate, the name of the programme, or even which kind of programme – indeed sometimes he doubted he had actually seen him at all. It didn't seem worth passing this on to Downing either, so, having called the office and found nothing that couldn't wait for a few hours, I set out for Limerick.

I really missed my mobile phone – it's amazing how quickly you become dependent on them. I stopped at a phonebox, but couldn't find the phonecard I could have sworn I'd seen in the glove box only the day before, so I drove on to the next; this one accepted coins. I rang Hilliard's private number. Annie, the maid, answered. I told her who I was, and asked to speak to Miss Molly.

'Hello?' Molly said cautiously, as though she was wondering what nasty piece of news I might spring on her this time.

'Hi! It's Frank Samson. The vet.'

'I know. What can I do for you?'

'Well, I'll be in your area in about half an hour and, as I'm going to be in dire need of a cup of coffee, I was wondering if you – being a local – could recommend anywhere better than Cottlestone's. Their coffee was terrible.'

'They'll be devastated to hear this. Why don't you drop by here? I'm sure I can rustle up something a little less awful.'

'Now why didn't I think of that?'

She laughed. 'I'll put the kettle on and tell the guards you're coming. I'd hate you to get shot on sight.'

'Despite everything, huh?'

'See you.' She hung up.

I drove on, delighted at the transformation I could hear in her.

I didn't recognise either of the gatemen, so I had to go

through the Q.&A. routine again – despite Molly's promised smoothing of the way. I signed the book, waited for the gate to be opened, then saluted smartly as I whizzed through.

She was on the front lawn, throwing a stick for a spaniel which looked as if he could go on all day, he was having such fun. She was dressed in a tartan shirt and faded jeans and she looked much better than the day I'd met her, even before the tragedies. Her blond hair was caught by a simple clip at the nape of her neck, and she wore no make-up. She came towards me with a welcoming smile, her blue eyes crinkling. If I hadn't known better, I'd have said that this was a young woman who'd never had a bad day so far in her life.

'Yo, Frank.'

'The same to you. You're looking very well.'

'So are you.'

'You should see me on a Sunday morning.' That got a laugh out of her and made me feel a bit like Bobby Young.

'I don't know about that but I have it on reliable authority that you're a knockout in blazer and slacks. Even if they're not your own.'

'My, my. News travels fast, I see. How've you been?'

'Oh, under the circumstances, fine. Just fine. Downing sends a report to my father every day, but so far, I don't think they're very close to finding Marc's killer. I believe that the longer a case goes unsolved, the less chance there is that it will be?'

'I wouldn't know about that.'

'Really? I thought you were quite the Sherlock Holmes. Wasn't it you who worked out that Marc was the one who'd infected Frosty?' I thought the mention of both names in one breath was going to be too much for her, but her gaze remained calm.

'I'm sorry it turned out like it did, Molly.'

'Oh don't be. It seems you did me a big favour. Gerry Downing explained it all to me – how Marc deliberately set out to trap me, how he was actually paid to do it, and all so that they could poison poor Frosty. And here was I, gormless simpleton that I am, madly in love with him, while he was just . . . doing a job.'

'Don't be too sure it was just a job, Molly. It may have started that way, but the "job" was over the moment he passed that apple to Frosty, and that was six weeks ago. If it was just a job, then why were you still together?'

'Thanks Frank, but the truth is, a cabinet minister's daughter has very few doors closed to her *or* her friends. Marc saw me as his ticket into what he would have considered establishment society. Downing showed me the wallet, Frank. All those women and not even one single picture of me. Not even *one*?'

'They've probably been in his wallet since the year dot.'

'Maybe some have, but not all, that's for sure. I actually know one of the "ladies". She arrived from Australia about a month ago. With her long-suffering husband, God help him.'

I spread my hands. 'What can I say? I'm sorry.'

'Yep.' She made a little grimace, half-sad, half-angry, then clapped her hands together. 'So how about that coffee, then? Ready?'

'I'd murder a cup,' I said and wished immediately that I hadn't. But Molly didn't seem to notice.

When she had poured and done the honours with sugar, cream, and little biscuits coated in sugar, she said: 'So. What's on your mind, Frank? Cottlestone's coffee can't be that bad. It's about Marc, I presume?'

'I just wanted to know what clothes he was wearing that night you came from Dublin.'

'Let me think . . . Jeans and a yellow shirt with wide sleeves which I'd never liked – I thought it made him look like a gigolo. Can you believe it? What's more, I actually told him so!' She shook her head and blew an ironic snort of annoyance. 'Why do you want to know?'

'Tell you later. Did he change after you got to the Summers'? Did he, for instance, take a shower and put on fresh clothes?'

'Neither. He didn't shower or change. What's the big deal about his clothes?'

'Like I said, I'll tell you later.' I smiled mysteriously at her.

I stayed for a second cup of coffee as I wanted to check a bit further. Molly was full of talk and, wherever it came from, optimism for the future. She was going to go back to college, finish her degree, possibly get involved in politics, help her father in the constituency or even in the Dáil . . .

'That's a lot of hard work,' I teased. 'If I were you, I'd rough it here in this impoverished hovel for a while, then marry some rich local scion. Like Pinky Summers.'

'Pinky? Marry Pinky! Not even to spite him. Scion he may be, but rich? Pinky hasn't two pennies to rub together. Which wouldn't matter if he was even half decent. He sleeps all day and his only form of exercise is racing – not in the running sense, horse racing. Bertie told me he loses a fortune to the bookies – did you see his car, for God's sake. He's mad! He even borrowed money last year to buy a few broken down nags, which would have been rejected by any self-respecting cannery. Pinky's bone lazy, a fool, and a piggy glutton . . . and they're the only nice things I can think of offhand to say about him. Pinky? Jeez!'

'But he must have some job, surely? This thing about him sleeping until noon has to be exaggerated.'

'Oh, no, it's not.'

'Every day?'

'Unless he's been boozing the night before. Then his bladder gets him up. He's got some crackpot theory which he's tried to explain to me a hundred times, but I never listen. Marry Pinky Summers? Jeez!'

Soon after, I left. Molly came to the Land Rover with me and waved until I'd rounded the first bend in the driveway. Beside her, the spaniel, holding the stick in his mouth, wagged his short tail and looked up encouragingly into the face of his mistress.

I rang the bell of the Summers' front door.

'Good afternoon, sir,' said Maeve, who must have checked the time before answering my knock, because it had just barely gone twelve.

'Good afternoon, Maeve. Anybody home?' The Mercedes and the Fiat were both on the forecourt, which made my question a bit foolish.

'Yes, sir. Miss Roberta is about but Mr George is still asleep. He should be waking up any minute now.'

'Hard night, had he?'

'Sir?'

'A man still in bed at this hour . . .'

'Mr George always sleeps until this hour, sir.'

'Good Lord! He's not sick, is he?'

I could see her getting uncomfortable with the private stuff. 'Oh no, sir.'

'Surely, he can't be asleep at this hour. He's probably writing a Booker prizewinner or running a multi-national company or something. Some people do that, you know.'

'Not Mr George, sir. He's asleep.'

'How can you be sure of that?'

She hesitated, perhaps wondering if I wasn't salaciously inferring some reason as to why she might have secret knowledge of what went on behind Pinky's bedroom door. 'Because, sir, when Mr George awakes, the first thing he does is ring the bell. Then I know it's time to start his breakfast so it'll be freshly cooked and he won't have to wait.' From the kitchen area came the faint sound of a buzzer. Maeve looked at me triumphantly. 'There, sir! The bell. Excuse me while I fetch Miss Roberta.' And she hurried off, leaving me standing in the doorway.

A moment later, Bertie appeared in the hall.

'Frank!' she said, coming towards me, looking half-delighted, half-worried. 'This is a surprise. Come in, come in. I did try to ring you but you were out and your secretary told me your mobile is kaput.' She had on a different swimsuit, a different kimono, and a different tan than last time.

'Afraid so. I'll have to take it into Limerick – there's

nowhere in Ward that can fix it.' I nodded towards the beachwear and grinned. 'Back in uniform, I see. The tan is coming on a treat.'

She smiled, then self-consciously gathered a fistful of kimono lapels. 'There's nothing wrong is there? You still okay for tonight?'

'I'm looking forward to it.'

'Well then . . . It's great to see you, but was there any special reason? I take it you haven't come all this way to bring the worming tablets?' She bit her lower lip, lowered her head, then, with a tiny smile, flicked her eyes briefly up at me.

'No!' I laughed. 'Actually I was hoping to have a chat with Pinky about his horses. I'm told they could do with a bit of juicing up, and I may be able to help.'

'If you've invented some ju-ju that'll turn those crocks into racehorses, then you'll probably match my fortune in your first week! But you may have to keep the good tidings to yourself for a while – until Pinky descends from on high. Fancy a swim? It's lovely out there.'

'I don't have my trunks with me.'

'I'll close my eyes and promise not to peep.'

I grinned. 'Well if I did fancy a swim, and was feeling all coy, I suppose I could always borrow Pinky's trunks.' It was bit laboured but I wanted to work her slothful brother back into the conversation as soon as possible.

'No, actually. You couldn't. Pinky is not a Swimming Type of human being. Something about if God had meant us to swim, he would have given us gills or fins. Or at least webbed hands and feet.'

'Pinky seems to have his own theories on lots of things. Sleep, for instance.' There was no harm in checking it out, yet again.

She threw her eyes towards the ceiling. 'God! How he goes on. It's all Mother's fault. She maintains he's not well and needs all the sleep he can get. Look at him. It's a beautiful day and he's still stretched out up there, snoring like the pig he is.'

'I think he's awake now. His bell went just as I arrived.'

'Oh? If the bell rang then he is. That's the first thing he does – ring down to Maeve so that he can stuff his fat face as soon as he hits the ground.' She mimed a waking idiot, mouth hanging slack, vacant eyes fluttering open, and swung her arm robotically to push an imaginary button. I laughed. 'The only advantage to his "lifestyle" – if I may degrade the word by using it in this context – is that I get to have every morning of the year totally Pinky-free. And that's a blessing, believe me.' She cleared her throat with a delicate little cough. 'Has Claire arrived safely back in Dublin?'

'Yes.'

'She's very beautiful.'

'Funnily enough, that's what she said about you.'

'Really? I hope it wasn't ... awkward for you, us meeting on the platform like that. You didn't seem very relaxed when we had that hamburger afterwards.'

'Put it this way ... I don't think I'm her favourite man right now.'

'Oh ... It's like that, is it? Well, if it's any tiny consolation, you are mine,' she added quietly.

'Thank you, Bertie. You're not so bad yourself.'

She laughed it off, then said abruptly, 'Well if you won't come skinny-dipping with me, I'm going for a shower. I'm covered in suntan oil and I've got to go into Limerick later on. I'll tell Pinky you're here, get the lazy sod to hurry up.'

'Okay then. See you later. D'you mind if I use the phone?'

'Help yourself. See you this evening.'

I rang the practice – things were still quiet. There had been a call from Potter so I rang him back. He told me that the news blackout was to be lifted after the six o'clock news when Hilliard was going to go public with the whole story on TV. Having read Gordon Harris's letter, I thought they were daft to take the chance, but I knew they were running out of options fast. I wondered if I was going to be able to pass Downing a life-saving clue within the next half-hour.

Next I rang Claire's office but she was out (probably just as well) so I talked to her editor and told him to find her at once and get her to phone our friend, PP. She'd know who I meant. It was very important. Very.

I wandered into the sitting room and picked up a newspaper. When I heard footsteps in the hall I went to the door, but it was only Maeve, ferrying brekkers from the kitchen to the dining room. She made three trips in all. When, eventually, I heard the slower scrape-scrape of Pinky's shuffling slippers, I set the paper down and went into the hall.

18

'Ah there you are, Frank. Bertie tells me you've come to chat about the horses. At least I think that's what she said. Forgive me. I'm never at my best first thing in the . . . afternoon.' There was a significant pause while he let the 'afternoon' crack sink in. 'Come and have a bite – I won't be able to pay proper attention until I get some nutrients to the old grey cells.' He turned and led the way to the dining room. I followed. Brekkers would take at least twenty minutes, and if I couldn't work the conversation around in that time . . .

Pinky was loading his plate, making appreciative sounds as he raised the different covers. I followed behind, being abstemious, and wondering what happened to all the leftovers – they'd feed a dozen meals-on-wheelers. Pinky carried his piled plate to the head of the table and set to.

Nothing was said for a while as he bent his whole effort to staving off personal famine. I chewed my food and waited for a break in the total commitment on my right. At last the cutlery was laid down for a moment's rest, though the jaw kept chewing.

I smiled amiably and prepared to get the ball rolling. 'Just what I needed. I haven't had a bite since breakfast. At six-thirty this morning.'

'Six-thirty! In the *morning?*' Pinky shuddered all over. 'God! How *utterly* uncivilised.'

'Oh, I don't know. You get used to it. In fact, on fine mornings, it can be really nice. What's your normal time? Eight? Half-past?' I speared half a sausage.

'Good God, man!' He almost clutched his brow. 'Perish the thought. This is my normal time.'

I was about to pop the sausage into my mouth, but didn't. 'But it's afternoon.'

'So? What's that got to do with anything? Look.' He laid down the cutlery. We were off. Crackpot theory coming up, and it hadn't needed much prodding. 'The way I see it is this: Why do we sleep? To restore the body and mind, no?'

'I guess so.'

'You know so. Now, given that basic biological truth, it follows that we should stay asleep Until We Have Had Enough Sleep To Restore Us.' He emphasised each syllable by stabbing the air with a pudgy finger. 'Then, and *only* then should we awake. It's all regulated by that wise old dame, Mother Nature, Frank. Look. You're a vet . . . Do animals go to sleep when the National Anthem plays on TV? Or wake up when the factory whistle blows? Or forty minutes before their commuter train is due?'

'I must admit, you have me there.'

'When do they sleep?'

'When they're tired.'

'And when do they wake up?'

'When they're not tired any more. Hey! I never thought of it like that.'

'We sleep when we're tired and we wake up when we've been restored. It's that simple, Frank. That simple. I rest my case.' Pinky looked smug, and picked up the cutlery again.

'Pinky, you're some lucky stiff – wake up, stretch a bit, potter about the room, read a bit, doze a while.' All of a sudden, I felt very sorry for Pinky Summers. The whole thing was a pathetic pose, a childish, attention-seeking affectation, the sole purpose of which was to provide something – anything – memorable about a totally unmemorable person.

He had been looking alarmed as I went on. Clearly there was some heresy which needed rectifying. He laid the knife and fork down again. 'No Frank. I'm not talking about "pottering about the bedroom". No hanging about the bedroom for me, unless, of course,' he added with a pantomime-lewd wink, 'it happens to be the bedroom of some naughty, nubile nymph, what?' And he threw off a man-of-the-world laugh. I grinned a cheesy one and inclined my head, deferring to his wide experience in these matters.

'No. There's a second, equally important, part to all this. We sleep to rest our bodies and minds, okay? So the converse is also true. We awake to use them! Now, I don't need to tell you, a vet who has, I presume studied physiology?' – I nodded – 'that you're not going to get much mileage out of either mind *or* body unless you provide them with an energy source, air – oxygen – and food. The air we get automatically, so all we have to worry about is the food. That we have to provide ourselves. You probably think I'm living in luxury, that I'm a spoilt brat, breakfast ready for me the moment I come downstairs? But,' he wagged the fork at me, 'I have no wish to be running at anything less than full power, and, if I don't fuel my cells immediately, then that is exactly what will happen. Do you follow me?' Like a large, florid, overweight lemming, Pinky headed unswervingly onwards towards the precipice.

I nodded and chewed thoughtfully.

'So you see, Frank, I'm neither the lazy bum that my sister makes me out to be, nor the greedy pig that some people might think I am. In fact, if you think it through to the end, I'm actually treating my body responsibly. I would consider any shortcuts in my routine to be a danger to its general health and wellbeing, and a threat to its longevity.'

I forewent a snappy retort about the health, wellbeing and prospects for a long life of the whole working population of the world. I was too busy reeling him in. 'Do

I gather then, Pinky, from the foregoing, that you are not in any way partial to the alarm clock?' I asked dryly.

Pained, Pinky closed his eyes. 'Don't *mention* the abominations! Not even in jest.'

'Oops, sorry.' He'd already said enough but, as he had no idea where this was all leading to, I decided to cut off all escape hatches. 'But what happens, Pinky, if something wakes you? A sudden noise; Maeve drops a bucket outside your door; you need the loo? There must be lots of things.' I wound him in another notch.

'I suppose there have been one or two instances, but I'm a resilient sleeper. I've got my bladder under strict control. I can sleep through phones ringing, Maeve clattering about, cars coming and going outside, you name it. Actually, I used to sleep at the front of the house and cars sometimes were a problem, but I moved rooms.' He smiled, smug at his ingenuity in having outfoxed cars. 'To the west side, of course – the sun makes an east-facing room sheer hell.'

'Indeed.' It had to face west, I realised, because the entrance to the forest path was to the west and Pinky must have watched from the shadows of his room as Glasser, below him, set out upon his last fatal walk. If his room had faced any other direction, then I'd seriously have had to consider the possibility that Pinky was the killer or had at least been present. Again, I decided to press on, let him paint himself into an escape-proof corner.

'So if you're disturbed, you just roll over and go back to sleep, is that it?'

'No. Unfortunately I have not yet developed the ability – divine gift, more like – of sleeping at will. If I *am* awoken by something totally unusual, then, that's it. I'm awake. And it's breakfast time. I ring down to Maeve and we move the whole routine forward. But this hasn't happened in months, probably not since last year.' The lemming had just put his front paws over the cliff.

'This is amazing! What a strange ability.' Pinky popped some food into his mouth and tried to look amazing and strangely able. I couldn't believe that he was still unaware of the implications of what he was saying. 'Let me get this straight,' I said, giving him yet another chance to see where he was going, 'if you wake up, even say at eight, eight-thirty, nine, whatever . . . then you ring the bell at once?'

'At once, Frank,' he replied, relieved that I was getting his drift at long last. As far as Pinky was concerned we could have gone on forever discussing his theory over and over. He reminded me of Molly Hilliard's spaniel – as long as I was willing to throw him the same few daft questions about his 'theory', he was game to go haring off, yapping excitedly, fetching the same few daft answers back, and dropping them at my, presumably, appreciative feet.

'You never lounge about for an hour or two? Reading a book, writing a letter, clipping your toenails . . .?'

'Never! As I said, even those tasks, mundane though they may be, could not be undertaken properly, without having first fuelled the cells with food.'

'So – you'll excuse my denseness, Pinky, but this is totally fascinating! – no matter what, your never-changing motto is: "Wake Up And Eat At Once"?' The guy had to be mentally blank.

'Yes.'

'Without exception.'

'Without exception. As you say, "Wake Up And Eat At Once". That's not a bad motto, Frank.'

'You have my permission to use it. On all occasions where it seems apt.'

'Thank you.' Pinky smiled, toasted me with a laden fork, then shovelled its contents into his mouth.

I sighed. Despite my heavy-handed, oft-repeated clues, it seemed I'd have to put it in simple English for him after all. 'I think you've forgotten one recent exception to your rule, Pinky: when I met you that first time, the day Marc was killed, you were just starting breakfast. It was after one o'clock . . .'

Unbelievably, he still didn't see the abyss. The lemming created a hamster-like cheek pouch for the food and gave me a long-suffering look. 'Because, Frank,' he mumbled, 'as I've *explained* to you, several times, I had just woken up, ten minutes beforehand, and my motto is . . . Wake Up . . .'

'You didn't let me finish, Pinky. It was after one o'clock, nearer one-thirty, yet you were able to describe to me exactly what Marc had been wearing when he walked into the woods nearly four hours earlier. So the rule isn't one hundred per cent, obviously. Can't be, can it?' I smiled disarmingly and took a forkful, not wanting it to look like I was accusing him of anything.

Pinky didn't know what had hit him – one second he'd been busily trotting out his lunatic theory, the next, he was being challenged about a very suspicious lie, turgid with the gravest of implications. He swallowed painfully, his fat face blanched, and he began to shake and hyperventilate so badly I thought he might faint.

It suddenly struck me that I was now in a bit of a bind, too. In my original plan, Pinky was supposed to look briefly and slightly furtive, just enough to show that I'd touched a raw nerve, then come suavely up with a 'plausible' answer which I would, just as suavely, 'believe'. It didn't require much ingenuity to come up with a story: for instance what was wrong with claiming that the morning of the murder had been the first time in many many years that he had awoken to go to the loo and then managed to get back to sleep again? It would have fitted the bill nicely. Then we would begin to chat about something neutral, his horses or such, and, after a reasonable interval, I would take my casual leave, and, once round the corner, set Potter on him. But, for whatever reason – panic, or because the fuel he'd just been stuffing hadn't quite reached his brain cells yet – Pinky screwed up monumentally, and ruined my clever, naive, little plan.

His wide-eyed gaze, which had been fixed unseeingly on his plate, transferred itself slowly and unnervingly on to me, and held while he fought for breath. Then he began to whisper in a horrible dry, rasping voice filled with venom: 'You can't prove anything! It wasn't me who did it. Marc was my *friend*! I didn't think it would go this far. It was totally unnecessary!' He shot up from his chair and took off around the table, clutching his temples. As he came up along my side, I stood and faced him. Not to block him – I just didn't want him getting behind me.

By this time I was shaking too. What the hell was I going to do now? This had got totally out of hand.

'Fuck it, anyway,' Pinky muttered, distraught, and flopped back down onto his chair.

My sentiments exactly, I thought as I watched him twisting in torment. There didn't seem to be much point in feigning innocence now, not after Pinky's incredible reaction, so I more or less had to go for broke. 'Look, Pinky,' I said gently, 'I realise you wouldn't have wanted anything to happen to Marc, but your *other* pal, Mr Anthrax, Glanders, Foot and Mouth . . . Now, he's a totally different proposition, isn't he? He's a really tough bastard.'

Pinky's eyes widened in amazement, which rapidly gave way to raw, naked fear, then confusion and panic. Five minutes before, he'd been unsuspected by anyone, as far as he knew; now he was a major suspect in a brutal murder investigation. How much did I know? How had I found out? Who else knew? What should he do? What *could* he do? How much did I know, again? Around and around in horrifying circles . . .

'Think about it, Pinky. I'll bet murder was never mentioned when you guys were hatching up your little scheme, but now see what shit you're in.'

He made one attempt, a very feeble one that not even he expected to work. 'Of course I knew what clothes Marc was wearing! I talked to him for hours the night before. We ate . . .'

'. . . pasta and played pontoon. I know all that, Pinky. I also know that Marc was wearing a sexy yellow gigolo shirt and jeans, and didn't change them. Molly told me. You went to bed first, then Marc, and he was fast asleep before she left. So when did you see his change of clothes, eh?'

He stirred a bit. 'You can't prove a thing!' he repeated, though without conviction.

He was dead right, but, to keep him rattled, I said: 'If I were you, I don't think I'd take that chance. A bit of help now could make a big difference come sentencing day.'

'I don't know what you're talking about.'

I wasn't exactly sure myself. 'Bullshit, Pinky,' I scoffed. 'Pull the other one! The only things we're not sure of are: Which of you came up with the idea first. Who decided to kill Molly Hilliard's horse? Why bring Marc Glasser in when you could have done it? After all you are reasonably friendly with Molly and could, presumably, have got into the Hilliard place without too much hassle. Which of you decided to write it all down in poem-form, who actually wrote the poems, why you decided to address the first poem to Molly's mother, stuff like that.' I paused for about five seconds, then resumed quietly. 'I notice, Pinky, you didn't ask: "What poems?"'

'What poems?' he rushed guiltily.

'Too late. Too late. Tell you what, Pinky ... In gratitude for two great brekkers, I advise you again to help out with the last bits. They're on to you, Pinky. Use your head, man.'

'You're bluffing! If anyone else believed this ... this *preposterous* fairy tale, then the place would be swarming with cops, not some chancer ...' To his credit, he managed to work a thin layer of contempt into his tone.

'Oh they'll be here soon enough, don't you worry. I'm just trying to give you the chance to make things a whole lot better for yourself before the law arrives, by going to them voluntarily and telling them your conscience made you do it. You can probably bargain away like hell. If you can save the country from all these plagues, shit, they'll probably give you a medal instead of a spell in gaol. You'd probably end up with nothing worse than a suspended sentence.'

'Just why are you here?'

'I told you – to warn you.'

'And why should you want to ... *warn* me, as you put it?'

'Because of Bertie. She's a fine person and a good friend, and she deserves better than you. I felt that the least I could do for her was give her brother a chance to limit the damage. You can thank your sister.'

'Does Bertie know?'

'Not unless you told her – I certainly didn't.'

As I watched him, it began to dawn on me that I was now worse off than ever. I'd told Pinky all I knew, and I still hadn't a clue who the killer was. There was a very slight chance that the killer might be Pinky himself, but somehow I couldn't quite see the slothful and unfit Pinky carrying out such an energetic murder, even assuming he'd be able to overpower Glasser in the first place, which I doubted . . . Also he couldn't have been in Cloughbeg between eight-thirty and nine – he'd have had to use his car to get there and so the household would have known he was up and about and would have expected him for brekkers. Nor did he fit the description of the man who'd been knocking on the door of the public callbox. Nor would it explain the blue Renault 16. Besides, Glasser would have known his voice.

As I saw it, I had little choice now other than to phone the police and guard Pinky until they arrived, or actually try a citizen's arrest, however that worked. Downing would be furious at my going it alone, but what the hell. I still thought that if he had arrived to ask Pinky about the slip up in his timing, he'd have clammed up and Downing would be left empty-handed. All he'd have would be my word against Pinky's, which was no good, and a Pinky on the loose who would warn his partner in crime that they were under suspicion. And at that point, who knew what his response would be? One thing was for sure – all gentlemanly agreements with the government would be off. He might panic. Or turn vindictive and unleash his arsenal of bugs straightaway. In fact, the same might happen if Pinky was hauled in. The news of his arrest would spread so quickly that, within an hour or two, it might reach his accomplice . . . Same potential result. Biological warfare on a grand scale.

I gradually came to the unpalatable conclusion that I might as well be hung for a sheep, now that I'd come this far. Maybe the safest course now was to stick with it to the end, cut the panicking Pinky enough slack and see where he bolted to. For this to work I had to frighten him off using the phone, force him to drive. Then I'd tail him – the Land Rover could easily keep up with his little rusty blue Fiat. *Then* I'd call Downing.

'Pinky,' I said, 'you and your mate are trapped; your phones are tapped, every cop car in the country has your registrations taped to its dashboard . . .'

The phone in the hall rang suddenly, making both Pinky and me jump in our seats. As it rang and rang in the silence, Pinky began to look like one of these characters who have spent Hallowe'en night alone in the haunted attic. Maeve arrived after five or six rings and picked up the phone. Pinky's jaw fell even further open, and he gave up breathing.

We heard Maeve say that Mr and Mrs Summers were still away and would not be back until the end of the week, could she take a message, then wait for a moment and say she would tell them on their return about the phonecall, goodbye. Pinky was shaking like a jelly.

'That was a close one!' I said. 'If you don't have enough brains to give up now and cooperate, then you deserve whatever you get. Do yourself, Bertie, and your parents a favour. I'm off. I don't want to have to see the look on Bertie's face when they cart her stupid brother away.'

Coming out of the Summers' gate, I turned right and drove slowly along the road which led towards the Limerick motorway, looking for somewhere to tuck myself out of sight. After a couple of hundred yards I found an unlocked gate in a thick hedge and, a minute later, I had driven the Land Rover into the field and settled down to wait. Within seconds, I became impatient and, before another minute had passed, I'd decided I could stand the waiting no longer. Keeping low, I crept back through the field until I arrived opposite the Summers' gate, and there I hunkered down, peering through the thick hedge, waiting for Pinky to come wheezing through in his ancient Fiat. I didn't have long to wait.

When he came, he wasn't wheezing. Nor, for that matter, was he in his ancient Fiat. Nor, as it happened, did he turn towards the Limerick road. I could only stare in stunned disbelief as, tyres spinning, he shot off up the hill towards the boggy uplands, punishing Bertie's Mercedes up through its gears. I felt almost physically sick as I watched him diminish into the distance, and cursed myself for dreaming up the inspired all-car-alert for his number plate.

'Now what?' I wondered frantically. Downing would skin me alive. What Pinky and his accomplice might do now didn't bear thinking about, but I thought about it just the same.

Bertie! He'd surely have told *her* where he was going, especially as he'd borrowed her car. I raced back to the gate and drove like a maniac the short distance to the house.

Maeve looked puzzled as she re-admitted me; she left me in the hall and went off to find Miss Roberta, glancing back over her shoulder a few times as she went. I made a conscious effort to calm down.

Bertie arrived wearing a short towel bathrobe tied loosely in front; her hair was wet and tousled. 'Excuse the shape of me,' she grinned, 'but I've got this *mega* date tonight.' Smiling teasingly, she gave her hair a few pummels with the damp towel she carried.

'Bertie,' I said. 'Do you know where Pinky has gone?'

'Gone? I thought he was here with you . . .'

'I left a while ago. Then I remembered something urgent, but when I came back, he'd left.'

She shook her head. 'Sorry, Frank. Blood relations we may be, but the man is a complete mystery to me.'

'But he took your car.'

'What!' She rushed to the door and looked out. 'Aw shit!

He *knows* I've got to go into Limerick this afternoon. It's my own fault, I suppose – I keep forgetting to hide the keys. I'll kill the . . .'

'Bertie . . . please. It's really very important that I talk to him. D'you have any idea at all where he might be? He didn't pass me on the road, so he probably went up the hill. Do you know who he might be going to see over in that direction?'

'No. He . . . The mountain road?' she grinned suddenly with malicious satisfaction. 'The Merc's almost empty and there isn't a petrol station until the Mallow road, eighteen miles away.'

I couldn't suddenly get that lucky, I thought. 'Does he have friends living along the mountain road?'

'No. There's hardly a soul living along there. It's really only a shortcut to the main Mallow road – a lot quicker than going into Limerick and back out again. I hope the slug runs out of juice exactly halfway. He'll pass out at the thought of a nine-mile hike.'

'So who might he be calling on over that way?' I continued doggedly, all the time painfully aware that Pinky was getting further and further away by the second.

She shrugged. 'I'm sure he knows lots of people over there, but I wouldn't be able to even *guess* which of them he might be going to see. I'll *kill* him if he doesn't bring the car back soon.'

I'd run out of options. It was time to call in Downing. He would not be pleased, but what the hell. 'May I use your phone?'

'Sure. Go ahead.'

'Eh . . . It's a bit . . . private . . .'

Sudden hurt dulled the sparkle in her green eyes. I suppose she thought I was calling Claire. 'Oh? Sorry. I'll just go and finish the beautifying. See you later.'

The phone was dead. Already knowing what I'd find, I reached to the back of the instrument and hauled gently on the cord. It rode freely up through my half-clenched palm until, some three feet along, it ended in a clean diagonal cut. The fuel, it seemed, had eventually reached the grey cells – to make sure his partner couldn't call him, Pinky had, very sensibly, cut the wire. Once again, I'd outsmarted myself, and this time I really was on my own – no fall back, no Downing waiting in the wings in case I came unstuck. I rushed out on to the forecourt, gunned the Land Rover into life and turned in a shower of gravel, but it wasn't until I was out through the gate and facing the hill that I really floored the accelerator, hoping fervently that Pinky *had* run out of petrol.

I covered the eighteen miles in a little over twenty minutes. There wasn't a single phonebox from which I could call Downing. At least, I thought with grim consolation, Pinky can't have called his man either. Though I reckoned, on reflection, he wouldn't have anyway; serendipitously, I'd told him his accomplice's phone was tapped too. Maybe my luck was changing.

The road was almost deserted and ran across and between the brown crests of hills, with infrequent green patches – small fields clustered around isolated cottages. There were no trees or hedges, walls or fences, and oncoming traffic was visible for miles. Each time I crested a rise, I anxiously scanned the terrain beyond but, as the last few miles rolled by, I began to accept that I'd lost him. Pinky was probably already gasping out the whole story to his psychopathic pal.

Approaching the T-junction with the busy main road, I eased off. If my chances on the mountain road had been slim, on this busy main road, they'd be almost non-existent. Where to now? Left or right? Did it matter? How about a U-turn and head back across the hills? I reckoned I should first find a phone and get through to Downing. I turned left for no other reason than that it was easier to go with the heavy traffic than to cross it, and I was as likely to find a phonebox to the left as to the right. Within the first mile I came upon a flag-bedecked service station which I assumed would have a public phone. I indicated, slowed down and was just about to pull in when, to my astonishment, I saw Bertie's Mercedes in a line at the inside row of pumps. It was second in a queue of six or seven cars. Pinky had probably been stuck in the line for ten minutes. For me to have caught him up, he must have had to nurse the Merc this far, coasting down hills, keeping the revs low, driving slowly all the way . . . There was a God after all. Changing my mind abruptly, I jinked back out into the traffic and drove on, picking up speed as I went. I'd no idea how far he might be going but I reckoned that Pinky would be moving fast when he passed me and I'd be as well to get started – it would be hard enough to keep up with him on the open road. If he opened her up, I'd have no chance; if he kept within the speed limit (and I thought that, today of all days, he just might do that) then I should be able to keep him in sight.

In fact, he wasn't going far at all – a couple of miles after he'd flashed past, he indicated right and moved to the centre line, waiting for a break in the oncoming traffic. I had no option but to pull in behind him and I huddled so far down in my seat that only my eyes showed above the dashboard. But Pinky was totally focussed on crossing the road and didn't once look back.

Suddenly he was gone. Drawing a cacophony of outraged horns and flashing lights, he catapulted the Merc suicidally across a tiny gap, and vanished into a narrow sideroad. I eased up to the break in the centre strip but had no option but to sit and wait and look across at the small road with its signpost which read 'Bunacrick 4 mls.'

Bunacrick is a better-than-usual Anglicised attempt at Bonn an Chnoic, which, in Gaelic, means Foot of the Hill. The eponymous hill was visible a long time before the village itself came into view. I'd passed no side turnings off the four miles of narrow, twisting road so I knew that Pinky had to be ahead. It was now highly probable that I had lost him, but I didn't feel too bad; Downing should have no trouble now finding Pinky's destination – after all, just how many people could anyone from twenty-five miles away know down this tiny road?

As I was about to enter the one-street village, I braked to a sudden stop. There, up ahead, not more than a hundred yards away, was the Mercedes. It was parked outside what looked like the one and only pub in town. As I sat and wondered how to take it from here, Pinky came out of the pub, carrying a small brown paper bag, then got back into the car and rolled away, seemingly not in any hurry. As I watched him gain the end of the street, I saw him raise his left hand to his face and, after a few seconds, draw it across his mouth. Pinky had bought himself a half-naggin of whiskey! As soon as he vanished over the hump-backed bridge at the end of the town, I let out my clutch and drove after him.

The road ran along the floor of a valley, until it reached the butt of the hill, which it hugged closely from then on. On the right, a small river twisted its sluggish way towards the distant Atlantic. For a few miles Pinky drove slowly, swigging regularly. Then he sped up and was soon lost to my sight. I was thinking of turning back when I caught sight of the Merc again – she was headed straight up the flank of the hill. Another mile and I came upon the left turn-off which Pinky must have taken, swung onto the tiny potholed road and immediately began to climb.

The hill had the characteristic unhealthy look of a north-facing slope, and I hadn't gone many yards before the rich greenery of the valley gave way to sedgy tussocks and clumps of rushes, with the occasional small, stunted furze bush. Though it hadn't rained for days, the black ground between the islands of unwholesome vegetation had a slick greasy look to it. I changed down for yet another hairpin, tacking my way upwards, until at last, some fifty feet short of the summit, the road levelled off and ran, more or less horizontally, on a step cut into the slope.

Less than a mile on, I rounded a shoulder and, in the fold which followed, came abruptly upon impressively large, but ill-kept, gate pillars; from them hung heavy iron gates, leprous with burst rust blisters in their once-bright silver paint. As I drove slowly past, I peered through at a large country house, somewhere in the middle stages of dilapidation. It looked deserted.

I drove on and had gone a hundred yards or two when, with a sudden tingling in my scalp, I realised that the faded lettering on the flaking pillars had a vaguely familiar ring to them.

I had just passed Northfield House.

19

The flood of possibilities arising from this almost made me stall, but I drove on, now with an uneasy feeling that I was being observed from the hill, my erratic driving being noted. When I rounded the next shoulder of hillside, and the house slipped off my mirror, I stopped, engine idling, and tried to figure it all out.

My first thought was that Joss Murray, he of the scarred horses, was an ideal choice for Anthrax Man. He was certainly violent enough, assuming that he had knocked those horses about and had hired the three thugs to do me over. He was also bitter enough – he was broke, he'd just lost his licence, and he had a huge chip on his shoulder against society in general. As an ex-vet student he'd have a more than average knowledge of all the diseases he was threatening to unleash, and would have been well-versed in bacteriology, virology and lab work. Also, being a trainer, Bobby Young might very well have seen him on TV ... But what was his connection with Pinky, other than that Pinky, while fleeing in a blind funk, had driven along the same road on which Murray lived? Maybe he had trained Pinky's horses for him?

It was back to options. Give up and ring Downing? Drive on and see if I could catch sight of Bertie's Merc again? Or take a quick peep and see if the Merc was parked round the back of Northfield House? It certainly hadn't been parked at the front or the sides. In the end I plumped for a quick peep over the hill – it would be safe, swift, and sure. The house stood some fifty feet below the summit so I'd just drive back the way I'd come, pull over when I got well past the gate, take a quick stroll to the top of the hill and look down. Simple. If the Merc was parked anywhere there, I'd see it from my crow's nest. Then I'd drive back to Bunacrick and phone Potter. Another fifteen or twenty minutes wasn't going to make much difference at this stage. Executing a perfect seven-point turn on the narrow road, I headed back.

Half a mile beyond the gate, I came across a double row of dilapidated sheds running at right angles to the road, on an outcrop which jutted out over the valley. I stopped, backed up, and looked; the sheds looked long-abandoned and, all things considered, the short street between them was as good a parking place as I was likely to find on the exposed, narrow road. I drove in until my front bumper was almost touching the solid five-bar gate at the end; beyond the gate, the land fell steeply away towards the valley floor, far below. Satisfied that the Land Rover would be hidden from casual, passing traffic, I locked it, crossed the road, and climbed the dry-stone wall which separated road from hill. Ten minutes later I was crouched, just below the skyline, looking down on the house below. There were no cars round the back either. I still couldn't be sure that Pinky was here. Blankly, from dark windows like empty eye sockets, the shabby house stared back up at me. A chilling breeze rustled and stirred the dry sedge in a dead, whispering susurrus.

I had begun to edge my way back towards the road when I heard the noise of an engine – distant, indistinct, but unmistakable. It didn't seem to be coming from the direction of the road and there were none of the rises and falls in pitch which one would expect from a moving vehicle. It stopped abruptly and, a moment later, I heard a door slam. It was this latter, sharper noise which gave me a fix the sound's direction – it had come from across the hill, from the south-facing side. Belly-crawling through the sedge, I reached the cover of some furze bushes, and, using them to screen me from the house, made a dash for the summit. I crawled the last few feet and gingerly peeped over the top. Due south of me, splashed in sunshine, were the paddocks and stables of Northfield House.

The air of neglect was in keeping with the house, but in their day they must have been quite a sight. The railings of the paddocks, their white paint almost vanished, were nevertheless more or less intact. Each paddock, though now overrun with thistles, nettles, and brown, brittle bracken, had a single, large deciduous tree smack bang in the middle, and I could almost *see* the horses in neat compositional groups in the shade, à la Stubbs. The stables made a large square and, across the roof of the side nearest me, I could see a strip of cobbled yard and the buildings along the far wall. These consisted entirely of a row of broken-down loose boxes. I could also see the top corner of an arched entrance – it pierced the wall on the right. Immediately outside the gate was an oak wood, and, beyond this, a slice of road – presumably linking house and yard; the road hadn't been visible from my first vantage point, above the house. The yard, paddocks, and indeed the whole shallow valley, were splashed in the chiaroscuro of a sunny afternoon, and I wondered why the founder of Northfield had built his stables in the sun, but his residence on the dreary, gloomy northern slope.

Suddenly Pinky appeared in the strip of yard which was visible to me. He was walking briskly, talking over his shoulder. I could hear him but couldn't make out the words. Then he vanished. Another door banged, there was the sound of conversation, then silence, and finally Pinky and a man whom I took to be Murray came into view on the road beyond the oak wood, heading for the house. A small dog trotted ahead of them, short busy legs almost a blur. I watched until they rounded a bend. There was no urgency in their walk, no sign that they were going to make a run for it. Hopefully, they'd be sitting there, unsuspecting, when Downing and his troops arrived.

Mission accomplished. I'd done my bit, and it was now time – not to mention politic – for me to bow out, head back to the security of the Land Rover, drive away, and hand it all over to the pros. A warm sense of relief flowed over me.

Some five minutes later, palms sweating, heart thumping, adrenaline by the pint coursing through me, I slid from behind the safety of the last oak tree and dashed through the arched gate into the confines of the yard. Inside, I stood with my back to the wall, cursing whatever perverse lunacy had made me come here, and waited for my breathing to return to normal. At a glance, I saw that the gate was the only way in, or, for that matter, I thought grimly, out.

The yard was a large cobbled square, choked with weeds and surrounded by buildings. The side opposite the arch was one long shed without windows upstairs or down – it had probably once been the carriage house with hay loft overhead. There were two sets of large double doors in the centre of the building, modern, painted blue; judging by the 'V' of vehicle tracks which led from them and converged at the gate, the carriage house had now become the garage. The side walls of the yard were lined with loose boxes, those to my right (the ones I had seen from the hill) totally dilapidated. To my left, the boxes nearest the archway were in a similarly sorry state, but the nine or ten nearest the garage were in better nick; missing slates had been replaced by flat roofing tiles of different colours, and the doors seemed to work – they were all closed, with their upper halves fastened back to the wall. There was a long-dead clock on a tower on the roof of the loft, and on top, a weather vane. From one of the good boxes, a horse's head appeared, looked around, saw me and whinnied. Three other heads appeared almost at once, watched me for a few seconds, jaws chomping away busily, then simultaneously, withdrew.

I reckoned I'd start with the garage. If I could find the blue

Renault 16, then I could be on my way, no more evidence required. The double door at the end of the right arm of the 'V' had a Judas gate in it so I made for that and, a few seconds later, depressed the thumb–plate of the latch, and stepped through. I felt along the wall on either side of the door but found no light switch. No matter; in front of me I could feel the taillights of a car, so I groped my way along to the driver's door and opened it. The interior light showed me the headlight switch of Bertie's Merc and flicking *that* on showed me the main switch by the door – for some reason it was fixed very high. I turned it on, waited for the fluorescent tubes to flicker into humming life, then turned off the lights of the Merc.

The garage ran the width of the yard. At the far end was a horse transporter covered in the dust of disuse, then a Land Rover like mine, only blue; next came a large Opel, and then, between the Opel and the Mercedes, a pale blue Renault 16. I walked behind it and ran my finger along the vertical crease in the bodywork beside the broken taillight. Squatting to read the number plate, I noticed that the screws holding it on were clean and bright, in contrast to the plate itself, and I reckoned that on her sallies through the country, the Renault carried false plates. Not that it had mattered in this case, as nobody had taken the number, but it had still been a wise move. On a hunch I went to the workbench and there, wrapped in newspapers less than a week old, I found another set of number plates. As there was no way of knowing which set was the false one, I wrote both down on a piece of oily cardboard, using a stub of yellow crayon – the type used for marking holes in punctured inner tubes. There didn't seem to be much point in taking the numbers of the other vehicles as it was surely all over now, and the cops would be along in an hour, max. As I got ready to leave, I wondered if I should put all the cars out of commission, but what was the point? They didn't look as though they were about to make a run for it and, if they happened to discover that the cars had been tampered with, it would only spook them. I paused by the door, took one last look, then switched out the light. Pressing my ear against the wood, I listened, then lifted the latch slowly and eased the door open a crack; nothing appeared in my limited vertical line of vision so I eased it a crack more. Still clear. Taking a deep breath, I emerged cautiously into the sunny brightness of the yard, and moved quickly towards the shadow.

The buildings on either side of the archway looked like offices, but just in case one of them was doubling as a temporary lab, I felt, as I was here anyway, I should check. If they weren't locked. I had a momentary flash of me striding heroically into Downing's office and casually placing a plastic bag containing the entire arsenal of lethal organisms on his desk.

I was making my way towards the first door when the dog trotted through the archway.

Our reactions were almost identical. The dog pulled up with a jerk and stared; I did the same. His hackles rose; so did mine. For several seconds he did nothing; I waited for him to make the first move. When he turned and shot off out the gate, yelping, I shot into the nearest loose box and retired into its darkest corner to observe the gate. My pounding heart was just getting back towards normal when, to my horror, I saw Murray framed in the arch, moving cautiously. He was on his own. The dog followed him, slinking along at his heels – if his master had even glanced at him, he'd have seen the dog staring fixedly at the spot where he had seen me. But Murray's gaze ranged slowly around the square of buildings as he walked sideways towards one of the office doors. Reaching behind him, he turned the knob, then dashed in. In a matter of seconds he was back out again, carrying a shotgun. My heart clamped in my chest as I watched him; without once lowering his searching eyes, he broke the gun and loaded both barrels. Then, with the chilling sense of purpose of the professional soldier, he snapped the gun shut and set out on patrol. The dog lay down by the door and looked anxious.

Eyes darting alertly from side to side, Murray headed for

the row of boxes across from me and I changed my position to watch. The first three boxes had no doors so he stepped quickly into each, gun at the ready. The next one had a rickety door, sagging open on its lower hinge; this he leaned over and checked the floor by its front wall before moving on. All the time his gaze darted randomly about the yard, sweeping over it every couple of seconds. I shifted position again and wondered if I shouldn't try making a dash for it. In my heart, I knew I wouldn't make it, but it seemed better to take my chances running in the open than to get shot cowering in a dark corner. I wondered if he'd search the garage before coming down along my row of boxes; if he did, that would occupy him for a good thirty seconds. It would be enough. I'd make a dash for it and to hell with the dog. Once in the oak wood . . .

The Judas gate in the garage door was at the limit of my vision – if I wanted to see beyond that, I'd have to poke my head out into the open. I saw him come to it, hesitate, then reach for the latch. 'Go in, you bastard!' I almost screamed. 'Go in!' He opened the door, stuck his head in briefly, then, to my horror, closed it again. Then he passed out of my sight and, a few seconds later, I heard him mumbling something to the first horse in my row, about six boxes away. By this stage, trapped in my small bare loose box, I had to force myself to think, to explore. His voice, talking now to another, nearer horse spurred me on and, in the next few seconds I came up with all kinds of desperate plans – crouching under the door until he poked the gun over, then grabbing it and wrenching it from him; or jerking it so hard that his fingers would accidentally press the triggers and the shots would pass harmlessly over my head; or stooping beneath the door until he was right outside, then shoving the door violently out, toppling him over and rushing him before he could regain his balance . . . Then I noticed the dividing walls between the boxes. One block wide, they were just high enough to ensure that neighbouring horses couldn't get at each other. There was a gap between the lean-to roof and the top of each wall, a

237

substantial gap at the back, which decreased as the roof sloped forward until it narrowed to a mere three feet or so at the front. Almost without thinking, I hauled myself up onto the dividing wall on my right (the one farthest from Murray), and crawled along on all fours until I was at the front. Then I stood as best I could, turned, and, backing my way funambulistically along its single block width, managed to mould myself into the awkward angle formed by the roof and the front wall of the stable. Having now committed myself irrevocably, the obvious vulnerability of my position struck me – he now had two chances to see me, one from the box on either side, and, if he did spot me, I'd be too far away to grapple with him for the gun – the most I could do would be to jump down on the other side, which would merely postpone the inevitable by seconds. Wishing I had gone for pushing out the door instead, I took a deep breath, thought a quick prayer, froze myself into angular immobility, and waited.

Suddenly his shadow appeared on the floor of the box to my left; my eyes slewed left and I saw his head and shoulders hunch over the door. He looked down first, scanning the floor, but his inspection didn't travel beyond the butt of the dividing wall; he didn't raise his eyes and, in a moment he was gone. I changed the air in my tortured lungs, mentally repeated the prayer, and froze again. He did the same on the other side and, in a year-like few seconds, miraculously, he had passed on to the next box. I stayed where I was until I heard him say: 'You must be seeing things, eh, boy?' to the dog which had obviously rejoined him, then I took a long deep breath, then another, and another.

When I thought he was far enough away, I lowered myself carefully down from my perch and retreated to the back corner of the box to see what I could see. The yard was flooded in sunlight and I reckoned that it had been the saving of me – he hadn't allowed time for his constricted pupils to adjust to the gloom in the boxes and, whereas he wouldn't have missed me if I had been crouching in a corner or lying along under the door, his peripheral vision had to have been impaired. I saw him cross the yard, back to the room where he'd got the gun, take one last suspicious look about before going in, then emerge a few moments later, carrying nothing more menacing than a green manila folder. He pulled the door to, took another, unconvinced look around, then hurried out through the gate. I stayed in my loose box for some time, not willing to take the chance. Could he be lying in wait for me? Why had he acted so suspicious and searched so thoroughly, yet ignored the garage? Was he hoping that an intruder, believing himself in the clear, would now show himself and try to get away? But if he was thinking of setting up an ambush, then why had he left the gun in the office?

After many minutes, I decided to risk it. I crept out into the yard and, with no further thoughts of investigation, silently headed into the archway. I took one quick peek through, darted into the cover of the oak wood and, a few moments later was squirming thankfully along through the sedge, making my way unchallenged, back up the hill. The sky had begun to cloud over, the wind had picked up, and the exposed hillside had become noticeably cooler. But inside, I was feeling all warm and glowing as I belly-crawled out of sight of house and stables, then stood and made my way stiffly and thankfully back to where I'd left the Land Rover between the sheds.

20

I sat, preheating the engine, and thinking what a hell of a man I was. Another mystery solved, the country saved from the spectre of hundreds of thousands of animal deaths; the best bit of preventive medicine that any vet had ever done – in any place or in any time, and probably also as smart a bit of detective work as had been done since the days of Sherlock Holmes. Not to mention saving the national chest from losses which would undoubtedly have run into billions . . . They'd probably name a big important street after me.

Though admittedly it had taken a not-so-clever length of time for me to twig Pinky's error, and I'd been incredibly lucky in the last few hours not to have cocked up everything – on several occasions. I turned the key and let the engine warm in its own time, without my customary revving. When it was running smoothly and tuneful to my ear, I engaged reverse. As I turned in my seat to back the twenty-odd yards back to the road, the prospect of immediate departure from Murray's doleful environs boosted my feeling of warm wellbeing. Twenty yards, a few seconds.

When the three sharp raps came from in front, I thought I'd snagged something. I braked and turned to look forward, and my heart lurched in disbelief and horror when I saw Pinky standing there, left palm on the bonnet, right hand pointing a double-barrelled shotgun unsteadily, but unmissably, at me. He seemed to have materialised from nowhere but, as my initial shock ebbed, I noticed the door of one of the sheds ajar; I knew they'd all been closed before – an open one would have had me all nervous and jumpy. Momentarily drained, I followed his mimed order and switched off the engine; in the ensuing silence, we eyed one another warily. They'd probably name a headstone after me.

Pinky looked ill at ease and unsure as I waited for him to make the next move, but all he did was wave the gun about, lick his lips a lot, and gulp painfully once or twice. That seemed to be it. Action postponed. It was obvious from his owl-like stare that he didn't have a clue what to do next.

I watched him and tried to think some positive thoughts, but I could find little cause for optimism. The fact that he had waited so long before challenging me was worrying – maybe he'd been using his head and holding off until I was in the worst possible tactical position; or maybe he was scared witless, and had just been waiting for Murray to arrive, knowing that he would take the whole nightmare off his hands and handle it in his own inimitable style. Opting to take my chances with Pinky, I decided to force the issue, and began by opening the door. Instantly he panicked.

'Stay where you are!' he squeaked. 'Don't move!' The gun began to swing in agitated arcs.

'Or what?' I chanced a touch of scorn, the beginnings of defiance, but at the same time, just in case, smartly closed the door. Nothing. Back to the impasse. I gave it another few seconds, then slid open the window. 'Are you going to *shoot* me, Pinky?' I didn't think he would, at least not intentionally, but with the way the gun was jerking about, an accident was not out of the question.

'Don't move!' he repeated, searching anxiously beyond me. So he was expecting Murray. He was almost frantic.

So was I, but I tried to sound cool, in charge. I had to keep talking, keep trying to fluster him. I also had to get the hell away before Murray arrived. 'Don't you think you're in enough trouble as it is, Pinky? You want to add a murder now, do you? Be as good as Joss?'

'Shut *up!*'

'If you pull that trigger, Bertie will never forgive you.'

'If I pull this trigger, then who's going to tell her it was me, aye?'

The man had a point. 'Listen. I don't want to end up dead any more than you want to end up in gaol for the rest of your days, so do us both a favour and put down that gun before there's an accident. Then you can come with me.'

For a moment he looked perplexed, as if he couldn't quite work out why his message wasn't getting across. 'What d'you mean: come with you? I've told you, you're not going anywhere.'

I had an almost irresistible urge to check in the mirror, to see if Murray was stalking up behind me, but I had Pinky locked into a kind of mesmeric stare and didn't want to break it. 'I'm going to start the engine, Pinky. I'm going to back out onto the road and drive away. If you have any sense at all, you'll throw away the gun and come with me.'

'I'm *warning* you! Stay right there! I'll *shoot!*'

I felt he was trying to convince himself more than me; still, as I reached for the key, I wondered if perhaps this wasn't just dangerous wishful thinking on my part – suicidal wishful thinking. 'No you won't, Pinky. You're no killer. I trust you. I'm starting the engine now.'

'Just you fucking well *try!*' He was in a rage, probably at his own impotence. For a moment I thought he might shoot me, though for all the wrong reasons, and it struck me how ironic it would be to get killed for nothing more than grinding whatever morsel of machismo he possessed into the mud of the mountainside. I thought I'd better get the real reason for our present impasse back up front again, and quickly.

'Pinky. Listen to me. What they've got on you is minor stuff, a few bugs here and there – nothing much. A couple of years; less if you cooperate. A couple of years is nothing, Pinky. You can do it easy. Molly Hilliard,' I lied, suddenly inspired, 'told me you're a pretty tough guy, though you try to hide it, and I believe her. Now for the last time, don't screw up. Not now when it's all over. I'm starting the engine, Pinky, so . . . shoot, if you're going to.'

With a silent prayer, I squeezed my eyes shut and turned the key. When I opened them again, I could see that Pinky was in a torment of indecision. 'I'm leaving, Pinky,' I said and, feigning a confidence I didn't feel, turned in my seat, looked out through the rear window, and resumed reversing. He kept with me, slapping the bonnet with the flat of his hand and shouting at me that he would shoot if I tried to drive off down the road. I didn't know whether, faced with my final irrevocable departure, he mightn't actually be panicked into doing it, and I wasn't looking forward to putting it to the test, but what else could I . . . Suddenly I had an idea – a chancy one, but probably offering a shade better odds than betting my life against having read Pinky's agitated mind correctly.

I stopped again and urged: 'Last chance. Cut your losses and . . .'

'You start down that hill, you cocky bastard, and you're a dead man. I *swear* to you. Don't underestimate me!'

I sat and tried to judge his shifting mood, and was suddenly struck by a very uncomfortable thought: Pinky, if he realised it, had just found himself a foolproof method of becoming a really interesting character, in fact a household name. A cold-blooded killer has a million times more street cred than a lazy lie-abed. 'I'm not underestimating you. A fool would shoot now and think of the consequences later. But you're no fool, Pinky.' With trembling hand, I put the gear shift into first, turned my head again, away from my prospective victim, and forcing myself to look steadily through the rear window, revved the engine. Praying that Pinky hadn't moved, I released the clutch sharply and felt the Land Rover surge forward like a great, pouncing cat. I felt the bump even as I turned my head and was just in time to see Pinky's horrified face vanish from sight as I rolled inexorably over him. The gun flew free when he threw up his arms in a puny effort to fend me off and clattered into some nettles by the sheds. I knew I had to stop for it. Pinky wasn't hurt – certainly not seriously – and, if he could retrieve it and catch up with me before I made it to the road, retribution would be unthinkingly instant for someone who had made a fool of him twice in the one afternoon. I braked quickly so that the Land Rover stopped, straddling him menacingly like the winner of a dogfight, then leapt out to pick up the gun. As I bent, I took a quick look under – Pinky lay facing me, in a kind of sideways foetal position, hugging his right leg to him, and even over the knock of the diesel, I could hear his hollow groans.

'Pinky!' I called, but all he did was moan. Raising my voice, I called again, but there was still no answer. I knew I couldn't have hurt him – it wasn't as if the wheels had gone over him. 'Pinky! You've got two seconds to make up your mind. Come with me now or keep your head down. One . . . Two! Time up. Too late. Keep your head down.' I jumped back into the driver's seat, slammed the gearshift into reverse and started back. Pinky reappeared as I went, rolling out like washing from a wringer. Once clear of him, I increased speed, backing straight onto the road, taking my chances that there'd be no traffic.

There wasn't. What there was instead was Joss Murray, lounging almost insolently against the gable end of the sheds, an evil grin on his face, a shotgun, rock-steady and unwavering in his hands. As he stepped over to the window, I thought fleetingly of making a grab for Pinky's gun on the seat beside me, but I didn't – I knew it would be useless. He read the intention in my eyes and my rejection of it. Still smiling evilly, he shook his head, indicating that I'd got it right. Before I could consider any further options, I had meekly obeyed his order to unlock the passenger door and watched him reach in and take the gun off the seat. He removed the cartridges, which he left on the seat while he flicked the gun shut again; then he put the gun in the back among my medicines, and pocketed the cartridges. He accomplished all this one-handed; his gun never wavered, his stare never left my eyes and the leering grin never left his face.

When he spoke, his voice sounded like the voice of the dead, devoid of any emotion. 'Go back down,' he ordered in a matter of fact tone, sitting in and pressing the shotgun against my cheek. 'In reverse. Oh . . . And mind Pinky,' he added in a mocking whisper.

I reversed as ordered, mechanically and carefully, the chilling, smiling, axe murderer sitting malevolently beside me.

'Stop!' I braked hard even though we were still yards away from the stricken Pinky. 'Now get all this stuff out of the back. Make room for poor Pinky. Uh-uh!' he warned as I went to open my door, 'this side.' He climbed out, gun trained on me and I slid across to comply. Then he waved me to the back. Pinky had sat up by now, but he was still hugging his right leg and still moaning. I didn't know what to say so I just stared at him until Murray looked at me: 'Well? What are you looking at? Get on with it.' As I began moving Gino's medicines and equipment out on to the ground, he said to Pinky: 'So what happened to you, then, Action Man?'

'That bastard ran me down!' Pinky, arm outstretched, hurled melodramatically at me, the picture of outraged innocence.

'It was an accident, Pinky. A mistake. First and reverse are very close together in Land Rovers.'

'Don't mind him,' Murray said mildly to Pinky, 'they are not.' Then I remembered that he too, had a Land Rover. 'He was trying to kill you. The "accident" is that you're still alive.'

I stared at them, from one to the other, but couldn't think of anything to say. Murray looked at me sharply. 'Is it empty yet?'

It wasn't, so I got back to the task. Along with the equipment, I removed the now useless gun. Pinky's eyes dilated in terror when he saw it in my hands; Murray threw his arms wide in mock horror, then laughed at Pinky and told me to put it back in the jeep. When everything lay in a heap on the grassy street between the sheds, Murray said: 'Now help poor Pinky up. And try not to damage him any more than you have already.' I wondered if Pinky noticed the sarcasm – it was obvious that he couldn't have cared less if I'd cracked Pinky's skull, broken all four of his limbs, and fractured half his ribcage. Pinky, who had resumed his steady moaning, broke into agonised howls about ten times as I manoeuvred him into the back of the Land Rover. I knew the bastard was hamming it up, going for the sympathy vote, but, in the circumstances, all I could do was try to make life easier for him, and so, hopefully, for myself.

At this point, with Pinky only half inserted into the back of the Land Rover, there was the sound of an engine approaching, then a second one, and my heart began to beat faster. Maybe Downing had worked it out from another angle. From the description of the car, maybe. Murray, suddenly worried, growled: 'Shut up, Pinky!' and stepped behind the Land Rover. He grabbed my elbow, put the gun under my jaw and we stood there, watching tensely through the windscreen. The noise grew louder and then two cars passed, the elderly driver of the first going much too slowly for the driver behind who had a look of extreme frustration on his youthful face. Neither of them even glanced our way and, as soon as they'd passed, Pinky started groaning again.

'Drive to the house.' Murray ordered, slamming the rear door and following me down along the driver's side. He waited until I had got in, took the key out of the ignition, then, walking alertly around the front, slid into the passenger's side, and passed me the key again. Even if he hadn't removed the key, I knew I wouldn't have considered running him down.

On the short drive, Pinky found several reasons for anguished yells and, as I swung in the gate, he emitted one extra-long 'Aaagggggh' and asked me if I wasn't having a second go at trying to kill him. I didn't bother to answer as

I was doing about ten miles an hour, but Murray replied that, no I wasn't, but that I definitely had been last time. Pinky considered this silently for a moment, then started moaning again.

The passage from the Land Rover to the front door, up two steps, through a corridor and into a large kitchen, was even more harrowing, with much wincing and bellowing from Pinky. The longest howl came when I lowered him into an armchair beside a warm Aga range. As it seemed to me to be in an uncomfortable position, I tried to re-position the injured limb, but this caused such a scream that I sprang back. 'Jeez, I'm sorry, Pink,' I found myself using an even more hideous abbreviation of his already awful nickname. 'It really was just an unfortunate accident.' But Pink looked unconvinced.

'Are you calling me a liar, Samson?' Murray asked. Recognising that I was snookered, I said nothing. 'Are you?' he persisted, and I said: 'No, of course not. Just misinformed.'

Pinky, who had gone silent during this brief exchange, gave it another few seconds to see if anything would develop, and, when nothing did, started up again. At a loss for something to do, I stayed kneeling in front of the fat stricken figure and, in my most professional bedside manner, said: 'Perhaps I can help. Where exactly does it hurt?' Abruptly he stopped moaning, looked at me incredulously, then gave another, even louder wail. 'Alright, alright!' I said, standing up quickly, palms towards him. 'Only trying to help.'

Murray jammed the gun into my back and directed me towards a door, one of two (besides the one we'd entered through) which opened off the kitchen. 'Open it,' he ordered curtly. I pressed down on the thumb plate of the latch and pushed the door in. I was pushed roughly through, then Murray pulled the door to and shot home the bolt with a click of awful finality.

The next hour was probably the worst I've ever experienced in my life. I sat in a tiny dim and dank room, a larder of sorts, on a sharp-edged shelf, obliged by the shelf above it to lean forward at an uncomfortable angle, and listened in horror to a dispassionate discussion on the best way to murder me.

It was almost a monologue from Murray, Pinky taking very little part because of his continuous moaning. Three or four times Murray told him to shut up, not to be such a baby, and, for a while, he would. But always, after a short break, he would try a tentative, testing one, and if he got away with that, would soon be hard at it again.

'Isn't it a fright how things go astray, no matter how well you plan?' Murray waxed philosophical at one point. 'I mean, who would have thought that that little prick, Glasser, would have had the nerve to try to blackmail us?'

'Blackmail *you*, Joss. Not me.' Groan, moan.

'Well . . . both of us really. Just 'cos he didn't know you were involved.'

'I still think you could have paid him off, Joss. Or at least scared him . . .' He broke off to hiss inwards with pain.

'Nobody fucks me around Pinky. *Nobody!* He got what we agreed and he should have been happy with that. But the greedy little nancy-boy had to look for more. Who knows where it would have stopped?'

'Yeah, but now the cops are all over the place . . .'

'What do you mean, all over the place? You haven't seen one since that first day, have you?'

'No . . . but . . .'

'Are you worried about Samson? Is that it?'

'Well, if *he* worked it out . . .' Ow! Oh!

'He had a lucky guess, Pinky. But he obviously kept it to himself or we'd have had a million cops here by now. And now he's not going to have a chance to tell anyone. Or have another lucky guess either. Ever.' Pinky said nothing to this and there followed a long silence, broken by the odd moan.

'We can't have blood about the place,' Murray said suddenly, 'not with the possibility that the cops *might* come checking here at some point. You can scrub and scrub and scrub, but there's always something left, inside or out, it doesn't matter – between the floorboards, on the underside of a blade of grass . . . somewhere stupid like that. If they're looking for it, then they'll find it for sure. One miserable minuscule spot, and they have you by the balls. DNA tests, genetic fingerprinting, they'll be able to tell you what the bastard had for his lunch. And all from one tiny erythrocyte . . .'

'One tiny *what*?'

'Erythrocyte. Red blood cell.'

'Oh.' Ouch, groan, oh.

'Anyway, why the fuck should we spend hours scrubbing? There must be an easier way.'

There was another silence, during which Murray struggled with the conundrum, and I almost saved them the bother of murdering me by dying, unassisted, of horror. He wasn't stuck for long.

'I know!' he said suddenly, brightly. 'We'll shoot him in the stream and leave him in it until he's fully bled out. Then we can put him in the car and take him somewhere and dump him. Into the sea, maybe. But hang on . . . It's almost dark now and it'd be just our luck that some bastard would be passing on the road outside – and might wonder what I was shooting at in the dark . . . better not use the gun at all.' This technical hitch didn't stump him for long either. 'Suppose we just cut his throat in the stream? He'd bleed out a lot faster too, as long as we went deep enough to get the carotid arteries. Gash those two boyos and it'll come *spouting* out of him. Like a fuckin' fountain!' After another few moments' thought, he seemed to make up his mind. 'That'd be the way, alright. Do the business nicely, it would. But you're going to have to help me, Pinky – to tie him up.'

'I can't, Joss,' Pinky pleaded. 'My leg . . .'

'Fuck your leg, Pinky. It's not as if it's broken. I won't be able to do it on my own. He's going to struggle like hell. Leg or no leg, you'll have to help.'

Suddenly his footsteps were coming towards my door and the skin shrank in icy dread on me as I stood up and, without any idea how, prepared to face him, to fight him to the last. Nobody was going to cut *my* throat, in a stream or anywhere else for that matter, not while I had a conscious breath left in me. The footsteps stopped and, a moment later, receded again. 'Here,' he said, 'take these. They'll have you right as rain in no time. You'll be fit to bull cows, so you will.'

'Maybe I can just keep him covered with the gun.'

'Shit, Pinky! I've just told you. We can't use the gun, not in the dark.'

'But he doesn't know that. If you tell him we're just tieing him up to move him somewhere else, he'll stay quiet. He'll obey the gun because he won't know that we can't chance using it . . .'

'Don't you believe it! I bet the sneaky bastard is listening to every word we say. Some people just have *no* manners!' he exploded into laughter. Pinky said something which I didn't catch as it was drowned out by Murray's laugh.

'A glass of water, bejasus?' he mocked, recovering from his bout of mirth. 'Can you not swallow two tiny aspirins without a bleedin' glass of water? A man with a powerful swallow like you? *Christ*, Pinky, but you're a real baby!'

I'd been trying to think of some plan of escape, but my train of thought was being constantly fragmented by the horrific discussion on the other side of the door, and it was useless. And useless was going to find me, in the very near future, lying with my throat slashed open, and my hot life's blood eddying away in weakening spurts into the stream which would carry it into the cold depths of the North Atlantic. I covered my ears to block out the frightful conversation from the kitchen and tried to think.

I had already checked the small unglazed window and found that its three vertical bars, though flaking and rusty, were nevertheless, solid; anyway, it looked too small for me to squeeze through, even if I did manage to remove the bars. The only way out was through the door. But it was also their only way in. If I could block it, then I might be able to buy some time, some precious, life-saving minutes. In the depths of my soul, I believed that, spurred to greater efforts by the approach of D-day, Downing would work it out sooner or later, and I thought my only chance lay in trying to stay alive until then.

In the rapidly-fading light, I examined the door. It opened inwards, I remembered, so if I could wedge a slat from one of the shelves between it and the thick upright support post of the shelves, then I could jam it shut. Eagerly I checked the slats but I found one after the other securely nailed down. I could easily hammer one free with the heel of my palm but the noise would surely draw Murray, probably before I could work the slat free, and as this would probably only hasten my gory end, I scrapped the whole idea. After several minutes, I came up with a compromise. I removed the lace from one of my boots and used it to lash the latch of the door into its bracket on the jamb so that it couldn't be raised by pressing on its thumb-plate on the kitchen side – at least now, when they eventually came for me, there would be a few minutes delay before they could actually get at me. And those might be the few minutes during which Downing would arrive. Also, as secrecy and stealth would no longer be required at that point, it would give me time to bang some slats free – they might come in handy for something, though I couldn't quite think what. I sat and unlaced my other boot, bit the lace in two and used the resultant halves in the top few eyelets of each boot – if there was a chance of making a break for it, I didn't want to have to sprint with my toes all curled up, trying to keep one laceless boot from flying off.

I sat and waited and listened to the conversation outside. My fate was no longer being discussed – presumably, it had already been agreed upon and they would get around to it in their own good time. I tried to guess what their reactions would be when they found the door locked; hardly any, I supposed – it wouldn't take them more than a few moments to smash it open. Murray would no doubt have an axe handy and, I swallowed painfully and thought back to the shed in the woods, he was well able to use it. I toyed with the possibility of the axehead coming through the door and becoming stuck, and me grabbing it and wresting it from his grasp and . . . and then what? Then nothing. I'd be locked in (with an axe) and they'd be locked out (with shotguns) and the door through the kitchen would still be the only way in or out.

Some time later, I had a bright idea, slightly farfetched, but definitely bright. If they were afraid of erythrocytes on the premises, I'd give them erythrocytes. I lifted the drying scab off a knuckle which I had grazed badly the day before and, when I managed to get blood oozing, pressed the raw flesh against the timber in several places. One of those little stained patches might be the only proof that I'd ever been there; one of those little stained patches might end up nailing the bastards . . .

It was at that point that the glow of a car's headlights, driving up the short avenue, shone in through the ventilator, briefly illuminating my cell. Darkness returned as the car passed round to the front of the house and came to a halt by the door.

21

Neither Murray nor Pinky heard the car until it was passing the kitchen window, but then there was consternation.

'Who's that?' squawked Pinky, his voice breaking into a panicky half-whisper.

'How the fuck should I know?' I could hear the tinge of worry in Murray's voice as he scraped back his chair.

'What are we going to do? Oh, sweet *Jesus*!'

'Just shut up, will you! It's probably a neighbour. I'll get rid of him. You turn on the radio as loud as it'll go – in case Samson tries to make a racket.' But he sounded neither confident nor convinced.

'It couldn't be the cops, could it?' Pinky was almost in tears.

'How the fuck should I know?' he repeated angrily. 'And why should it be cops? If he'd tipped them off, they'd have been here hours ago. And there'd be several cars. This is just one.'

The shrill peal of the doorbell almost gave Pinky a heart attack. He squealed and then whimpered: 'Jesus H . . . I knew I should never have got involved.'

'Well you fucking well did, you fat greedy bastard . . . now *do* something!'

'I don't know what to do,' wailed the fat greedy bastard forlornly.

'I told you – turn on the bloody radio! And hide that

shotgun, for Chrissakes! Put it in the corner, there, down beside the dresser.'

The doorbell sounded again, this time a longer burst.

'Coming! Coming!' shouted Murray.

I could picture him taking one last glance around the kitchen, staring a stern warning at the snivelling, gibbering Pinky, then heading for the hall door. I heard Pinky's heavy breathing as he approached my door, then a dull clunk – the shotgun, I presumed, being hidden as per instruction. Then a radio came on full blast and I could hear no more.

Afraid to hope, I was even more afraid not to. It probably was just a neighbour, looking for the loan of a trailer or some such. Murray would stall him at the door and that would be that; my cell would be bathed briefly in the red glow of taillights as the car left, growing fainter as it went down the short driveway, a brief intensification as the brake lights blinked at the gate, then . . . nothing. Oblivion. I'd be alone again in the dark and, moments later, they'd come for me. There'd be no more delays, not after such a close shave. I checked that the binding on the latch had stayed tight, tried to quiet the thumping of my heart, and strained my ears to catch some telltale sound over the din of the radio.

Vague and distant, there were voices which I judged to be coming from the corridor. There seemed to be an argument of sorts in progress, and one of the voices sounded like a woman's. Then they were in the kitchen and, radio or no radio, I had no difficulty in recognising Bertie's voice.

'For God's sake, Pinky, turn down that radio! Are you deaf or something?' Pinky turned it off altogether. 'That's better. Now will someone please tell me what's going on?'

'What do you mean, "what's going on", Roberta?' Murray asked.

'Well, where's Frank for a start?'

He hesitated, no doubt expecting me to answer for

myself, but I didn't, so he decided to go for it. 'How should I know? What makes you think he might be here?'

'His Land Rover is parked outside.'

'That's *my* Land Rover.'

'No it's not, Joss. Yours is blue. What's wrong with your leg, Pinky?'

'He fell. He'll be okay. Why this interest in Samson all of a sudden?'

There was a brief silence before she answered and when she did, she sounded unsure, as if she'd suddenly detected the strained atmosphere. 'Frank and I were to have dinner this evening and he didn't show. His office didn't know where he was, hadn't heard from him since mid-morning. He was at the house today to talk to Pinky about the horses, so I thought he might have come here to look at them and forgotten our date . . . I phoned a few times but nobody answered.'

I recalled hearing the phone on a couple of occasions but it had been ignored.

'Let me get this straight, Roberta. You rang a few times, but got no answer? Now, any normal person would assume that that was because there wasn't anybody here, yet you decided to come on out anyway just for the heck of it? Why?'

'What's got into you, Joss? What's with all the questions? Pinky, what's going on?' When there was no response from either of them, Bertie hesitated, then said, even more unsurely – and unconvincingly: 'Actually, I came to swap cars. In case you hadn't noticed, Pinky has mine. He took it without asking me, and . . . I need it.'

'At this hour of the night? You came all this way . . . just for your car?'

'Where's Francesca? Is she here?.'

'Never mind Francesca,' Murray replied, momentarily thrown by the change of subject. 'She's . . . eh out.'

'Is she away?'

'Why d'you ask that?'

'I'm surprised she'd leave the kitchen in this state – she's so house-proud. Look at all those dishes. And how come there are none of her clothes on the airing frame? Not even a pair of tights? Unless, of course, Francesca has suddenly taken to wearing off-white Y-fronts?' She laughed nervously, frantically trying to change the subject and the tone. She was only making things worse.

'Actually she's gone home for a holiday. I left her to Shannon last week.'

In my cell I wondered if Murray hadn't murdered Francesca too, whoever she might be – hard-working wife, daughter, mistress or girlfriend. I was also wondering what my captors were making of my continued silence; they probably thought I'd hanged myself.

'Oh! She's gone back home to *Argentina*?' Bertie continued. 'You made it sound like she'd slipped down the road for a cup of coffee with a neighbour. Or gone to Bingo. Or . . .'

'Roberta! I asked you why you asked what was going on? I'm waiting for an answer! Now *why* did you think that there was something . . . going on, as you put it?'

'I . . . I . . . Pinky! What are you doing with that gun?'

So Pinky had picked up the gun. Interesting . . . There was silence from the kitchen. I could picture Murray trying to figure out this new move, and not liking what he came up with. Into this silence, I decided to throw my tuppence worth.

'He's protecting you, Bertie!' I shouted. 'Let me out!' I pounded on the door with my fist. 'I'm in here.' There was a deeper silence in the kitchen. 'Bertie? Bertie! Let me out!' I began to unwind the bootlace from the latchplate as I spoke.

'Frank?' She said hesitantly, as though she didn't believe her ears.

'Get me out of here, quick! Open the door but, whatever you do, don't walk between Pinky and Murray.'

With indescribable relief, I heard her approach the door. 'Frank?' she asked again, still at a loss.

'Open the door, Bertie.' I clicked the latch up and down impatiently.

There was no sound from the others. No doubt they were trying to figure some way out of this sudden, awful dilemma which Bertie's arrival had placed them in. For there was now a second witness – another throat to be slit open in the stream, Pinky's sister. Joss would have no qualms, but for all his cowardice, I didn't think Pinky would put up with the murder of his one and only sister. Which was why he'd picked up the gun. He also may have realised that he too would be for the chop – after all, Joss could hardly kill Bertie and expect Pinky to continue on as if nothing had happened.

'Come on, Bertie,' I urged. 'Open up!'

Suddenly the door was opening and Bertie stood in the widening gap, wide-eyed with bewilderment. She looked totally incongruous in her elegant dress. Without a word, I brushed past her, my eyes immediately seeking out Murray. Pinky might be the one with the gun, but Joss was the dangerous one. He was off to my right, standing alone, eyes intently studying the fingernails of his clenched hands, tongue flicking in and out between pursed lips, like a hunting snake. I didn't take my eyes off him, but he didn't look up, didn't raise his head to face up to his rapidly deteriorating position.

Pinky and Bertie were to my left. He stood protectively, slightly in front of her, a belated, accidental, and distinctly off-white, knight. As usual, he hadn't the guts to look at anyone – he had located an interesting spot on the opposite wall, above the range, where Murray would be well within his peripheral vision, and was absorbed in studying that. He was whisper-whistling softly, blowing unconnected, tuneless little notes into the silence, making it up as he went along. He lounged against the dresser and tried to look nonchalant, but the knuckle of the finger which was wrapped round the trigger, was taut.

Bertie was looking from one of us to the other, still befuddled. I decided to break the standoff.

'It's over, Pinky,' I said, taking a step towards him. 'Give me the gun.'

Murray's head came up with a jerk and he glared at Pinky, but Pinky had already swung the gun towards me. 'Stay where you are!' he warned. 'Right there!' This time there was no waver in his hand.

'*Pinky!*' cried Bertie, shocked.

'I mean it! Nobody's to move.'

Murray spoke for the first time. 'Nobody, Pinky? Not even me?'

'*Especially* you, Joss.'

'Jeez, Pinky!' He looked hurt, as if he couldn't believe what he had just heard. 'Listen to me, Pinky.' He held up his palms in a reassuring way. 'There's a way out of this, you know. An easy way.' He paused, then, when Pinky showed no interest, said: 'And no one will be hurt. You can be in control – keep the gun at all times . . .'

'Go on,' said Pinky, sounding none too hopeful.

'We lock Samson and Roberta in the larder, you and I leave with the stocks, go into hiding for a few days until we can get Hilliard to deal. Of course, as soon as we're far enough away, we ring the cops and tell them where they are. That way, no harm comes to Roberta . . .'

'What he means, Pinky,' I interrupted, 'is you lock us in the larder and leave us there until such time as he can disarm you. Then he'll kill you and come back and finish us off. We'll be waiting in the Death Cell that you, Pinky, will have put us in.'

Joss glared at me, his dark deepset eyes smouldering with hatred. 'Don't listen to him. He's just trying to put the wind up you . . .'

'True,' I said to him. 'Just like Marc Glasser was trying to put the wind up *you*.'

'Joss killed Marc?' Bertie squeaked in disbelief.

Pinky began shaking his head. 'No, Joss. It wouldn't be the same. We'd be on the run all the time and even if we did manage to get the money, how could we ever enjoy it?'

'We can demand a plane out of the country, to anywhere we like! Anywhere, Pinky!'

'Yeah. And get extradited the next day.'

'There are lots of countries which don't have extradition treaties with Ireland.'

'Oh, sure! But I don't think I'd fancy living in any of them. Neither would you, Joss. I know you.'

There was a long silence. 'So what happens now, then?' Murray asked after a while.

'I'm staying put, Joss. Here.'

'That'll mean doing time. You realise that, don't you?'

'I think that's inevitable now, no matter what I do. But the sooner I give up, the less time I'll have to do.'

'I see,' said Murray, leaving the next question unasked.

'How about you?' Pinky asked it.

'Emmm . . . What are my options, Pinky? As you see them, like?'

'That's up to you. I've made my choice, you make yours.'

Murray thought for a moment. Though I could only see him in profile, I was almost certain that a fleeting cunning look came into his eye and was almost immediately extinguished. 'I can leave?'

'Sure. If that's what you want.'

'Pinky,' I warned. 'Do that, and you start adding on time. Are you willing to do three or four extra years for him?'

'Well, I'm not going to *arrest* him, if that's what you mean. He's a friend.' Pinky, it seemed, had developed a sudden noble streak.

'Yeah. Like Marc Glasser was your friend,' I said dryly.

'I appreciate this, Pinky,' Murray said, oozing comforting sincerity. 'A lot. I won't forget you for giving me this break. There are just one or two things. How much of a headstart do I get and what about the . . . em . . . stocks?'

'How much time do you think you need?'

'How about three or four years?' Murray grinned boyishly, trying hard to be the good ol' boy.

'Seriously, Joss.' Pinky managed a wan smile back.

'Acch! I don't know. Couple of hours? Three?'

Pinky shrugged. 'You can get to almost anywhere in the country in that time. Especially at this hour of the night. No traffic.'

'True. True. What about the stocks?'

Pinky thought for a moment. 'I don't want to know, Joss. But I'm certainly not going to search your baggage.'

Having stirred the embers of the old rapport, Murray gave it one last try. 'C'mon, Pinky!' he cajoled. 'I tell you, it'll *work*, man . . .'

'No, Joss. I'm no good at all this high-energy, high-risk stuff. You know that. You're the one who's always telling me what a wimp I am. Whatever chance you have of making it on your own, you'd have none at all if I was with you. Now . . . you probably should get going, Joss.'

'Yeh,' he said with suspicious enthusiasm, 'I suppose you're right. I probably should.'

I expected Murray to head straight off down the corridor towards the front door, but instead he went in through the third door off the kitchen. A back door, I assumed, until I heard the opening and closing of doors and drawers, and the hum of a fridge suddenly disturbed into life. He was in the actual laboratory!

'Pinky!' Bertie whispered urgently. '*Did* Joss kill Marc?'

'Well . . .' said Pinky, uncomfortably.

'Then are you raving mad? If you let him leave, you'll get twenty years! For God's sake, act your age! Give the gun to Frank if you're not willing . . .' She broke off guiltily, aware that the sounds of activity from the lab had ceased, scared that Murray might be listening. Which he probably was.

'Pinky,' I moved closer to him and whispered. 'If he has a gun in there then we're all goners. Either give me the gun or else cover that doorway. Well!'

'There's no gun in there.' But just the same, he shifted the shotgun to point at the door.

Murray's jacket was hanging on the back of a chair across the table from me and I suddenly remembered the cartridges which he had removed from Pinky's gun, the gun which now lay empty in the back of my Land Rover. So *that* was why he'd had the short-lived cunning leer! Seconds after leaving the house, Murray would have reloaded, and be blasting at us through the kitchen window. I moved casually around the table, removed the two cartridges from his pocket and put them into mine. Significantly, Pinky didn't try to stop me.

Murray came through from the lab, carrying an aluminium case. When he saw that I'd moved to the other side of the table and was now standing between it and the range, blocking his way, he hesitated and looked nervously at Pinky, as though he suspected that Pinky might have changed his mind; but Pinky, managing another wan smile, said: 'Good Luck, Joss. Mind how you go.' Immediately, I moved aside and stood by the table. Murray eyed me suspiciously for a second or two, then came to a decision – presumably he thought that if Pinky had changed his mind about letting him leave, then the gun would have been brought into play by now. Squaring his shoulders, he set off. His eyes were fixed on the jacket and it was clear that, next to his 'stocks', this was the single most important item on his list. Shifting the case to his right hand, he picked up the jacket with his left, with hardly a break in stride. At this stage, heading for the door to the corridor, he probably thought he was away with it; at any rate he didn't even glance at me as he passed. If he had he might have seen the tension on my face as I prepared to stick my foot out, and been warned of the danger. But he didn't look, so he missed the warning.

As he stumbled, I leaped on his back, wrapping my arms round his upper arms and my legs round his. For a moment, he swayed, nearly succeeding in regaining balance, but then, almost gracefully at first, he keeled over and we crashed heavily to the ground. He tried to twist as we fell, but by some frantic and totally instinctive legwork, armwork and counter-adjustments to my weight, I managed to hold my position and, when we did fall down, I was firmly on top, my arms locked about his upper body. What followed could hardly be called a fight; it was more like an arm wrestling bout, periods of grunting stillness as power was summoned and concentrated at one particular point. I strove to anticipate his sudden concentrated efforts to free his arms, while his senses were honed to recognise, milliseconds in advance, the moments when I'd have to ease off slightly. In the end, I managed to hold out. All the fight seemed to drain from, and he began to moan: 'Oh, Pinky. Pinky,' in reproachful exhaustion.

'Bertie,' I panted, 'get the case.' Beneath me, Murray stiffened but when I locked my arms even tighter about him, he gave up the idea and let himself go limp again.

'I've got it, Frank,' she said, her ankles coming into view.

'Take the top off the range, the fire box.'

Murray's voice came shrilly from beneath me, jerky because he was panting so hard. 'Christ, Pinky! Can't you see what they're doing? Stop her!' He gave a single desperate heave, but there was little strength in it.

'What do you suggest, Joss? That I shoot her? Or just bludgeon her senseless with the gun butt?'

There was the dull clang of iron on iron which must have sounded like the death knell to Murray. Then came the acrid smell of anthracite.

'Okay,' said Bertie. 'It's open.'

'Will the case fit through the opening?'

'No. No way.'

'Then open it and see what's inside.'

'Test tubes,' she said after a moment. 'With different coloured tops.'

'Right. I want you to throw them into the fire. They're probably clean, but if you can get a piece of cloth or paper to handle them with, all the better.'

'A dishcloth.'

'Perfect.'

There was a pause and I imagined her gingerly reaching

into the case. 'The test tubes with the same coloured tops are bound together with rubber bands.'

'Anything written on them?'

'Yes. These are three blue ones with labels which say . . . Swine Fever.'

'Throw them in.' There was a plop and a hiss and a stronger stink of anthracite as the brittle crust of magma was broken.

'Four tubes with red stoppers which are . . . Newcastle Disease. Drop them in?'

'Yeh.' Beneath me, Murray had gone flaccid.

'Black stoppers, four. Rabies. Jesus! *Rabies!*'

'Drop them in.'

'Okay. Gone. Next is a group of . . . three-four-five-six – six vials, green tops with F&M on the labels. Is that Foot and Mouth Disease?'

'Yes. Throw them in.'

'Then there are three with purple stoppers – Anthrax – and finally one, just one single one on its own, with a white top, and it says Glanders.' She threw the last of the deadly vials into the range and said: 'That's it. They're all gone.'

'Good. Now, throw the dishcloth in as well, put the case in the oven and go and check if there are any more tubes in that room.'

A few moments later she announced that the room was clear except for a glass tank seething with 'disgusting creepy-crawlies.'

'The Colorado Beetles.'

'Whatever. But I'll fix them. I've found a can of fly spray.' Her steps receded back into the laboratory, there was a prolonged hissing sound, and she re-emerged, coughing.

'Now search his pockets.'

When she had done this as best as she could with my weight on top of him, I turned to Pinky. 'Do you have any rope?' I asked.

Pinky shook his head. 'Uh-uh. Let him up. A deal's a deal. I gave my word.'

Beneath me, I felt Joss give a mirthless laugh of despair.

'Don't be daft, Pinky!' I said urgently. 'The man's a psychopath. He doesn't need favours . . . Treatment is what he needs.'

'The man's a friend,' Pinky corrected me icily, and I wondered if my tone had been wrong, had sparked off a mini-rebellion. 'I gave him my word. Three hours.'

There was a contemptuous snarl from beneath me. 'You didn't even give me three fucking *seconds*! You are a rotten turncoat bastard and you'll regret this night's work as long as you live. I promise you that. "Three hours", you said, you unspeakable shit!'

Pinky began to show signs of agitation, not comfortable with being everyone's enemy, not man enough to commit himself to one side or the other. He hobbled across to where Joss and I lay on the floor. 'Now hold on there, Joss . . . If you can't keep out of trouble, then that's not my fault – I'm going to pay dearly enough for your headstart as it is, but there's no way I'm going to start shooting anyone for you. If *you'd* been getting the better of it, I wouldn't have interfered either.'

'Face facts, Pinky. You're a coward, a yellow rat. A fat, lazy, yellow, despicable rat.'

'Well, fuck you!' Pinky squeaked, outraged. 'I'm facing years extra in gaol to give you a chance and all you can do is abuse me because you were outwitted! Well, if that's your attitude, then maybe I *should* turn you in. Maybe I'd get a few years taken off instead!' He paused, staring at Joss, breathing heavily. Then he shouted: 'You've still got your three hours!' and hurled his great bulk straight at my neck.

I was taken totally unawares and went backwards. I heard Bertie scream '*Pinky!*' as I rolled to the floor, pressed down by his heavy body. My first instinct was to fight him off, but I realised at once that in the scuffle, Joss would very likely end up with the gun – Pinky couldn't fight me and keep Murray covered at the same time. I lay prone and shouted: 'I'm not going to struggle, Pinky. Just don't let him get the gun. Hang on to that gun or we're all dead!'

I didn't know what was happening until Murray stood up and I could see him over Pinky's obscuring shoulder. For a few seconds he stood there, clothes dishevelled, chest heaving, glaring malevolently at each of us in turn; then he picked up his jacket and, turning on his heel, made for the corridor. We listened to his steps echo along the wooden corridor then pause in the hall for a moment. Suddenly the front door slammed and we could hear footsteps crunch on the gravel.

'Pinky,' I whispered. 'Shhh! Listen carefully – he's going to open the door of my Land Rover to get your gun. He doesn't know I've taken the cartridges out of his jacket . . .'

On cue, the footsteps stopped, the back door of my vehicle was audibly wrenched open. Seconds later there was a loud oath, the door was slammed again and there was a string of infuriated curses as his steps ran past the kitchen window, crunching through the gravel, heading for the stable yard.

'He's headed for the yard. He's got another gun there – I saw it. Now, would you please get the hell off me!'

Pinky rolled aside. 'He's only gone for his car,' he panted. 'You don't expect him to *walk* for three hours, do you?'

I snorted. 'He'll be back in a few minutes, believe you me, and he'll be armed to the teeth. I'm not staying here a moment longer, in a lighted room on a dark night. We're sitting ducks.'

'Me neither,' said Bertie and we both moved towards the door.

Pinky took one look at the window, another at our retreating backs, then hobbled rapidly after us.

Outside, low, scudding cloud obliterated any sign of the moon. With only the light streaming from the kitchen window to guide us, we made our way across the weed-choked gravel to the lawn, and into a dark clump of shrubbery. There we stood and waited for the lights of Murray's car to come over the hill from the stables.

'He's taking a long time,' Pinky said after a while. 'What's the delay?'

'No talking,' I whispered.

In the cold night, Bertie searched for my hand. 'I'm freezing, Frank,' she whispered in my ear.

I put my arm around her. I could feel her shivering through the clinging fabric of her mini-dress.

Sliding her arms around my waist, she pressed her head to my shoulder.

'I'll give you my sweater in a moment,' I whispered, my lips touching her ear.

At that precise moment, all three of us caught the faint glint on the front of Murray's Opel as it glided like a shark out of the murky depths. He had crept up the road in pitch dark, nosing his way along. When the interior light came on briefly, we could see that he was carrying a gun. When the car door closed again, he became just a shadow, a faint, almost invisible, presence edging along against the darkness of the house. Suddenly he appeared in full startling silhouette in the rectangle of yellow light, gun raised to fire. He stared motionless for a moment into the empty room, then dashed silently through the open front door. We could hear him moving about the house, going from room to room, and see lights switching on and off as he went. When he was upstairs, I disengaged Bertie's arms and made a dash to his car, but he'd taken the keys. I was probing under the steering column for a skein of wires which I might be able to tear out and thus immobilise the car, when his figure appeared briefly in the light from the kitchen. Slamming the door, I dashed off towards the top of the stables road and fell into some bushes. In seconds came the roar of a shotgun but none of the pellets came anywhere near. He bellowed: 'Pinky! Pinky!' into the dark night a few times, then began to chortle to himself. 'Pinky, me bucko! You're doin' alright! You'll learn!' There was a short hysterical laugh which quickly died to a strange burbling sound until it was finally chopped off by the closing of the car door.

Then, with great revving and blowing of the horn, he was gone.

We trooped out the gate, across the road, and stood in the dark of an imminent storm, leaning over the ditch, watching his tail lights descending all the way to the valley floor. Only then did we venture back inside. Bertie, wrapped in my sweater and Pinky's jacket, was snug and warm; I was shivering, but Pinky was positively trembling.

Of course he had more than just the night chill to shiver about.

22

I picked up the phone in the hall.

'What the hell do you think you're doing?' demanded Pinky, trying to pull the receiver away from my ear.

I brushed him off like an annoying fly and stuck my fist in front of his face. 'Don't you *ever* lay a finger on me!' I glared at him until he lowered his eyes, which didn't take long. 'I was trying to ring Downing,' I dropped the receiver back in its cradle, 'but the line's dead.' I reached behind the instrument and hauled in the line – no neat cuts on this one; it had been yanked unceremoniously out of the wall. 'You and Joss must have gone to the same school for assholes.'

I brushed past him, contemptuously dismissing the gun, and followed Bertie into the kitchen where I found her warming herself by the range. She looked miserable and dazed. When she saw me, she began to cry. I put an arm around her and rocked her back and forth. 'What's going on, Frank?' She turned her tear-stained face up to me. 'How is Pinky involved?' At that point, Pinky hobbled in. 'Why, Pinky?' she asked him tearfully.

He shrugged, laid the shotgun on the table, pulled out a chair and flopped down heavily on to it. 'You'd better let him tell you. I don't feel up to it, right now.'

I told her all I knew, which, by now, was practically everything. Bertie stared at her brother, sometimes in horror, sometimes in pity, and, when I'd finished, demanded confirmation from his own lips. Refusing to meet her eyes, Pinky nodded and made a small strangled 'yes'. Then Bertie wanted again to know why – which he couldn't (or wouldn't) answer. If it was for the money, why hadn't he asked her? Pinky said it wasn't for the money. Then why . . .?

Anxious to reach a phone, I broke the cycle. 'Look. You can go into that later. Let's get out of here before Murray has second thoughts and comes back to finish us off.'

The first few raindrops were falling as we dashed to the Land Rover and climbed in. Seconds later we were climbing out again. Murray had taken the keys.

'The Fiat,' I said, and we dashed through the strengthening rain towards the tiny car, Pinky struggling along behind. But Joss had taken the keys of that, too. 'Are you sure you left them in the ignition?' I turned to Bertie.

'The only time I take keys out of a car is when I'm in town. I certainly don't have them on me.' She patted her thighs through the wet and now even more clinging dress. 'No pockets.'

'Did you have a handbag?'

'Yes, but it's been in the glove compartment since I left Limerick, so they're not in that.'

'So, that's that then,' I said. 'We're stranded.'

Towards the east, a pale quarter moon appeared briefly in a sudden tear in the fast-moving cloud cover; it ought to have been reassuring but somehow, my fanciful mind illusioned it into a bloodless fingertip poking a peephole through the fabric of the cloud. 'Let's get out of this rain,' I said, heading for the door.

Pinky and Bertie made straight for the warmth of the kitchen again. I followed, reckoning it should be safe for a few minutes more, even if Murray was already on his way back.

'Okay. War council. Any brilliant ideas?'

'Eh . . . About what?' Pinky asked hesitantly.

'What do you think? About reaching a phone, of course. And,' I looked a warning at him when I saw a tiny gleam of protest begin in his eye, 'don't give us any of that three hours rubbish. You reckon we should become accomplices, too?'

He darted his eyes away from mine only to turn them into the path of his sister's even more venomous glare, then dropped them to study the floor, his usual ploy; the close study of walls and floors seemed to occupy a disproportionately large part of Pinky's few waking hours. Downing was into ceilings and windows, Pinky into walls and floors.

'You know this area, Pinky,' I said. 'Where's the nearest telephone?'

He cleared his throat. 'The village. Bunacrick.' So much for honour among thieves.

'What about neighbours? The ones Joss thought might be at the door when Bertie rang and almost gave you both massive coronaries?'

He shook his head. 'Bunacrick's the nearest. The next house is about nine miles in the other direction, over the top of the mountain.'

'Are you levelling with me, Pinky?' I glared. I thought he probably was. I couldn't recall any houses between the village and Northfield and I'd seen no houses when I'd overshot the gate by a good mile.

'It's the truth. Why should I lie now?'

'Just don't mess, okay? What's the transport situation?'

'In the garage,' he answered sullenly. 'Lots of vehicles. Take your pick.'

'He's probably taken the keys for those too. Can either of you hot-wire a car?' Neither of them even knew what 'hot-wire' meant, let alone how to do it. That made three of us.

'Trust you not to start out on your criminal career with the usual apprenticeship in car theft,' Bertie snapped. 'Too much like hard work, I suppose.' She turned to me. 'Maybe we could hitch a lift?'

'Maybe that's exactly what Joss wants us to do,' said Pinky, suddenly coming fully over to the side of the angels.

'Butt out, you!' his sister rounded on him.

'It could be why he took the keys. If he actually has taken them.'

'You're just scared that we'll leave you and your hoppity leg behind!' She turned again to me, 'Still, maybe it's not such a great idea after all. Who'd give us a lift? Who'd be out on a night like this?'

Joss Murray is who, I thought, reflexively glancing at the black rectangle of the window, now awash in streams of raintrails which winked the kitchen light back at us as they snaked their way crookedly down the panes. In the flue of the range, the wind had risen to a loud moan, shot through with the tattoo of raindrops being drummed by gusts against the glass. Between them, they would drown out any sounds from outside. 'Pinky,' I said, 'we haven't got all night. Do you know where there might be spare keys to the cars? Or is there a motorbike, scooter, pushbike? Anything like that?'

Pinky thought a while, eyes still on the floor. 'Spare keys, I wouldn't know, but there used to be a bicycle. I don't know where it is, though. I haven't seen it lately. Maybe in the garage?'

'No. I've been in there. How about the offices in the yard?'

He shook his head. 'Those offices are small. I'd have noticed it.'

'Any other sheds?' I asked, without expectation. Apart from the loose boxes – and I'd already looked into most of them – I hadn't noticed any outbuildings during my extended surveillance from the hill.

'No.'

'Then, let's have a look – maybe it's right here, in the house.'

It was. In a small, impossibly cluttered room inside the back door was a long-disused, heavy, black bicycle with a crossbar – what used to be called a gent's cycle. I disinterred it, wheeled it out into the corridor and inspected it; to my delight, I discovered that it had a working dynamo – when I held up the back wheel and spun it, the bulb produced a faint glow. Bertie located a suit of yellow oilskins in a large cupboard in the hall, smelling of tack-leather, horse-cubes and hay. I struggled into the oilers, wheeled the bike outside, and, advising the others to find somewhere safe and barricade themselves in, threw my leg over the dry and cracked saddle. 'I wouldn't stay in the kitchen, even with the light off. Try upstairs,' I said. 'I'll go to the garage first and if I can get any of the cars to go, I'll come back and give three blasts on the horn, then two, then one, okay?'

'Take care, Frank,' Bertie said as I wobbled off clumsily into the dark.

None of the vehicles had keys in the ignition. I switched off the garage light, closed the door behind me, and wondered why the fugitive hadn't thought to click down the button on the Yale lock which would have locked the garage. He'd probably been too intent on getting back to the kitchen to finish us off.

Leaving the ghosts of my near death in the dark yard, I pedalled out through the archway, the lamp giving me light for about five feet ahead, barely adequate. On the climb back towards the house, however, the dynamo slowed as I slowed, until, in mid-hill, it was producing scarcely any light at all. Standing on the pedals, swaying from side to side, blinded by darkness, driving rain and the non-functioning dynamo, I began to see potential snags in my strategy. The whole point was to raise the alarm as soon as possible, by reaching Bunacrick before Murray got too far away; if I rode at a safe pace, the wan orange glow from the bulb would barely illuminate the wet front mudguard, never mind the road ahead, and the journey could take an hour or more. If, on the other hand, I went for speed, especially down that steep, twisting hill into the valley, I'd have lots of light, enough to see, whole yards away, any looming obstacle; the drawback was of course that by then I'd probably be travelling so fast that I'd have little chance of avoiding it. As I neared the house, I wondered if I oughtn't to stop and look for a torch, but then as the hill levelled out I picked up a little speed, the bulb began to glow a little more hopefully and the moon made another brief appearance. Seduced by their combined false promises, I pressed on. Murphy's Law. Clouds closed down the moon before I'd gone more than a few hundred yards.

It was a badger that delivered the final *coup de grâce* to my faltering progress. Just past the row of sheds where I'd earlier parked the Land Rover there was a gradual downhill slope which I recalled was straight, and I was pedalling hard, wind at my back, oilskins pressed clammily against me by my speed, dynamo humming out some quality light, when what looked like a largish boulder at the side of the road exploded suddenly and disastrously into life, and darted out into my path – a mature boar badger, snuffling in the ditch for slugs and other wet-night creatures, startled at my previously undetected approach. A split second later and I'd have been past him, but he hit the space between the wheels, the rear wheel climbed his powerful shoulders and the bike and I floated almost gracefully into a horizontal position parallel with the road. We landed in a knot of twisted legs and wheels in the ditch, several skidding yards along, and, through the click of the spinning rear wheel I could hear disgruntled grunts as the badger scampered indignantly off. I picked up the bicycle and checked it quickly – the chain had come off but it took me less than a minute to stand the machine on its saddle and handlebars, and coax the slack links back on to their toothed cogs. Postponing a check on a dull throb in my right ankle, I righted the bike, remounted, and pushed off. At once, a steering wobble forced me off again, and my exploring hands soon found a buckle in the front wheel which brushed the fork (also bent), with an ominous click and scrape, twice per rotation. Hopes fading, I tried another hundred yards or so but the buckle quickly worsened and, when I heard some spokes fall out, I decided that the bike was never going to make it, not even halfway. I stood, seething with frustration, buffeted by the wild, sodden night and tried to make up my mind whether to go on on foot or turn back. As Bertie had said, the chances of getting a lift were slim to nil, while walking all the way to the village would take so long as to make it pointless. I'd only made it some half-mile from Northfield so I decided to return there. Maybe I could find the spare car keys, another bike, or, as a last resort, ride one of Pinky's horses . . . Cursing the badger, I left the bicycle – and with it my most realistic chance of heading off Joss Murray – propped against a dry-stone wall, and turned back into the wind and rain. Knowing that, like the badger, I couldn't hear anything coming up behind me, I kept turning my head to probe suspiciously, from beneath the dripping brim of the rain hat, into the blindness of the foul night. The walk didn't help my ankle any and I hobbled through the gate in considerable pain.

Pinky and Bertie had barricaded themselves into an upstairs room, a bedroom with two single beds. It was cold but it was reasonably secure and afforded a good view of the road. Or at least would have done had it not been pitch black outside – Bertie had been watching the gate and hadn't seen me, though I'd walked through in full sight in my bright yellow rain gear.

'Crashed the bike, just a bit down the road,' I said. 'The front wheel was totally banjaxed. I suppose neither of you happened to come across car keys?'

'We've been here all the time, Frank, since you left.'

I caught my breath for a few moments, trying to think of some intelligent plan, but getting nowhere much. 'Pinky, d'you reckon I could ride one of your horses?'

He snorted derisively. 'You've got to be joking! They wouldn't even let you tack them up! Nobody except Joss has handled those horses in ages. Even I can't get near them.' I was inclined to believe him. From what I'd heard of Joss, he wasn't the best man to engender in other species a love and trust of the human race.

'Right, then,' I said locating the chair in the dark and wedging it back under the door handle again. 'I'll rest a short while and then set off on foot.' It would be little more than a token action, but it beat the hell out of sitting around helplessly. Maybe after all, I would get a lift.

'Don't be daft, Frank! He could be anywhere in the country by the time you get to a phone. And anyway, unless he has another stash somewhere, we've got the bugs . . .'

'Well, Pinky? Any more bugs? Some other place?'

'No.'

'You're sure?'

'Yes.'

'Pinky?' Bertie's voice came softly through the dark. 'Is that the truth?'

'Yes!' he said testily. 'It's the truth.'

'By the way, Pinky,' I said, feeling my way to the chair by the window, 'what about the three guys who attacked me? Who were they?'

Pinky seemed genuinely mystified. It was, he claimed, the first he'd heard of it. 'I swear, Frank! God's truth!'

Bertie was lying on one of the beds, shivering. I stood up, bumped into a large wardrobe and felt blankets inside. I flapped two of them over her and she lay, absolutely quiet, not even bothering when Pinky began a long, jumbled monologue of regret for his past life, his laziness, his '*lu*dicrous theory of sleep' and so on, ad nauseam. When this was over, he said, when he had repaid his debt to society, he'd be a new man. His family would be proud of him. We might find that hard to believe right now, but we should just wait and see. On and on and on. Saul of Tarsus, I recalled, had had something of a similar experience on the road to Damascus, only, one suspected, not quite as profound. The Corinthians and the Ephesians, I reckoned, could start watching the post for Pinky's letters any day now . . .

I sat by the window on the dressing-table stool and tried to look beyond the moving curtains of rain which distorted and fractured the infrequent lights which appeared down on the valley floor. At one point, a car actually turned up the hill, but it didn't come more than a hundred yards before stopping and turning off its lights. Probably a courting couple, or a farmer out to see how his stock were weathering the storm. No telltale interior light came on, so I opted for the courting couple – nobody had got out. In the meantime, Pinky droned on, repeating himself, re-repeating himself.

I'd pulled the oilskins back on and was testing the ankle tentatively when lights came fast along the valley floor, a chain of them. Because of the streaming panes I couldn't count them accurately. Three? Four? Behind me, Pinky was shuffling about, waffling on about the future, how maybe, if she still thought he was (nervous laugh) 'What was it she called me, Frank? A Pretty Tough Guy?' (second nervous laugh), he and Molly, eh . . . Hilliard might . . . eh . . . get together . . . you know . . . eh . . . time to settle down . . . a man could do worse . . .

'You poor, gullible, pathetic, pitiable bastard,' I thought guiltily as I watched the cars speed along, waiting for them to get to the turn off to the hill. I heard Bertie mutter 'Jesus!' – in pity rather than annoyance. It was muffled and I reckoned she'd pulled the blankets over her head.

As the cars reached the turn off and began swinging in, another came racing up behind, blue light flashing. 'The cops are coming!' I announced excitedly. 'They're on their way up the hill!'

Bertie sat up and said: 'The *cops?* They must have caught Joss already, then . . .'

Pinky subsided onto the bed and, suspending all talk of Molly Hilliard and her fairy-tale role in his fairly distant future, told me, after a brief silence, that I could now have the gun. I said thanks and, warning him to pass it to me stock first, explored with my hands until I felt the smooth wood. Immediately I felt silly for saying thanks, so I said wickedly: 'At least I think it's the cops,' and brandished the gun with a triumphant little shake. Which made me feel petty, petty and silly, as Pinky couldn't even see me. But he was beyond caring; with the surrender of the gun, the shedding of the last worldly trappings, his transformation into St Paul mode became complete, and he began in a pious voice, to try to convince us, and more likely himself, that he was willing to embrace with *joy* whatever retribution the good Lord might visit upon him. Hallelujah, brother. Yea!

They were climbing the hill now, travelling as fast as the gradient and the sharp bends would allow. 'It's the cops, alright,' I said. 'At least four carloads of them.' A sudden squall sent great soft gobs of rain plopping against the window, like a drum roll heralding the denouement. 'Pinky,' I said, 'if you want to concoct a whitewash story, you've got about three minutes.'

'A story? Like *what*, for fuck sake?' he demanded, reasonably enough, though in singularly un-Pauline fashion.

'How the hell would I know, like what? But you're surely not going to tell them you gave your pal three hours . . .'

'Better leave that out,' agreed Bertie, suddenly on the side of the family criminal, 'unless Joss has already told them . . .'

'In fact,' I continued, 'as far as I'm concerned, you gave yourself up, surrendered when you could have gone on the run. You refused to let him take the bugs with him and oversaw their destruction. You also prevented him from murdering us – there can be no argument about that. Kept him covered.'

'If I kept him covered, then how come he's not still here?' objected Pinky.

'Ah!' I said. 'Good point. I'm not concentrating.' I wasn't concentrating because basically, I didn't give a damn. No skin off my nose if Pinky got life, three times over. Still, the poor dumb bastard . . .

The cars had now disappeared behind the brow of the hill to our right; next time they came into view, they'd be a mere two hundred yards away. I wondered if they had Murray with them or if he'd already been lodged in a cell somewhere. Bertie began talking in a low, counselling mutter to Pinky. I looked out into the black void and left them to it.

Shrouds of rain slanting towards the valley floor, suddenly reflected faint swathes of light and, moments later, the convoy snaked round the outcrop, painting the dark walls of our room with moving white light and rapid bursts of blue. The whisperings behind me ceased briefly, then resumed with last-chance urgency as the first car turned in through the gate, blue roof-light flashing. I turned away from the window as car doors opened and slammed below. 'Time to go,' I said. 'Ready?'

In the half-light, Bertie squeezed her brother's arm, studied his still, downcast face for a moment, then looked up and nodded for both of them. 'We're ready.'

The landing and hall pulsed with blue light as I descended the stairs, gun in hand, reaching the bottom just as the first pounding reverberated through the dark house. 'Open up in there! Open up, Murray! This is the Gardai!'

Had he just said *Murray?* I wondered, turning to see where the others were. St Paul and Bertie had just set reluctant foot on the top step; the throbbing light and their step by step descent made the scene eerily jerky. On the other side of the thick timber, a different voice said: 'Maybe there's nobody here, Super. God! I'm gettin' soaked through to me knickers!'

As I reached for the doorknob there came renewed pounding followed by Gerry Downing's voice. 'Joseph Murray! Open this door at once! It's the Gardai!' Clearly they had *not* caught the fleeing Murray. Then how . . .

I opened the door and was immediately blinded by the beams of several powerful spotlights, not to mention the strobic blue pulse. 'Hello, Superintendent,' I said, turning my head away and raising a palm to ward off the lights.

'Drop that gun, Murray!' screamed a warning voice out in the wet night. 'We've got you covered!'

For what could have been a fatal moment, I hesitated. I

thought Murray had suddenly re-appeared, with a gun, and my first instinct was to raise my own gun protectively and dodge back inside.

'Don't shoot!' Downing's voice was almost a scream too. 'That's not Murray!'

It was then that I realised the deadly ambiguity of my situation and I dropped the gun as if it had suddenly become electrified. Standing there, pinned in silent, suspicious lights, I didn't know what to do; for want of a better idea, I began to raise my hands.

'I *thought* it was your Land Rover,' Downing's voice came from an ill-defined silhouette out in the streaming, pulsing night, 'even without the medicines in the back.' He didn't sound too hostile so I lowered the half-raised arms again. 'Would you just step away from that gun, like a good man . . .' When I had done so, he asked: 'Now. Where's Murray?'

'Gone,' I said.

'Gone where?'

'I don't know.'

'When did he go?'

'About an hour ago, maybe a bit less..'

'So, who's here now, just you?'

'No. There's me, Mr George Summers, and his sister, Mrs Roberta Garrison.'

'What are they doing here? In fact, what's any of you doing here?'

'It's a fairly long story. Perhaps you should come in out of the rain?'

'Does either of the others have a gun?'

'No. Neither.'

He thought a moment. 'Where are they?'

I looked over my shoulder. 'Right here. Behind me.'

'Ask them to step forward please, so that we can see them.'

When they had done so and we had all stood in the doorway to be inspected by unseen eyes, Downing resumed the questions. 'Why is the house dark? Why no lights?'

'We were afraid Murray might come back and try to kill us.'

'And why should he want to kill you?'

'Because he killed Glasser and he knows that we know it.'

'Can you *prove* that he killed Glasser?'

This was where Pinky was going to have to start paying his bill. 'Yes. More or less,' I said, reaching for Pinky's elbow and steering him to the front.

'How?'

I gave Pinky a nudge. 'The superintendent just asked you a question . . .'

'Eh . . . I eh . . . was aware of what was going on.' Squeakily, Pinky broke his uneasy silence.

'Oh? . . . Is that a fact? Were you now, begod?'

'Yes. I was.'

'How, may I ask?'

'My brother,' inserted Bertie, 'has been through a harrowing ordeal, and doesn't feel at all well. I think, before he answers any further questions, he should have a night's rest and then perhaps see his doctor.'

'*And* lawyer,' added the guilty one in true Pinkine fashion.

'Do you mind my asking,' I asked anyway, 'how come you're here? I thought you must have caught Murray already, but obviously not.'

'What about the germs?' Downing ignored my question.

'They've all been destroyed. Incinerated.'

'You're sure?'

'Yes.'

At that point Downing decided that it was safe to come in – or maybe it was just that the deluge was getting to him. Anyway, after a brief, whispered consultation, he emerged from the darkness, flanked by two armed plainclothes men, one of whom I recognised. 'Hi!' I said, as he passed me in the doorway, for we had exchanged pleasantries the day of Glasser's murder, 'whore of a night, isn't it?' But he ignored me totally and turned to Downing for orders. The superintendent sent him and the other one off to search the house.

'Now then,' he turned to me. 'D'you mind telling me how *you* happen to be here.'

Fifteen minutes later, fifteen minutes during which the pale eyes roamed over and inspected the kitchen ceiling minutely, dropping occasionally to glare long and hard at the squirming Pinky, he had the whole story. Bertie interrupted a few times and I didn't have the heart to argue with her: when I was telling Downing about their plans for my disposal, she broke in to inform him (and me) that Pinky had at that stage decided to play along, only because Joss had the gun beside him. But Pinky was already planning to save me as soon as he got hold of the gun, which had been part of Joss's plan – Pinky was to cover me with the gun, while . . . She offered as proof the fact that I was still alive – had Pinky not been stalling, they'd have gone ahead straightaway. When I came to the part about how Murray had managed to get away, she shoved her oar in again. 'And it was during this time, while we were throwing the vials into the fire, Superintendent, that Murray managed somehow to sneak away. Perhaps my brother's vigilance was distracted for a split second, which was all that Murray needed to slink away into the dark . . .' She'd have made a brilliant shyster lawyer.

Downing stared hard at her for a long time and Bertie stared innocently back. I knew he'd ask me for confirmation and, when he at last did, I said, yes, it was, in substance, more or less, true.

'If you didn't intercept Murray,' I asked again, 'then how did you manage to get here.'

'Does it matter?' he was being deliberately awkward, continuing to glare at Bertie, and none too pleased with me either, I suspected.

'It does to me.'

'Oh? Why?' He broke off hostilities with Bertie.

'Because I'm dead curious.'

'I see. Okay then, through Interpol. About an hour ago

we had a reply from the Argentine police. They had news of a man who is technical manager at a large vaccine plant, who visits Ireland regularly – almost every year – and whose sister is married to an Irishman . . .'

'Francesca Murray,' Bertie said.

'Exactly. Then one of the men, who seems to have an encyclopaedic knowledge of racing, recognised Murray as George Summer's ex-trainer. So, we now had Murray connected to a source of germs in South America, to Glasser, who almost certainly had passed these same germs on to Miss Hilliard's pony, and to George Summers, whose horses he had trained and on whose property Glasser had been murdered. This, on its own, would have been enough, but our man also knew that Murray had all but completed a veterinary degree, and that he had fallen on hard times, so there we were. A triple coincidence spanning an ocean, the equator and two continents. Also, the sample we'd sent to the lab turned out to be a strain associated mostly with South America. Did *you* know about the different strains of Foot and Mouth virus? I ask because it might have been handy if we had known from the outset – it would have given us some limiting factor in our . . . worldwide search.'

I went on the defensive. 'Look, I'm no expert on Foot and Mouth Disease. I've never seen a case and we don't get it here. Like any vet, I'd think of it if I came across a salivating, lame, cloven-hoofed animal, with blisters in its mouth, on its tongue and on its feet, but that's about it. I'd then just report it to the government vets. That's what we G.P's are supposed to do.'

He looked at me a moment then slapped his hands together. 'Right, then! I think we should go and have a look at that lab now.'

23

The cloying reek of fly spray hung in the room, another larder, or perhaps a scullery. A large sink, square and white, with pitted concrete draining boards on either side of it, occupied the back wall, one ancient tap hissing incessantly as it dribbled a brown stain down the cracked enamel, the other almost overgrown by verdigris. Above the sink was a small window. Cupboards, topped by stained and chipped work surfaces of pale yellowish formica, stood against the side walls. A fridge/freezer and a laboratory incubator flanked the door; both were brand new, both had their doors open, and both were empty. A waterless plastic aquarium on the worktop to our left was three deep in dead beetles, their limbs angled in the rigor of terminal flexion. I shuddered as I imagined them back into seething life, a scuttling mass of hard-shelled, spike-legged insects, antennae ceaselessly feeling and probing as they crawled and scrambled blindly over and under and past one another.

'What's ND?' Downing asked as I hunkered down to check the cupboards. He was holding an empty test tube rack, reading from labels stuck on its base.

'Newcastle Disease. It affects poultry. Don't worry – we've destroyed it.'

'Good. And I presume F and M stands for Foot and Mouth?'

'Correct. All gone too. Into the fire.'

'That's a relief. Then there's Anthrax, Glanders, Rabies . . . All gone?'

'Up in smoke.'

'And SF?'

'Swine Fever. A feverish condition of swine, would you believe? That's gone too.' The cupboards contained the usual tins of floor cleaner, furniture polish, bath scourer et cetera. plus a selection of laboratory apparatus, glassware, plastic petri dishes, reagents and selective media, none in use.

'Good. And EIA?'

For the space of a single heartbeat, it didn't register. Then it did. With a bang. 'EIA?' I echoed, standing up slowly.

'Here.' He tilted the rack towards me. 'Look. There's a single empty space, coloured yellow, and a yellow label with EIA written on it stuck beside it. What does EIA stand for?'

'Equine Infectious Anaemia,' I said, feeling drained.

He looked sharply at me. 'Do I gather from your expression that there wasn't a vial of EIA.'

'No. There wasn't.' I wondered where the EIA could have been. It hadn't been in the case so perhaps, for some unguessable reason, he'd had it in his pocket. I ought to have made sure that he'd had a thorough going over, not the cursory up and down which, in fact, was all Bertie had been able to do. 'I don't remember EIA being mentioned in that letter of the minister's,' I complained indignantly, as if Murray had suddenly pulled a fast one, introduced a hitherto undisclosed wild card, without so much as a by-your-leave. 'Damn!'

'It wasn't. It named all these other things, even the beetles, but not EIA. The only other discrepancy is that the letter said there wasn't any more Glanders, whereas you say you destroyed some. Was there much of it?'

'Just one vial, as far as I remember. You could check with Mrs Garrison. She was the one who actually handled the vials.'

'It's not important. One vial would be correct according

to this. There's only one space marked "Glanders" – a white one.'

Downing set the test tube rack down, hitched one hip onto the worktop, and folding his arms, said: 'So, the position is that our friend is now on the loose with a vial of EIA in his possession.' He called one of his men. 'Is our plump bird singing?'

'He's cooperating sir. He hasn't refused to answer so far.'

'I'll be back in a minute,' he said to me and went out, leaving me to contemplate the latest shambles I'd got myself into.

When he came back he said: 'Summers knows nothing about the EIA. He knew about the others, but had never heard this one mentioned. Tell me about EIA. Is it a virus?'

'Yes. Of horses and other equines like donkeys and mules.'

'Let me guess. A virus that's not usually found in Ireland?'

'Correct. And because of that, I'm not exactly well up on it either – just like Foot and Mouth. As far as I remember, the virus can survive for ages in drops of dried blood. It's spread by insect bites or skin penetration by contaminated needles or the like. I *think* the incubation period is something less than a month. The disease itself can take four or five forms. There's an acute form with ninety-five to one hundred per cent rapid mortality; a less acute form, with a slower and slightly lower mortality rate; a chronic form, causing months of debilitation, then death – actually this form can also flare up suddenly into either of the two acute forms; finally, affected animals can recover – but as they remain carriers, so-called "recovered" horses should be put down.'

'In that case it sounds as if, one way or another, EIA is pretty much one hundred per cent fatal?'

'You could say that.'

'Didn't you tell us, in connection with the Glanders case, that horses would be difficult creatures to organise an epidemic for?'

'That's right. And an EIA epidemic would be even harder to arrange than a Glanders one, because, whereas Glanders would spread pretty much on its own, once it got into a yard, in the case of EIA you'd have to inoculate each animal individually – or pray for swarms of biting or sucking insects.'

'So if it's not a suitable agent for spreading about, and it wasn't listed in the letter as a blackmail threat, and Summers knew nothing of it, then it seems legitimate to assume that this EIA is, as it were, for his own private use, no?'

I shrugged. 'For what, though? Spite? Jealousy of another trainer? Revenge?'

'Murray is a violent character. Maybe he doesn't need much of a reason, though I suppose, if he took the trouble to order EIA from his brother-in-law, then there had to be an element of premeditation in it – he must have placed the order for his "stocks" months ago.'

The two men who had been searching the house returned. I half-expected them to report the decaying body of Francesca Murray in a trunk in the attic, or semi-dissolved in a bath of acid, but it seemed there wasn't anything untoward to report, and when, after a few cryptic words, Downing went off with them, I went in search of Bertie.

She looked up when I entered the dilapidated dining room. She was seated at the end of a long, dusty table, in the dubious gloom of a single candle-shaped bulb, the only one working in a chandelier of at least twenty of them. She had been crying. She stretched her arms out to me.

'What's happening?' I asked, taking her hands.

She shook her head. 'Nothing. I've been questioned and now I'm free to go. You?'

'Me too,' I said. There was a longish silence, until I asked: 'Were they hard on you?'

'No. Why do you ask?'

'Well, you seem to have been crying again . . .'

She gave a mighty sniff. 'I was just thinking about my parents. This is going to kill them. They don't deserve it, you know.' She wiped the tear tracks from her cheeks with the heel of her palm and sniffed loudly. 'Or maybe they do. They've always spoiled him rotten.'

'They'll get used to it. So will you.'

'I suppose so.' She sniffed again and then managed a wan smile. 'It might actually be better having a swashbuckling brigand for a brother than a boring lie-abed zero.'

'Bertie,' I said solemnly, 'I owe you my life. If you hadn't turned up when you did, I'd be dead now. I don't know how to thank you. I don't even know if there is a way to thank someone who has just saved your life.'

'It was accidental, Frank. I was looking for you for purely selfish reasons, and I found you. Pinky had the sense, for once, to grab the gun, so he probably saved both our lives.'

'Pinky's mind change only came about when you appeared out of the blue and placed him in an impossible position. It had nothing whatever to do with remorse. I owe *you*, Bertie. Nobody else. And certainly not one of my would-be killers.'

Perturbed at being reminded that there was nothing swashbuckling or cutesy brigandly about her brother, Bertie looked towards the hall where there was the sound of people moving about. 'It's all very well being told we can leave, but how? Joss has taken your keys and, even if mine were still in the. Merc, they've impounded it – until tomorrow evening, at the earliest.'

'Give me a minute,' I said, and went off to see how we were supposed to get home. I was referred at once to one of the men who was usually attached to Vehicle Thefts. He hot-wired the Land Rover in less than a minute and even rigged a crude switch which would turn the ignition on and off. Then I went in search of Downing to ask about Gino's abandoned equipment which was still lying, soaked, on the grass between the sheds. He said he'd have it collected and delivered to the surgery next morning. 'If you're taking

Mrs Garrison home, you'd better not stop. She's had a bad shock.'

When I went back for Mrs Garrison, she had repaired all of the damage wrought by the rain and her ordeal. She'd even found some make-up. 'Francesca's,' she explained, noticing my look of surprise. 'It was on the dressing table. She must have left in one hell of a hurry.' She took a last look around, then said: 'I wonder if she'll ever come back, now.'

'C'mon,' I said. 'Let's go. This place depresses me.'

It took almost ten minutes to get us to the road. So many cars had arrived that the place was now gridlocked, with my Land Rover stuck right on the inside, by the hall door. Drivers had to be rounded up and each had to be directed back onto the road and up onto the grass before I could worm my way back through the twisted channel which gradually opened up behind me; with a streaming back window and wing mirrors almost useless because of the rain, there were lots of warning shouts from without, hand slaps on the back and sides, and directions to 'go forward again', and 'left hand down a bit'.

'Where are we going?' Bertie asked when we finally wriggled free and I was negotiating my way down on to the valley floor.

'Well, first I'm going to drive you home, then I'm going to drive me home.'

'*Home?* You've got to be joking! I'm not going anywhere near home while that lunatic is still on the loose. Not even for a toothbrush. And I think you'd be crazy to go back to your hotel, too. Right now, he probably hates you more than anybody else in the world because you screwed it all up for him.'

'Downing would have got him anyway. With or without me.'

'But Joss doesn't know that, does he? He'd left before the law arrived.' She shivered. 'I'm cold, Frank.' She moved across towards me, caught my arm and put it around her shoulder. 'Please? Just until the heater warms up,' she murmured, snuggling up to me. 'Poor old Pinky . . .' she sighed after a while.

'Yeh. Pinky. He's not the worst.'

She pushed herself away slightly, so that she could look straight at me. 'Actually, he is. But still he's my brother, my only brother, and we used to have great times together when we were kids. Stuck in a cell for years. He'll die. Or go mad.'

'It'll probably do him the world of good.'

'Maybe it will and maybe it won't. You know, Frank, I couldn't have faced it if you hadn't been with me.'

'Of course you could. In fact, if it hadn't been for me, you mightn't have had anything to face. Downing had the goods on Joss only.'

Bertie was silent for a while, though she was still regarding me closely in the dim light of the dashboard lights. 'You just haven't a clue, do you, Frank, what a difference you've made to my life? Though, how could you? You hardly knew me before we went to Stella's awful dinner party.' She gave a little laugh 'It's funny. I find it hard to remember a time when I didn't know you, and I suppose I just expect that what was a pretty seismic encounter for me, would have had the same effect on you.'

'Bertie, you say the nicest things, but you ought to be careful not to sell yourself short in this transformation of yours. Don't let the idea take root that it's all thanks to someone else. You're a hell of a person, and you did it all yourself.'

'Let's not argue. When you're around, I feel I could move mountains. Do you know why I had to go to Limerick this afternoon? I went to shop for a new outfit. I felt I had to. I didn't want to wear anything that I'd ever worn before. I wanted to be, for tonight, as near as possible to being a new woman. Do you like the dress?'

'It's beautiful. You look spectacular, stunning – even after half an hour in a freezing downpour. So you bought a new dress for our date? I'm flattered.'

'A new dress, new underwear, new shoes, new everything! Very symbolic, no? And all for you.'

'For me? Wow! But what am I going to do with the shoes? They'll never fit me. Miles too small.'

She laughed: 'To hell with the shoes. I'm just delighted that you're in no doubt as to what to do with the rest . . .' Then she burrowed under my arm again and this time, whether she had planned it or not, my hand came to rest against her breast; as if it was the most natural thing in the world, she covered my hand with hers and pressed it gently against the soft full curve. 'I think,' she said in a sleepy monotone, 'that tonight, we should keep far away from anywhere that Joss might expect us to go. What I think is we should go the opposite way, towards Mallow, or even beyond, then check into a hotel.' Slowly she led my hand to her nipple which hardened at the first touch of my fingers.

I tried to think straight. I wanted Bertie as much as she wanted me, but Claire was there in my mind. Not the disapproving, stern, censorious Claire I'd last spoken to – it seemed like months ago, but in reality was less than twenty-four hours – but the Claire I loved, beautiful, warm, witty and serious, an intellectual one moment, a frivolous prankster the next . . .

Bertie was whispering in my ear, nuzzling my neck and earlobe. I think she could sense my struggle. 'Frank . . . I need you to be with me tonight. It's more than just physically wanting you until I almost ache. You've made me come alive again, Frank . . .'

'Shhh,' I said, meaning nothing in particular. My head was in chaos. I was almost aching for Bertie, too, but Claire was still in my mind – the loyal, trusting, constant Claire; the evening we met; falling hopelessly in love with her within hours; Claire slowly coming round to admitting that she loved me too. Then there was this unknown Claire, the distant and frigid stranger who was to let me know within the next few days, if she bothered to, what punishment I was to have meted out to me for my so-called crime, the impossibly high-minded Claire who, for all I knew, might already have decided that she never wanted to see me again. I was totally confused.

'I'm a new woman, Frank; I'm my own person for the first time, not the relict of a ghost or a memory. Do you know that until I met you, the thought of making love with any man was repulsive to me? I was dead inside, terrified I'd be like that forever. Oh . . . Frank!' She leaned towards me and then she was kissing me with an incredible devouring hunger, driven by two years of pent-up passion. Keeping my eyes swivelled on the road, I pulled over and yielded myself to matching her voracity, my thoughts wiped out by the fever of the moment.

Moments later, with both of us panting and trembling with desire, Bertie put her hand to my lips. 'Not here, my love. There's a hotel a little way further on. Let's wait.'

We drove in silence with Bertie clinging to me. The first words she said were: 'It's just up ahead. On the left.' As I swung in through the gate she squeezed my arm. 'Just think,' she breathed in a dreamy voice, 'nobody in the whole wide world knows we're here.' Then she looked straight up into my face and repeated, firmly: 'Nobody.'

As we drove past the entrance towards the car park at the rear, she said she wanted to freshen up, so I let her off. Suddenly alone, Claire was there before me again, my beloved Claire. That is, if she hadn't decided to give me the boot. Maybe I was already a free man, only I didn't know it.

When I entered the foyer a few minutes later, it was empty. As I crossed to the reception desk to ring for the night porter, Bertie emerged from a door marked LADIES. 'Don't bother ringing the bell Frank. I've already looked after it. Are you hungry?'

'Starving. I had this dinner date, but something else came up . . .'

She laughed. 'I'm ravenous too, but never mind. We can have a huge breakfast.'

Arms around each other, Bertie and I headed for the lifts.

Only I knew that Claire was an unshiftable third, unseen companion. Observer.

24

I was dog-tired. At some ungodly small hour, I'd made my way to the phone in the hotel foyer and rung the flat; there was no reply, which churned up all sorts of negative emotions in me. Next I rang the night editor, Walter Webster, and gave him a full update on the story. On several occasions, Claire and I had been out for an evening with Wal and his wife, Cora, so I had no problem in establishing my credentials. As he thanked me for the tip-off, I asked casually if he knew if Claire's phone was out of order, because she wasn't answering. He told me that Claire was in Paris covering a World Bank meeting, and seemed surprised that I didn't know this. As I hung up, I could imagine the inferences already beginning to ripple out from my question.

EIA figured prominently in my thoughts, too, though I wasn't too worried. With a country-wide alert out for him, Murray would surely be picked up within hours and then they'd find the missing vial. Perhaps they'd already caught him.

At some point during the long night, I'd also begun to feel that, even at this late stage, I owed it to Bertie to tell her exactly how things stood between Claire and me, and, apart from one dry remark about my fabulous sense of timing, she accepted what she chose to call my 'caveat emptor' sensibly, and decided 'to wait and see what happens'. All was fair in love and war. I almost told her that if Claire and I *did* split up, then she'd be my top choice as a replacement, by a mile, but how the hell could you say something as insensitive and insufferably patronising as that to anybody? I felt like a total creep for even thinking it. Still, I wanted her to realise it – whether for her sake or mine, I didn't know – and I tried to tell her through touch, body language, and roundabout, jokey, teasing talk.

The huge breakfast never materialised – Bertie was too worried about how she was going to break the news about Pinky to her parents, relations, Maeve, and friends, while I was wondering what state Gino's practice was in – I'd been away and out of communication since midday the day before. I dropped her off at her house, promising to phone soon, and hared back to Ward as quickly as the Land Rover could get me there.

I'd showered at the hotel so I went straight to the surgery. Joannie had kept things together in my absence but she still gave me a stony look and said that I might at least have phoned. I gave her a very brief resumé of the previous day as I scanned the day book. Most of the calls had been left over, but there had been three calls which couldn't wait so she'd passed them on to Jamey Mulligan, the other vet in town. I decided to pay him a visit first and make my apologies. On my way, I bought a copy of *The Daily Instructor*. It carried the story I had called in on the front page – with Walter Webster's by-line. None of the other papers had it.

I stood across the operating table from Jamey, Gino's opposition (and friend) and watched him place the last suture in the incision through which he had just removed the collie's uterus and ovaries. I had begun my story as Jamey picked up his scalpel, and rather neatly, but totally coincidentally, finished it with the last stitch. Beneath the green drapes, the bitch's chest moved rhythmically in strong, steady respirations. 'Joey Murray, bejasus!' he said. He gave the neatly sutured incision a few final dabs with a swab. 'Well, I can't say I'm *too* surprised . . .' He glanced at the nurse who was examining the patient's gums. 'Colour okay, Lena?'

'Fine.'

'Good. Give her the usual and put her under the lamp. She'll probably be okay to go home this evening, but don't let her go until I've had another look at her.' He moved to the sink and, nudging the bar tap with his elbow, began to wash his hands. I watched his broad back and wondered why he and Gino didn't go into partnership. Both were well-liked and respected in the town, they were both better than average vets, neither was afraid of hard work, they got along well, met socially, covered for each other, lent each other drugs and equipment, called each other in for second opinions; it seemed an ideal combination. He turned and pulled disposable paper towel from a large roll – Gino had a hot air blower. 'What else do we have lined up, Lena?'

'The Black Lab pup with the dew claws, Mrs Nash's tom with the dodgy tooth – you said it'd have to come out, but she says it's improved a bit since then . . .'

'Well, we'll take another look.'

'Then you've to take the pin out of the spaniel's femur. Then, that's it.'

'Ah we're not too bad, then. C'mon Frank, let's get a coffee.'

'If you're rushed, Jamey, stay at it. I just came to apologise for being away so often. I couldn't help it.'

'Say no more about it.'

'No seriously,' I followed his bulk through the door, 'I know you and Gino cover for each other and all that, but I don't want Gino paying back *my* time off, so, if it suits you, I'll do a week for you some time.'

'A week?' He stopped so abruptly that I almost bumped into him.

'Whenever you want, as long as you give me a bit of notice. And it'll be on the house.'

'You hardly owe me a week, Frank.'

'Well, it can't be far off it. Anyway, you deserve a week.

I didn't give you any notice or anything – just took off as and when it suited.'

'It wasn't exactly on a whim, now, was it?'

When we were seated, with steaming mugs of coffee on the desk between us, I asked him why he hadn't been surprised about Murray. 'You sounded almost like you expected it.'

'I wouldn't say expected it; I wouldn't put it that strong. But he's an odd fish sure enough – odd enough for anything.'

'You know him?'

'Know him? Apart from seeing him in Northfield almost once a week for the past eight years or so, we were in the same year at vet school. Not that we were great friends or anything – he was a bigshot, nephew of a famous trainer and all that, while I came from and moved in far less rarified circles. We wouldn't have mixed much socially, but in college we were always together, in the same group for lab work, post mortems, large animal ops, whatever. Mullen Liam, Mulligan James, Murray Anne, Murray Joseph . . .' he intoned, then grinned. 'I can still recite the roll-call. Almost next to each other on the roll. Only Anne Murray between us. God, but I was mad about that Anne Murray.'

'What was he like as a student?'

'Not bad. He did his bit and passed his exams. As I said, I didn't mix much with him; he was a social animal, but not in the sense of the few pints and the odd rugby or tennis club hooley that the rest of us called a social life. Parties with the racing fraternity and high class girlfriends, who never stayed long. He always carried the *Financial Times* because it was unmissably pink; he probably carried the same one for a week. He always wore handmade suits, oxblood brogues, that type of thing. He joined the right societies – The L&H, The Poetry Society, and the like. He was a leading member of the Drama Society and if there was a play on he'd strut about like he was Sir Henry-fucking-Irving himself . . .'

'Did he have any close friends in the class?'

'Naw. You know the type yourself – he was never even going to look at anything other than classics winners. And he'd refer to those of us with less lofty aspirations as "the cow, sow, miaow and bow-wow-wow mob".' He tried a haughty, aristocratic accent which missed by a mile.

I laughed. 'We had a few assholes like that in my year too.' I sipped my coffee. 'Ever notice a streak of cruelty in him? Or any kind of badness?'

'Can't say I did. Of course everything was going his way in those days. He hadn't been tested, if you get my point. I'd say he only began to change when his dream world started to slip away. When Georgie died and Joey inherited the lot, he pulled out of college like he'd just won the sweepstake. Which, I suppose, he probably had. But the bloody idiot had only a term to go, three months to finish his degree, and he couldn't put off his glorious destiny even for that long. I remember his "farewell speech" when we had a kind of a send-off booze-up for him. He told us – admittedly when he was well-jarred – that none of us should be thinking of making a fortune out of him in the years to come as there wasn't even one of us good enough to drive into his yard, never mind treat his horses.'

'Charming . . .'

'Except for Anne Murray. Joey was mad about her too. The whole class was. Probably half of us still are. Or would be if only we knew where she was.' He laughed and raised his coffee mug in a toast. 'Ah! Youth!'

I responded, sipped, then set my mug down. 'So what happened the glorious destiny?'

He repeated more or less what Bill Howell in Nenagh had told me, though, as Jamey actually did some work at Northfield, he had a different slant. 'Let's say he coasted along for a few years on his uncle's name and goodwill, not to mention staff, but it couldn't go on forever and the cracks began to appear in earnest four, five years ago. In a big way.'

'How?'

'Basically he treated his owners, especially the smaller ones, patronisingly – he as much as told them that they were fortunate that he had deigned to take on their useless nags. If a horse won, it was because he, with amazing skill, had managed to get it to perform way beyond its abilities; if it lost, then of course it was because not even he could perform miracles with such woeful dogmeat. Well, with that attitude, even in the early days, one or two owners moved away; then a few more and so on. He was a bit more careful with the bigger owners, but not a lot, and it was inevitable that sooner or later, one of them, too, would go. It also became noticeable that quite a few horses, as soon as they left Northfield, began to win every race they entered, the most famous, I suppose, being Banjo Master. He went to Herbie Jones's yard.

'To explain away these results, Joey started blaming his staff, some of whom had worked for Georgie and had forgotten more about the game than Joey would ever know – if only he'd let them run the place instead of interfering in everything, the place might still be open, but he didn't. Some left, he sacked some others and he was reported to have been only livid when a few of the better ones were snapped up at once by none other than the selfsame Herbie Jones.

'But a few biggish owners stayed on, mainly out of respect for old Georgie. He'd made most of them what they were, at least in the racehorse line – advised them right, bought them good horses at the right prices which he then trained to the tops of their capabilities, picked his races carefully, all the skills Joey didn't have. Later on he started messing around even more. He'd bill owners for stuff he hadn't given their horses, tonics, worm doses, that sort of thing. At one point he was inventing illnesses and presenting forged, receipted vets' bills. He pulled that one on me a few times. He got hold of my bill head, made photocopies and began to churn out bills which he would then mark paid and claim back from the owner.'

Same technique as the sheepscab letter, I mused, as

Jamey went on. Photocopy the heading and you could fool anyone.

'He did it with other vets, too. Anyway that neat little earner came unstuck when he got greedy. He put down such an exorbitant fee on one bill that the owner rang the vet to complain and, of course, the shit hit the fan. He'd choked the goose that laid the golden eggs. The very next day, even before *that* news broke, an owner who was a client of mine, rang me to see if she shouldn't have her horse put down. "What horse?" says I, not having a clue what she was talking about. "The horse you've had to visit seven times already this month," says she. Of course I hadn't had to see the horse in the previous six months!'

'The guy must be crazy! How could he expect to get away with that?'

'Believe it or not, he nearly did. A few more people took their horses away but refused to press charges. George Harty was such a widely-respected person, you wouldn't believe it.'

'Did your client take her horses away?'

'No. At least, not right then. You probably know her – Madeleine Fingal-Symms?'

'I know of her.' Even to a non-racing man like myself, her name, like that of Banjo Master, was famous in the racing world.

'Well she was his biggest, and most loyal, owner. For some reason, presumably the uncle again, she stuck with him almost until the end, though she had plenty of cause to leave him.' Almost like a non sequitur, he added: 'He was almost done for cruelty once, you know?'

'So I've heard. Couple of years ago?'

'Thereabouts. Again, one of Mrs Fingal-Symms's – a young horse, frisking about a bit, being bolshe, reared up and Joey jerked so hard on the bit that he almost sliced the tongue off. Caught it between the bit and the teeth.'

I grimaced and sucked breath in through my teeth.

'But he got away with it, said it was an accident. And the two stable boys who saw the incident changed their testimony. Bought off, or threatened more likely. Then the following spring he broke a pitchfork handle on another of her horses, fracturing its nose in the process. Another accident, he claimed: the horse had jerked its head up suddenly, for no apparent reason, mind you, and banged its nose on the door jamb. And again the witness changed his mind. He'd only talk about what really happened after a few pints in the local of a Saturday night.'

'And that was when she took her horses away.'

'No. It wasn't. Mind you, I advised her to – I mean, even if they were accidents, two in six months smacked, at best, of pretty lousy management – but she wouldn't. She's as gentle an old dear as you could ever meet and she refused to believe that 'young Joss' was not the chip off the old block that everyone had hoped he'd be. Actually, strictly speaking, she herself never took them away at all – it was her husband who insisted in the end, and that came about because of a disgraceful episode at the end of last year, which I happened to witness. I still blush.

'We were in the members' bar at Leopardstown, after a race in which one of her horses, despite being hot favourite, had finished fifth. It was the shock of the day though it was clear to a blind man why it had happened. The horse was First And Almost, a horse that likes to lead from the start, as everyone knows, but Joey had given explicit instructions to Tom Healy to hold him back until the second last from home. He was absolutely adamant about it, lots of people heard him. So Tom did as he was told – and came fifth. Fifth in a six horse race. When Joey came into the bar later on, Mrs Fingal-Symms said, mild as could be, something like: 'Hard luck, Joss. Perhaps Tom should have moved just a *fraction* earlier . . .' Or something even milder, which, in the circumstances, I would have thought was being extremely restrained.' He stopped, remembering, then shook his head. 'Then she asked him what he wanted to drink. He didn't reply at first, and I thought he was trying to decide, but when the silence went on, I looked up at him and saw that his face was black with rage. He was staring at the poor woman like he was a madman, the eyes sticking out of his head, and suddenly he started shouting. He told her to stop effin' meddling in something she knew eff all about, that she was a spoilt, fat, useless bitch who knew eff all about anything and that as far as he was concerned she could shove her advice and her interfering comments she knew where, if she could still reach around that far!'

'Never!' I said, aghast.

'I swear. That's word for word. Sure wasn't I *there*! The bar went silent – needless to say – then Joey turned and bolted. Herself was red with embarrassment – the poor woman didn't know where to look; then everyone started talking again – you know? – saying anything at all that comes into the old head, even if the words make no sense. A few days later, the husband, who lives in Hong Kong most of the time, got to hear about it, the other side of the world, and the very next day the transporters arrived at Northfield. Bye-bye Mrs Fingal-Symms.' Jamey sipped again and made a wry barking noise. 'Bugger him anyway! Joey and his shenanigans cost me one of my biggest clients, too – those horses are over a hundred miles away now, up with Lucas McDonald on the Curragh.' He shook his head in a mixture of regret and disgust. 'Anyway, be that as it may, that left the stupid bastard with some twenty horses, spread over about nine tiny owners and, over the next couple of months, a lot of them too, left. Geoffrey Fingal-Symms is a rich and powerful man and not even the late, great Uncle George could save Joey this time. Geoffrey lodged an official complaint, pushed it hard, put money and legal heavyweights behind it and, bingo, Joey lost his licence. It should have happened years ago. And that was that – an empty yard.'

'Except for Pinky Summers's four.'

'You wouldn't call them horses! They're only there on livery now. Summers claims he trains them himself.'

'They haven't caught Murray yet, you know – unless they've done it since the nine o'clock news. Let me ask you a question, Jamey. He probably has a vial of EIA virus with him . . .'

Jamey gawked at me. 'Oh shit!'

'They reckon it's for private use only, because he never mentioned it in connection with the blackmail. Who would he want to use it against? Who does he hate most in the horsey world?'

'I don't know. There could be many.'

'What about Herbie Jones? He made him look bad by turning Banjo Master into a winner and then employed his sacked assistants . . .'

'Possibly. But that was a long time ago. I'm sure he's developed other hated ones since. I reckon it's probably Madeline Fingal-Symms or possibly Lucas McDonald, the one who got her horses. But I'd go for Madeline or her husband. When she pulled out, the slide became terminal. And he was the one who finally had Joey's trainer's licence revoked.'

From the direction of the theatre came the sound of the surgery being prepared for further action, Lena indicating pointedly that coffee break was over. I took my leave, repeating my insistence that I'd do a week for him, and went out to devote my last day in Ward, one hundred and one per cent, to looking after Gino's practice. He was due back next day.

In contrast to the previous twenty-four hours, the period between my leaving Jamey's surgery and Gino's return, was one of the most humdrum times I have ever spent, but perhaps it only seemed so by comparison – I must have had equally unmemorable days in the past, only I can't remember them.

The highlight of a shortish list of routine calls was to a heifer that had somehow managed to get a bottomless enamel bucket stuck over her head and was going noisily frantic, charging blindly about, scaring herself silly with the new metallic echoing sound of her lowing, being a danger to herself and all in her immediate vicinity. Her herdmates were also at high doh, keeping with her all the way, sniffing anxiously with concerned and worried expressions, generally trying to suss out just what, in the name of all that was wonderful, could be going on here. Cattle being their incurably inquisitive selves again. I ended up running along athletically in the middle of the general stampede, waiting until there were a couple of strong ones running alongside on her *other* side to prevent her from swerving off, then jabbing three ccs of xylazine into her rump as we ran. That accomplished, I retired from the race and waited the few minutes for the drug to work. As soon as she lay down and passed out, I let her owner – and the ten or so neighbours who had miraculously materialised – loose on her with wire-cutters, tin snips and hacksaws, and, ten minutes later, Old Buckethead was back to normal. This was my most exciting and professionally-challenging case that day. Enough said. I had an early, troubled, night and awoke feeling grotty.

On the criminal front there was nothing doing. Murray seemed to have vanished into nothingness. His car was found in a back street lot on Dublin's north side, its engine still warm. The gun was in the boot but no vial of EIA was found. All the taxi firms and ranks in the area had been contacted but no one had reported picking up a fare in the dwindling hours of the night. The airport, ferry terminals, railway and bus stations were covered by the gardai, and, as no one answering his description had tried to go through, it was assumed that he was still in the country. Hotels and guest-houses were being checked today, plus all cars reported stolen during the night from the north Dublin area.

'What about the three guys who attacked you?' Sergeant Rhea asked me – Downing had skedaddled back to Dublin now that the 'rural phase' of the case was over. 'D'you think he might have linked up with them again?'

I shrugged. 'It's a possibility, I suppose. Why?'

'I had GHQ send me a printout on any big blond thugs

with records of violence, who were also known to have an interest in racing. It's a long shot, I know, but worth a try. The file arrived a couple of hours ago.'

He spoke to an intercom and asked for the file. When it arrived, he spread out fourteen mug-shots on the desk, which had been miraculously cleared since the day that Downing and I had first faced each other across it. I'd have picked out my blond at once if he'd been there but he wasn't. There was only one with any resemblance at all but he was ten years too old, ten kilos too heavy, scarfaced, and balding. He was also, Rhea told me, in Mountjoy, serving the second year of a five-year sentence for armed robbery with aggravated assault. But even if he hadn't been in the 'Joy, he wouldn't have been taking on little rough-up jobs like mine, because he was a medium-sized player in Dublin's criminal community, running his own gang of 'sub-contractors' doing the dirty work for some of the really big fish, and a job like mine would have been beneath him. His name was Brady, Kevin Brady, so, almost inevitably, his gang was called The Brady Bunch.

'My guy had a Dublin accent,' I said. 'I forgot to tell you at the time, but I can distinctly remember noticing it.'

'Listen, Mr Samson. Ninety per cent of these characters,' he tapped the photos with the back of his hand, 'have Dublin accents, and ninety per cent of *that* ninety per cent have Dublin accents which come from three small areas in Dublin.'

'Oh.'

'Still, it's strange that you should have picked Brady because *his* racing connection was that he was once arrested for, but not convicted of, viciously laming the favourite in a race which a horse of Joss Murray's subsequently won. The horse he attacked had to be put down. He had his knee smashed with an iron bar, broke some of the small bones in it.'

'God! Are you sure he's still in the 'Joy?'

'"Records" double-checked when they found Brady and Murray coming up together. And Brady is definitely still in the 'Joy. But it smelled fishier than a pelican's breath to me, so I asked them for the details of that old case.' He shrugged. 'They found nothing at all suspicious to connect the two men at the time.'

'How come Brady got off?'

'The usual. The main witness developed sudden amnesia on the stand. Couldn't recognise the defendant at all.'

And that was that. I left the station feeling somewhat miffed at having had my three-against-one attempted murder, or at least GBH, described as a 'little rough-up job'. With that attitude, no wonder they hadn't found the rougher-uppers.

On the social front, there was an invitation to dine at home with the Hilliards the following evening and, though – apart from the embossed government crest and the gilt rim – the card looked much the same as any other formal invitation, I felt that there was a distinct air of the Command Performance about it. But perhaps it was just me. Anyway it fitted in nicely; I'd be finished the locum, heading back for Dublin, and Hilliard's was on the way. It would delay me a mere three or four hours. I RSVPed that I'd be delighted.

Claire hadn't called at all and I began to fear the worst. Even if she wasn't back from Paris, so what? She phoned from all over the world when she was on assignment – Santiago, Anchorage, Vladivostok. Paris was a breeze. If she wanted to. With a start I realised that it had in fact been less than forty-eight hours since Claire's call after she'd got back to Dublin on the train, and, to be fair, this was not an unusual gap. Still, I felt, in these unprecedented circumstances, she ought to have called – she must have thought it through by now, must have decided whether she wanted to give it another go or call it a day.

Bertie phoned later and I got myself worked up into a lather of passion just hearing her voice, but she was tied up with her hysterical mother and I was occupied with catching up on my work and preparing for my departure so, to both my intense relief and equally intense disappoint-ment, we decided that there was no way we could meet that evening.

An hour or two later, Claire phoned. I did not get myself worked up into a lather of passion on hearing her voice, for it held an ominous and chilling edge which made it sound as if passion would be pointless.

'Thank you for ringing in the story,' she said coolly, as if I was just any old Joe Soap. 'Walter had a scoop.'

'I saw that. You're welcome. He's welcome . . . How was Paris? Or are you still there?'

'No, I got back a few hours ago.'

I waited a moment. Nothing happened. 'How're things?' I said.

'Fine. And you?'

It went along like this for a while, wary, stilted, pussyfooting. When would I be finishing the job (as if she didn't know – the diary was right beside the phone); how was Gino? Fine. Sylvia? Also fine. Then she asked me if she should accept an invitation for us to late supper with some friends, what time did I expect to be back? When I told her about my prior commitment to the Hilliards she sounded cheesed and said, that in that case, she might as well go on her own. I said, why not and she sounded even more cheesed. Then she said she presumed that she'd see me when she saw me, whenever I decided to put into port, provided, of course, that I actually deigned to clock in at all, and I said that if she felt really bad about it, then I could invent a plausible excuse for passing up on the Hilliards and she said that she was in no doubt at all that I could, without any trouble whatsoever, as I had shown a remarkable, hitherto unsuspected, flair, almost genius, for plausible excuses, but not to bother on her account, thank you. She couldn't figure me out – I didn't even like Hilliard for God's sake! She paused to let me have my say, but only briefly – if I'd realised that the brief pause was about to occur, then I might have been ready to kick off, but I hadn't, and the split second passed, over before I realised it had begun. She hoped that I would have a very good time with my friends, though she didn't sound as if she really meant it, then hung up. I called her back but she'd either been ringing from somewhere else or she was refusing to answer the phone.

The holidaymakers arrived home around five o'clock. About an hour later, Gino, moving gingerly, opened the door and greeted me with a careful handshake. On our way to the kitchen I could hear the TV blaring, so I shoved my head into the sitting room and found Ben and Lucy engrossed in Wile E. Coyote's latest (doomed) effort to trap the Road Runner with the aid of some fiendish contraption from The Acme Fiendish Contraption Co. 'Hello!' I called and waited. A second 'Hello?' met with equal lack of response, so I honked 'Mee! Mee!' and followed their limping father on into the kitchen.

It had been an outdoor adventure holiday, an almost endless procession of rock climbing, abseiling, canoeing, dinghy sailing and orienteering and, as the children were a bit young for many of these arduous activities, Gino had spent the entire time demonstrating. Knowing his irrepressible enthusiasm, I could just picture him, launching himself with totally unwarranted panache at the most difficult and dangerous-looking obstacles, as the children sat, watching dutifully but thinking of video arcades with loud music and monosodium glutamate by the packetful, while Sylvia rolled her eyes to heaven and tried to whip up a bit of hero-worship for the man they all loved and who was now stuck, clinging in terror to a sheer rockface fifty feet above, entangled in ropes and little metal things.

When he winced as he lowered himself carefully on to a kitchen chair, she didn't actually say 'I told you so', but there was a distinct lack of wifely sympathy for his wounds. Sylvia had maintained from the outset that the children weren't old enough for such a holiday, but Gino had insisted that this was cissyish nonsense – it was past time to foster in them a deep feeling for the great outdoors, a love of the hand-held compass and the soggy map, an early acceptance of the grazed knee, the wet boot and sweaty sock. He had been more than a little dismayed when the first thing they did on returning home was race for the TV – they had been doing cold turkey for the entire holiday and, so their father thought, not even missing it. Nor, Gino informed me, with hurt bafflement in his voice, had weeks of muesli and yoghurt, wholewheat bread and wild honey, weaned them on to 'the gifts of nature's bounty.' He waved his hand in defeat at the Manhattan skyline of beverage cartons and cereal packets already clustered in the middle of the kitchen table. 'There's enough MSG in that lot to turn them into mental vegetables. Did they even *speak* to you just now, Frank, when you came in?'

We drank the ubiquitous coffee and talked. Gino and Sylvia were agog at what had been going on in their own backyard almost since the moment they had left – they had eschewed papers, TV, and radio for the duration – and their coffees went cold as I related the saga. I stayed for an hour or so, helping them to unpack and answering questions, then I borrowed a suit, shirt, tie and shoes from Gino and we went to the surgery to unload his stuff from the Land Rover and fix up our business. I gave him a rundown on any problems which needed his attention and he gave me a cheque. I felt almost guilty about taking it and told him so. 'I've been away so often.'

'Couldn't be helped, Frank. You did right.'

'But don't worry . . . I'll be doing a week for Jamey to pay him back. It's all arranged.'

'Yeah? When?'

'Whenever he wants. Within reason.'

'It'll be funny having you about the place while I'm here as well.'

'I imagine it'll cause all kinds of confusion amongst your respective clients.'

He laughed. 'Anyway,' he said, 'you're in a hurry. Get going.' He held out his hand. 'Thanks again, Frank.'

'*De nada*, Gino. Always a pleasure. Give us a shout if you're up in town.'

'Will do.'

I pocketed the cheque, promised to send back his clothes at once, dry-cleaned, said: 'See ya,' and left.

An hour later, showered and dressed in Gino's best, I left Mrs Foley waving at the door of the hotel, and, via the Hilliard's dinner party, headed for Dublin.

25

The dinner party was something of a non-event. I hadn't formed any serious preconceptions – I just hadn't expected it to be like it was. Maybe I thought there might be a speech or two congratulating all concerned for saving the country from the ravages and ruination of the plagues which had been headed off with less than twenty-four hours to go. But if that was so, then I was wrong. There were no speeches or eulogies, no ministerial handshakes and no public applause. It seemed that I'd been invited to fill the role of performing bear for three political cronies of Hilliard's, and duly gave them, as per ministerial request, a first hand account of 'The Murray Affair', followed at once by a similarly minute treatment of 'The Catamaran Business' of last year. Hilliard's designations, not mine. Downing arrived as I was answering questions arising, and I was thankful that he hadn't been there for the narrative – my accounts had, perforce, been one-sided, and he might have misconstrued my lack of emphasis on the role played by the Garda Síochána as vainglory on my part, rather than the real cause, my ignorance of the work they had done. From the outset his attitude towards me had been, at best, ambivalent – the pro's niggling jealousy of the bumbling, but lucky, amateur. When I eventually managed to get a quiet word with him I asked him about Murray. 'No sign of the fugitive?'

'Not so far.'

'What about Mrs Fingal-Symms? Jamey Mulligan, the other vet in Ward, told me he hated her with a vengeance. Maybe the EIA is for her?'

'Rhea told me you'd mentioned that. But we already had it covered. Her horses, yard and house are under 24-security watch. She's hired private security as well.'

'Of course, it doesn't have to be her.'

'Of course not. But she is by far the most likely candidate. Other possible targets have also been warned, like Lucas McDonald. Whose stables, by the way,' he added as if he suspected I was about to check up further on him, 'we are also keeping a close eye on.'

'So. What happens now?'

'We'll get him. He can't have vanished. Sooner or later, he'll slip up.' Someone engaged Downing in small-talk so I muttered something about getting myself a top-up and excused myself.

Bertie, looking her ultimate best in a close-fitting lime-green dress that flicked out into a ruff several inches above the knee, had arrived while I was partway through 'The Catamaran Business', so I hadn't had a chance to talk to her. I'd caught her eye several times and she looked totally at ease as she chatted and laughed her way from group to group on her way to where Molly was doing her bit at the far end of the room to get the evening off to a flying start with the 'younger set'. I was at the bar-table, recharging my glass before joining Molly's group, when our hostess, Veronica Hilliard, summoned us to table. She came towards me and touched my arm. She was a remarkably handsome woman with high cheekbones, deep blue eyes, a straight, no-nonsense nose and a wide, generous mouth which seemed to be always on the verge of breaking into a smile; her oval face was tanned and unlined and her short, swept-back hair looked like straightened steel-wool. She was at least an inch taller than her husband, with the body of an athlete, and I reckoned that she had to be a daunting act for Molly to follow.

'Mr Samson. I hope you'll forgive me, but I've changed

your place. I did have you between Molly and Roberta but Clayton is making such a fuss about sitting beside Roberta, that I've told him he may. Do you mind terribly?'

'Not at all.'

'Thank you.' She smiled a dazzler, and, by way of explanation, said: 'Clayton is such a D.O.M. I can't for the life of me see why my husband will insist on inviting him to almost every party. Look. He's already latched on to the girls.'

I followed the direction of her eyes and instantly worked out that D.O.M. was politespeak for Dirty Old Man. A very elderly and scrawny specimen was leering shamelessly through a walrus moustache at Bertie; two yellow, beaver-like, front teeth rested on a lower lip that receded at once at an acute angle towards the prominent Adam's apple. The original chinless wonder. His hand made a few passes at Bertie's rump, but due to a combination of his poor timing and lack of brain-hand coordination, and Bertie's pelvic agility, no contact was made. Mrs Hilliard shook her head disapprovingly, clicking her tongue. 'That's Jenny, his long-suffering wife, standing beside him and suffering some more. After dinner, be sure you avoid him – he's harder to get away from than the Ancient Mariner. God!' she said, giving me a playful, if not actually flirty smile. 'The girls will be furious! Instead of you, they get Clayton.' I decided not to let it go to my head – compared to the lecherous Clayton, almost anybody not actually dead, would have been a bargain.

As we trooped into the dining room, Bertie managed to dig me in the ribs from behind. 'A *suit*, bejasus, Samson! How come I never got that treatment?'

'The blazer was out on hire tonight,' I explained. 'I just had to go with the mohair.'

I ended up sitting between Jenny, the long-suffering wife, and the *très chic* wife of one of the politicians that I had held riveted by my stories. Across the table, a few places down, Clayton sat between Molly and Bertie and proceeded to get more and more tipsy as course succeeded course. Molly was engrossed with the young man who sat, lovelorn, on her other side and didn't help at all with Clayton whose randy mumblings, in the loud whispers of the hard of hearing, were becoming steadily louder and more reckless, much to the barely-disguised mirth of a widening audience of diners and waiters. Mercifully, Jenny seemed not to notice; perhaps she, too, was hard of hearing. Bertie, for her part, handled the smutty outflow with the consummate aplomb with which she had fielded Stella's unsubtle innuendoes at that first party. As dessert was being served, Clayton was staring rheumily at her breasts, rueing the fact that he wasn't fifty years younger and telling Bertie that she was a loser too, because, in his youth, his sexual prowess had been legendary. In fact, nothing less than Olympic.

'Sure,' spat the supposedly deaf Jenny. 'Once every four years!'

The table erupted. Jenny became instantly deaf again and began to rail quietly to me against Tom Hilliard, whom she referred to as Sow's Ear, for inviting Clayton to these affairs which always ended up in Clayton making a fool of himself. And her. Veronica (Silk Purse) was a darling, and much too good for that rascal husband of hers, minister or no minister . . .

Over dessert, which she hardly touched, Jenny told me an anecdote about the young Joss Murray, who'd been the main topic of conversation locally for the past day or so. She referred to him as Joseph and told me that his mother had been one of her best friends. 'He was about twenty and I remember that he had a big crush on the daughter of a neighbour of ours, even though he had met her on just one occasion, the previous year when he'd stayed with us. Well, Joseph asked her if he could take her to our local hunt ball but she had already accepted an invitation from another young man so she declined. I don't think she wanted to go with Joseph anyway – he wasn't the easiest of people to get along with – boastful, not a good mixer or talker and certainly not what you would call handsome. Not exactly ugly, mind you, but not handsome either – a bit nondescript, I suppose.

'Now, it may or not have been a coincidence, but the young man who was to be her escort was unaccountably set upon one night by some thugs and sustained a broken leg. The very next morning, however he had come to hear about it, Joseph telephoned to ask the girl – Joanna, her name was – to go with him, now that she was without an escort, but she told him that she had decided, under the circumstances, not to go at all. At the last moment, her sister and friends prevailed upon her to join their party, especially as she had had a new frock made and everything, and her young man, the one with the broken leg, nobly urged her to go. So she went.

'Joseph was there, squiring a cousin, and I'm told that when he saw that Joanna had gone to the ball after all, he was livid. When the soup was served, he said he wanted to complain to the kitchen about it, stood up, and began to head for the kitchen door, carrying the soup. On the way, he decided to say hello to Joanna but tripped just as he got there, and sent the hot soup all over her dress. Oxtail, it was, and the dress was white. She was lucky it didn't get on her face or arms, because it was scalding hot. If one of the men at the table hadn't grabbed Joseph by the elbow to steady him, they say that Joanna *would* have got it right in her face.

'I often wonder if that really was an accident. I try to think the best of it, that he just wanted to ruin her dress so that she couldn't dance with anyone else if she wasn't going to dance with him. But somehow, I don't know . . .'

'Surely there was nothing stopping him from asking her to dance? What makes you think it wasn't an accident?'

'Joseph carrying soup to the kitchen to complain? Ridiculous! He would have called a waiter and given the poor man hell. He believes in making staff earn their money. His tripping was no accident, believe me. I'm just wondering about how close the piping soup came to disfiguring Joanna's pretty face . . . The unforeseeable accident, I think, was when the other boy managed to grab Joseph's arm in time.'

I tried to pump her for more background on Murray. Was there, by any chance, some quiet family retreat – a low-roofed cottage on a hidden Connemara inlet perhaps? An eyrie perched high in the mountains of Kerry? A lodge in the woods of Wicklow? An old houseboat on some turgid backwater of the Shannon? A studio flat in Dublin's dockland? That sort of thing? But I got nowhere. All of a sudden, presumably alerted by the persistence and direction of my questions, she made the connection that I was *the* Frank Samson, *that* Frank Samson, at which point she stopped talking to me altogether, refusing to respond even to neutral comments about the delicious choice of puds on offer, and edged her chair closer to the diner on her other side, from which distant remove she directed sporadic evil looks in my direction.

I began to get restless – I was already looking at a two o'clock in the morning arrival in Dublin – and this looked like a party that was going to stay at table until the small hours. I finished coffee, declined a brandy or port and managed to distract Molly's attention from her besotted companion. I tapped my watch and my chest and made walking fingers at her. She nodded and rose from the table. I said my farewells to the guests nearest me, received an icy glare and a melodramatic snapping away of the head from Jenny, and made my way to my hosts. After several minutes of fulsome eulogy from Tom Hilliard, I managed to extricate my hand from his grip and left. When we got to the door, Bertie was already there.

'I'll walk you to your car, Frank,' she said.

'Well, sure, but it's probably turned cold out there.' I was aware of Molly looking from one of us to the other; then she shrugged, said her goodbyes and returned to her new love life.

'I think I'm blocking you in anyway.' Bertie jangled her keys.

She was. Though there was lots of space on the forecourt

– and, as nobody had yet left, presumably there had been when she'd arrived – she had backed the Merc tight up against my front bumper. We talked a while and I didn't feel good when she told me that she had never felt for anyone what she felt for me. She buried her face in my jacket and I knew she was crying but chose to pretend I didn't. I just waited for it to pass – there wasn't a lot I could say or do, I reckoned.

'I can't believe I'll never see you again.' She held my elbows and looked into my eyes.

'Never say never, Bertie. I'm sure we'll meet . . .'

'But if we do, it'll be by accident. Who am I going to take to dinner, now? Who can I try to impress when I buy myself a new outfit? Who can I talk to or even think of when I need a boost?'

'Well, you can still *think* of me . . . if you reckon that's a help.'

'It'll be because I've been thinking of you, dummy, that I'll need the boost.' She managed a wan smile.

I smiled back. 'I'll ring you,' I said, thinking instantly that I shouldn't have said it, though somehow not regretting it much that I had.

'If only you would.'

'I will. I promise.'

She sighed and squeezed my hand. 'Before you go, tell me again. How serious are you about Claire? I just find it impossible to believe that it can be better than what you and I have had over the last . . .'

'I know. I know. But I told you the other night, I'm one hundred per cent serious. It's not even something I've got any control over. At this stage, though I might have to soon enough, I couldn't even visualise a life that didn't include her. I'm sorry, Bertie.'

'It's not as if you're married,' she pointed out.

'We just haven't had time to do the ceremonial bit. Or much of an appetite for the paperwork and the fuss. But it's the same. De facto, if not actually de jure.'

She seemed about to argue, then changed her mind, said:

'The jammy bitch!' and put her arms quickly around my neck. I gave her a squeeze and released her, the signal for her to do the same. Then I kissed her cheek and unlocked the Land Rover.

'Move along there now, young lady,' I said in my PC Plod voice. 'You're causing an obstruction to traffic.'

I waited while she moved the Merc a few feet. Then she came back to me, and clung to me desperately for a moment. I placed my hands on her hips and gently eased her away from me, then wordlessly sat into the Land Rover.

As I rounded the curve in the driveway, I took a last look back at the tall, beautiful woman standing beneath the porchlight, a lissome silhouette with one arm half-raised in farewell, and I felt lousy. In an elated, flattered sort of way. I couldn't remember ever having been so lusted after before – by anyone. Except Avril Harrington. But that was in playschool so it didn't count.

The roads emptied after midnight and I made good time. By one o'clock, I was alone in a world of dark, featureless countryside, sleeping villages and unlit houses. Somewhere in County Kildare a row of low cottages across a mile of fields was all lit up – without another light to be seen anywhere, it looked like a train stranded in a dark wilderness.

Unsure of my reception and feeling guilty that I hadn't given the dinner party a miss and come straight home to go with Claire to Bernard and Sally's, I opened the garden gate and walked up the path to the front door. I let myself into the dim hall, lit only by the orange aura of street lights which seeped through the half circle of Georgian fanlight, and headed for the stairs.

I'd been relieved to find her car parked outside – the way things were between us, she might have taken it into her head not to come back to the flat at all. Passing the car, I'd laid a palm on the bonnet – warm, though not hot; at least she'd driven herself there and back. And she hadn't been very late home either. Finding myself checking up on her had made me feel even more of a louse.

The key slotted sweetly into the door of the flat – so far, so good; she hadn't changed the locks. I tiptoed to the bedroom door and pushed it tentatively open. The bedside light was on but Claire had fallen asleep, the book she'd been reading lying aslant beside her propped knees, its pages fanning out from the spine. Her reading glasses were askew on her nose and her head had turned away from the light, away from the door. Her nightdress had slid down along her arm, exposing her shoulder. The auburn hair was a tousled mass on the pillow and, as ever, I got a lump in my throat just looking at her.

'Claire?' I whispered. She stirred a little and wrinkled her nose like a rabbit, but she didn't wake.

Having made the effort, albeit tentatively, I retired to the kitchenette and plugged in the kettle, which, I noted, like the car engine, was still warm.

She came padding into the kitchen a few moments later, on bare feet.

'Hi!' I said. 'Sorry if I made a noise. I didn't want to wake you.' I tried to act normal, as if this was just another homecoming, a pointless effort since we didn't make a beeline for each other. Which we'd always done before. And so, tacitly and mutually, we recognised the new baseline of our altered relationship.

'How are you?' I asked, sparring exploratively.

'Fine.'

'Did you go to Bernard and Sally's?'

'Yes.'

'How was it?'

'Fine.'

'Good supper?'

'Fine.'

Three 'Fines' and a 'Yes' didn't sound too hopeful to me. I decided to get a bit more specific. 'Who was there?'

'The usual bunch. Who was at your party? Anyone I'd know?'

'Just T.F. Hilliard and his wife, who, by the way, are referred to, amongst their inner circle, as Sow's Ear and Silk Purse respectively . . .' I paused for the smile which this should have elicited, but it didn't come.

'And?'

'Molly, their daughter, girlfriend – amongst many – of the late Mosquito; Superintendent Gerard Downing; and Bertie Garrison . . .' That hit the spot. Claire didn't flinch or anything; there wasn't even the flicker of an eyelid, she just seemed to suspend breathing and her eyes on mine became a stare. I paused, thinking she wanted to say something, but she didn't and then I decided that my pause could be misinterpreted as guilt, so I said: 'You wouldn't have known anybody else, I think. Two or three politicos, party hacks.' More silence. 'Gino and Sylvia send their love.'

'Frank?'

'Yes?'

'Tell me the truth. Did you make love with Bertie Garrison?'

I looked long and hard at her. 'No. What gave you that idea?'

She returned my lengthy look time before answering. 'That evening, at the station, d'you remember?'

I nodded. 'Could I forget? What about it?'

'She looked at you as if she could have eaten you alive.'

'Can't say I noticed. You ought to have tipped me off!' I chanced a disarming grin which missed by a street, its purpose shrivelling and dying in the parched air between us.

'I still can't understand why you had to pretend that she was unattractive. Or why you pretended not to recognise her at the railway station . . .'

'That's not fair, Claire. I told you why I had played down her attractiveness and, as for the station, if you remember, I *did* recognise her and introduce you.'

'Yes, but there was a short time beforehand when your face looked panic-stricken, trapped. In view of what happened next, it can only have meant that you were gauging your chances of getting away with treating your recent date as a total stranger. I know you, Frank. I know you better than you know yourself.'

I decided to come clean with her. 'Claire. I'm going to tell you all about whatever relationship developed between Bertie Garrison and me, and how and why. It'll be the truth and I hope it never comes between us again.'

'We met the day I discovered Marc Glasser's body. As you already know, she wrote to me a few days later asking me to escort her to a dinner party because she was fed up having partners organised for her and she wanted to show some independence. It was a lousy party so we left early and sat in a caff for an hour or so during which she talked about her problems and I listened. You know me: Frank, The Universal Earhole. Everyone's father-confessor and amateur shrink. Then we went our separate ways. A few days later she asked me to go to dinner with her, on the grounds that she had felt so relaxed on our first meeting and it would do her even more good to have another evening out. I said I'd think about it because, as I'd told her straight out on our first 'date', I wasn't exactly footloose and fancy-free. She took my response to mean I'd accepted her invitation and planned accordingly and, as I was just providing a friendly ear for a nice but mentally screwed up woman, who badly needed a friendly ear, I saw no harm in it. Certainly not enough to make a fuss about it. So I let it go.'

'When was this second date supposed to be?'

'The Monday after the meeting at the station.'

'You mean the following evening? The very next *night*?'

'Put like that, it sounds really bad, but basically, yes.'

'And you never thought to mention it to me?'

'Oh, I did. A hundred times. D'you remember asking me what was wrong with me and me telling you I had a cold or 'flu or some such? Well, I hadn't. I was worried sick about keeping something from you for the first time ever. But I was afraid you wouldn't have understood, and I saw no reason to cause a fuss over what I regarded as nothing more than a therapy session.' I stopped to let Claire reply but, apart from a very dubious look and sniff, she said nothing. Reserving judgement. 'Anyway, that meeting never took place because at the time that I was supposed to be meeting her at a fancy restaurant in Limerick, I was, in fact, locked in a tiny larder, waiting to have my throat slit. It was Bertie's arrival that saved my life.' And I gave Claire the whole story. She was horrified and actually reached across the table and took my hand in both of hers. 'I'd have told you this, but you were in France and, when you rang this evening, somehow . . . it didn't seem to be the right time. Or atmosphere.

'Anyway, as I was saying, Bertie's unexpected arrival and the sudden shifting of alliances it caused, saved my life. When at last the cops allowed us to leave Northfield, we decided that, with Murray on the loose and in murderous mood, the prudent thing would be *not* to return to our respective homes. So we drove in the opposite direction and booked into a hotel.' I could feel Claire stiffen as I went on. 'While I was parking, Bertie booked a double room. At this point, she said she was in love with me and wanted to start a relationship. I kept telling her I was committed to you – like I had all along, but she, I suppose, reckoned that all was fair in love and war. In fact she said those very words.' I faltered a bit, stuck for the next bit.

'So that's the mousey widow's part.' Claire said, clipped. 'Now what's your excuse?'

'Pretty lame, or reasonable, depending on how you look at it. I, too, if you remember, was recently bereft. When you left on that train you wouldn't even look at me . . . For all I knew, that view of you as the train pulled out might have been my last ever. I was worried sick, lonely, and as down as I've ever been. I suppose I was vulnerable . . .'

'Well I'm flattered to see that your period of mourning lasted so long. Almost twenty-four hours!' Her eyes narrowed to warning slits. 'Are you trying to lay all this on me, Frank?'

'No. I'm just trying to explain my state of mind at the time . . .'

'So you thought we were history at this point, did you?'

'I thought it was a distinct possibility, yes. In fact, maybe that's still a possibility . . .' I hesitated to see if she wanted to reassure me that this was not the case, but my hopeful glance was reflected by a stony, hurt, bewildered stare. '. . . and on top of that I'd just been rescued . . .'

'By the little mousey old widow-woman . . .'

'Whether you like it or not, Claire, she did save my life. That whole Northfield business was totally disorientating. The point I'm trying to make is that I was anything but myself that night . . .'

'Oh! So it was somebody else altogether. I see.' She pulled her hands back to herself leaving mine lying pathetically in the middle of the table, like a dead bird.

I wanted to tell her to shut up and listen but I was hardly in a position to call the shots. 'You're not making this any easier, you know,' was all I said.

'Too right, I'm not.'

'Okay then, no more frills, but I swear what I've told you is true. So that was my state of mind. Her's was no better; she'd just found out that her only brother was in big trouble, had been involved in a murder, even though indirectly, and had been holding the country to ransom. So put those together. She fancied me; I found her attractive . . . So the stage was set for a night of grand passion. But it didn't happen.'

'D'you expect me to believe that?'

'I swear, Claire. I'll admit we kissed and cuddled a bit, but we never made love.'

'I'm going to bed.'

'No, Claire. Wait! We have to finish this now. I swear to you that we never made love. Oh the flesh was willing, alright, but the spirit couldn't get rid of you. I couldn't get you out of my head and I knew that if I was unfaithful to you, even just once, something basic in our relationship would have changed forever. The honesty and the trust

327

would have been gone for all time. You were like Banquo's ghost, materialising out of the background every time it seemed that I needed reminding. Even when I tried to fool myself by telling myself that it looked like it was all over between you and me anyway, I couldn't ... All I kept thinking was that, even if you had decided to break up, I'd still love you the same as ever, for a long long time to come, and it was too early to think of other women, even one as beautiful and willing as Bertie Garrison ...'

Claire was having trouble coming to terms with this. She stood up and looked at me.

'I swear, Claire. I did not make love with Bertie Garrison. It got close, but it didn't happen. As if that makes much difference.'

'I don't know, Frank. I don't know what to think.'

'Claire ...'

'Shh. Don't say another word. You've said enough.' She headed for the corridor, then turned in the doorway. 'Would you tell me if you ... had made love with her?'

I thought for a moment, then shook my head. 'Probably not. No. I wouldn't.'

She gave a little laugh of despair, then said to the wall: 'Great! Oh that's just *great*, isn't it! That's just fucking dinky!'

'Listen to me, Claire. If I had, I don't think I'd have the courage to tell you. In case you threw me out. I'd die if you did.' I stretched my hand out towards her, but she didn't come to me and I let it fall again.

'I've made up the bed in the spare room. I thought you'd need a good night's sleep. After all your exertions. I'm going to bed now. I'm very tired.' And she went into the bedroom and closed the door firmly and pointedly behind her.

I finished my coffee, washed the cups and went to the small back bedroom, where I tossed about for some time before eventually falling into a troubled sleep.

In the early hours, as the rectangle of the window was

328

turning pearl grey, Claire came into the room and wriggled in beside me. Then I held her and whispered to her and stroked her hair until she stopped crying and fell asleep.

26

Next day was a wary one, at least the morning part of it. There was no point in talking again about the topic that was filling both our heads, yet there was nothing else to talk about. Anything I could think of would have seemed in very bad taste, like frivolity at the bedside of the terminally ill. Claire could have brought it up if she'd wanted to, but not me. I'd had my chance and, as Claire had said, I'd already said enough. Maybe even too much. So we went about the flat making stiff little efforts at being normal, formal enquiries about mundane things, and smiling politely and nodding at each other when we met in the narrow hall. Like two strangers sharing a train carriage. At one point, meeting Claire coming into the kitchen as I was exiting it, I found myself saying: 'Ah! I was just going into the next room . . .' It was horrible.

By noon, I'd had enough. 'I'm off to the pub for lunch,' I told her hyperenthusiastically. 'I'm going to celebrate! And I'm officially inviting you.'

'What are you celebrating?'

'The fact that you haven't thrown me out.'

'Yet!' she scowled, but the corners of her mouth crinkled momentarily.

'C'mon.' I grabbed her hand and pulled her up from the armchair, sending the newspaper tumbling to the floor. Suddenly I was holding her to me, admittedly with the buffer of her arms between us, her palms flat on my lapels. 'May I kiss you?' I asked seriously. 'Please.'

She didn't reply. She just looked into my eyes for a few seconds, as if she was trying to work out her own feelings, then slid her hands up to my face and pulled my mouth down to hers. We made love where we fell, among scattered sheets of newspaper and hastily discarded clothing, on a kilim which was just a fraction too small and slid inopportunely about on the waxed floorboards. We made love with a wild and exhausting abandon, at times almost fighting one another, our eyes locked in some defiant contest which I didn't even begin to understand, until they squeezed shut in the runaway explosion of the final, agonising ecstasy.

For me, our lovemaking was the final proof that everything was better again, that we were back to normal, but for Claire, it seemed to be the trigger which released all the tears she hadn't shed last night, and wracking sobs shook her as we lay on the floor; I did my best to reassure her, as I had when she'd crept into my bed before dawn.

It was too late for a pub lunch, and anyway it was suddenly much nicer to be together at home, so we sat and had tea and Corn Flakes at the kitchenette counter. Seán Berry, the chief crime reporter on Claire's paper, rang to see if he could pop around to talk to me, so we removed the signs of our recent orgy, dressed, and prepared for his visit. Claire put on the percolator while I went to the corner shop and bought chocolate biscuits. I didn't know if they were what Seán liked, but they were my favourites.

I'd known Seán for almost as long as I'd known Claire. His long, spindly frame sprawled untidily in an armchair, limbs looking as though they'd been inexpertly folded away. Knobbly shoulders stuck up like a bat's, almost as far as his huge ears, and his thin face gazed immobile at me, only moving when he spoke or chewed one of my biscuits. Claire hovered about possessively – the rumour that her love life had gone down in flames had been nudging around her office since my call to Wally Webster, and she was stopping it dead in its tracks.

Seán had an encyclopaedic knowledge of the Dublin criminal scene, and, like Claire, had known Marc Glasser socially.

'What do you know, Seán, about a gang called the Brady Bunch?'

'Why?'

I told him my story, that the only mug-shot I had seen that looked even vaguely like my blond attacker was one of Kevin Brady, present address, Mountjoy Jail.

'They're a bunch from the south side. They were biggish, and growing, until Kevin got sent up, but they're just ticking over now. We're all expecting war when he comes out – some of the newer outfits have muscled in on his old turf, and he won't give it up that easily. The thing is, he left no real boss to look after things while he's in the 'Joy so now it's just a bunch of family and a few hangers on. There were over forty active soldiers in Kevin's heyday, but all they do now are odd little jobs.'

'Like giving me a hammering?'

Seán shrugged. 'Tell the law.'

'I did.'

'And?'

'And nothing. If I wanted a "little job" done, where would I be likely to find them?'

'Most nights you'll find a few of them scattered over about four different pubs, along with other freelance scumballs.' And he named off four pubs. 'That's where I'd start if I wanted to find a Brady man.'

'More heroics, Frank?' Claire asked with a resigned sigh. 'One of these days, you're going to get yourself killed.'

'You nearly did last week,' said Seán.

'Indeed he did, Seán. But he was rescued by a passing widow. Weren't you, honeybunch?' She tugged my earlobe, painfully. Stoic that I am, I kept on a fixed smile of homely pleasure for Sean's benefit.

I ignored the laden comment and pushed the rapidly

dwindling plate of biscuits over to Seán, who polished them off, washed them down with fresh coffee, then left. I thought Claire might want to take up arms again but she didn't. When she'd seen Seán to the top of the stairs, she decided that it was a beautiful day and that we should drive out to Howth Head and walk round the summit.

We were almost back to normal by the time we got back to the flat – I'd stopped being excessively polite, attentive, and over-considerate and Claire was giving me fewer and fewer speculative side glances, all of which I affected not to notice. That evening we took our postponed celebratory mood out to Dublin's newest, and supposedly best, Chinese restaurant. We left the waning daylight and entered the red dimness of the restaurant, and before our eyes had adjusted, I heard our names called – Claire's first, and mine, a very unenthusiastic second. I immediately recognised the deep virile bass of Paul Markham and managed to distinguish his excellent body uncoiling itself from a table slightly off to the right.

'Paul!' Claire squeaked in evident pleasure and submitted to a kiss on the cheek from the Adonis who was now visible in all his ghastly glory. But I spotted her little grimace as the lingering kiss continued to linger. Once, in our early days, Claire had described to me how Paul Markham's lips on her cheek always made her feel like she'd been attacked by a small, persistent and very self-opinionated sink plunger. 'It's that little *suck* that goes with it,' she had shuddered.

'Hey! It's been ages! Great to see you!' I watched as his eyes sparkled at hers and his smiling teeth dispelled the dimness for several feet around. 'Frank.' He at last extended his hand and I submitted to the vice-like squeeze, refusing to squeeze back, wanting nothing to do with such childish dominating tactics. Next thing I'd know, he'd have cleared the nearest table and we'd be arm-wrestling to the death. He and I had already been through the mental version of all that, last year and, against all the odds – his looks, his wealth, his sophistication, his ability to discuss Kafka, Camus and Spengler, his fascinating theories on subliminal meanings in Dahl, the aplomb with which he could dash off any Chopin prelude or Jerry Lee Lewis rocker and make an out-of-tune upright sound like a concert Steinway or a honkytonk – I'd won. Claire herself, no less, being the prize.

Needless to mention, Paul insisted that we join him, and Claire was off before I could get a word in edgewise.

Paul's beautiful but vapid date was called Tippi and was, she told me, in fashionable cockney, a moddzau.

'A what?' I asked. Claire and Paul were so engrossed in some discussion involving current affairs that they were letting Tippi and me get along with whatever trivia might amuse us.

'A moddzau . . .' She looked at a loss as to how to explain it, but only for a few minutes. 'You know? Swimsuits and . . . fings? For magazines?'

'Oh! A model?'

'Yeh. 'S woh ah said. A moddzau.'

We ordered and sipped drinks while we waited. Paul and Claire were still going strong, the conversation having swung now to historical precedents for whatever they'd been talking about before. Tippi and I got on as best we could, given the language barrier.

When the food came, there was an almost ceremonial Unsheathing Of The Chopsticks.

'Could I have a spoon please?' I asked the waiter. 'Oh. And a knife and fork.' He looked at me as though wondering how I'd managed to sneak in.

'Not into the old chopsticks, Frank?' Paul smiled across the table at me and delicately clicked the ends of his at me several times in a second. They were like extensions of his sensitive fingers.

'Awoh . . .' said Tippi, sorry for my affliction but not really up to expressing it.

'Naw,' I curled my lip. 'I reckon that if, after God knows how many centuries of much-vaunted Chinese civilisation, the best they could come up with as a means of transferring food from bowl to mouth was two small pieces of straight stick, then . . . it's a pretty poor look-out for their future.' I picked up the spoon which the waiter had just delivered and made paddling, ladling motions at him. 'See? Much more efficient and practical. Well, *bon appetit*, or, as they say in China, Tzu Ling *Wuk*.' I looked at Tippi. 'You're supposed to answer "Hoi *Wuk* Ling!" It's extremely bad manners not to.'

Tippi didn't hesitate. 'Hoi *Wuk* Ling!' she said, giving a great squeak on the 'Wuk' part and hopping a little in her chair. 'C'mon Paou,' she urged, 'let's 'ave some manners, then!' She kept at him until he said it, then decided he hadn't said it with enough brio and made him say it again until he got it right. He was fuming, but Tippi didn't notice a thing.

Claire, with barely suppressed laughter, said: 'And a hearty Hoi *Wuk* Ling! to you too!'

'*Now* we can eat,' I said and scooped up a great spoonful of the excellent fare.

Having reclaimed Claire's attention from Paul, I decided to have a go at Tippi, too, and by the time we'd finished our meal, I had her hooked. I reduced her to helpless giggles when I told her that the difference between a buffalo and a bison was that you couldn't wash your hands in a buffalo. Later, when the ambient muzak changed from Shanghai A Go-Go to saccharinely romantic piano, she told me that Paou had played the piano for her, 'just like Richard Clayderman, 'e was' and asked me if I too could play the piano?

I hesitated a thoughtful moment. 'I don't know,' I said. 'I never tried.' This sent her off into hysterics again. Claire laughed, Paul Markham pretended he couldn't hear above the busy clicking of his chopsticks, and I made a mental note to remember it for Bobby Young next year.

Over herbal tea and lychees, she asked me about her poodle whose nails were extra-long. I told her that fair was fair and that I'd give her an after hours, private demonstration of my professional skills, if she gave me a similar demonstration of hers, and I'd bring my own camera. She laughed uproariously again, thumped me on my biceps and told me I was '*awful*' and asked me if that was an example of my bedside manner. When I told her that the poodle's problem would probably resolve itself if she took it for walks on rough surfaces like pavements, and didn't confine it to a carpeted flat twenty-four hours a day, she looked at me like I'd discovered the cure for cancer just in time to save the life of a beloved granny . . .

Paul Markham hardly spoke to me when we parted outside the restaurant. Tippi hugged me and gave me big smackers on both cheeks and kept wagging little finger waves at me and smiling and wrinkling her cute nose fetchingly as Paul and Claire ponderously said Goodbye, See you around, and so forth.

On our way to the car, Claire hugged my arm and kept touching her head to my shoulder. She was laughing out loud. 'You're such a bullshitter, Samson! You and your rampant chatting-up. You should have seen Paul's face!'

'I did.'

'You could have stolen his woman from him. Just like that, I reckon. He's such a pompous ass behind it all. What the hell does Tippi care about his deep thoughts?'

'Do you want us to run back and swap? I'll take Tippi and you can have Paou?'

She tightened her grip on my arm. 'No thank you. You'll stay right here, with me. C'mon, let's get back to the flat. I didn't sleep much last night and I want to get to bed.'

'Tired?'

'No.'

When I turned in the wrong direction, away from the flat, Claire said: 'Hey! Where are we going?'

'On a pub-crawl. A *four*-pub-crawl.'

'To those pubs Seán told you about?'

'Yes. There'd be no point in going tomorrow morning; they'll be empty then. Okay?'

'Hoi *Wuk* Ling!'

On the third pub we got lucky. Just as well as it was almost closing time. I didn't spot my blond but I did find one of the other two, the one who had been talking to the blond that night as I approached, not the one who'd been skulking in the doorway with the length of timber. Though I hadn't been able to give a very good description of him to the cops – because the blond was demanding most of my attention – I recognised him instantly. He looked like a slightly decrepit Phil Collins and was standing with a group at the end of the bar, a half-empty pint glass in his hand. He looked towards Claire, as did the whole bar, and stared at her long enough for me to get my back turned before they began to check up on what kind of lucky guy had scored the gorgeous chick. I edged Claire towards a small table and sat with my back to the bar. A waiter came and we gave him an order.

'When you get a chance,' I whispered to Claire, 'take a look at those guys at the end, there.' I bobbed my head in their direction. 'There's one guy, five-eight or nine, balding, wearing a denim shirt with a white vest in the gap of the collar, and a black waistcoat, open. He's holding a pint of Guinness.'

Claire looked over her shoulder after a minute or so and turned back. 'The one who's a ringer for Phil Collins?'

'That's the one. He was one of the three who attacked me.'

'What are you going to do about it, Frank? There's about ten of them and he looks to be the only gentleman amongst them.' She looked at me, worried.

'Don't worry, love. I can handle them all with one hand tied behind me back,' I said, but I was smiling so that she'd know that I was joking. 'We'll finish our drinks and get out of here. In the meantime, do you think you could draw a quick likeness of him? Seán might be able to put a name to the face.'

Claire had a gift for making quick sketches, especially of faces. She'd taken a course to hone her raw talent and had done a stint in her early days on the paper as the person who went with the court reporter to do the work that cameras were barred from doing. In a matter of minutes, peeping cautiously over my shoulder, she had produced a very passable likeness, but, being a perfectionist, she insisted on going to the Ladies, so she could get a closer look for the finer details. On her return, she added the final touches. As far as I could see, the result was as good as a photograph.

Next morning, Seán was able to name him immediately. 'Dinny Hayes,' he said. 'And he is a member of the Brady Bunch.' He pushed the paper back towards me then retrieved it. 'Let me see that again . . . Jeez, I never noticed it before, but he's the spittin' image of Paul Simon.'

'Paul *Simon?* You mean Phil Collins, surely.'

'Naw! Paul Simon,' he said and pushed the paper back.

As I was walking out I could hear him whistling 'Me and Julio Down by the Schoolyard.'

27

I hung about the flat, waiting for the summons to the line-up. It had gone midday before the phone rang. A cop with a sense of humour, looking for me.

'Speaking.'

Bad news. Hayes had an unbreakable alibi and an uncooperative lawyer. 'About twelve witnesses all put him at a party in Dublin at the exact time you report being attacked. Ten of them didn't have the brains to even *pretend* to think back. You know . . . "Where were you on the night of so and so?" "Oh I was at a party which Dinny Hayes was at from at least nine p.m. to three a.m." I asked a few of them "Where were you *last* night, and they hadn't a clue, couldn't remember that far back. A couple said they were at a party which Dinny Hayes was at from at least nine p.m. to three a.m." just in case they'd got the dates wrong . . . Sometimes you have to admire them. But that's it. According to them Hayes was there from nine p.m. to three a.m. on the night you were attacked, and never left. So there . . .'

'They're all liars.'

'Oh, undoubtedly! But that's as much as we can do. Sorry.'

'Well, thanks anyway.'

I rang Downing next. Nobody had told him anything about Hayes – obviously the assault on me, and the missing Murray were in two separate files. He agreed that Hayes might be a lead to the fugitive – if Murray had hired him and the others once, then maybe he'd hired them again, this time to hide him. He took down details and said he'd get back to me.

Claire was at the office so I decided I'd have yesterday's postponed pub lunch – at Seán Berry's fourth pub, the one we'd missed out on last night. I located it, parked the Land Rover a discreet distance away, and walked back.

I found my blond almost as soon as I entered. I glanced in the mirror behind the bar and there he was, grinning over my shoulder at me, pleased as punch with himself. I stared at him for a few moments then, sliding off my stool, went for a closer look at the large framed photograph on the wall. It was him alright. Beaming smugly to camera, he cradled a fancy trophy in one hand and held a set of darts in the other. The caption, in fancy type, read:

Scott (The Blond Bombshell) Brady.
Southern League Interpub Champion 1994.
Dessie McCarthy Perpetual Trophy.

Even through the depersonifying photograph, I could see he was posing, role-playing, and I wondered who he was imagining himself to be this time. Maybe Errol Flynn or Kevin Costner as Robin Hood.

'Is old Scotty still getting one-eighties every second throw?' I asked the young barman when he brought my soup and sandwiches. He looked perplexed so I indicated the picture.

He shrugged: 'I'm new, me. On me third day,' and went back to stocking his shelves.

I rang Downing from the payphone beside the door to the GENTS and told him I'd found the leader of my attackers.

There was a delay before he demanded, in a tight voice: 'And just *how* did you do that?'

'Happened to see his photograph on a pub wall – he's a champion darts player.'

'I see.' More disapproving silence.

'D'you want his name?'

'That *would* be helpful . . .'

'Scott Brady. They call him The Blond Bombshell. He's a member of the Brady gang.'

'Oh! I suppose it mentioned *that* on the photograph, too, did it?' he said sarcastically.

I drew several deep breaths, but I was still angry when I answered. 'Listen! I'm trying to find the guys who beat me up, and the only reason I have to do it myself is because you people aren't even vaguely interested. So if that's how you feel, then fine! I'll continue on my own-i-o. I only rang in case you might be interested in tailing him to see where he goes. I thought you were of the opinion that he might be a lead . . .'

'Yeah. You're right. I'm sorry. I'm under a fair bit of pressure right now.'

'Okay. Just as long as you understand that this isn't some kind of glory trip for me. Now, what do you want me to do about . . .' I dropped my voice and turned my face to the wall as a customer passed by and pushed open the door, liberating a noisome waft of ammonia and urine into the pub. 'What'll I do about the darts man?'

'Nothing. Just go home and leave it to us. What's the pub?'

I told him. He apologised again, then thanked me for my help.

'Hey! Forget it. But can I ask you one favour? Do you mind if I keep in touch, just to see what's going on, like?'

'Sure. I think you've earned that much.'

That's what I felt, too.

I managed to get hold of Downing about noon next day and half-expected to get a very curt reception for my persistence – I'd been phoning every twenty minutes or so since nine. Instead he invited me to share a sandwich in an hour's time at a pub near his office. I walked the mile or so and found him sitting in a corner doing a crossword. He moved his coat off the chair he'd been keeping for me, invited me to sit, and summoned a waiter.

'So!' I said after we'd been through the inevitable meteorological preliminaries, 'any news?'

'A bit,' he conceded after a silence. I said nothing. He was either going to tell me or not. 'I called on a pretty unsavoury contact of mine last night and he told me that Brady has moved out of his mother's house, where he has lived in pampered luxury for years. It seems he took this unprecedented decision the very next day after Murray went missing.'

'Some coincidence, hey?' I said, thinking that if only the cops had paid a little more heed to my assault, they'd have already been aware of Brady's moves and not have had to wait for a stoolie to tell them, five days late. 'Where has he moved to?'

'My contact didn't know that. He's going to try to find out and I've put men on it, priority, so, one way or another, we ought to know pretty soon. If we're lucky, Murray just might be holing up there, too. Another interesting tidbit he had was that Brady has just, in the last couple of days got himself an "honest" job as a groundsman. In the RDS, no less.'

'The RDS!' I whistled. 'During Horse Show Week! Now, *there's* a worthy candidate for the EIA.'

The Royal Dublin Society's grounds provide an ideal venue for many of the biggest events in Dublin's calendar, from trade fairs to industrial exhibitions, from classical concerts, ballet and opera to mega-gigs by mega-stars and for international sporting fixtures like the Aga Khan's Nations Cup Trophy, the main event during Horse Show Week. The reason that *that* was significant in this instance was that the star of the Irish team, a grey gelding called West Kong Wizard, was owned by none other than Madeline Fingal-Symms, though for some reason, probably to do with tax, the horse was held in the name of one of her husband's companies, West Kong plc.

'You mean The Wizard?' he asked. 'I agree, and that's

344

why he's under guard every minute of every day. He's at the home place and when he moves to the RDS, we'll have men in the horsebox with him, men in his stall, men outside his stall, men on the door to the stalls, men on all the entrance gates, scrutinising everyone coming through, men all over the grounds, men watching the walls to make sure nobody scales them. And finally, if we haven't located Murray by the time the Aga Khan starts, then we'll pull in Brady, lean heavily on him, and see what he knows of Murray or his plans.' He took a fastidious nibble out of his sandwich and looked to me for my comment.

'Why not arrest him now? Surely the more time you have to "lean" on him, the better?'

Downing chewed methodically, then swallowed and dabbed his lips. 'If I had my way, I wouldn't go near Brady at all.'

'Why not?'

'Because if Murray gets to hear of it, he'll know we're getting close, and might just decide to cut his losses and leg it. And then we'll have lost him.' He inspected the inside of the sandwich, then reached for the ketchup. 'However, my orders are that keeping EIA at bay is the top priority, far more important than bringing a murderer to justice, so that's what I must do.'

'Surely they go together? Find Murray and you'll find the EIA, too.'

'Not necessarily. The current thinking is that, when Murray sees that there isn't a hope in hell of him getting within a mile of The Wizard, he'll deputise Brady to act for him. If that is so then it follows that if we don't pick Brady up, we'll be taking an unacceptable risk that he just might pull it off, and we'd have EIA chewing its way through the entire bloodstock industry. I'm going to try to get them to agree to hold off just a little longer before arresting Brady. We'll watch him like a hawk and see if he does anything which might give us a clue as to where Murray is.'

'You really want Murray, don't you? No matter what.'

'Well? Don't you?'

'I want all five of the bastards – Murray, Brady, Hayes, the other guy *and* the EIA.'

He smiled at me. 'You know? You're right. And we'll get them.'

I'd been wondering about his change of heart, why he was now keeping me so assiduously updated; eventually I asked him.

He shrugged. 'I've got no end of police doctors I can call on, but you're the nearest I have to a police vet.'

Back at the flat, I suddenly remembered my promise to Bertie and, after a brief inner tussle, stretched guiltily for the phone. I didn't even have to look up her number.

She was glad I'd rung, but sad I'd gone. I told her that Claire was in great form, but only because she asked. It wasn't the answer she'd hoped for, she said. I told her I respected her greatly for her candour, then changed the subject by asking about her family. Pinky had been let out on bail but was now back in jail because he'd been unable, even once, to meet the ten o'clock sign-in deadline at his local police station; their (still-hysterical) mother was phoning all over the country to the great and the good, trying to have the time shifted to three in the afternoon on medical grounds, but had, so far, got nowhere; Molly Hilliard, she hadn't seen since the night of the dinner. Switching the subject back again, Bertie asked me if I'd be down the south-west on another locum soon and I said no, I wouldn't. Then she asked me *where* I was going next, and suggested that perhaps she could take a drive and visit me and I told her that would not be a good idea. I said I'd ring her again, but that it was going to screw up my life completely if we started to meet. She said that when I left it was like being widowed all over again, only this time, worse. I told her that she was on the rebound and that she should be very wary of getting serious about the first bloke she went out with. We argued that a bit and then, with me promising to ring her again, and not to rule out, for all time, a future meeting – she couldn't bear the thought of that right now, she said – hung up. I sat and stared at the phone and felt guilty as hell. Perhaps, though I had spent the whole time trying to put her off, I oughtn't to have spoken to her at all. It bothered me so much all afternoon that, come evening, I had developed an irrational fear that some perverse death-wish was going to make me address Claire as 'Bertie' before the night was out, with unimaginable consequences. When Claire arrived home, I became so convinced that the mother of Freudian slips was but a sentence away, that I started calling her gooey pet names – sugar-puff, sweetness, lambkins, and the like. She looked at me oddly once or twice but made no comment. Later, when I felt myself to be truly on the verge of disaster, I began to call her *real* names like Prunella, Phoebe, Beryl, Monserrat, Ngaio, or Assumpta, affecting a funny Goon-show type voice each time. I suppose I thought that, if the dreaded B-word did slip out, I'd already be halfway to a semi-plausible explanation. She took it as part of a game and joined in, calling me different names, too. And so the evening passed, almost unbelievably, without catastrophe.

'Goodnight, sweet Verbena,' I murmured as we began to fall asleep.

'*Oíche mhaith*, Festus,' she whispered back, then smiled without opening her eyes.

I lay there with her head resting on my shoulder, and waited for the guilt to come bursting up through the calm surface of my drowsiness like a Polaris missile.

We shuffled towards the turnstiles, borne slowly along in a stream of people which seemed to comprise half the population of Ireland. We paid our money and, having been peered at suspiciously by two gardai, clicked through into the hallowed grounds of the RDS. A few paces ahead, a man who bore the vaguest resemblance to Murray (similar build and hair-colour) had been taken aside and was being asked for some ID, a possibly tricky one as nobody in Ireland carries ID. His wife was giving the gardai stick, while their three children looked on in puzzlement.

347

The paths were thronged with people in bright summer clothes dawdling along in the late summer sun, relishing the atmosphere and the spectacle which made the Horse Show one of the sporting and social highlights of the year. In railed-off or hedged-in practice paddocks, horses were being put through their paces, and we stopped to watch a group of ladies riding sidesaddle, bobbing gracefully around in a canter, in long dresses and headgear which had been fashionable in days when one either walked, took a hansom, or rode. A few paddocks along, a lone, graceful horsewoman practised dressage, as near one with her beautifully-groomed mount as it was possible to be without being a centaur. We moved on, in no hurry, stopping wherever took our fancy. There seemed to be hundreds of groundsmen, all in yellow overalls with RDS stencilled on the backs. I kept a sharp look out for Brady. When people began to head for the jumping enclosure, Claire and I followed – on a fine afternoon, the stands would soon fill for the highlight of the week, the Nations Cup Competition for the Aga Khan Trophy. We found good seats and settled in. Out on the bright, springy turf, a visiting troop of Mounties began an exhibition of perfectly synchronised horsemanship. Up at the end of the arena, the band struck up what the bandmaster proudly announced as a 'Rose Marie Medley.'

'Well, fancy that!' Claire drawled, tendering a bag of crisps. 'Here. Put out your hand . . .'

'"When I'm calling you–oo–oo–oo–oo–oo–oo . . ."' I sang with the band, my eyes wandering off towards yet another yellow overalls I had registered at the far end of the arena.

'I didn't know you were into Rose Marie.'

'My mother is one of Nelson Eddy's greatest-living fans. I was weaned on dawn to dusk Nelson Eddy. Many's the night I fell asleep with Nelson Eddy in my ears.'

'Look at them! They look like there's a rod running through them, like a kebab.' Down on the greensward, the kebab split in two and described a perfect figure of 8 at a slow trot, then began some very intricate in-and-out weaving manoeuvre which suddenly became two concentric circles rotating in opposite directions. The crowd loved it and burst into enthusiastic applause as the medley segued into 'Here Come The Mounties'. Another ten minutes of complicated set-dancing on horseback, and the chief Nelson Eddy raised his arm and led them all off in two straight lines, all looking very stern, square-chinned, and unyielding. The crowd sang at the top of its collective voice, telling Rose Marie it loved her, was always dreaming of her, and so on, raucously, until the high note at the end. I sang too, picking out yellow overalls as I did, studying any that looked even vaguely like the right build for Brady. I was relieved to see that there were almost as many blue uniforms as there were yellow ones. In purposeful pairs, the police patrolled the paths and paddocks.

Uniformed fence builders had begun to amass on the sidelines towards the end of the Mounties' display and, as soon as the last pair of rumps passed through the exit, they surged onto the arena, spreading out like a stain towards the jumps. Judges and assorted officials, all topped by bowler hats, moved between the jumps, checking heights, spreads, the stability of top poles or blocks, and gathering in little groups to discuss and point at things. Some riders appeared and walked the course with their *chefs d'équipe* and they all spent extra time at a treble at the top end which, from where I sat, didn't look particularly difficult, but from their point of view, clearly deserved the number thirteen which was on a little rigid flag beside it. This busy preamble to the main event was fascinating in itself, in the same way that the sound of an orchestra tuning up has a beauty and excitement all of its own.

The band, which was now working its way through South Pacific, stopped abruptly in the middle of Bali Hai, and the opening drum roll of the national anthem brought work in the arena to a halt, and the crowd to its feet. The president and her party had arrived. The show was on its way. With the end of '*Amhrán na bhFiann*' the few remaining seats quickly filled and, moments later, from the pocket opposite us, the first horse, with a Brazilian army capitano astride, entered the arena. The crowd got ready to be entertained.

The rider settled the horse with a short canter around in the bottom half of the field, then approached the president's box and turned to face it; rider and animal came to attention, the slim young officer snapped a smart salute, and they were off, first to go. A few minutes later they were headed back into the pocket after an impeccable round – except for the middle section of the treble, the obviously much-feared number thirteen. The crowd which had groaned when the striped pole fell, showed its appreciation with polite applause. The next rider, a Swiss girl, who had been cantering and settling her mount at the end of the arena while the Brazilian was still jumping, now set off, but she knocked both the second and third sections of thirteen for eight faults and again got a good round of applause as she went disgruntledly off, patting her horse's neck. I was doing my best to relax but I kept feeling that I'd prefer to be prowling the grounds looking for Scott Brady. Downing was probably right; very likely, Brady had been appointed Murray's hit man. He himself could never have got past all that security at the entrance. Brady had to be the one with the EIA, unless Murray had called the whole thing off and decided to sneak meekly away. Somehow I didn't see that happening – there was nothing meek about Murray.

As the day wore on, I began to notice that the applause of the crowd (except in the case of clear rounds) was in inverse proportion to success on the field – unlucky four-faulters were given polite applause whereas one hapless young Frenchwoman who flattened up to half the course almost got a standing ovation and turned, for some reason beaming widely, into the pocket, followed by good-natured cries of '*Encore! Encore!*' Needless to say, the only fence she *hadn't* had trouble with was number thirteen; she'd cleared it as if it was a mere practice jump for Connemara ponies, and then, five seconds later, put all four hooves into the water jump, the only competitor, so far, to even ripple its mirrored surface. While they were rebuilding the course in the wake of Hurricane Marie-Alice Adès – everyone, including me, had dived for their programmes to check the hapless one's name – I took the opportunity to go and stretch my legs.

On my way back up to the stand, I noticed, from the height of my vantage point, a man in yellow overalls rounding a corner of a long shed in one of the more remote areas of the grounds, some distance off. He checked and doubled back a few paces when he saw two gardaí thirty or forty yards in front of him. He stood, back to the wall, for a moment, then cautiously edged forward to the corner again. A quick look showed the gardaí still in view so he withdrew his head and waited another few seconds. He was far away and wrapped in shade, so I couldn't see him clearly, but there was nothing about him which precluded him from being Scott Brady. Another peep, and he set off back along the way he'd come, glancing constantly over his shoulder.

I raced back down the stairs and headed towards the two cops, but, when I got there, they were nowhere to be seen. Almost without thinking, I reversed direction and sprinted to where I'd last seen the furtive groundsman. When I came to the end of the long shed, I had to guess which way to go. Presuming he'd continue the journey which had been cut off by the blue uniforms, I headed in that general direction, and, within a minute, had him in view. Slowed by having to check around every corner, he hadn't travelled far. I followed discreetly, acting the same aimless way as most of the small scattering of people who were roaming in this remote area of the grounds. His stop-start progress meant that I inevitably gained on him. A loud cheer went up from the jumping area, another clear round, or a disastrous one. Brady glanced back nervously several times but seemed satisfied that he was not being followed. I kept my distance, waiting for him to get near a couple of gardaí before I showed myself; I reckoned I should have some help close at hand before I started any physical stuff, just in case I screwed up. Again. Strictly speaking, I supposed, I should leave it to the cops altogether – they were the experts – but I wanted a crack at him, too. I owed the bastard.

My quarry made his wary way towards the busier areas, becoming more cautious as the crowds got bigger. At one point, spotting a pair of blue uniforms up ahead, he bent down behind a piece of farm machinery, ostensibly to check it, but probably just biding his time to see if there were any more about. When I saw the police stroll away into the crowd, I decided that this was as good a time as any, so I kept walking until I was almost abreast of the stooping figure. I thought of shouting for the gardaí and then pouncing on him, then decided to do it the other way round. Giving him as much fair play as he had shown me, I stepped silently up behind him and said: 'Hey, Scotty!' As he slewed around towards me, eyes widening in alarm, trying to rise, I kicked him hard in the kidney, sending him back down with a great grunt. He tried to rise again, so I hit him again, this time with a closed-fisted rabbit punch just behind his right ear. He went down, poleaxed. Reckoning I'd had enough revenge, I stood over him and shouted. 'Police! *Police!*'

The message flashed along until the two policemen saw me gesturing, and began to run towards me. No doubt in groggy response to the electrifying words, 'Police! *Police!*', Scott tried once again to get up, but I kicked him hard in the belly, and he turned over onto his side, making retching noises and gasping for air. I searched his pockets while the gardaí were trying to figure out who I was and what I was doing. His pockets were empty, at least of an EIA vial, or anything remotely like it.

'Where is it, you bastard?' I shouted. 'Where's the EIA?'

'Where's *what?*' asked one of the cops.

'And who are you?' asked the other.

'And who's he?' asked the first one again.

I asked them to get Downing here as soon as possible, that I wanted Brady arrested for assault.

Further questioning about the EIA got me nowhere. Scott wanted a lawyer.

'What's your address, Scott?'

'Fuck off. You want to ask me out on a date? You one of those?'

'I already had a date with you – in Limerick, remember? And it didn't work out. Where have you been living since you left your mother's house last week?'

'With a chick.'

'What chick? Where?'

'None of your fucking business.'

'Where's Joss Murray?' The two cops looked at each other when they heard this. This was heavy stuff.

'Who?' asked Scott, the picture of innocence.

'Joss Murray, the trainer who paid you to beat me up.'

'I never saw you before in my life.'

'Heh, heh! Very smart. What about Murray? Where is he?'

'Never even heard of him. What does he train? Boxers? Footballers?'

'What's this EIA, then?' asked one of the cops.

'The *CIA?*' Scott slipped into tough-guy, slick-talking James Cagney mode. 'Ain't it bad enough having the fucking *CID* around without callin' the CIA?' The show must go on. Like the cop had said of Hayes's preprogrammed witnesses, you just had to admire him.

'Smartass!' I hissed.

'Dickhead!' he snapped.

I was going to give him one last kick, in the head, but I reckoned that that might get *me* into chokey so I just gave him a withering look and turned away. There were six cops there by now and, while we waited for Downing, I told them what was going on. From his seat on the kerb, Scott scoffed theatrically at each revelation.

They took Scott Brady away. They had to drag him the first few steps as he cursed me and them, demanding to know why he was being treated like a common criminal, protesting his innocence, and insisting that his rights as an honest citizen be respected. If he lost his job because of this, he warned, he'd be looking for hundreds of thousands in damages – false arrest, defamation of character, loss of earnings . . . His protests began to fade as they hustled him towards the nearest exit. Downing watched him go. 'Don't worry. I'll get him to talk. There's loads of stuff I can throw at him and most of it he's probably guilty of anyway. He'll talk.'

'D'you think you'll get him to finger Murray? Honour among thieves and all that?'

'You don't believe that rubbish! It'll be strictly cash between them, and Murray doesn't have much of that right now, does he?'

'What about the EIA, then? He didn't have it on him.'

'We'll get that too, don't you worry! He probably has it hidden somewhere here in the RDS, just waiting his moment . . .' And he went off, almost rubbing his hands together.

I agreed with him. Until he was out of sight, that is. Then I began to think that if I was the one intending to inoculate West Kong Wizard with EIA, I wouldn't be lurking about behind sheds with, at most, thirty minutes to go before my quarry was due in the arena. I'd be in position by now, EIA at the ready, not miles away from the arena or the stabling area. Thoughtfully, I headed back up to the stand to join Claire, who asked me where I'd been and informed me that I was missing it all, then, without waiting for reply or comment, turned her attention back to the action.

I tried to focus on the jumping but it was useless; my mind wasn't on it. If what Downing said about the impenetrable security surrounding West Kong Wizard was true – and I had no reason to believe that it wasn't – then, barring one of the guards being bent, there was no way that anyone could get to the horse in the RDS. The only time West Kong Wizard would be alone and exposed would be when he was jumping in the arena, and he'd be well out of reach there. Neither a dart gun nor a blowpipe, nor for that matter an ordinary pub dart tipped with the virus, would be a practical option; in the first place, the target would be moving fast and, in the second, it would be impossible to make the attempt without being seen by a huge audience, and probably captured on TV as well.

However, it was hard to see how the horse could be got to at any other time because, as soon as the jumping was over, he'd be off back into the pocket across from us, back into the charge of his minders, off to his stall, and so safely out of reach again. And maybe for good – unless a tie forced a jump-off against the clock, none of the horses would appear again, except as part of the final pageant parade. So I figured it was almost inevitable, if an attempt was to be made, that it would have to be made between his leaving his stall and getting back to it. And, presuming that his vigilant guards accompanied him to and from the entrance to the arena, then . . .

The realisation slowly dawned on me that, in view of the fact that Brady had been neither equipped with the EIA nor in a position where he could deliver it, there was very likely another hit man in the grounds, waiting, watching, ready to strike as soon as his chosen moment came.

28

The obvious suspects were Hayes and my third, as yet unidentified, attacker. I narrowed my eyes and looked speculatively across at the chaos in the pocket. The place was thronged with people – rushing busily about, making final checks and adjustments to bridles, stirrups and girths, giving last minute advice to riders; it was busier than a beehive. Slight, dark, excitable Latins milled around amongst tall, fair, stolid Teutons and I could just imagine the Babel of tongues. Gradually I began to recognise people, especially the ones who were performing specific regular functions, like the gateman, a lanky youth in a white coat. There was an older man in a bowler, who wrote things on a clipboard every time a horse came back in. There was another man, also with a clipboard, who talked briefly to each rider as he or she dismounted – it seemed he asked a question to which the answer was 'no', because invariably the riders shook their heads in response, at which point he would nod his head and make a tick on his form. There was a man making videos of the return of each horse. At various times, the yellowish overalls of ground staff members would appear, busily trying to keep the pocket tidy and clean, but none that I saw looked anything like either of the remaining suspects. At one point I actually saw someone I knew – Will Johnson, a vet from Bray, just outside Dublin. I'd worked for Will in the past, in fact during this very week; he was one of a panel of vets who did duty at the

Horse Show, year after year. Another horse came back in and was immediately fussed over by its attendants.

With the competition nearing its climax, attention was focusing on the ring. Normal duties seemed to have been suspended and, all round the arena, I could see officials drifting towards the sidelines; with Brady safely out of the way, the few policemen who were still in evidence sauntered along or even stopped patrolling altogether, their watchful eyes drawn to the ring; groundsmen leaned on their brushes and brooms; vendors stopped vending because no one was buying. Across in the pocket, there were now even more people about – as attendants got their charges tucked away, they came back to watch the final action – but again, I saw nobody even vaguely resembling either of my two remaining assailants. I began to think that maybe we'd got it wrong after all, that there wasn't going to be an attack today, at least not here.

A vague uneasiness disturbed me, a feeling that maybe we had indeed got it wrong, only in another direction. With a cold shudder, I suddenly realised just how wrong. Downing's assumption sounded logical: if Murray was after West Kong Wizard, then today had to be D-day. Today, he'd creep out of his hideout and try to get within striking distance of his quarry. But what if this assumption was wrong? Then mightn't the strategy he had devised on the basis of it also be wrong? What if Murray had been hiding in the RDS since he'd vanished? Or even since only yesterday, when there'd been no extra security? When Downing hadn't known about Brady's timely move or most fortuitous new job? There were hundreds of buildings, outbuildings, sheds, stables, in the grounds. If Murray stayed quietly out of sight in any of those, he'd never be spotted, and with Brady coming in daily to supply him, he could hole up for months. I stopped looking for Hayes and his mate and began trying to superimpose the figure of Murray himself on the people moving about in the pocket across the arena from me.

People came and went, all looking very busy, but there

were about twenty who seemed to stay in the pocket; of these, only three could possibly be Murray. Some half-dozen were women, another few were far too short, some too tall, others too skinny or too plump. One of the three possibles, the most likely one, was dressed in the clothes of a competitor, and seemed to be known by everyone, so I discounted him. That left two – if I was right. One was the man who asked each competitor the question to which the answer was invariably 'no' and the other was the arty type with the video camera. He had long greying hair, a pair of round, steel-framed glasses, and a Fu Manchu moustache. I borrowed binoculars from the man sitting next to me and studied the faces of my suspects. Either could be Murray with wig, make-up, hair dye and cheek-padding. I recalled Jamey Mulligan's remark about Murray being a leading member of the Drama Society and wondered how good he'd been at make up. Probably, I thought, he'd been known to one and all as The Man Of A Thousand Faces.

I studied their actions. The man with the clipboard seemed to have an almost pointless task, and, when he'd asked his question and jotted down the 'no' answer, he'd lose all interest and lean against the wall until the next rider came in. The man with the video camera didn't have a whole lot to do either: his sole function seemed to be to record for posterity the return of each competitor through the gate, until the horse drew level with him, at which point he would lower the camera, give the horse a slap on the rump and wander off into a corner where, the picture of boredom, he would await the return of the next warrior. His handheld camera looked just like any I had seen wielded by hundreds of amateur video-makers, and I wondered briefly if a pro shouldn't be using something more sophisticated. Apart from these observations there seemed to be little to notice about the two men: they looked equally innocent or suspicious, depending on how you looked at it – both got right beside the horses; either could strike with a contaminated needle and be gone before anyone realised what was going on. The one with the camera actually made contact with each horse but then so did half a dozen others; the man on the gate, gaunt, pimply and not a day over twenty, did it; so did the horse's pit-crew, several times, as they followed their charge on into the inner regions. As I watched, my suspicions slowly ebbing, I saw the man with the video camera start suddenly, turn his head aside, and pull from his pocket a handkerchief which he put to his face as if to blow his nose; however, instead of sneezing or blowing, he just held it there as if he was trying to avoid a bad smell. A moment later two uniformed gardai appeared, took one officious turn about the area, then, without glancing to left or right, left. With handkerchief to face, the video man watched their departure, then, very slowly, as if he was afraid they'd return, he removed the handkerchief.

'How soon before The Wizard goes?' I asked the man whose binoculars I'd borrowed.

'About ten or twelve minutes? Depends on how many fences have to be rebuilt . . .'

I touched Claire's arm, told her I reckoned the video man was Murray, that I had to go and find a cop, and left before she had time to assimilate this, or question me about it. 'Keep an eye on him, will you,' I called as I took off down the steps in search of Downing.

When you need a cop, you can't find one. Perhaps with Brady arrested, they'd all gone suddenly off duty. Not one did I see on my brief tour, so, trusting that the pair who had scared the video man would still be in the pocket, I headed straight there. It took me the best part of five minutes just to find an entrance, and when I did, it was locked. Security. Knowing that the gateman would probably have strict instructions to keep people out, I prepared a plausible tale as I pounded loudly on the stout door.

A head appeared. 'Yes?'

'I need to give a message to Mr Johnson, Will Johnson, the vet. They told me I'd find him here, in the pocket.'

'Who told you?'

'The people at the vet station. It's urgent.'

'Can I see your pass?'

'Pass? They didn't mention anything about a pass.'

'Sorry, pal,' he shook his head. 'No pass, no in. Rules.'

'But it's urgent!'

He just looked at me and shook his head again.

'Look,' I said, pressing a palm against the closing door, 'I haven't time to go back for a pass. Can you give him a message?'

'I'm not supposed to leave here.'

'Just tell him I need to see him urgently at the gate. Tell him it's very urgent. Please!'

He looked over my shoulder as if there might be a queue forming which would tie him up for hours, then, seeing that there wasn't, said: 'Okay. I'll tell him. Who are you?'

'Frank Samson. Another vet,' I added, in case Will might have forgotten me.

'Okay. Wait here.' And he closed the door in my face. I stared at the blank timber and wondered why I hadn't just asked him to fetch the police, but that would have been too simple, and anyway, by the time I'd convinced them . . . An outbreak of clapping from the stands signalled the end of another round. I wondered if the doorman had bothered going to look for Will at all. Surely it couldn't be taking *this* long.

I hammered again, but there was no response. Perhaps it was a good sign – maybe the doorman *was* away looking for Will. Or maybe the bastard was just ignoring me, hoping I'd go away. Christ! There was *another* burst of applause! Already? Another round over. I was just about to look for some other way in when the door opened and Will Johnson came out.

'Will! Jesus, Will, am I glad to see you!'

'What's the emergency, Frank?' He wasn't looking overjoyed at the renewal of our acquaintance. The timing was lousy.

'Listen, Will. Don't ask questions, but Joss Murray is in there.'

'Joss Murray? In the *pocket*, d'you mean?'

'Yes. I saw him. He's going to inject The Wizard with EIA.'

'What? How?'

'It's too long to explain but that's what he's going to do. When The Wizard comes back in from his round, Murray will pat him on the rump, but he'll have a syringe or a contaminated needle in his hand . . . We have to get in there Will and find the cops.'

'Jesus, Frank . . .' he began doubtfully.

'Please, Will! Please!' I clutched his arm. 'Now!'

'Okay,' he said, making up his mind. 'But we'd better hurry. The Wizard will be off any moment.' As if to underline his words, there was another bout of applause, but this time it was followed by a full-blooded partisan roar as the crowd heralded its champion to the field of battle. The gloves were off, this was serious; no more polite magnanimity towards the opposition. I could hear the bloodlust in the war cry that rang around the grounds. 'Would you just listen to that,' Will said, his dark eyes gleaming, 'He's off already.'

'Oh shit! C'mon!' I hammered at the door but it didn't open. 'Hey!' I shouted, slapping it hard with my palm, 'Open the gate!'

'He'll be watching The Wizard,' said Will. I looked at him in horror. 'But,' he said, 'we can probably get in through the horse gate.'

'Will,' I said with barely contained desperation. 'We've got three minutes. Max. Now for God's sake, *run!*'

We hared around the back of the pocket and came to tall double gates. Thankfully one side was open, letting a horse out. He was limping badly and being led by a worried-looking groom. The gateman recognised Will and waved us through into the pocket.

There wasn't a person in there who wasn't gathered at the fence watching the great horse. They seemed to be four deep, more in some places. A huge 'Ooooh!' went up as The Wizard had a close shave somewhere along the line.

I turned to Will. 'Find as many cops as you can and get them over to the gate in a hurry. That's where he is. *That* gate,' I pointed.

There was another oooh from the crowd, but no groan. It seemed that The Wizard was leading a charmed existence. The excitement was palpable as I rushed towards the gate – I knew he was coming to the last few fences. Then there was a huge intake of breath – the last fence – a pause, then a sudden, mighty roar which rang round and round and round the grounds. In the pocket, the Irish contingent went wild with glee. We must have won, I thought, pushing on. At the gate itself, the crowd was packed ten deep and I panicked momentarily when I couldn't spot Murray – I'd been so sure that he'd be lounging by the wall. But, I realised, he'd never be able to reach The Wizard from anywhere but the centre of the crowd, so I searched, trying to identify the back of his head. It was useless. The heads kept shifting about, each person straining to see the horse, weaving back and forth in response to the movements of the heads in front.

Suddenly The Wizard was approaching the gate, a huge beaming smile on the flushed face of his young rider. I stood transfixed as they approached and I knew there was no way I was going to be able to save the horse – there were too many people, I couldn't tell which one was Murray – and in another five or six seconds, The Wizard would be passing slowly through the crowd, running the gauntlet of congratulatory slaps and pats, one of which would be his death sentence. The crowd began to part like the Red Sea for Moses. Suddenly I saw his profile, and, for the first time, was absolutely certain that it was Murray. About halfway down, on the left side, grim and purposeful, he stood immobile in the front row, the only face in the whole place which wasn't smiling. There was no mistaking him. This time there was no effort to raise the camera. Even as I watched, I saw him take his hand from his pocket, adjust something in it, then turn towards The Wizard, now only feet away.

'*Murray!*' I roared. But he couldn't hear me above the cheering.

Frantic now, with only seconds to go and no chance of battling my way through the mob, I backed a few steps to see if there was any sign of Will or the Gardai, but there wasn't and I turned back to see, to my horror, that The Wizard's head was almost abreast of Murray. There was a chilling fanatical gleam in his eyes, the lustful leer intensifying as he watched the horse draw ever closer. Now the rider's knee was nearly touching him and I could see the almost orgasmic excitement on Murray's face as he licked his lips in unholy anticipation, and waited for The Wizard to move the last fateful few feet. Impatiently, he raised his right arm but had to let it fall back as the horse's progress was interrupted yet again. Then, as I watched in horror, the Wizard took the final step, Murray's arm came slowly up again and, fresh out of options, I yelled a hoarse battle-cry, ran at the crowd, and launched myself into the air above them. In something like slow motion, I felt myself hurtling above the startled heads, my outstretched hand reaching for Murray's raised arm. My fingers curled round his wrist just as it began its forceful descent and I held grimly on as I fell onto and between the shocked heads and shoulders of the bystanders.

'Move the horse!' someone shouted, obviously thinking I was trying to get at The Wizard. Half-lying on heads and shoulders and half-slipping down between them, I clung desperately to the wrist, dragging it with me as I slid clumsily to the ground. I released it only when I was sure that the Wizard had moved to safety and the crowd had closed safely in behind him. An unsympathetic circle of faces looked down at me as I lay, half-winded, on my back and none of them seemed too shocked when Murray suddenly appeared, hugging his twisted wrist, and with a venomous oath, kicked me viciously in the ribs. By the looks on their faces, they thought I deserved it.

I might have got more but there was a sudden call from

close by: 'Move aside there now! Stand back! Gardaí. Make way there!'

I smiled angelically up at Murray, who gave me one last look of absolute hatred, then turned and went the only way that was open to him, through the gate, and out onto the arena. I shouted at the crowd to stop him, but they were too confused to know whose side they should be on. I got to my feet, wincing as my ribs reacted, and tried to push my way towards the gate, but the crowd had not yet decided who the good guy was, and I made no progress. Between heads I could see Murray running out across the arena. I turned and shouted to the two uniformed gardai: 'C'mon, men! Follow me! He's getting away across the arena!' That settled it: I was one of the good guys, and I was allowed to pass without further hindrance, through to the gate.

29

He had a fair headstart and should have been long gone, but, in his initial confusion, he'd run the wrong way, heading straight across the arena instead of sharp right towards the gate through which the Mounties had exited. That dog-leg had cost him precious time. The gate facing him was high, solid and wooden, but Murray launched himself at it gymnastically, hauling himself over just as I arrived; a few seconds earlier and I could have grabbed him by the leg. I scrambled up after him and straddled the gate, teetering precariously, scanning the crowd below. From my precarious vantage point, I soon spotted him, forcing himself to walk casually, trying to blend in. I watched him turn and twist along the intersecting paths, glancing surreptitiously back every time he turned a right angle. Nearing the back of the stands, where the crowd was thinner, he stopped and turned for a few seconds, scanning the crowd, then, seemingly satisfied, he darted suddenly into the dark mouth of a tunnel.

'He's gone into that tunnel under the stand,' I called down to the gardaí who had just caught up with me, two middle-aged men, puffing heavily, neither of whom looked as if he'd be able to get over the gate, let alone keep up with the fugitive. 'I'm going after him,' I said and jumped.

I made up time easily. Murray had had to walk in a zig-zag which would not attract attention, but I could run flat out, cutting diagonally across paddocks, clearing their low boundary railings like a champion hurdler.

Gaining the tunnel entrance, I peeped quickly in, just in time to see the bright sunshine paint detail onto Murray's silhouette as he exited at the other end. He went right. I counted to five, then, footsteps echoing loudly, pounded the length of the concrete passage, stopped at the exit, and peeked cautiously round. Murray was standing, some fifty yards away, outside a back door of the main Exhibition Hall. I watched him until he started to examine the area around, then withdrew my head. Next time I peered into the sunlight, I saw him pull open the door and enter. Once in the Exhibition Hall, I knew he could exit through any of several front doors onto the forecourt, and from there, through any of several gates, out of the RDS grounds and on to the Merrion Road, the whole of Dublin, and the entire country. Obviously I couldn't just let him walk free out the main gate.

But should I rush him and bank on being able to restrain him until help arrived, or tail him and take a chance on being seen and losing him altogether? I decided to go for the element of surprise and the sooner the better. I'd tackle him in the Exhibition Hall where, hopefully, a brawl would instantly attract the law. Quietly, adrenaline pumping, I slipped into the huge hall.

I couldn't have been more than fifteen seconds behind him, yet he had already vanished among the ranks of display stands which began just inside the door. Suddenly foiled, I groped for a Plan B.

He was probably on his way to the nearest exit and he was probably not running because he still didn't want to be noticed; besides, there was no need to run – as far as he knew, he was safe from pursuit. So, if I ran, I could get to the exit as soon as him. But what if I actually got there first? Then he'd probably see me . . . A lousy plan, Plan B. Settling on a compromise, I set off as fast as I could for a more distant exit. Brushing people aside, I reached it at the gallop, shot through onto the forecourt, and flattened myself into a narrow band of shade against the wall. There was no sign of my quarry on the long forecourt which fronted the building so I assumed that he was still inside. On the other side of the heavy railings, traffic rumbled past on the main road to Blackrock, Dun Laoighre and Bray. On impulse, unhappy with the narrow shade I hid in, and the unnaturally flattened posture I had to adopt in order to do so, I moved quickly to a small grassy patch and lay out in the full sunlight, my forearm covering my eyes – almost. My other arm raised my head just enough to give me a good view along the entire length of the building.

Suddenly, he was there, a mere twenty feet away. He came unhurriedly through the exit I'd predicted he would, and without even a glance at the sleeping sunbather, turned away from me, towards the main gate. There was nobody else on the forecourt except the two of us and, as he kept glancing behind, I had to postpone my attack. A group of six or seven men came through the same door, laughing and jostling in horseplay, and turned in his direction. Bending slightly to keep them between him and me, I rushed up behind them and walked along as if I belonged. They were talking about West Kong Wizard.

Murray walked out the main gate and turned right. A few seconds later my group followed, but they turned left, probably heading for one of the many pubs along that stretch, beating the crowds to the counter. I hung back, partially hidden by the railings and the gate.

When I pushed my head round the gate, I saw Murray, one foot on the pavement, the other on a zebra crossing, and waited until the sluggish traffic came to a grudging halt. As he crossed, so did I; thirty yards short of the zebra crossing, I snaked through the traffic and reached the far pavement at an angle going away from Murray, as if I was heading into town. Ten steps on, in the shade of an overhanging laburnum, I bent to check a shoelace and squinted sideways along the path at him. Murray was looking back towards the RDS, and didn't even glance my way.

Reassured, he moved on. He walked the few yards to a sideroad and turned in, entering the quiet and prosperous suburb of Ballsbridge. I dashed to the junction and took a quick look around. He had crossed the peaceful suburban road, and was walking along, hands in pockets, seemingly without a care in the world, though he must have been seething with frustrated rage. I watched until he came to a crossroads in the quiet residential suburb and turned right, then sprinted to the junction and chanced another quick peek; Murray was thirty yards away, walking, hands in pockets, totally unremarkable, a resident out for a stroll.

The next twenty minutes went the same way. Luckily, Ballsbridge is laid out in a fairly regular grid pattern, so it was easy to follow him and still stay out of sight. The whole place was as deserted as it would be at five a.m. Only once did he carry straight on through a crossroads and that left me with a longish sprint. He didn't seem to be headed in any direction, and he certainly wasn't worried about pursuit.

After many turnings, he crossed a railway line, then made a left onto a road so short that he had vanished by the time I peeped around the corner. The road, no longer than the gardens of the two houses between which it ran, ended in a T-junction with the sea road that parallels Sandymount Strand, the great curve of sand which forms the south-west corner of Dublin Bay and stretches for miles along its southern shore. When I checked round the corner, I found myself with little more than a few yards view to either left or right as the sea road formed a concave curve at this point. Dodging across to the beach side, I turned, my back to the sea, to search in either direction along the road for my quarry. I gasped in disbelief when I found myself looking straight into the face of Joss Murray. Almost directly across from me, a picture of suburban normality, Ireland's current most wanted man was quietly sharing a bus shelter with two elderly ladies. Almost at the same instant, he saw me. His jaw sagged open owlishly and he gawked at me as if I was an apparition.

Recovering from my initial surprise, I began to wonder what the hell to do now. Clearly, discreet pursuit was no longer an option. I'd have to rush him at once, while I still had the advantage of surprise. Hoping that the elderly ladies, chatting peacefully in the shelter, wouldn't get heart attacks when the rough stuff began, I started for the kerb, but a stream of cars stuck on the long blind corner behind one slow one prevented my crossing. While we waited for them to pass, Murray and I glared at each other like two boxers in a grudge fight waiting in the ring for the opening bell. His face was now a mask of narrow-eyed loathing, murderous rage – the same face, I thought with a shudder, which had been Marc Glasser's departing view of life, the visual image he had carried with him into eternity. His breathing was heavy, his nostrils flared, the muscles in his jaws bunched ominously and he began a rhythmic clench-ing of his fists. I told myself dryly that I just couldn't *wait* for the traffic to get out of the way and hoped to hell that the ladies, or somebody, anybody, would call the cops at once. His hatred for me – his own personal, persistent nemesis – coupled with his instinct for survival, would maximise his strength, and, though I reckoned I could still take him, it could turn out to be a long, brutal brawl.

And still the carcade moved slowly along without a sign of a gap in it; the Horse Show crowd would soon be adding to it. Seeing the possibility for escape which the seemingly endless traffic might afford him, Murray suddenly left the bus shelter and, keeping a wary eye on me, began to sidle rapidly away, his pace increasing with each crab-like distancing step. I didn't like this development at all – for one, given a couple of minutes headstart he could vanish back into the labyrinth of leafy, suburban roads; for another, he could lie in ambush and take *me* by surprise, which would, if successful, most likely be fatal for me . . .

To complicate any nasty plans he might be considering, I thought I'd be wise to heap even more pressure on him, spook him into near panic. I pointed straight at him with one accusing hand and beckoned athletically with the other up the short, empty road I'd just come down. 'He's here, Sergeant!' I shouted loudly, confidently, urgently. 'Hurry. He's making a run for it!'

Murray fell for it. He glanced in fear once towards the exit of the short road, then turned and fled. Gesticulating wildly at the traffic, I perched on the edge of the kerbstone, fixed one driver with a suicidal stare then stepped in front of him. I could read his lips perfectly as I made him choose between braking hard and hitting me, and grimaced apologetically at him as I left my handprint on the polished bonnet of his car before dashing across to the other kerb and setting off at speed after the fleeing Murray; I wanted to tackle him before he realised that there were no policemen, no sergeant – if he expected hundreds of cops to descend upon him within seconds, he mightn't, if I was lucky, put up any resistance at all.

I was gaining rapidly when fate intervened. Around the curve, coming towards us, there suddenly appeared a squad car. Murray, presumably believing he was being trapped in a pincer movement by whole droves of gardaí, faltered once, then veered straight across the road in front of it. I thought he'd had it, but the driver braked heroically, avoiding him by millimetres, and Murray, gaining the opposite kerb unscathed, vaulted the wall down onto the beach with scarcely a break in stride. The car lurched forward again as I flagged it down and I was dumbstruck when I realised that, shocked by their near miss, the occupants hadn't notice me. All I could do was stare in dismay as they accelerated on around the curve and vanished.

Now thoroughly disgusted with the vagaries of fate and fed up with the chase, I crossed the road and looked over the sea wall. Down on the beach, some hundred yards along, Murray was running. He was running towards the city. He had discarded his disguise somewhere on the beach. For some odd reason he was running in the white, powdery sand above the highwater mark; ten yards further down he'd have hit damp sand, firm as a tarmac road.

Despite the fine afternoon, there were few people about. The tide was flat out, almost half a mile away, and a thick bank of autumnal fog sat on the sea and sent intermittent probing tendrils onto the beach. Jogging almost at walking speed, I kept pace with the figure stumbling along below. Suddenly he seemed very small, very forlorn. He no longer looked back, but, like a punch-drunk boxer, kept grimly going because now that was all he knew. Twice I saw him fall, but he struggled back to his feet each time and continued to fight his way through the dry yielding sand, his feet sinking inches into it with each faltering step. I wondered if he had ever been to the seaside in his life.

I saw the phone box a hundred yards ahead and sprinted. I dialled 999, asked for the Gardai, and was put through at once. While I gave my message, I was actually able to keep watch on Murray through the perspex canopy. Yes, I confirmed, I was sure it was Murray. Near Sandymount village. Towards the city. They'd know *exactly* where when I flagged them down. I'd be on the road, waiting for them.

I ran a short sprint to catch up, then dropped back to an easy jog to pace his exhausted stumble through the sand. I began to look around for approaching squad cars, my ears straining to detect the faint whine of distant sirens but, instead of help, I found a problem looming ahead – a wedge of houses came between road and beach, separating them. If Murray reached those before the police arrived, our trails would part and he'd be lost to my sight, hidden by the row of redbrick homes. I waited until the last possible moment, but when no squad cars had yet arrived, decided I should stick with Murray – I didn't want to lose him, not now, not at this stage. The cops would have no trouble in locating us – you could see for miles along that beach. A flash image of Murray, exhausted and unhinged by despair, breaking into one of the houses and taking hostages hurried me on. There was hardly need for caution at this point. He'd be so sapped by now that I'd only have to push him over and sit on him.

I raced across his footsteps in the dry sand, crackled over the band of sandflea-infested seaweed which marked the high-tide line, and, as soon as my feet touched firm sand, turned to follow him. Inside a couple of strides, I was trotting along easily on the sea side of him, just behind the limit of his peripheral vision. I had to slow to a near walk to keep my distance and I was considering how best to take him when he stumbled again and went down. In regaining his balance, he turned his head and saw me. Features twisted with hatred and the pain of his futile exhaustion, he swayed on trembling legs, panting and heaving, and stared fixedly at me. I glanced back along the miles of sand. There were no gardaí on the beach.

'It's all over,' I said almost gently. 'You can't run any further. I just called 999 a few minutes ago.' I pointed vaguely towards the road. 'From a box up there.'

He continued to glare at me in silence, physically drained but defiant in the face of the inevitable, like a spent bull as the matador approaches with curved sword. I reckoned he'd reached the end of his rope. Physically, he could just about stay on his feet; mentally, he must have been wondering if I wasn't some kind of supernatural being, a shade who kept materialising out of nothingness: at Northfield House, in the pocket at the RDS, on the sea road in front of him, and now again after he'd been ploughing through the sand. His head was drooping, and his breathing sounded painfully laboured.

I saw him look suddenly beyond me and chanced a quick glance over my shoulder; there were four gardaí on the beach now, though they were still a fair way off.

'See?' I said, looking back at him. 'You may as well give up.'

The hatred in his eyes was uncomfortable to look at, so, after a few moments, I glanced back along the beach again – there were six uniformed men now, two of them closing quickly. In the corner of my eye, I registered a movement and I snapped back in time to see Murray pull a handgun from his pocket. Reflexly, before he could even level it at me, I was off, haring back the way I'd come, jinking and dodging like a mad thing. I heard three waspish reports in quick succession and saw a spurt of sand kick up some five feet away, but I was drawing away rapidly and no more shots came. Checking quickly over my shoulder I saw that he hadn't moved, so I stopped when I considered that I was out of range. Then I had second thoughts and backed off some more.

Murray stood alone now, facing the sea, seemingly no longer interested in me or the approaching gardai.

From the distant road came the rumble of traffic; in front of him, the wet wall of fog had crept appreciably closer and a few chill wisps stretched tentatively towards us; unseen, out along the tideline, sea birds made their plaintive cries. He turned round once, twice, three times, taking it all in, then, gun pointed in our general direction, began to make his way slowly down the beach towards the sea. At the limit of the fog, he turned towards us again, raised the gun and seemed to fire a shot, though I heard no report.

'Did you hear a click, Mick?' I heard one of the men behind me ask quietly.

'No, Sarge. I didn't.'

'I wonder did he just change his mind about pulling the trigger, or is that gun empty? Are you sure you heard no click?' Action, if any, would depend on the answer.

'I am, Sarge. No bang, and no click.'

'Here come the Ringsend crew,' another voice intervened, seeming to hold the suggestion that nothing should be done until the Ringsend crew arrived.

'Late, as usual,' sighed Mick.

Now there were tendrils of fog licking about Murray; his body seemed to attract them and wraith-like tongues undulated up and down along his frame as though they were live things, tasting him. He took a step into the fog and had all but vanished, when he suddenly re-emerged, and called in a half broken scream: 'I'll get you Samson! Some day, when you and yours think you're safe, I'll suddenly be there. Damn you to *Hell!*' Then he stepped back into the fog, became a shrouded shadowy man-shape for a moment, and vanished. It was a powerful performance – if I'd been superstitious, I'd have gone into an immediate decline, like a tribesman when the shaman points the bone at him.

The Ringsend crew arrived and the general consensus was that nobody in their right minds would go blind into impenetrable fog after a desperate madman armed with a loaded gun. True, nobody could swear for sure that it *was* loaded, but nobody felt like putting it to the test either. Various suggestions were tendered during the ensuing pow-wow. Some wanted to send for the dog squad, let the dogs sniff the discarded wig, if they could find it, then set the pack loose in the fog; that point of view was gaining support until someone pointed out that there might be innocent citizens strolling about in there, digging lugworms for bait or even just taking *their* dogs for a walk. Small dogs maybe. Poodles and the like. Did anybody know how a pack of excited Alsatians and Dobermanns, even very well-trained ones, might react to the sight – or scent, more like, because of the fog – of a poodle? Nobody seemed to, not even me, so at last it was decided not to disturb the Dog Section at all, but to mount a kind of coastal defence instead, to station a man every hundred yards or so along the wall up on the road so that anyone coming up from the beach would be visible to at least two of the watchers. The same one who had raised the question about the dogs objected again: if, he pointed out, the fog continued to roll across the beach and up onto the road, then they'd need a man every *six inches* to cover the whole beach, you could forget your hundred yards, and there weren't enough men in the country, never mind, Dublin South, for that. I didn't take any part in the war council. My opinion, apart from the matter of the dogs, was not sought.

As we headed up the beach towards the busy road, I kept glancing uneasily over my shoulder, back at the following fog.

30

By the time we reached the road, a large task force had assembled and men were immediately strung out along the wall as had been suggested. The chain stretched unbroken, all along the coast, from the Liffey estuary to Dalkey, but no one came up from the sea. Within an hour the fog dispersed under the onset of a stiffish evening breeze and it was clear that there was nobody lurking at the water's edge or in the shallows. Two inflatables were launched to search an area up to half a mile offshore, but found nothing. A search of the beach turned up a shoe swirling at the tide's edge and, a little further along, a light jacket. The shoe might or might not have been Murray's, but the jacket certainly was. The pockets contained a little money, a handgun (with two rounds still in it), and a small vial of liquid, which subsequently proved to be virulent EIA virus. There was also a curiously adapted syringe – a normal, plastic 10cc syringe with its barrel sawn off at the 1cc mark. The plunger had been proportionately shortened and the ensuing sharp end had had a coat button glued onto it to protect the palm when the plunger was depressed. The whole apparatus fitted neatly into the tented palm, the plunger being depressed simply by flattening the hand. A short, wide bore needle completed the assembly, the wide bore being essential to allow rapid passage of liquid and so permit of a very fast injection. West Kong Wizard wouldn't have felt a thing, and even if he had, it would have been over before he could react.

Murray himself proved more elusive. The news of his dramatic vanishing spread like lightning and, for the next few days, the media made hay. There were more reported sightings of him than there were of Elvis or Lord Lucan. Most of them were crank calls but a few were investigated, and could neither be proven nor debunked.

In the absence of a body, the rumours and the sightings went on: A passenger on the incoming mailboat reported seeing what she thought was a man swimming in the middle of the bay right by the ship, but, as it was quite dark and she wasn't one hundred percent sure, she didn't raise an alarm. She did, however, mention it to two people who were close by, strangers, and they confirmed that she had told them, though they themselves had seen nothing. Whether she was right or wrong, she certainly couldn't have been acting under the influence of suggestion – she could have known nothing about the incident until next morning's papers. A 'source in the coastguards' was quoted as saying that if there had been a man as close to the ship as the lady described, then he would have been drawn into the propellers and mangled to death. The next day, complicating matters even more, a report appeared which quoted the Chief Engineer on the mailboat as describing a 'sudden interruption' in the smooth running of one of his engines at about the same time. This sometimes happened, he explained, especially near port, and was usually caused by some large piece of drifting flotsam temporarily fouling the propellers. That had been about 9.45p.m.

A young couple, snogging in a car among the dunes on Bull Island, across on the other side of Dublin Bay, had reportedly been terrified when they saw a man wearing a shirt and jeans struggle from the sea a few yards in front of them and stagger off up along the beach towards the bridge to Dollymount. This had been about ten-thirty, or perhaps a little after. At least three other witnesses, in no way connected with each other, reported seeing the same soaking man further along the strand. One man, out walking his German Shepherd, felt brave enough to ask the man, who looked 'distraught', if he needed help, but the man passed on without reply; in fact, he gave no indication that he had even heard the man with the dog or indeed been aware of his presence.

In the following days and weeks, news about Murray faded from the papers and now, it would be hard to find anyone who could tell you just who Joss Murray was. Or is.

I won't say that I worry all that much about him, though I admit that I would be relieved if he was found. On the other hand, I can't claim to be unaffected by his parting malediction – only last week, Claire was twenty minutes late for a lunch date and I was shaking with anxiety by the time she finally did turn up.

Then there is the annoying habit I have developed of seeing significance in even the most tenuous of references. Though, I suppose some haven't been that tenuous, really. For instance, take last week. Wednesday was Bloomsday. I've made umpteen efforts to read *Ulysses*, but have never managed to finish it. It's a bit beyond me. Nevertheless, for Claire's sake and because it was Bloomsday, and this is Dublin, I started it, yet again. By the end of the first chapter, I had come across:

'The boatman nodded towards the north of the bay with some disdain.
– There's five fathoms out there, he said. It'll be swept up that way when the tide comes in about one. It's nine days today.
*   The man that was drowned. A sail veering about the blank bay waiting for a swollen bundle to bob up, roll over to the sun a puffy face, saltwhite. Here I am.'*

And then, ten pages later:

'Am I walking into eternity along Sandymount Strand?

379

Crush, crack, crick, crick. Wild sea money. Dominie Deasy kens them a'.

> *Won't you come to Sandymount,*
> *Madeline the mare?'*

I give up on *Ulysses*. Again. Maybe I'll have another go next year but, for now, enough is enough.